W9-BYK-673

COWBOY WOLF
OUTLAW

KAIT BALLENGER

sourcebooks
casablanca

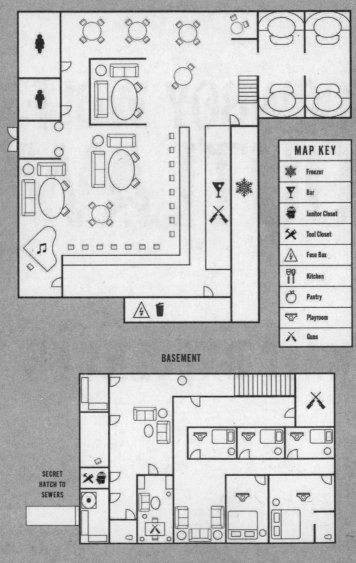

THE BLOOD ROSE

MAIN FLOOR

BASEMENT

SECRET HATCH TO SEWERS

MAP KEY

❄	Freezer
￦	Bar
🪣	Janitor Closet
✕	Tool Closet
⚡	Fuse Box
🍴	Kitchen
🍎	Pantry
▽	Playroom
✕	Guns

THE MIDNIGHT COYOTE

BASEMENT

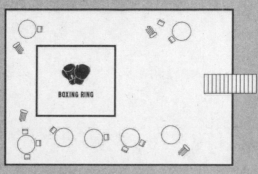

MAIN FLOOR

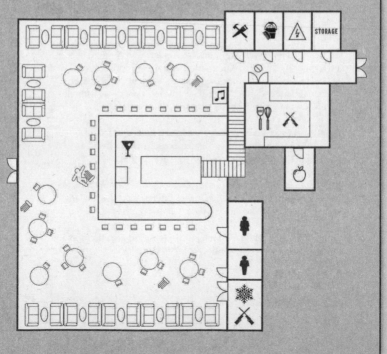

Published by Sourcebooks Casablanca, an imprint of Sourcebooks
P.O. Box 4410, Naperville, Illinois 60567-4410
(630) 961-3900
sourcebooks.com

Printed and bound in Canada.
MBP 10 9 8 7 6 5 4 3 2 1

To all my readers, thank you for carrying this series so far. I'll be forever grateful.

Chapter 1

THE CAVE REEKED OF DEATH. MALCOLM STOOD AMONG his packmates, blade in hand, watching as the final layer of dirt covered Austin's corpse. Each smack of steel shovel against the frozen top rock felt oddly sickening. Among the pack, tension hung heavy in the air. This wouldn't be their last burial before winter.

Malcolm's grip tightened around the hilt of his executioner's blade, the smooth leather handle stalwart and reassuring. Death had never intimidated him. Most days, he *was* the reaper, sickle in hand. But tonight, the violent promise of his packmate's bloodshed shook him.

He'd never feared anything more.

A thrum of anger coursed through him, sharp and heady. He hadn't been allowed to help lay his friend to rest, and his hand ached to do *something*. Work, move, kill. It didn't matter. But pack custom dictated the females of their kind handled their dead, which meant he had to stand here in the cavern's stillness, although he'd seen enough death to know that sentimental niceties like burial rites and ceremony proved meaningless.

What a load of bullshit.

Blaze placed a hand on his shoulder and squeezed.

Malcolm tensed beneath the other man's touch without turning away from the grave. He might not be a fan of Blaze and his normal attention-seeking jokes, but they were pack-mates all the same. Somehow, in the face of the battles to come, that meant more now than it ever had.

Malcolm had barely survived the last time he'd buried the man he'd loved.

He wasn't certain he could do it again.

"He wouldn't have wanted to see you like this, brother."

"You mean Austin?" He turned toward Blaze. Their deceased packmate's name sat heavy on his tongue. He and Austin had been no more than friends, but that didn't lessen the pain, and it didn't stop him from remembering the man he *had* loved.

"I mean Bo." Blaze cast him a knowing look.

First his mate, and now his friend. Both buried beneath the cave floor. Malcolm frowned, his wolf stirring inside him uncomfortably. *Fuck.* He didn't want their half-hearted pity. He mourned two souls today and the whole pack knew it. It'd been nearly three years since he'd lost Bo, but the grief never went away. It simply lay dormant.

Until the next time someone drew close to him.

Malcolm nearly snarled at the thought. He shouldn't have been surprised to lose Austin, too. Death followed him like the damn plague. He knew it. Blaze knew it. They all did. He saw the way they looked at him. Like he really *was* the reaper, even though he'd never asked to be.

The animals in them sensed it.

Blaze lowered his voice, drawing close, although every

other packmate who'd stood near Malcolm at the start of the ceremony had already drifted away. "Bo wouldn't want this."

"Wouldn't want what? Cut the cryptic bullshit," Malcolm growled, his eyes flashing to his wolf.

At the harsh sound, several of their surrounding packmates glanced up. Wolf shifters had impeccable hearing. Not to mention, everything in a damn cave echoed. The other pack members glanced nervously in his and Blaze's direction, quickly lowering their gazes and refusing to meet his eyes as soon as he stared back.

Malcolm bared his teeth. *Cowards.*

Pack mentality was brutal. They only respected him, feared him, because they couldn't understand him. They never would.

With a beckoning nod, Blaze stepped farther away from the burial ceremony, beyond the glow of the cave's torches. Malcolm gave a reluctant shake of his head but followed nonetheless. If Blaze had lost a mate like he had, the whole pack would have run to his aid, supported him, coddled him. But the love of Blaze's life was still living and breathing, while Malcolm's was buried six feet under and rotted to bone, only a handful of feet away from Austin no less.

Malcolm lowered his voice to a whispering hiss. "Save any feel-good niceties for someone who cares. Asking me not to grieve Bo? Hell, Austin too?" Malcolm shook his head, jaw clenched and features nearly feral. "I can't. I won't."

"That's not what I mean. I mean, he wouldn't want you to resign yourself to it."

"To our enemies?" Malcolm snarled. "Never."

"To the grief." Blaze reached out, gripping Malcolm with both hands by the sides of his neck and forcing him to meet his gaze. "He'd want you to move on. Stop living in the past."

Malcolm scowled. "You're one to talk."

Blaze had his own share of demons that had haunted him for years, the most recent of which had ravaged their pack, killing sixteen in the process. Injuring even more. It was why they were here in the pack's godforsaken graveyard, burying yet another one of their own among the limestone and gypsum walls.

"The Volk left us weak, but we won't stay that way. They wouldn't have been nearly as successful without the help of those bloodsuckers, without their knowledge about how the pack operates." Blaze's eyes burned gold, the glare of his wolf sudden and searing in its intensity. His unusual seriousness gave his words even more urgency. "Think of everything those leeches have taken from you," he whispered. "What they still stand to take from you, from all of us, if this goes on any longer."

Malcolm placed his hands overtop Blaze's, lowering them from his neck. From the murmurs nearby, the last rites had finally ended and their packmates had started to disperse.

Blaze stepped away briefly, returning to the main crowd and retrieving a small cloth parcel wrapped with string from next to the stone staircase that led down into the caverns. In the foreground, Maverick, the Grey Wolf packmaster, made his way toward the stairs, leading the pack's exit. He nodded at Blaze, his gold wolf eyes glowing through the darkness, before the weight of his stare turned toward Malcolm.

Malcolm felt the beast inside him stir in response like a caged animal beneath his skin. He didn't need words to understand that Blaze's order came directly from their alpha.

A moment later, as the last of the pack exited, Blaze returned, looking like nothing but a pair of lupine eyes staring at Malcolm through the dark. "I took care of the Volk. I made my peace. Now it's time for you to make yours." Blaze passed the parcel toward him. "Make it swift, brother."

Malcolm stared down at the package in his hands, the evening's events weighing heavily on his shoulders. The pack may not have loved him, cared for him, but he did have their fear, their respect. But was that enough? He'd never been certain.

Every movement in the cave caused a cacophonous chorus as he listened to the sound of Blaze's steps ascending the staircase. The stillness and silence that followed were deafening.

He was alone with the dead once more.

Instinctively, Malcolm crossed the cavern to Bo's grave, only a single torch at the cave entrance leading him. The orange glow pulsed and flickered over the cavern rock, casting shadows on the centuries-old stalagmites. There was an ancient history here, but it'd never be his. Not truly. Standing over his mate's grave, with shaking hands he removed his Stetson, casting it onto a nearby rock. Malcolm pulled the tail of the string, allowing the parcel to fall open. It was exactly what he'd hoped—and feared.

He lifted Bo's blade into his hand, the once familiar weapon feeling at home in his palm as he allowed the cloth wrapping to drop to the cave floor. Upon death, it was custom among the pack for a warrior's weapons to be burned. Years ago, he'd requested—no, pleaded—that Bo's be left untouched, that they remain with him where they belonged, but Maverick had refused.

"No," the packmaster had said. *"Not yet."*

At the time, Malcolm hadn't known what the fuck that meant. He wasn't one of them the way the others were, hadn't grown up among them, didn't belong, and he still didn't care about customs that had never been his to uphold. All he'd wanted, all he'd thought he needed then was some way to be close to the man he'd loved. But that hadn't entirely been the truth. Not really. He understood that now, as his packmaster had then.

He'd been too ravaged with grief, too broken to take his vengeance.

But he wasn't any longer.

Crouching beside Bo's grave, Malcolm used his mate's knife to slice against the sensitive skin of his palm. Pain seared through the wound as warm blood pooled, but he welcomed the stinging sensation. He didn't so much as flinch. Palm filled with his lifeblood, he pressed it into the dirt above Bo's final resting place, before he repeated the same with Austin's.

Leave it to him to make a blood oath with the dead.

As his blood sank into the soil, Malcolm stood, closing his bleeding hand over the weighted blade and bringing it momentarily to his lips before he tipped on his Stetson. The wound would close before long. But through the pain, he could almost feel Bo's presence there. He tried to find words, something eloquent to say, but that wasn't what they needed from him. Bo, Austin, their pack. This was the pack's open declaration of war against the vampires, against the Volk. They didn't need eloquence.

They needed destruction. The annihilation of their enemies.

For once, they needed him.

So he'd do what he did best and allow chaos to reign.

Malcolm growled, his oath echoing out into the cave's darkness. "This ends now."

Chapter 2

THERE WERE TWO KINDS OF MEN FOUND IN THE
Midnight Coyote saloon—cowboys and bikers—and
by her estimate, the asshole taking up her corner booth
was both. Trixie Beauregard leaned over the bar top,
damp microfiber soaking her hand from where she'd been
wiping up yet another spilled beer. The yeasty scent lingered. In the dim lighting of the neon bar signs, all that
was visible of the freeloader in the corner was a black
leather jacket with nondescript biker patches paired with
a dark Stetson.

She glanced at her watch. Boss had ordered her to get
her "sweet ass" hustling on Stanislav's drink order nearly ten
minutes ago, but first she'd been held up by a mess left over
from a bunch of drunken, idiot cougar shifters, and now this.

Money wasn't conjured on trees. Trixie tossed the soiled
rag into the suds bucket behind the bar top and grabbed a
fresh one from the stack.

"Don't even bother," Dani said, waving a hand toward the
alcove, clearly recognizing what she was thinking. "Shawna
and I already tried to get his order—twice now—and all that
pissed-off bastard did was growl at us."

At her coworker's rebuke, the dark Stetson in question

tilted slightly in their direction. If Trixie hadn't been looking, she might have missed it.

The beast could hear every word they said.

Not surprising in a place like this.

She shoved off the bar top. Tucking a new cleaning rag into her belt loop, she straightened her apron and the girls before placing her hands on her hips. By her guess, from the sheer size and breadth of the shadow hunkered there...

"Shifter?" she asked Dani over her shoulder.

Seven years working in this hellhole and she could size up any supernatural in two seconds flat. Shifter. Vamp. Warlock. Demon. It didn't matter. Name it, and she had poured it a tall one.

Dani shrugged as she held a Bombardier pint glass beneath the tap, pouring yet another Coors for the group of rabble-rousers belowstairs. "Probably. If you ask me, he looked like one of those Grey Wolves you like."

Trixie shook her head. Figured. "'Like' is a strong word, darlin.'"

She could count on one hand the number of shifters she truly "liked." Snarly bastards. Still, her *thing* for them was well known. She'd dated more than one over the years. They may not be likable, but they were her favorite toys. Rough, passionate, wild. No holds barred. A woman could get used to that. There was a brutish honesty in them that a witch like her could appreciate.

But if bartending didn't make a witch cynical real fast, being a woman in a place like this sure did, considering it was her job to wait hand and foot on a bunch of drunken supernatural assholes who thought she was no more than a pair of legs and a nice rack.

And half the time, they *still* left a shitty tip.

Trixie huffed, throwing her dry rag onto the bar top in frustration. She'd lost this particular game of chicken. Hell, she'd hadn't won a round yet. This time, he'd been there nearly a half an hour and *still* hadn't signaled her. But she could feel him watching her every move.

The heat of his gaze burned through her.

Damn him.

She frowned. "If he's gonna take up space on a Friday night, he's gonna drink."

Dani scoffed. "Good luck with that."

Trixie glanced at the human woman, taking in her appearance with a shake of her head. The bruised puncture wounds on Dani's neck were more than enough to piss off any wolf shifter within a fifty-mile radius. She sighed. *Humans.*

"A word from the wise, honey." She stepped in front of Dani, gently pulling the brunette's silky hair forward and positioning the long locks over the fang marks on Dani's neck. "Grey Wolves don't like bloodsuckers or their feeders." She patted the other woman on the cheek. "Next time, cover up your vamp stamp and you might actually get his order."

Dani blushed, deep and crimson.

Poor girl. She'd get herself drained dry within a year at this rate.

Trixie shook her head in disappointment as she made her way over to Mr. Tall, Big, and Brooding in the corner. His dark silhouette stirred as she drew closer, but the shadows of the bar still cloaked him. Not that it mattered.

Grey Wolf or not, they were all the same in the end.

And there was only one shifter she knew who could fill a booth like that.

Leaning against the edge of the wooden tabletop, she crossed her arms under her breasts, framing her cleavage in a way she knew he'd appreciate. She'd never catch him looking, but she'd felt his eyes there plenty. "I hear you've been pissy with the other staff. Must mean you were hoping to see me." She cast him a coy, knowing grin. "What can I get ya, sugar?" she said, laying it on extra thick.

The Grey Wolf executioner growled.

A real talker. As always.

Trixie huffed an annoyed sigh, momentarily cutting the bullshit. She didn't have time for his games tonight, even though she wanted to. "Look, I don't make the rules, darlin'. I'm just paid to follow 'em. So Grey Wolf or not, if you're gonna take up one of my tables, you're gonna drink, and when this is all over, you're hopefully gonna tip—big." She gave him a quick once-over, purposefully lingering on the massive breadth of his chest and shoulders. She might not have been able to see his face, but the man was the size of a friggin' tank. All muscle. "A bad-boy wolf like you probably knows a thing or two about *big*, don't you, Malcolm?" She flashed a suggestive grin. Just enough to rile him up like she always did.

It was part of their game.

The voice that finally answered raised the hairs on the back of her neck. "I'm not here for a drink."

Trixie lifted a brow. Lord, she'd never get used to that voice. Rough, graveled in timbre. A girl could get behind a voice like that, or on top of it. It'd taken her months to first get him to speak to her. Now, it was too much fun not to provoke him.

"So he *can* speak after all," she drawled sarcastically. "And he gives good voice, too." She flashed her fakest smile. All white teeth and ruby-red lips.

Malcolm didn't so much as grin.

Tonight he was going to make her work for it.

Leaning in, she lowered her voice to a conspiratorial whisper, giving him a prime view of her chest as she let a little extra Georgia-sweet slip into her voice. Most of the cowboys who came through here liked that. It made them feel like they were real tough stuff. "Look," she whispered. "Nobody's here for a drink, darlin'. They come for the secrets and stay for the fights. I don't make the rules." She sat back again. "The overpriced liquor is just a bonus."

"I said, I'm not here for a drink." The shadows of the bar shifted as he leaned forward into the light, wolf eyes flashing.

Trixie grinned. She never forgot a face, but his was especially memorable. Harsh, hardened features. Black hair. A permanent scowl. From the dark tan of his skin, he was maybe Italian or some other Mediterranean mixed in with those big, bad wolf genes. The gold wolf eyes gave a touch of dramatic splendor as if they'd been rimmed in ebony eyeliner, though she doubted that was the case. The Grey Wolf executioner was pretty but too much of a brute for that— withdrawn and brooding. The kind of shifter who could kill a man in seconds if someone looked at him wrong.

Death was his trade after all. Lord knew she'd heard the stories. No one this side of the Mississippi wanted to see this assassin's face staring at him from an alley's shadows. The Grey Wolves took no mercy on their enemies.

Malcolm's gold wolf eyes fell to the offered view of her chest, lingering for barely more than a second. That single look was so scorching that a less experienced woman would have mistaken it for rage. But she didn't. With or without her magic, she knew *exactly* what did it for him.

His eyes quickly shot back to hers. "Are you done yet?" he snarled.

Trixie stuck out her lip in a fake pout. "Not in the mood to play tonight?"

It was rare a man surprised her, a wolf shifter especially. It was the way he denied the tension between them that caught her intrigue. Like he wanted her but wouldn't let himself indulge. It made her want to test him, bend him until she saw him break. That was the game.

But she hadn't won...yet.

"It's been a while since you've come to see me," she crooned, recovering quickly. "Last time was your packmaster's reception, remember? You were sitting with that real cute Texan with the curls and that handsome, goofy one with the mischievous grin."

She'd been hired to bartend the private affair on account of the fact that she'd once saved the life of the Grey Wolves' second-in-command and his human mate for funsies. Plus, the Midnight Coyote was the only supernatural bar this side of Interstate 90 with a large enough liquor license to supply enough booze for a whole pack of wolf shifters to drown themselves.

He growled. "I don't come here for you."

"Sure you don't." She lifted herself up to sit on the hard booth top. Veritas witch or not, she didn't buy that for a second. "Says the man who always sits alone in my section, growling at all the other staff while he can't keep his eyes off me."

He leaned closer, face tight with anger and wolf eyes glowing. "What will it take to get you to leave me the fuck alone?"

She laughed, twisting toward him and placing her boots in the cushioned seat on either side of his lap. "The truth." She leaned forward, drawing nearly nose to nose with him, until she could feel the warmth of his breath. "You'd save us both a lot of time if you'd just admit you want me and we could get this over with."

There was only a hairsbreadth between them. All he'd need to do was lean in to kiss her. But he wouldn't. Not again. That'd be too easy.

She watched the muscles of his throat contract, saw how the rise and fall of that large chest increased.

Those gold wolf eyes fell to her lips, lingering, before he scowled. He still wanted her as badly as that night in the alley, but he was disgusted with himself for it. "I don't fuck humans." He growled.

Trixie laughed. After all this time, he still didn't realize? "That's the best you got, sugar?" She reached out and touched him, trailing one sharp, glowing pink fingernail across his cheek. Her magic hummed through like a charged, live wire. "I'm *not* human."

"A witch." He sneered, pulling away from her touch as if she were poison. The growl that rumbled from him was downright feral. Like she was a curse word. "Might as well be human."

She started to laugh, slowly leaning back.

But something dark flashed through his eyes.

Without warning, his hand darted out, tattooed knuckles capturing the gold locket on her necklace to hold her in place. Roughly, he yanked her forward, using the sturdy chain around her neck like a lead. The metal dug into the back of her neck. Trixie froze, a mixture of shock, excitement, and adrenaline holding her in place. He'd moved so fast she'd barely seen it coming.

"Is that what you want to hear, witch?" He snarled, his voice harsh and feral. He tugged her down even closer, positioning himself between her legs. His gaze raked over her, hot and assessing. "Will that get you to release me from your spell?"

One large hand clamped down on her bare thigh and spread. She could feel the thrum of her pulse there and no doubt he could, too. He stared up at her, holding her captured as he snaked a welcome hand up the opening of her skirt.

"You want me to tell you I come here to imagine bending you over the bar top while I tongue-fuck your pretty pink pussy?" His fingers brushed over the outside of her thong, scorching her. She shivered. She was already wet there for him and he had to feel it. "I bet you'd like that," he sneered.

"Ain't no shame in it," she whispered.

Abruptly, he released her, sinking back into the cushions of the booth. "Too bad I have more self-respect than that."

For a moment, Trixie couldn't bring herself to say anything. She could count on one hand the number of times she'd been caught speechless. But he'd done it—twice now. Her gaze traced over him, cataloging the moment for memory just like before. It'd be a while before she saw this side of him again. But for tonight, she'd won.

A slow smile spread across her lips.

"If you value your life, you'll stay the hell away from me." He scowled at her again. "Now fuck off, *witch*."

She blinked, both stunned and slightly amused. It was rare a man caught her by surprise, but that didn't mean she didn't enjoy it. Oh, he was fun to play with alright, especially now that she knew the beast bit back. The bigger shocker was that he truly believed his own dramatic bullshit. She didn't detect even a hint of a lie in any of his words. Most men in this bar lied as much as they breathed. But he didn't.

Interesting.

"I might have been offended if I didn't know you punctuate half your sentences that way." Finally, she collected herself, smile widening. "That was fun, darlin'. Truly. Only one problem with that plan, sugar."

His dark brow lifted in response.

She leaned in close to him again as she whispered, "I'm a veritas witch, not a siren." Her eyes fell deliberately to his lap and the large, visible erection straining against his jeans. "And that's all you, sweetheart."

His wolf eyes flashed in anger as he snarled. He wasn't amused by her in the slightest. And he didn't try to hide it this time. He wasn't embarrassed, just pissed. The man wore his pain like a statement. Too bad.

"Now, you gonna order a drink, Malcolm, or do I have to get Frank here to escort you out?" She nodded toward the bouncer who worked the door.

Most of the Coyote's patrons could hold their own in a brawl and she had no doubt this Grey Wolf could, but Frank had the brawn of being half-giant on his side. A rare breed these days, especially this side of the Atlantic.

Malcolm growled again. As if *she* was the one wasting *his* time. The gall of this shifter. "Will that get you and your little feeder friends to leave me the fuck alone?"

"Who says I'm friends with the feeders?" Trixie feigned offense before she crossed her fingers and placed a hand over her heart. At this point, she'd say anything to get him to shell out some cash so she could be on her way. Pride intact. "Witch's honor. Not that it's worth much."

Another growl, this time with bared teeth. "Laphroaig."

She lifted a brow. "A cowboy who drinks scotch instead of bourbon? You really are a man of mystery." She rolled her eyes and smirked. "One scotch comin' up, Mr..." Trixie hesitated. "What *is* your last name anyway?" she asked.

"Malcolm," he growled. "Just Malcolm."

Yeah, sure. She rolled her eyes again. "Everybody's got a last name, sugar. Even Prince, Madonna, Dolly."

"Not me," he nearly snarled. Clearly the subject was only pissing him off.

"Whatever. One scotch coming up." Trixie shook her head as she flounced back over to the bar, careful to put a little extra sway in her step. She could still feel his eyes on her, watching, wanting.

The man was an enigma.

"Did you get his order?" Dani asked, dunking two empty pint glasses in the dish sink. The soapy liquid sloshed over the edge, spilling into a small puddle below. From the innocent look in the human's eyes, she was none the wiser about Trixie and Malcolm's brief interlude.

If there was one thing the Coyote was good for, it was keeping her secrets.

"Don't you worry about him, darlin'. Just leave that one to me." Trixie smiled to herself, grabbing a clean tumbler and the bottle of Laphroaig off the backlit liquor shelf. Turning back toward the bar top, she was starting to pour as a familiar face approached.

"Hey, Trixie," Blaze said. The Grey Wolf security specialist flashed her that handsome white-toothed grin as he pulled out his wallet and shelled a few bills out onto the counter. "Jack Daniel's, would ya?"

She nodded. At least some of them were easy talkers. "Anything for you, sugar."

As if he were in a hurry, Blaze's eyes darted toward the corner to where Malcolm waited, but instead he turned back toward her, lips pressed together like he was burning with something to say. That look was more obvious than the flamboyant Hawaiian shirt beneath his leather jacket.

"Runnin' late?" She lifted a brow.

That wry grin pulled at his lips again. "Always. I didn't want to leave Dakota." He pawed at the back of his neck sheepishly.

"At least he's got someone to keep him company tonight." She nodded to where Malcolm sat among the shadows.

Blaze twisted the brim of his Stetson for a moment, fiddling with it like he was uncomfortable, before he leaned onto the bar top. "Yeah, about that," he said, lowering his voice to a whisper. "You know you're barking up the wrong tree with Malcolm, right?"

Dani may have missed her and Malcolm's little standoff, but clearly Malcolm's packmate hadn't.

Trixie couldn't help but chuckle. "If you mean do I know he was mated to Bo before Bo passed on? That would be a yes, sugar."

Blaze's blond brows shot up. "He told you?"

This time, Trixie shook her head. Wolves. "Honey, he didn't have to. Ain't no secret. Bo was a regular. When that one showed up a few weeks after he died, sitting in that same booth in that same corner..." She finished her pour of the Laphroaig with a shrug. "A witch like me knows." She placed the bottle back up on the shelf before grabbing another tumbler and the Jack.

"He's come in here 'bout every month since. Missed a few when we relocated from Billings out to this godforsaken hellhole, but now that he's back, he sits in my section every time." She poured the amber liquid into the waiting glass, the whiskey's scent hitting her, before placing the bottle back on the shelf. "But that's what I love about you wolves.

Everything is so black and white. You don't even realize the rest of us live in a sea of gray." She pushed the glass of Jack toward him, giving him a pointed look. "And you don't know your boy like you think you do."

Blaze glanced toward Malcolm, brows drawn low in confusion.

Trixie tried not to let her gaze follow his but failed. Malcolm's dark form stirred with awareness. The brute knew when he was being watched, by her especially. She'd been with her fair share of men, shifter or otherwise. Enough that he shouldn't faze her. It'd been one damn kiss in a back alley nearly a year earlier, and yet…

The heat of it still burned through her.

She frowned, turning away as she cleared her throat. "You boys want to start a tab or you want me to ring you up now?"

Blaze grabbed his glass. "Ring us up. With any luck, this won't take long."

He moved to grab Malcolm's Laphroaig, but Trixie placed a hand over it. "I got this one." She took the glass in her hand and sauntered back around the bar top, Blaze trailing her as she made her way over to Malcolm's booth.

At her approach, Malcolm reached into his back pocket, pulling out his wallet before dropping a wad of bills on the table. "Keep the change." From the expression on his face, he might as well have told her to fuck off again. Lone cowboy was his shtick after all.

Trixie slid the glass toward him as she plucked the bills off the wooden surface, giving him a quick once-over. "At least you're a decent tipper." Thumbing through the stack of twenties, she turned to leave but then stopped at the last second. She couldn't resist.

Turning back toward him, she placed a hand on his booth and leaned in to whisper against his ear, dropping her voice to low and sultry. "If you change your mind about wanting company..." Her voice trailed off.

She said it mostly to toy with him because she'd won their little game tonight.

Not that she'd say no if he agreed. He might have wasted her time on occasion and been rude to her and her staff, but no woman in her right mind would turn a wolf like this away. He was a mighty fine sight, dark and dangerous. Who didn't want the kind of man who was as wild and untamed in the bedroom as he was in life? A wolf with the face of an angel but all the harsh passion of demon fire.

Something told her that wasn't all there was to him though. He was too complex for that. He'd be more of a giver than a taker. She was certain of it.

The harsh golden glare of his eyes would have cut a lesser woman down to size. "I won't," he ground out. He turned away from her, looking toward his packmate who was sliding into the booth across from him.

She clicked her tongue in mock sorrow, walking away as she pocketed her tip. "A shame." No surprise there.

Her favorites were always a disappointment.

Chapter 3

MALCOLM TILTED HIS GLASS TO HIS LIPS, THE PEATY liquid coating his tongue as Blaze slipped into the booth across from him. For a moment, the dim drop-hat lights and neon liquor signs that decorated the western saloon cut through the darkness, clashing against the opening of Blaze's jacket to reveal... Was that an orange pineapple pattern?

"You're late." Malcolm scowled before he took another large swig of his scotch. Maybe he *did* need the liquor after all.

"I'm always late." Blaze shrugged before fidgeting with the glass of amber liquid in front of him. Jack Daniel's, from the smell of it. Blaze glanced at the drink like he didn't really want it.

That made two of them.

Malcolm shook his head. Blaze *would* order the same as every other cardboard cowboy in this joint. He and Trixie were that much alike. All show. No substance.

"Did you actually *expect* me to be on time?" Blaze's brow lifted in confusion.

Malcolm shot his packmate an annoyed look, turning his attention instead toward Trixie. She sauntered across the bar, her perfect Georgia-peach bottom swaying. When she reached the jukebox, she pressed several buttons, and a moment later, Dolly Parton's "Dumb Blonde" thumped through the speakers.

Trixie was nobody's fool.

Spinning back toward him, Trixie cast him a pointed look and fluffed her loose blond curls. Even from across the room, he could practically smell the gardenia scent of her hair, and she knew it. The woman lived to taunt him.

And he hated how much he craved it.

Malcolm swore under his breath, his cock instantly responding, even as his hand clenched into a fist. He'd let himself get caught up in her spectacle, and already he regretted it. *Fuck.* Tonight, he didn't need any distractions. No matter how tempting.

Still, the memory of the last time he'd tangled his fingers in her silky hair gripped him. She'd been soft and pliable in his arms, sexy as hell. Nothing like the hard, world-weary woman who now glared back at him. He needed to let it go. Lord knew he'd tried more than once to forget it. But for some reason, he couldn't. He wouldn't make the same mistake again.

With one final bat of her eyelashes, Trixie hoisted a large tray from the bar top onto her shoulder and sashayed toward the basement stairs, clearly finished with her little show. For now. There'd be more. There was always more. At least until close.

Malcolm twisted in his seat, his lower head aching.

There wasn't anything real beneath all that cheap glitz, but the fact that he wanted there to be still angered him.

Blaze's eyes followed his. He smiled a knowing grin as Trixie disappeared into the darkness of the saloon's stairwell, the scent of her hair replaced by a stringent mixture of the bar's cleaning agents and spilled beer.

"So are you and Trixie…?"

Malcolm growled, harsh and warning.

There were some things even *he* didn't share with his packmates. His poor taste in women being one of them.

Blaze sniffed the air, scrunching his nose like he'd taken a whiff of something disgusting. "Ugh. Never mind. I can smell the pheromones on you from a mile away. Get a damn room." He waved a hand in front of his face. "Didn't realize you swing both ways."

"I'm about to take a swing at your face if you don't shut the fuck up," Malcolm shot back. "And that's called bi erasure. Look it up."

The last thing he needed was Blaze making less-than-subtle wisecracks about his sexuality for the better part of the evening. Though in Blaze's defense, he joked about *everything*. But that didn't piss Malcolm off any less.

He leaned back in his seat, shamelessly adjusting himself. Goddamn, witch. Like he needed any other reason for his packmates to see him differently. The Grey Wolves had always accepted him, hadn't blinked an eye at him and Bo, but that didn't mean any of them actually *understood* him. Wolves were too focused on hierarchy, on binaries and reproduction for that.

Yet another reason he'd never quite belong among them.

"So where are our motorcycle-riding brethren?" Blaze asked, glancing around the bar expectantly.

Malcolm scanned the room. The nomads of the Detroit

Rock City MC hadn't yet shown their faces. The neon-lit ground floor where he and Blaze sat was mostly empty. Sprinkled throughout the booth and table seating, only a handful of patrons remained beneath the pale-blue glow of the Coors sign script. The multicolored flash from the updated jukebox screen colored the crowd pink or green. But Malcolm could hear the thrumming chatter of the crowd belowstairs, the roar of partygoers preparing for the cage fights. It was down the darkened stairwell, where Trixie had disappeared, that the true action reigned.

"I told them 9:00 p.m."

"So you *did* expect me to be late?" Blaze flashed him that stupidly handsome grin of his.

As if on cue, a moment later, the door to the Midnight Coyote swung open. Two leather-clad wolves strode in, eyes combing the space for them.

"This is the perfect setup for a really bad joke," Blaze muttered, finally sipping his whiskey. "But I'll save you from it."

Malcolm growled, willing Blaze to shut up.

The wolf-headed reaper patches on the backs of the wolves' leather jackets marked the two shifters as Rock City MC as clearly as the Grey Wolves' Stetsons did.

"Shit. They're punctual. Right on the dot." Blaze glanced toward his watch. He slid out of the booth, raising a hand to flag the other shifters down before rounding to Malcolm's side of the table. Blaze perched next to him, bumping Malcolm with his elbow as he smiled that wry grin. "Try to look a little less like you want to kill someone, okay, Mac?"

Malcolm scowled. "Don't ever fucking call me Mac."

This meeting was his doing and his alone. He'd set it up as a service to their pack, despite Blaze having been tasked with cementing the potential alliance, not Malcolm. "You wouldn't be here if it wasn't for me."

"Now you sound like my mother." Blaze rolled his eyes.

As the other shifters approached, both Malcolm and Blaze stood, slipping out of the booth.

Blaze was the first to step forward, readily extending his hand. "Blaze Carter," he said, introducing himself before he lifted a brow. "Have we met before?" he asked one of the men. "You're a Yellowstone ranger, right?"

"I was. For a season. Been to Wolf Pack Run a time or two." The younger of the two bikers nodded. He looked at Blaze's palm wearily before he finally shook hands. "Dom Reyes." He nodded to the man on his right. "That's Rigs. Not all the rangers that protect our terra firma are former MC, but I was for a time."

Which meant Dom, at least, would know several of their packmembers and maybe even be sympathetic to their plight. The Grey Wolves had a vested interest in protecting terra firma, the lands of Yellowstone National Park, considering Wolf Pack Run bordered the vast landscape. Over the years, wolf shifters from various pack allegiances had taken up the mantel of protecting the reintroduction of true wolves into the forests that had once been their home. It was their species' collective dream that someday, they'd call terra firma their homeland again. That singular cause united their kind across pack lines. A pipe dream if anyone asked Malcolm, but a beautiful, albeit tragic one.

Malcolm scanned their guests, quickly sizing the other two men up. Tall, wide, muscled like most shifters. Their kind was built for the wicked wild of the forest, not humanity's cagelike walls. The two men's patched leathers marked them as MC, the accompanying tattoos as pack. From the loose-limbed ease of how he carried himself, the wolf with the buzz cut, Dom, was keener and more eager, less controlled. But the second, Rigs, had seen his fair share of violence, too, felt it more deeply, more personally. He simply hid it behind a too-scraggly beard and world-weary eyes that saw and felt too much.

Malcolm knew the feeling.

"Pleasure." Blaze touched the rim of his Stetson, then tilted his chin toward Malcolm. "This is..."

"Malcolm," Rigs finished for him, gruff voice rumbling as he readily extended his hand.

The unexpected ease of the gesture caught Malcolm off guard. He wasn't used to anyone feeling anything close to *ease* in his presence. But among their kind, the gesture was still abnormal.

Malcolm extended his hand and the other man pulled him in for an unexpected brotherly hug. Malcolm stiffened, hand falling to his blade. As he pulled back, his confusion must have shown, because the other wolf chuckled, low and deep.

"You saved the life of our club's pres. You wear our patch." Rigs gestured toward Malcolm's leather before he glanced toward his packmate, who signaled his agreement. "You're one of us."

Malcolm nodded, despite the hollow feeling in his chest.

They wouldn't say that if they truly knew him. He wore the leather out of necessity, because he was too cheap to buy another to use on his own bike. Growing up as a poor Chicago South Sider was a lifelong affliction, and it'd been years since he freelanced for the MC, long before he became an elite warrior.

He'd been hired to take out the bastard threatening the life of the MC's pres. It'd been an easy payday. He'd taken the other contract killer with a .44 to the back of the head. Amateur fool had never seen it coming. The kill had barely fazed Malcolm, the memory little more than the familiar tinge of cordite in his nose. But from the looks of it, the passage of time hadn't lessened the Rock City MC's gratitude for protecting their leader.

"Pres?" Blaze quirked a brow at the other wolf's phrasing. "You mean your packmaster?"

The two shifters slipped into the opposite side of the booth. Malcolm and Blaze did the same.

"No. Pres," Dom corrected. "He rules by the vote of the club." Those intense, wild eyes narrowed. "We serve no master."

They may have been the same species, but that didn't mean their worlds were the same. All the more reason this meeting needed to go well. If the vote of the MC's membership mattered more than their club pres, they needed to get these shifters before them to see eye to eye, to understand the mutual threat they faced. Malcolm glanced toward Blaze, the concerned look in his packmate's eyes indicating he, too, understood.

The fate of the Grey Wolves fell on this alliance's shoulders.

"We won't waste your time with small talk then," Blaze said, leaning forward to place his elbows on the table.

Dom and Rigs both nodded.

"We heard about the"—Dom hesitated, searching for the right word—"recent incident at Wolf Pack Run."

Malcolm felt Blaze tense beside him. *Recent incident*, his ass. The Volk had decimated them. Malcolm wasn't one for niceties, and neither was Blaze. Not when it came down to it.

"'Slaughter' is the more appropriate word," Blaze hissed. The easygoing expression on his face faltered, replaced by a glimpse of the tortured soldier who lay beneath. A stark contrast to Blaze's normal grin.

Malcolm glanced toward his packmate, taking the true Blaze in. He'd seen more signs of the real shifter that lay beneath the obnoxious, comedic facade of late, and while he couldn't say he was pleased with the reason behind the change, he was glad for it. Malcolm wouldn't exactly call his packmate a friend, but he knew firsthand Blaze had done everything in his power to protect their pack from his past.

Time had revealed that the Volk's attack two months prior had been a bid for the twisted, cannibalistic shifters to claim the Grey Wolves' territory. The Grey Wolf Pack had provided the weapons that MAC-V-Alpha—a shifter-only unit of the U.S. military that Blaze had served in—used to nearly annihilate the Volk years earlier. It didn't matter that Blaze had done all he could for Austin and the pack. The Volk still got their revenge.

Malcolm remained silent, looking toward the other

wolves across from them. The sound of another old country song played in the background. He sensed an uneasiness in the bikers, a subtle tension in the tightness around their leather-clad shoulders. He didn't need to talk in order to speak, to communicate, and neither did they. An expression, a look, spoke volumes. That was something few ever seemed able to understand.

Blaze inhaled a deep breath, releasing it slowly through his nose to keep himself steady, careful as he chose his words. "If you think the vampires are a plague, wait until you face the Volk," Blaze said. "They're like us but twice as strong, twice as fast, and twisted and corrupted from feeding on the flesh of men—like those damned bloodsuckers only worse." Blaze lifted up a single finger for emphasis. "One can wipe out several wolves in a handful of seconds."

Rigs nodded, but Dom eyed them skeptically, leaning back in the booth. "You're asking us to place faith in you, to believe these...creatures exist?" Dom shook his head. "They're legends, both in our world and yours, the fodder of our elders' long-ago stories."

"I'm not *asking* for your faith," Blaze spat out. "Faith requires belief without proof. I'm asking for your understanding." He slid to the edge of the cushioned bench seat, exchanging a knowing glance with Malcolm.

Malcolm nodded his agreement.

Leaning down, Blaze rolled up the pant leg of his jeans, exposing his wounds.

Reddened stitches marred the misshapen curve of Blaze's thigh down to his knee. One of the Volk had taken a chunk of flesh there. Thanks to their kind's ability to heal, the injury hadn't been life-altering. Blaze was finally up and walking again, but still, the sight of the wound there, angry and inflamed with pain, months after their kind normally would have healed, spoke volumes.

Blaze would sport a permanent limp.

"They're a threat we all face." Blaze's blue eyes darkened, turning grim.

For a brief moment, Malcolm could see what Dakota, Blaze's mate, saw in him—something deep and real that the rest of the world rarely saw.

"Blaze served in MAC-V-Alpha. Two tours," Malcolm grumbled, voicing what he knew his packmate wouldn't.

Their worlds might be different, but Malcolm knew the MC held one thing dear—service to one's pack, club, country—something greater than themselves. There were plenty of MCs, both human and otherwise, who had warped values, especially among the one-percenters, but even among the worst, that respect for service remained true... for men and women who chose to live by their own rules.

"Those beasts were hiding, bidding their time for centuries until they came for us again," Blaze explained. "We took out their leadership. Only a handful remain. There wasn't enough"—he hesitated—"food," he said, choosing his words carefully, "for them to proliferate out in the Russian tundra. That's why they want Wolf Pack Run, Montana, our mountains near Yellowstone, terra firma." He nodded to Dom pointedly. "They want all the territories ruled by the shifters of the Seven Range Pact. Those areas are remote enough that they can find humans and feed, and no one would be the wiser to it."

Disappearances in the state parks, in the wild of the forest and mountains, happened all the time. The terrain made it easy enough to explain a few missing tourists, and in a low-population state ruled by livestock agents, the difference between a human dead from the Volk or a drop from a high rock was all the same.

It was why, led by the Grey Wolves, the seven shifter clans that ruled the Seven Range Pact made the foothills of the Absarokas their home territory, both because that was native land for their species and because the mountains hid them from the prying eyes of humanity.

"Now, they've partnered with the bloodsuckers," Blaze continued, "and with our pack severely weakened, we need more than our alliance with the other Seven Range shifters."

The vulnerability of that statement hung heavy in the air. *We need you.*

Malcolm felt the weight of the phrase. The lives of their packmates depended on it.

"That's all well and good," Dom answered. "We may be a mutual species. The Grey Wolves have our respect"—he nodded toward Malcolm—"but when it comes down to it, we're not pack. Not brothers. Why should we stick our necks out for you?"

It was a reasonable question, but the callousness when Austin and so many other wolves lay buried six feet under the rock of Wolf Den Caverns snaked through Malcolm. The mildewed scent of that damn cave still lingered in his nose. He knew Blaze would feel the same.

"Empathy isn't something you can beg for. You either have it or you don't," Blaze nearly snarled.

"What say you, Reaper?" The question came from Rigs, who'd proved nearly as quiet as Malcolm.

The other wolves' eyes turned toward him.

Malcolm took a long sip of his drink, considering. The green light from the jukebox caught like an emerald against the crystal. He set the glass back down on the tabletop with an audible *thunk*. "I think right now...our offer doesn't look very tempting to you. We're desperate and you know it. We don't have much to offer." He glanced down at his glass, to the amber liquid that seemed lit from within beneath the neon lights. That made it easier to rein in his emotions, appear unaffected.

"But I also know what a bad position a Grey Wolf defeat would put you in, both your pack and your cause to protect the homelands." He nodded to Dom. "If our pack falls, then who become the dominant shifters in this country? Who controls the land that borders northern Yellowstone? Now, maybe you want that. Maybe you think you're ready and powerful enough to handle it. After all, I grew up on the South Side of Chicago. I know your pack. From Detroit all the way down to Atlanta, you reign supreme. But your pack is still less than half the size of ours, and if we fall, then who stops the vampires from proliferating here out west? Who stops the Volk from regrouping and building their numbers? Who helps the rangers protect terra firma?

"Maybe the distance buys your pack a few years, but eventually the Volk will move into Yellowstone and eastward into your territory. Can you guarantee that in only a few years, you'll have the means to fight them while still keeping your own enemies at bay? If the Grey Wolves fall, where do you think the human hunters, the Execution Underground, will turn their gaze? With us gone, you suddenly have a target on your backs."

Malcolm lifted his head. His wolf moved beneath his skin, the canid gold of his true eyes flashing. "You may be powerful, but not as powerful as us. That's not posturing, that's fact. You may not need us to survive, but you do need us to *thrive*. In the long run, our success keeps a target off your backs, serves your goals, and when your pack is strong enough to draw further attention, when we've healed and your *own* enemies come for you, the favor will be returned."

He lifted his glass again, swirling the contents. "I say that's a fucking good deal," he growled.

He drew his glass to his lips, finishing off the last dregs of the smoky liquid. Even now that he was finished speaking, the other wolves watched him, base animal instincts assessing, evaluating. The reek of death on his skin, the pain in his eyes, the curl of vengeance in his lip. For once, what they saw there must have been enough.

Dom and Rigs exchanged a subtle look.

"The other rangers and I would do anything to protect terra firma." Dom's jaw drew into a tight line, his expression speaking volumes about exactly how far that promise stretched. He had done what he had to protect their homelands before and he would again.

"And it's in the MC's best interest." Rigs nodded his agreement.

Dom extended his hand. "We'll do our best to whip the votes in your favor."

Malcolm gripped the other wolf's hand in his, the skin on the hot spots of his palm nearly as coarse and callused as his own, from where they both rode the open road. "If you can whip the votes, the deal is the deal." He met the other wolf's golden eyes. "We seal it with the warlock."

Chapter 4

As soon as Trixie's high-heeled boots hit the basement concrete, Boss's hand was in the air, signaling her. The dark warlock snapped his large fingers with annoyed impatience as if she wasn't already headed straight toward him. Around her, the bar's basement felt too hot, stifling among the sweaty nearness of so many close bodies packed into one small space. The soured, stale scent of beer that'd been ground into the concrete floor one too many times never disappeared. The buzz of too many voices speaking at once and the basses of one of the same five or so godforsaken songs the patrons loved to drunkenly sing along to vibrated the floor. If she heard "Free Bird" again, she might go ballistic.

Thankfully, she'd made it back downstairs with the bottle of Ketel One and a tray of six chilled highball glasses with exactly one minute to spare before Boss completely lost his shit.

"Hold your horses, big man," she muttered under her breath, hoisting her tray higher on her shoulder as she navigated toward the large boxing ring in the center.

Fridays and Saturdays at the Coyote were the busiest. Come six o'clock, service always picked up. By nine, they were slammed belowstairs.

At the far side of the ring, Boss, Stanislav, and a handful

of Stan's Kamchatka bear shifter associates sat around one of the reserved high-tops, conversing. As members of the South Side Shifter Outfit, the supernatural equivalent of the Mafia, Stan and his men typically operated near Chicago. Too far east to be here in the middle of godforsaken Idaho. But despite the locale, for the past three weeks, the Triple S had shown up every Friday and Saturday night for the cage fights and to meet with Boss, which meant she'd had to hustle even more than usual.

Trixie waded through the crowd, making her way to the table. As she did, she muttered a spell under her breath, so low that not even the most attuned of shifters could hear. Instantly, the noise in the room dampened as she homed in on Boss and Stan, listening. When it came to meetings like this, there were more half-truths than not. The lies left a bitter taste on her tongue, but she'd long since mastered her poker face. A veritas witch like her was the perfect lie detector for a powerful warlock. But not for forever.

She inhaled a deep breath, steadying her focus.

Two years, seven months, and ten days and then she'd finally be free of this place and her contract. Selling your soul to the devil didn't have to be literal. Sometimes the devil was an ancient necromancer with heterochromia who had a penchant for binding spells.

"It could be worse. Could be the *actual* devil," she whispered to herself.

As she approached, one of Stan's associates was gesturing wildly. "And then she was so high on supe juice she said, I don't want to put that in my mouth, but I guess I have to!"

The Chicagoans roared with laughter.

Boss smiled that wide, white-toothed, easy New Orleans grin of his and forced a chuckle. She knew the warlock well enough to tell when he was being genuine. Out on the floor like this, those times were few and far between. Trixie came up beside him and set down the first highball glass as the men continued. Fly meet wall.

"No, no, no," the jokester said, waving his hand to quiet the group. "With all due respect, Boss. I think we have a mutual interest in our…lupus problem. Just make sure the fangers are on board."

Lupus. The word pinged around in Trixie's brain like a code. Her magic sensed the lie beneath. Even without her abilities, she would have known there was no truth in the word. Shifters like Stan and his goons didn't get human illnesses like lupus.

Lupus.

No, *lupine*, her magic instantly corrected as if another voice inside her head were speaking to her. If the "fangers" were involved, that meant they had to be talking wolf shifters—and there was only one pack of wolf shifters who ruled the West. She mentally cataloged the information, tucking it away for later use.

"I think they see eye to eye," Boss answered coolly.

"We'll see." Stan grabbed hold of his highball glass, pulling it out from beneath where she was pouring. Trixie jolted the cold bottle back upright, barely avoiding spilling it all over the tabletop, and quickly moved on to the next shifter in the group, another Kamchatka bear shifter who reeked oddly of earthy beets.

Stan drew a sip of his drink. "And we'll see how your little fighter boy does in the ring tonight."

Little fighter boy.

Trixie hesitated as she set down the last glass. The chilled rim started to sweat. There was only one young shifter she knew talented enough to be put in the ring that fit Stan's vague description. She shook her head, blond curls bouncing. She couldn't have heard Stan correctly, but as her eyes darted toward Boss, he didn't refute the comment. His dark features held firm, playing his hand close. Anger coursed through her, sharp and fierce.

Holding her tray against her chest like a shield, she inched over to Boss's side, her face betraying nothing. "Boss, a word," she whispered in his ear.

Boss nodded, patting her on the shoulder. Holding up a finger to interrupt Stan exactly when the Russian opened his big mouth to speak again, Boss pushed out his chair. "S'cuse me, gentlemen." He rose from his seat, buttoning his violet suit coat before he tipped his hat, then followed her away from the table and into the downstairs office.

The door shut behind them with a quiet *snick*.

"This better be good, girl," he muttered, his velvety voice tinged with annoyance.

Trixie whirled on him. "You promised!"

The darker of Boss's mismatched eyes sparked with fury. "You know full well I don't make no promises. Not even to you."

Trixie paced the length of the small office space, hands on her hips. Sometimes, she couldn't believe him. Boss might have saved her life once upon a time. Not without a cost, of course, but the warlock was her friend—and right now, an infuriating one. "You said you wouldn't put Jackie in, that he wouldn't be in the ring this season," she accused. "He's good, but not *that* good."

The young coyote cage fighter was a talent, but his bravado got the better of him when it came to estimating his skills, particularly against shifters who were older, nearly double his size.

"Circumstances change, cher." Boss was shaking his head now. "You know that."

"Not *this* circumstance." Unexpected tears stung the edges of her eyes. Immediately, she blinked them back, never allowing them to get past the thick layer of her mascara. "If you put him in the ring, he'll die. Mikey will slaughter him." Her voice wobbled slightly, betraying her.

"That's the point, cher." Boss let out a long sigh, perching against the edge of the desk. He eyed her, dropping the hardened face he wore among the crowd. He was at least thirty years her senior, the closest thing she had to a father, but with his magic, he didn't look it. Yet as he watched her, his handsome features looked tired, weary. In the past few months, a few crow's-feet had creased near his eyes. "And what's he to you now?"

She shook her head. Jackie wasn't anything to her, not really, but she couldn't say that. Instead, she settled on, "He's just a kid."

"Far younger been in that ring than that boy."

She knew that, but...

"Doesn't make it right," she countered.

Boss pushed off the desk. He stepped closer, closing the space between them. Placing both large hands on the sides of her head, he was careful not to muss her hair even as his thumbs made smooth, comforting circles. He leaned in and placed a warm, welcome kiss on her forehead. It wasn't sexual. It simply was. Acknowledgment that in their own strange way, they were partners, family. "His family will be taken care of, cher," Boss said, clearly recognizing her thoughts. "I'll do that for you."

She pulled away from him, the comfort she'd felt at the old warlock's touch no longer providing warmth. "Is that supposed to make it better?"

"That's why he got himself into these fights in the first place, why they all do. It's for the prize money, to provide, you know that." Boss was shaking his head again, as if she were being foolish to the ways of their world, and maybe she was. "We all do what we have to."

"Yeah." She turned her back toward him, pinching the bridge of her nose. "Doesn't mean I have to like it." She sighed.

Boss released a sigh of his own. "Take a moment, girl." She heard the twist of the office's metal door handle. "Then it's back to work," he said gently.

The office door latched shut behind him.

Trixie balled her hands into fists, letting out a silent, internal scream. Fuck this life. Fuck the hand they'd been given. Not a single one of them deserved it. Not her. Not Jackie. None of them. Yet here they were. And why? Because money equaled power and power made the world go round, even the supernatural world, and they'd had the misfortune of drawing the short end of the goddamn stick. She slammed one of her fists against the desk, hard enough that her hand stung.

Trixie swore several unladylike swears under her breath. Her sweet, southern mama was probably turning over in her grave from it, but Trixie couldn't bring herself to care. Collecting herself, she straightened her clothes, her apron, and the girls, double-checking her reflection in a picture of the New Orleans French Quarter that Boss kept on the wall.

Her makeup was still in place. Her face still on.

And she'd live to see another day, even if Jackie didn't.

That was what survivors did after all, and she'd be damned if she hadn't survived more than her share of adversity. What was one thing more?

All she had was the hand fate had dealt her. That was it.

Steeling herself, she pushed open the door, heading back out into the crowd. The patrons' rabbled roar was still quieted, muffled to her ears thanks to lasting effects of her spell. Moments later, she was at Boss and Stanislav's table again, topping off their already half-consumed drinks as if not a single word had passed between her and Boss.

But the old warlock hadn't returned to Stan and the other bear shifters. Instead, he'd detoured to the other side of the ring, where she caught sight of him shaking hands with Blaze, then Malcolm and two leather-clad biker wolves she didn't recognize. Some kind of MC. She stiffened. The bottle of Ketel One grew warm against her palm.

She hadn't even realized she'd been openly staring until Stan's hand snaked its way onto her lower back. A shiver trembled through her.

"What do you know about those Grey Wolf shifters?" Stan asked, his eyes following hers toward Malcolm and Blaze.

Trixie set the bottle of vodka on the table, leaving it for the group.

The question was spoken from regular patron to bartender, not to her abilities as a witch. There was no way Boss had let on to the Russian bear shifter about her truth-telling. That was a close-kept secret between her, Boss, and whatever supernaturals happened to deem God on any given day, and, well…now Malcolm. Heat filled her cheeks as she blushed, realizing what she'd let slip earlier. But she covered it from Stan by making as if she'd turned away to fix an earring.

It wouldn't happen again. She couldn't let it.

"Not much," she answered, straightening to her full height as a means of subtly brushing Stan's filthy hand off her lower back.

"Come on, Trixie. You expect me to believe that?" Stan teased. "You know everything that goes on around here." He flashed her what was meant to be a charming grin.

As if some half-assed compliment and a mediocre smile were supposed to mask the fact that Stan was a grade A dick who didn't tip. But she'd need to throw him a bone, keep him amenable, and prevent Boss from getting pissed. "The one in the Hawaiian shirt is the Grey Wolf security specialist." She shrugged a shoulder as if that didn't mean anything important. "Wouldn't know it from the look of him, but they say he's a double threat, a former soldier disguised as a real tech genius."

"And the other one?" Stan asked.

Trixie frowned as she turned away again, filling one of the other bears' glasses. She'd hoped throwing Blaze's credentials out there first would deter Stan from Malcolm. She didn't know why she felt a drive to protect the snarly bastard, but she did.

From the corner of her eye, she caught sight of Jackie, looking young and fearless in the far corner as he warmed up for the fight. Two jabs and a right hook across his body. She could barely stand to look at him, knowing he was going to die. And for what? All because the monster beside her needed bloodshed for entertainment.

"Bless your heart, he's the Grey Wolves' assassin," she answered Stan finally, "and from all I hear, you best not fuck with him 'less you have a death wish, *sugar.*" *Bless your heart* translated into a big, old southern *fuck you* and she made certain that *sugar* said as much. He could rot in hell for being the cause of Jackie's death.

She moved to step away, but Stan yanked her back toward his table with enough force to bruise her wrist. "Are you saying I couldn't take that asshole?" The bear shifter snarled.

Clearly, he wasn't from around here. It'd take more than a couple grumbles from a pissed-off shifter to fill her with fear.

She wrenched her hand away. She could feel Boss's gaze narrowed on her now, the tangy scent of his powers hanging in the stifling, close air as he watched over her. No doubt

Stan could feel it, too. Boss asked her to put up with a lot of shit from the patrons, but he wouldn't tolerate anyone hurting her. Not even a Triple S-hole. "I'm saying 'that asshole' eats men like you every day for his damn breakfast." She leaned in close to Stan's face. "There wouldn't even be a fight. Just you pissing yourself before he cut you."

Stan snarled, eyes flashing bear-amber. The loud and guttural sound was enough to draw other patrons' attention. She felt Boss moving toward her. The warlock's dark power wrapped around her like a protective shield, but she was already done. Trixie fled from the table, weaving her way through the watching crowd. Boss caught her on her way toward the stairs, linking her arm in his, just as her spell faltered and the sound of the crowd roared again.

"What'd that bastard say to you, cher?" Boss whispered into her ear.

"Nothing important." She nodded over her shoulder. "Ask him."

She freed herself from Boss's hold, carrying her now-empty tray with her. A second longer and she'd detonate. She couldn't stand to be in the stifling closeness of the basement another moment, and the fight was due to start any minute. One of the patrons careened into her, nearly knocking her on her ass, but she quickly recovered, staying her course. The toe of her heeled boot was seconds away from hitting the first stair when another dark figure blocked her path.

She hit the muscled plane of Malcolm's chest, hard, his large hands catching her.

"You okay?" he growled, low and rough against her ear.

He'd clearly witnessed her and Stan's exchange, yet the concerned question on his lips sounded strange, foreign. The feel of his breath against her neck sent a shiver down her spine in an entirely different way than Stan's grubby paw had. She felt her nipples stiffen, the girls growing heavy with need as she inhaled the welcome scent of lemony soap on his skin. Thyme and lemon verbena.

She tilted her chin, staring up at him. His face was only inches away from hers, close enough that if she wanted to, she could close the distance between them, feel the softness of his lips again. She wanted to fall into him, to let herself collapse into his arms, though she doubted he'd let her for long. Kindness, amiability wasn't like him, and she didn't truly believe his concern for a minute.

She felt her chin quiver.

Damn him.

She couldn't look weak, couldn't fall apart. Not now.

"I'm fine," she snapped, pulling away. "What's it to you?"

Malcolm's features went dark, concern instantly disappearing. She wouldn't characterize what she saw there as hurt so much as a subtle hardening, the mask she knew so well slipping back into place.

"You're right. It's none of my business," he said, turning away from her.

He disappeared, blending into the crowd, not bothering to glance back as he likely made his way toward Blaze and the other shifters. Trixie couldn't stop herself from glancing over her shoulder to watch him go.

She turned and barreled up the stairs, calves burning from

the strain of her heels as she climbed. With each step, she cursed Stan, Boss, Jackie, Malcolm—especially Malcolm—anyone and everyone, all for reminding her that her stupid heart wasn't nearly as disillusioned as she wished it were.

Chapter 5

MALCOLM DIDN'T ALLOW HIMSELF TO WATCH Trixie go.

Instead, he made his way back toward Blaze and the Rock City MC Wolves, the roaring sounds of the impending fight burning against his ears. The two fighters were warming up on opposite sides of the ring, the large, squared cage serving as the focal point of the room. A massive bear shifter, whose girth made it look as if he were part tank, wrapped his knuckles in preparation for the damaging blows he'd deliver, while his opponent, a young, lean coyote half his size, bounced and stretched, his movement highlighting how quick and agile he was on his feet. The dank smell of sweat hung in the air, already pungent with the adrenaline high of the watching crowd.

"Last call!" someone hollered.

The two demon bookies taking bets on either side of the ring were swarmed in a sea of supernatural bodies. An abundance of wasted green bills was waved in their faces as patrons placed the last of their cash on which fighter would be bleeding out on the ring's concrete floor before night's end. The crowd's growing rumble was loud enough in human form, but to Malcolm's wolf, the noise rattled inside his skull, echoing and amplifying his frustration. He couldn't be certain whether the cause of his anger was the surrounding din or the icy words Trixie had hurled at him.

She'd be back and serving more drinks in a handful of minutes, sugary smile in place as if nothing had happened. But he'd know the truth, see it hidden beneath every fake smile she gave, and that fake smile wouldn't stop him from wanting to cave that bear-shifter fuck's head in.

His eyes tracked to the bastard, still sitting on the far side of the ring. Caucasian. Bear shifter. Skinhead. A true piece of shit. He didn't recognize the fucker, but from the way Boss had catered to him, there was no doubt the asshole had enough power to think he was a major player on whatever turf he happened to piss on and mark as his own.

As he reached the other wolf shifters, Blaze clapped a hand on Malcolm's shoulder, drawing him back to himself. "Remember what I said about looking a little less like you want to kill someone?" he shouted into Malcolm's ear over the crowd's noise.

Malcolm *did* want to kill someone, but that was beside the point.

From beneath this Stetson, he shot Blaze a warning look. "You'd do the same."

Of that he had no doubt.

Blaze's brows shot up near his sun-kissed hairline. "Comparing Trixie to my mate, huh?" He let out a low whistle and flashed Malcolm that charming, too-handsome grin that made Malcolm want to punch him for being far more delicious than any heterosexual, mated packmate should be. "You're a goner."

Malcolm scowled, turning his attention back toward the ring. Maybe he was. But that didn't mean he had to like it.

Boss was weaving his way through the crowd again, heading back toward them. The dark warlock's mismatched eyes scrunched at the edges, the rage there barely contained. Malcolm didn't like the bastard, didn't trust the smooth talker as far as he could throw him, but Boss protected Trixie like she was more than his bartender, like she was family, and for that, the warlock had his respect.

"Forgive me, gentlemen." Boss straightened the purple fedora he wore, an exact match for his royal amethyst suit. "Always at least one…situation," he said, "on fight nights." The yellowed whites of his eyes crinkled amid a passing patron's smoke.

"That *situation* better not lay another fucking hand on one of the waitstaff if he plans to wake up tomorrow morning." Malcolm shot Boss a flat look. He didn't need to growl to get his point across. From him, such cold words carried a true threat. It wasn't pointless posturing. He meant it.

Sometimes there were advantages to playing the Grey Wolves' grim reaper.

A spark of intrigue lit Boss's face as he smiled, looking Malcolm up and down as if he were truly seeing him for the first time. "What's my sweet Trixie to you now?" he asked, the sound of New Orleans strong in his voice.

Malcolm didn't answer. His…whatever the fuck it was… with Trixie was no one's concern but his own, especially not her employer's.

Thankfully, Blaze swooped in, diverting the attention

away from him. "The Grey Wolves have never appreciated violence toward women. You know that, Boss." Blaze cupped the warlock on the shoulder. "No women. No children. You're familiar with Rogue's old rules. Best damn fighter you ever had in that ring." Blaze nodded to the cage at the room's center as if he were pleased with the prospect of the night's entertainment, though Malcolm was certain he wasn't.

Beside Blaze, Dom and Rigs nodded their mutual agreement with that rule set.

Violence was only enjoyed by men who seldom experienced it firsthand.

Silent, Malcolm watched the crowd, instantly spotting Trixie again the moment she sashayed back down to the basement floor.

She was holding a tray of flaming shots, the smoke billowing around her as she plastered that fake, red-lipped smile on her face. She carried the full tray over to a table of cougar shifters, who for all their drunkenness looked like thoroughly sloshed, slightly more muscular frat boys and probably blew through their pack's cash all the same. Cat shifters or not, the cougars practically howled their approval at her approach, snatching their shots off the tray Trixie carted. One of them passed a single small glass toward her. She accepted it with a coy smile and a little flirtatious shake of her shoulders before throwing back her head and downing the liquor to the cougars' jeering approval.

When she'd finished, she pounded the shot glass down on the table, the cougars around her too caught up in their own bullshit to notice that her fake smile was now gone from her face. Trixie glanced toward Malcolm, her eyes instantly finding his and settling as if she knew exactly where he stood at all times, no doubt to taunt him. But instead of the saucy grin she usually flashed him or the not-so-subtle bend to show off the ample curve of her mouthwatering cleavage, she simply stared back at him, eyes flat and revealing nothing, as if she'd rather be anywhere than the exact spot where she was standing. He recognized the feeling.

But as quickly as the moment came, it was gone again, one of the cougars beside her saying something to snag her attention before passing her a way-too-thin stack of bills considering all those damn flaming drinks she'd likely taken extra time to make.

A second later, Blaze's hand was suddenly on Malcolm's shoulder again. "This is your deal," he said, nodding toward where Boss and the Rock City MC Wolves waited. "Care to do the honors?"

With that intro, Malcolm supposed he didn't have a goddamn choice, but he didn't bother to say as much. He turned away from Trixie, stepping forward to shake Dom's now extended hand. Boss held his open palms out over their handshake. As the warlock chanted over them, Malcolm felt the searing brand of the binding spell sink into his skin.

The inky, midnight black of Boss's magic snaked its way over his and Dom's handshake, fierce and burning, like the heated end of a cattle prod, but Malcolm schooled his face to remain unfazed, unaffected. To Dom's credit, he did the same. The other wolf's eyes locked with his. Malcolm felt the exact moment the magic settled beneath his skin. The pain dulled considerably. He released Dom's grip, but the tangy scent of citrus and lemongrass mixed with the unfortunate smell of burnt flesh lingered along with the black magic markings that wrapped like a banded tattoo around his hand.

They'd remain until the pack's deal was completed.

Boss stepped back, tipping the rim of his fedora. "Pleasure doing business with you, gentlemen." The warlock smiled wide, pleased to be privy to the Grey Wolves and Rock City MC's dealings. That was how the Midnight Coyote's proprietor did his business after all, dealing and trading in secrets and betting lives beneath the bar stairs as if the weight of the two proved to be the same.

But the insurance that his magic provided—the guarantee that their pack wouldn't be double-crossed with the plague-like death that came with breaking a powerful binding spell—proved useful. The risk of their dealings being known outweighed the reward time and again. Boss's business model depended on it.

"A pleasure as always, Boss," Blaze answered, shaking hands with the other man.

Boss nodded his approval before slipping back into the fold of the crowd from which he'd come.

It was done then.

And perhaps, as a result, the Grey Wolves would live to see another day.

"It's settled," Dom said, smiling at him. The expression was easier, more genuine now that their deal was in place, and Malcolm was struck by how unexpectedly handsome it made the biker. He had more than a passing feeling that Rigs agreed.

Blaze plucked four beers that weren't his, two in each hand, off one of the passing waitstaff's trays. The feeder from earlier. At least this time, she had the shame to cover the fang marks on her neck. Though Malcolm supposed he shouldn't judge. Even the feeders served their purpose, staving off the bloodsuckers' hunger for other unwilling human prey, even if it'd eventually get her killed. The feeder started to protest about the stolen drinks but then immediately blanched when she saw Malcolm standing beside Blaze. Instead, she headed on her way, mumbling something about grabbing more and starting another tab for them.

Blaze passed out the beers to the other men before he held up his own. "For the first time in weeks, we have something to celebrate."

Malcolm glanced down at the brown bottle in his hand. Voodoo Ranger. Not the usual Coors. A surprising improvement. "Why didn't *you* seal the deal then?"

Blaze shrugged. "I promised Dakota I'd be back not long after midnight, and I've had enough pain for one day." He nodded to the stiffness in his leg before downing several gulps of his beer. "And with that, I'll leave you gentlemen to it." He grinned, throwing Malcolm under the proverbial bus by ensuring he'd have to stay.

And *that* was why Malcolm didn't like Blaze.

The charming bastard always knew how to get his damn way.

Blaze could have asked Malcolm to stay instead, and Malcolm would have obliged, but Blaze didn't. He simply manipulated, near effortlessly, no questions asked. A moment later, he slipped into the crowd, leaving Malcolm alone with the two biker wolves among the party's drunken masses. A newly released country song that sounded far too much like a mixture of pop and rock played in the background.

And the fight was about to begin.

Malcolm didn't have much taste for it, but he'd stay for the pack's sake. In obligation, thanks to Blaze.

"Who'd you place your bet on?" Rigs asked from beside him. The other wolf bumped shoulders with him, his large arms crossed over his chest as he watched the two fighters enter the caged ring.

"I don't waste my money on chance," Malcolm answered, drawing a sip of his beer. The hoppy taste slid down his throat.

"Growing up on the South Side will do that," Dom yelled over the noise knowingly. Malcolm had thought he'd recognized the familiarity of Dom's midwestern accent. He shot the other two wolves a look, confirming what he already knew.

They knew his background, his life before the Grey Wolves. No doubt because it'd happened within their club's territory. Didn't matter that it was decades-old news. Rumor proved timeless. Yet they'd made the deal with him despite him being a wanted man. He searched the other wolves' faces for some sort of disgust or censure but, surprisingly, found none.

It was one thing to kill for contract. It was another to kill someone with the same last name. A helpless human.

"We all do what we need to survive," Dom said,

acknowledging the unspoken tension. Based on that detail, the Rock City MC's sergeant had likely had some contact at the Chicago PD pull the human police reports.

Maybe these wolves *did* know him better than he thought, or at least what was detailed on his human rap sheet.

"So if you were the kind of wolf who wasted his hard-earned pack cash," Rigs said, nodding toward the ring, "who would you favor?"

Malcolm surveyed the two fighters as they circled the ring. It wasn't even a question. But off to the side, his eyes caught Trixie, scooping a tip off an abandoned table as she bused the leftover drinks. He took a moment as if to consider the fight while he watched her. "I tend to root for the underdog," he admitted, finally looking back toward the ring. "But anyone with half a brain and a realist's take can see the coyote's in over his head."

At that moment, the bear shifter landed a shot to the side of the coyote's jaw, sending his opponent careening. The crowd groaned a collective wince at the coyote's pain as a mix of spit and blood sprayed onto the concrete cage floor. But to Malcolm's surprise, the coyote quickly rebounded, quicker than he should have, throwing and landing a counterblow of his own. A true warrior. So much like another half coyote, half Grey Wolf he'd known, whose noted absence made Malcolm's chest ache. The crowd roared at the surprise hit, a mixture of amusement, pleasure, and jeering howls for the bear to throttle the young coyote shifter.

"You may be good at estimating our club's interest, but maybe not so much in the ring." Dom grinned behind the neck of his tipped-back beer. The coyote had rebounded nicely.

"Maybe so," Malcolm grumbled, his eyes locking on the true reason for his misestimation…on the far side of the cage, where Trixie stood, her eyes never leaving the coyote shifter as she muttered a heated spell beneath her breath.

Chapter 6

KEEPING JACKIE ALIVE WAS HARDER THAN IT LOOKED. Trixie whispered under her breath, her words a nonstop stream of spell casting as the crowd raged. The familiar scent of her magic surrounded her. Magnolia and honeysuckle. The hum of energy covered the crowd, engulfing Jackie inside the ring. She hadn't taken a full breath in several minutes. Having given up all pretense that she was busing the tables, she slipped toward the back of the crowd, hiding in the shadows. From the burning in her chest, her lungs were starting to feel it. But she didn't dare hesitate.

Her eyes tracked Jackie's movements as he fought with the ferocity of a naive kid who couldn't afford to lose. Fury rolled off his bear-shifter opponent, promising if her eyes left the young coyote, her friend would be bleeding out within seconds.

Her throat started to ache.

The crowd went wild with cheers from Jackie's supporters as he landed another unexpected blow. The smell of bar smoke, coppery bloodshed, and the sweaty, blinding rage from the bear's backers created a dangerous, heady mix. All it'd take was one spark from either side, the single strike of a flint, and the whole room would go up in a fire of fists.

But Trixie couldn't bring herself to care.

Fuck them. Fuck all of them. Every single patron here who thought violence was a sport, who wasted their money on watching innocent bodies drop onto the blood-soaked concrete, who made her and the other staff scrub the life of some poor bastard from the floor instead of using their privilege to help somebody, to do a damn bit of good in this godforsaken world. They didn't care if they destroyed the Midnight Coyote, her, or this person she loved, so why should she shed a tear if they destroyed themselves in return?

Her mama had always said fair was fair.

Trixie muttered under her breath, her words coming in a rapid-fire hiss like a cottonmouthed snake. She felt each sting of Jackie's wounds as her own, each hit the bear shifter landed on the coyote's bronzed skin.

Trixie had few good things in her life. Sure, she was more fortunate than most. She knew that firsthand. She had the basics. The roof of her shithole apartment over her head, enough money for food on the occasions she could muscle up the energy to cook for one, a well-stocked, skimpy wardrobe, and a sizable hair and makeup budget. Even an old beater of a car. In the words of her patron saint, Dolly Parton, it cost a lot of money to look this cheap.

It was more than she ever had as a child.

But none of that added up to a life that felt worth living, a life of happiness and satisfaction, of feeling as if she could look forward to each day when the rooster crowed. That wasn't the hand fate had dealt her. She knew that. Hell, she'd long since accepted it. Long before her contract with Boss.

She'd made her damn peace. Life was never going to be her oyster, so there was no point in griping about it.

But she'd be damned if she let Stan, Boss, these blood-hungry patrons, *anyone* take this *one* good thing from her, this bit of brightness in an otherwise dim world.

They were getting close now, the end of the fight drawing near. The bear shifter swayed on his giant feet, bobbing and weaving like he was about to collapse. Speckles of blood dripped from his mouth and nose, coating the cage floor. He kicked a stray tooth to the edge of the ring. Thanks to her, Jackie had landed several fierce, unfaltering blows. All she needed to do was hold the bear long enough for Jackie to deliver one final uppercut to his nose. Then Stan's precious bear's skull would cave in. She didn't feel the least bit of remorse about that.

If Stan and his goons could fix the fight, why couldn't she do the same?

Despite the fear in her gut, she didn't dare glance toward Triple S. They'd be too absorbed in their unexpected loss to notice her or the pull of her magic. But Boss would. No doubt he'd be pissed at her for interfering, but she'd caused him worse trouble before. Served him right for breaking his promise to her.

Jackie was in position now, had a clear opening.

All it'd take was one more punch.

Trixie stepped forward, away from the wall, stretching her power to her limit. She wasn't as strong as Boss. But she could do this. She *would* do this. For Jackie. For herself.

Her whispers held the bear shifter. Only a second longer.

This was it.

The hard blow of some drunken idiot slammed into her, his shoulder catching against hers. She lost her balance, nearly toppling to the floor. But bless his heart, Jackie didn't need it. He delivered the final punch she'd teed up, straight to the bear shifter's nose. The uppercut knocked the skinhead fucker into oblivion.

Still thrumming with rage, Trixie righted herself and shoved the asshole cougar who'd nearly knocked her on her ass, hard. He stumbled back, knocking into one of Stan's men at the exact moment the bear in the ring hit the floor. Stan's eyes found hers.

And in an instant, all hell broke loose.

The Kamchatka bear that the cougar stumbled into let out an earsplitting roar, throwing a punch of his own. Chaos rippled outward, fueling the fight like gasoline.

Trixie'd been in her fair number of brawls, but this one was a doozy. Fighting erupted around her. Glass shattered. She snatched a spare tray off the table she'd been busing, hunkering beneath it like it was a shield as she ducked beneath a table. Somewhere in the insanity, some idiot cowboy's gun went off, but it did little to calm the storm.

She needed to get the hell outta here—and fast.

Eyes scanning the free-for-all, she mapped a pathway to the stairs. But that was when she saw Stan crawling his way through the wreckage toward her, amber bear eyes blazing.

Shit. He knew. She didn't know how, but he did.

And he and his Triple S-holes were going to kill her for it.

It wasn't even a question.

Trixie yelped in fear. Scrambling from beneath the table, she used the plastic tray to shield her head. She barreled toward the stairs, diving through the brawling bodies, overturned tables, and broken bottles, nearly twisting her ankle twice in the process. To her relief, she made it to the back stairwell unscathed, only slipping when one of her heels caught the edge of a pint shard.

Righting herself, she raced upstairs with several gasps. The weight of the girls meant she wasn't built for running. No, sir. Adrenaline coursed through her. Her pulse thumped in her temple. Her hair was going to be a fucking mess, even if her waterproof mascara stayed in place. But she'd reach the top of those stairs if it was the last thing she did, damn it.

She *did* finally reach the top. Trixie's eyes darted over the scene. The brawl had traveled upstairs, leaving several tables overturned and the whole bar trashed. But the less crowded atmosphere and the swinging exit door from where some of the patrons had beat feet promised more safety.

She raced behind the bar top. If she wasn't so spiteful, she'd have hurried her sweet little ass out to her ancient hatchback and prayed that her key (plus a hint of magic) would cause the old vehicle's engine to turn over, but there was no way in hell she was abandoning the cash drawer and all her tips tucked beneath it. A girl needed to pay rent. Plus, once she'd let him cool down for a few days, the drawer would serve as a peace offering to Boss.

But saving Jackie's life had been worth it.

She punched a button on the register, and the drawer sprang open. She lifted the plastic cash tray out of its nestled hold, scooping up the bills beneath it and stuffing them into her pockets. It wouldn't be long before Stan would follow her up the stairs. Time didn't slow for anyone, even a witch.

Slamming the empty drawer closed, she was about to hightail it out of there when a cougar shifter twice her size came flying over the bar top. Trixie let out a shriek, missing the shifter by mere inches. On the top shelf, several liquor bottles teetered before they fell to the floor and shattered. But the cougar slumped against the tap wall, unconscious. Trixie's eyes darted to where he'd been thrown. Whoever had sent him flying had tossed the brute like he weighed no more than a rag doll.

At the sight of the culprit, she let out an unguarded squeak.

Malcolm stood on the other side of the bar, golden wolf eyes raging. Beneath his Stetson, his shadowed face was twisted with unruly rage. His muscled chest heaved from exertion, the sheen of his leather jacket catching against the neon bar lights. From the curled snarl of his upper lip, the cowboy wolf dared any other brawling piece of shit to stand in his way. Anyone who did had a death wish.

His gaze darted toward her, cold, unflinching eyes raking over her from head to toe. She felt her spine stiffen. He scowled, not bothering to say anything, before he headed toward the door. Clearly, he no longer gave two shits about her or her well-being. No surprise there.

She rolled her eyes, hefting the money drawer into her arms and scurrying after him. The big, wounded brute was Mr. Sensitive when it came to getting his feelings hurt. There were different kinds of weakness, and wallowing in the pits of hell because he didn't have the strength to pull himself back up again was one of Malcolm's.

She, on the other hand, had pulled herself up by the pointy heels of her stiletto pumps, and she had no intention of being pushed back down again. He likely thought her brittle in her cynicism, but it took true balls to brush herself off and keep fighting after she'd been knocked down time and again. Brooding was easy. Surviving wasn't.

The sound of several patrons laid flat and groaning, along with the muffled chaos from belowstairs, was the only noise that cut through the silence. From the bottom of the stairwell, a shout rang out. Stan. Or one of his idiot goons at least.

Shit.

She wasn't fast enough. In these heels, she'd never reach her car and get the thing started in time. She needed to hide, but with half the damn tables overturned, the only place was right out in the open behind the...

"Malcolm!" she hissed after him.

He hesitated momentarily but didn't turn to look at her. He must have decided that whatever had caused his stride to hitch, she wasn't worth it, because a second later, he kept going. *Damn it.*

"Malcolm, you big, burly idiot!" she whispered after him. "I've put up with enough of your shit and stayed till closing for you enough times that you could at least answer me."

An annoyed growl rumbled from the wolf shifter, but he cast a glance over his shoulder. "What?" The biting chill in his voice shouldn't have frustrated her. But it did.

How could he kiss her with more passion than any man she could conjure in her dreams and then act like the thought of it didn't keep him awake at night? For her, it certainly had. More than once. But she supposed the ache in her heart when she looked at him didn't mean anything. Not for him anyway. It never did for men in her past. That was how she'd been stupid enough to end up in her contract— wrongly thinking someone cared for her.

She wasn't the kind of woman a man took home with him.

"Stand guard over me," she said, pushing any sentimentality aside and slipping back behind the bar top, "or divert attention at least."

If Malcolm stood near the bar edge, she doubted Stan or any of the Triple S-holes would try to push past him. She slipped the cash drawer into the small gap underneath the dish sink. She'd need to squeeze herself into the cramped space between there and the mini fridge, but she hadn't spent all those years trying to meditate her way to happiness and find her center doing yoga for nothing.

"And why the fuck would I do that?" Malcolm growled again.

Trixie huffed, rolling her eyes as she started to duck behind the lacquered wood. "Out of the kindness of your brooding, bleeding heart?" The voices of the Triple S drew closer, growing louder with each green and pink flash of the cracked jukebox screen as they approached the top of the stairs.

Malcolm moved to turn away from her again.

"Please!" she pleaded, for once allowing the fear she felt to slip into her voice. "You may not like me, but I don't deserve to die."

Malcolm glanced toward her then, golden wolf eyes searing in their intensity. She wanted him to counter that claim, say he *did* like her, more than either of them would be willing to admit. But he didn't. That'd be far too easy, and she knew better than to think anything in her life would be tied up with a perfect, pretty bow other than the stitches of her G-string.

"Why'd you fix the fight?" he asked.

The abrupt question caught her off guard. Now hardly seemed like the time for that, but the answer tumbled from her painted lips before she could think it through. "Jackie's always been kind to me. Never pulled any bullshit. He looks at me like I'm a person, not some sexy plaything meant for his amusement."

Her eyes met Malcolm's, and for a brief moment, she thought she saw a hint of pity. The thought nearly killed her. She didn't need anyone's pity. His especially.

"Satisfied?"

Malcolm watched her for a beat. "No." He turned to leave again.

But Trixie could hear Stan coming down the hallway. The distinct cadence of his accented voice carried. Her pulse raced. She didn't think.

"Walk out that door, and whatever information I have about you and your stupid pack dies with me," she threatened.

That got his attention.

He'd no doubt find Stan's little lupus comment from earlier intriguing.

Malcolm snarled. "You're bluffing."

"Want to risk it?" She held his gaze for a prolonged beat, only breaking the standoff at the last second when the door from the basement burst inward. Time-out. She ducked behind the counter, folding herself into the small space and praying to Dolly, Patsy, and whatever witchy goddess had made twenty-four-hour lipstick to save her. She dug her heels into the hardwood flooring, urging them not to slip on the floor's sheen as she held her place.

The sound of a single pair of shitkicker boots drew closer, calmly making their way across the bar's wooden boards. Trixie tensed. Closing her eyes, she shivered but didn't allow herself to move, to even breathe. Whatever happened, she'd get through this. She always did. Even if it was by the skin of her teeth.

"Who the fuck are you?" Stan's voice accused.

Trixie's whole body sagged with relief when she heard Malcolm's graveled voice answer back. "No one." Thanks to her magic, the subtext of that statement rang clear inside her head.

No one you want to fuck with.

She bit her lips and smiled to herself. Reluctant hero he might be, but Malcolm wasn't going to leave her to the wolves...or bears, as it were. He had that going for him at least.

"You see that blond bartender bitch cut through here?" The hatred in those words was palpable. Her magic hissed.

She'd been called it all before, and Stan likely wouldn't be the last. America had no respect for strong women.

"She went that way," Malcolm grumbled, likely nodding toward the door.

Trixie winced. *Real original, sugar.*

No one had ever called the Grey Wolf executioner a smooth talker.

A silent beat passed, so filled with tension Trixie struggled to keep her breathing quiet.

"You two watch over this asshole," Stan finally ordered his men. "We'll find that bitch again, and when we do, don't hesitate. End her."

A moment later, she heard the distinct creak of Stan and three of his guys shuffling over the fluted brass floor separator at the entry door. But she and Malcolm were far from being in the clear.

The bear shifters would be back, and then…

"You're hugging pretty close to that bar top." The asinine comment came from one of Stan's men. Whoever it was, she heard him start to draw closer, as if to push past Malcolm and right near her hiding place. A few steps behind the bar top and they'd find her there—and if they did, she was dead. Stan had said as much.

One of Malcolm's large boots hit the floor as he blocked the other man's way.

Trixie's pulse raced.

A bearlike growl sounded. "Move out of my way, fuck-face."

"No."

She didn't know there could be such cold fury in a single word. Malcolm didn't need to growl or snarl for his point to be driven home.

"I'll give you one warning not to touch me again. I suggest you listen."

Trixie tensed.

"And if I don't?"

She could practically hear the sneer in the bear shifter's voice, the false bravado and confidence. But it was Malcolm's answer that chilled her.

"I'll bash your skull in."

Trixie stiffened. There wasn't even a hint of a lie in those words. He meant it.

He'd do that to a man *for her*.

She was certain she should feel more horrified by that, but she didn't.

The bear shifter laughed.

Trixie closed her eyes, silently pleading with the idiot not to be dumb enough to touch Malcolm again. But it was a worthless prayer. The moron lasted all of two seconds. The sound of cracking bone rang through the bar along with the sound of the two shifters scuffling and the shout of the other guard. Not far from where she hid, the distinct thud of a limp body landed beside her, followed by the other guard's repeated shouts.

"Shit!" he roared.

A loud clang followed, and a moment later, the fire extinguisher rolled to where she remained lodged between the sink and the mini fridge. Its base was covered in blood. From the corner of her eye, she could see a limp hand from where the body had landed. She dared peek out, only to be certain it wasn't Malcolm, and then instantly regretted it.

It wasn't.

Trixie clapped her hand over her mouth, struggling not to scream. There was violence and then there was *carnage*. A major difference. She whimpered.

He had, in fact, bashed the bear's head in. With a fire extinguisher no less.

A wolflike snarl rang out, harsh and feral, followed by the scrape of paws and claws against polished wood. Trixie closed her eyes, shaking and silent where she hid as Malcolm finished fighting his opponents. She'd never get used to the bloodshed, feeling every true emotion that came with it. The fear, the rage, the hatred. The only comfort that eventually came to her rescue was the silence that finally followed, and then a cold, wet wolf nose brushing against her face as it sniffed her.

Her eyes shot open. A massive beast stood before her. She'd dated plenty of wolf shifters, had even seen them shift, but never a Grey Wolf and never this close before. Trixie swallowed down her fear in favor of the mixture of surprise and awe that coursed through her. It was a wolf that stood before her, large, predatory, but the eyes were distinctly his.

Malcolm.

His muzzle dripped with blood. Still, she couldn't stop herself from reaching out to touch him, the dry spot of fur at his neck. The soft, bristled texture was both foreign and somehow distinctly his. Not at all like the monster she thought he'd be. No matter how violent and fierce.

She'd never be afraid of him.

At her touch, he grumbled, low in his throat in a way that was all too familiar, before he retreated. A moment later, the air around the wolf seemed to bend and shift, extending, changing, and then a pair of bare male human legs replaced her view.

Malcolm didn't say anything. Just stepped toward the sink beside her, turning the faucet on. She heard him splash some water on his face casually, cleaning the blood from his mouth before he pulled on his clothes again.

As if he hadn't killed two men without even a blink. No pity. No remorse.

Slowly, Trixie eased out from her hiding place.

"You okay?" he asked gruffly. His voice was even more graveled than normal, more wolf than man.

Breathing a sigh of relief, she nodded. "Yeah, I'm fine. Thanks."

He nodded to the floor beside her, where she was distinctly trying not to let her eyes stray. "Don't look," he warned.

"I already made that mistake." Bile stung the back of her throat.

If the carnage bothered Malcolm, he didn't show it. He shrugged back into his shirt and then his leather before replacing his Stetson, fully dressed again. His fallen clothes had barely gotten any blood spray. The Grey Wolf executioner killed quickly. Brutally and efficiently. She supposed with his reputation, that fit, but she didn't want to think about it too hard.

She was still struggling to breathe. "You…you killed a man for—"

"I didn't do it for you." Malcolm pegged her with a hardened stare.

"Of course you didn't."

A part of her wondered if he meant to protect her conscience from it, but if he did, it was a lost cause. They both knew it was a lie. At least in part, but Trixie didn't bother to acknowledge that. She felt some softened part inside herself tense and brace again at the tension. It was going to be like that between them again then. Nothing different.

She shouldn't be surprised. It shouldn't hurt, but if shouldn'ts were money, she'd be a rich woman. She had more than enough of them, especially for one night.

Trixie left the cash drawer hidden underneath the bar, fully abandoning it as she rounded the bar top. She could tell Boss where it was later. No one would find it there, and at least she'd nabbed her tips. That was what really mattered. Around them, the bar was in shambles, broken glass everywhere, tables overturned, and the kind of eerie stillness that came only after total chaos.

Beneath one of the booths, Trixie spotted Dani, pale-faced and shaking. Poor girl. She'd seen everything. Navigating through the wreckage, Trixie crossed the room before she crouched down beside the other woman. Dani flinched at her touch.

"You didn't see any of that," Trixie whispered, stroking a

glowing finger against Dani's cheek. She used the last of her magic to alter the other woman's truth.

Dani nodded dumbly, eyes wide and magic-struck. A moment later, she looked around with a startled blink. "What happened?"

Trixie smiled slow and sweet. "Don't worry about it, sugar. Boss'll come get you soon. Just stay right there, okay?"

Dani seemed to think this was a good idea. "Okay." She nodded.

Trixie rose to her feet, heading toward the door, but Malcolm blocked her way.

"You can alter memories," he said.

The unspoken question hung in the air.

Have you done that to me?

"I can manipulate truths. Seek them out, find them, change them. *Truth* is my thing," she said pointedly. "It's easier in humans. Doesn't work on shifters."

From the spark in his dark eyes, he seemed surprised by that. "You also fix bar fights."

She shrugged, trying to ignore the mess around them. In a few days' time, she'd no doubt pay for it. Someone would have to clean up. "On occasion," she answered. "But stuff like that drains me quick. Not my specialty." She eyed him up and down. "What deal were you making with Boss tonight anyway?"

Malcolm shrugged. "Pack business."

"Revenge or defense?"

He lifted a brow like he was surprised she could see straight through him.

"You don't get that heated up unless it's about Bo," she explained.

"Both," he answered. "For him and another friend."

She nodded. "Hope it was worth it then."

And she meant it. She'd liked Bo. Had mourned him in her own way. Truly. And she may not have known his other friend, but that didn't stop her from feeling sorry for Malcolm's newest loss. At least this time, he hadn't let it break him.

Without another word, she moved to brush past him, eager to leave. She needed to get the hell out of there before Stan came back and found his men dead, but Malcolm wasn't having it.

He stepped in front of her path again. "Tell me what you know about my pack."

Trixie glanced out toward the night, to the open doors and the stretching stars of Idaho's midnight skies and the orange glow of the streetlamps. Maybe her car would start. Maybe she'd make it home in one piece. But it wouldn't be hard for a guy like Stan to find her apartment if he asked around. Where did she go from there?

She shook her head. "No. Not till you get me to safety, darlin', and that ain't here."

Malcolm scowled. The gold of his wolf eyes had settled now, slowly shifting back to a brown so dark that the moonlight painted them near black. Two deep, midnight pools. Like he carried a hint of the night's shadows in his pocket with him. His gaze fell to her again. "Follow me," he said, finally relenting.

He led her out into the night, the faint outline of the mountains barely a shadow in the distance. They cut through several alleys near the Coyote, the ripe smell of the nearby businesses' garbage-filled dumpsters permeated the autumn air. A soft breeze ruffled her hair as Trixie breathed a sigh of relief.

Malcolm only stopped once they'd reached a large Harley, chained and locked far from the citrusy glow of the streetlights. He reached into the bike's saddlebag, trading his black Stetson for a helmet before shoving a spare at her.

She stared at the protective gear but didn't take it.

"You got a problem with helmets?" he mumbled. He mounted the bike, lifting its hefty weight upright with ease.

"I've got a problem with helmet *hair*, that's all."

"You look fine."

Fine. Not good. Not great. *Fine.*

Even after all the insanity of the evening, she had to admit that stung a bit.

"Not a single fake eyelash or tit out of place." His gaze darted to the girls.

In the midst of the melee, the already low neckline of her top had been twisted sideways, revealing a hint of the leopard-print bra she wore beneath.

She straightened herself while shooting him an incredulous look. "Excuse you, but these are real, asshole." She gestured to her ample chest like she was Vanna White. "I may look fake, but I'm real where it counts," she said. Another Dolly quote.

No one spoke truer to her heart than country music's queen.

She snatched the stupid helmet from his hand, jamming the hideous gear onto her head. Immediately, she felt her curls fall flat, but she didn't so much as bat one of her *very real* eyelashes before she sauntered over to him. She swung her leg over the Harley, settling onto the back seat pad as she wrapped her arms around him. She knew exactly where to place her high-heeled feet.

"Now shut up and ride toward I-90."

Chapter 7

MALCOLM COULD FEEL THE WARMTH OF TRIXIE'S ARMS wrapped around him. Her manicured hands settled against the front of his leather, the soft mounds of her ample breasts pressing against his back. Even as they sped toward the highway, finally free of the bar chaos, her touch felt like an embrace, a lover's caress. Far more intimate than it should be. But at the moment, he didn't have the mind to interrogate that.

He'd killed for her. That meant something. He didn't kill casually.

Not without being paid a giant sum anyway.

Around them, the Idaho night was inky black, a sea of swirling endless stars and constellations that stretched far beyond the dark mountaintops in the distance. His bike's muffler rumbled, filling the silence and quieting the thoughts in his head with it. His Harley's single headlight cut through the darkness. They weren't too far from the Montana border now, from the roads that would lead him back to Wolf Pack Run, to the ranch he was supposed to call home but didn't.

He twisted the throttle, speeding along the highway toward an upcoming exit. The mountain air was already thick with moisture. By sunrise, the autumn chill would cause the dying short grass to freeze, though snow was a few weeks off yet. Come winter, that same moisture would make for heavy snowfall.

The wind whipped around them, cold and fierce. It wouldn't be long before the other hands started complaining about the temperature and he'd have to kick on the bunkhouse heater.

But with the open road ahead of them and the sting of the wind on his face, he could almost forget the winter work that lay ahead. The long hours bringing in the cattle, the bite of frost against his skin, the ache in his muscles that never really seemed to disappear, even when he shifted into his wolf. Here, with the open road, the snowcapped mountains in the distance, and Trixie snuggled against his back, he almost felt calm, peaceful, like autumn wasn't the death of all the beauty summer wrought each year.

Like there wasn't blood on his hands again.

"Turn here," Trixie spoke over the wind into his ear.

Until now, he'd thought he'd known exactly where she was leading them, out to Black Hollow Ranch, Rogue's place. It was a near safe haven for wolf shifters and other supernaturals on the run in the middle of the night. Wolf Pack Run was several hours' drive, and Trixie was no doubt a friend of Rogue's from back in his fighting days at the Coyote. But that was one of the many frustrating things Malcolm had discovered about Trixie over the years. Faker than a three-dollar bill or not, she never failed to keep things interesting. No matter how much he despised his own intrigue with her show.

Malcolm followed her directions, tilting the weight of his

motorcycle beneath them into their next turn. In the minutes that followed, she whispered several more turns to him, the soft touch of her ruby-red lips brushing against his hair, the crook of his neck, his ear, each bit of nearness sending a warm shiver down his spine. His cock strained uncomfortably against his jeans and the bike's leather seat. With the wind whipping about them, he couldn't smell the gardenia scent that lingered in the blond curls of her hair, both too familiar and yet somehow foreign, like a memory he knew well but couldn't access, but he could imagine it, crave it.

His wolf stirred beneath his skin.

Damn, witch.

By the time they pulled off the road, he was equal parts horny and pissed.

"Right here," she said when they finally coasted to a stop outside a cheap, run-down motel that looked like some sort of cross between an old Econo Lodge and a Motel 6.

From the looks of it, the place was an even more endangered species—the kind of off-highway, nonfranchised, hole-in-the-wall that'd be damned if it ever left the light on for you. The building was sandwiched between what was, based on the name Kittie's Korner and the pink neon shape of a woman's silhouette on the sign, a twenty-four-hour sex shop and a long-since closed Cracker Barrel. In the empty dark, the abandoned rocking chairs and checkerboards on the overly sentimentalized country porch looked oddly ghostlike. The streetlights painted the scattered trucks in the parking lot a glowing orange that somehow tinged the olive hue of his skin a sickly green.

As soon as he threw down the bike's kickstand, Trixie slid out of the seat, the sound of her heeled boots against the concrete like sharp little clicks. She tore the helmet off her head, shaking her curled hair out in a way that was far too intoxicating even for him. He had to admit, she was effortlessly gorgeous, especially when she wasn't trying. She passed the helmet to him. Seconds later, she was strutting toward one of the rooms, heels clicking as she made her way toward a numbered door labeled with a crooked nine that appeared more like a six.

"What the fuck are we doing here?" Malcolm growled. He didn't know what the witch was playing at, but he didn't care for it one bit. He wasn't her errand boy.

He was here with one purpose: to get whatever information Trixie happened to have about the pack he was sworn to protect. Or at least that was what he was telling himself.

Standing at the door, Trixie reached into her bra, pulling a key from somewhere inside her cleavage before she wiggled it into the lock. "I live here, asshole. Not all of us can be as wealthy as the Grey Wolves, so mind your manners."

Malcolm scowled in response. Grey Wolf or not, he wanted to tell her that by no stretch of the imagination was he some elitist ass who'd look down on her for not having extra cash to spare or living in a motel. He still had far too many memories of windy Chicago nights where he'd had to choose between using whatever coins he could scrounge from beneath the cushions of their old plaid couch to venture out of their shithole apartment and find a meal to eat from the nearest fast-food dollar menu or watching over his mother, passed out in a drug-induced stupor on that same sofa, to make sure she didn't stop breathing.

She never had. She was still kicking as far as he knew, which wasn't very far, considering he hadn't checked the human obituaries in several years. It made all those nights watching over her feel like a waste, and wasn't that some messed-up shit...

Malcolm locked up his bike, quickly trading his helmet for his Stetson and dismounting before he followed Trixie through the still-open door.

Inside, her motel room wasn't anything near what he'd expected. Sure, the single queen-size mattress was propped up on four little white plastic wheels and likely sported a coin slot to make it vibrate, and the bedside drawer looked like it held multiple copies of some never-been-read Mormon bible, but clearly Trixie had taken care to try to make the space more homelike on what limited budget she had.

White lace doilies covered several of the old furniture pieces, giving an obvious old southern flare. They looked like subtle antiques passed down from distant family. An overabundance of fresh, green plants sat in terra-cotta pots throughout the room, a small hothouse worth of flowers. A vintage poster from an old Dolly Parton tour and another from Patsy Cline were framed on the far wall like shrines to the women depicted in them.

"You live here?" Malcolm mumbled. He realized how inane the comment was the moment it left his lips.

He watched as she pulled a small, pink leopard-print bag

from the top of the closet. She opened several dresser drawers and began shoving clothes into it.

"Obviously." Trixie rolled her eyes. "What's so hard to believe about that? I'm socking away every bit of cash I can for when I can get the hell away from the Coyote. Plus, my tips took a real hit when the bar moved from downtown Billings out here to the middle of fuckin' nowhere." She gestured out the open doorway to their remote Idaho location.

He knew bartenders in rural areas made shit for pay. It was why he always overtipped her, but...

"I expected something more..." His voice trailed off.

If he was honest, he wasn't entirely certain what he'd expected.

"Bar-like?" Trixie stopped what she was doing and turned to look at him. She placed her hands on the generous curve of her hips. Her waist was narrow, but she had curves to spare.

Curves he'd spent far too much time considering. Long nighttime hours in the bunkhouse with only himself, his thoughts, and his hand.

Malcolm shrugged. He supposed bar-like *had* been what he expected, though he didn't say as much. Conversation, small talk especially, had never been his strong suit. He was far better at ending discussions than starting them.

Trixie rolled her eyes again, letting out an annoyed little huff before she returned to her packing. "I work at the Coyote, darlin'. I don't need to live there, too. My mama always said you shouldn't shit where you eat, or live there in this case."

He supposed he could see the crass wisdom in that.

"What's with…?" He tilted his chin to all the surrounding greenery. He wasn't certain what compelled him to ask, but the questions kept coming all the same.

"All the plants?" she finished for him.

She was always two steps ahead, thinking twice as fast as he did. He supposed she had to. Bartenders needed to be quick on their feet to deal with the chaos around them while maintaining a level head.

"I don't have a pet or any kids," she said, picking up a purple plastic watering can on the small kitchen table and setting it in the tiny kitchenette sink. She twisted on the faucet to fill it. "Girl's gotta have something to care for other than herself."

Malcolm leaned against the doorframe, watching her. The thought of Trixie with a family seemed oddly…foreign. He guessed he'd never really pondered her existence outside the Coyote's tap-lined walls, and now that fact somehow seemed foolish. Narrow-minded.

"Would you want that?" he asked. "Kids, I mean."

The question came out far more personal than he intended it. Immediately, he wished he could take it back.

Trixie paused for a moment, staring down at a tiny bonsai tree in a bronze planter in front of her before she finally said, "No, I wouldn't make a great mother. Not with the kind of life I live."

But as Malcolm watched the way she gingerly cared for something as insignificant as a houseplant, trekking about the room with her plastic watering can in hand, careful not to injure even so much as one little leaf with her watering as she whispered little reassurances to the plants, he wasn't so certain. The thought made something inside him coil and tense, his perception of her uncomfortably changing with it.

He didn't like it one damn bit.

He wasn't entirely sure what he'd expected Trixie to be like in the comfort of her own home, but it hadn't been this. It hadn't been anything that would make him think perhaps there was something more caring underneath all that cheap glamour and glitz. That exactly what he wanted from her had been there all along, hidden beneath the surface. Inaccessible to him.

He scowled at the thought.

It wasn't as if a few houseplants and a couple of lace doilies somehow made a difference. She was still the same person. Still the same oversexed bartender whose outward appearance was as trashy and hot as her ruby-red lips and whose words were as cold and callous as the way she'd no doubt hurt him, break his heart.

Women like her always did.

But the image of her in the crowded bar earlier, risking it all on that coyote fighter who'd been little more than a kid, said different. The candid response she'd given as to why she'd bothered to save the kid was still ringing in his ears.

He looks at me like I'm a person, not some sexy plaything meant for his amusement.

When she'd said that, it'd struck some deep chord within him. He knew what it was like to have everyone around you perceive you as something you weren't.

Reaper. Killer. Predator. His own false labels played out in his head.

He pushed the thought aside, watching as Trixie continued to tend to her plants and pack her bag. He tried to see past it all now, all the fake glamour, to what really lay beneath. Suddenly, the heavy mascara that coated her eyes, the bright rouge on her cheeks, and her ruby-red lipstick didn't seem showy. Instead, it looked like a warrior's armor, meant to deflect and deter. The longer he stared, the more he saw the real woman beneath. Maybe she wasn't some sexed-up, callous witch of a seductress who'd break his heart in an instant.

Maybe she really was what he'd seen glimpses of underneath—a scared, insecure woman, as hurt and wounded as she was fierce, a sad soul who'd been savaged by the world around her, unwilling to give anyone the benefit of the doubt, not because she was cruel but because life had taught her it wasn't worth it.

And maybe she was right. Maybe he wasn't worth it.

He'd played right into all her fears after all.

"What?" she said, turning to look at him.

He hadn't realized he'd been staring so long until she said it.

Malcolm cleared his throat. "I know a thing or two about shitty moms," he admitted, harkening back to their last point of conversation. "I was thinking you might not be so bad at it. If that was something you wanted, I mean."

Trixie's eyes widened, dark lashes fluttering, and she looked at him as if he'd grown two heads. "I–I think that's the nicest thing you've ever said to me."

Malcolm tensed, pawing at the back of his neck as he glanced toward the floor. He suddenly felt naive, foolish, hell…worse. Like exactly the kind of monster everyone wanted him to be. All for the way he'd treated her. He'd never been kind, never made it easy to be near him.

Which like her was by design, of course.

He was exactly what he needed to be, to stay guarded, protect himself.

Bo had seen right through it, and maybe so had Trixie.

Thankfully, Trixie took pity on him, turning back toward her packing and plant care. She was putting little white bits of plant food in the soil of each pot now. She looked toward him. "You're hurt."

He glanced down. There was a decent-sized gash on his hand where one of the bears had sliced him after shifting their meaty hands into those long freaking claws of theirs. The bleeding had slowed, but it'd be closed within a day. His kind mended quickly. He still remembered the alarm on his mother's face when whatever wounds his monster of a stepfather had left on him as a kid had disappeared the next day.

"It'll heal," he said.

Trixie shook her head, ignoring him. "I'll get some antibacterial and some gauze." She flitted into the bathroom, returning a moment later with the supplies and pointing toward the bed. "Sit."

Malcolm grumbled, but he didn't fight it. "I'm no dog." He sank down onto the mattress.

"Wolf. Dog. It's all the same, innit?" she teased. With him sitting on the bed and her standing beside him, the curve of the cleavage she'd put on display tonight was far too close to his face. It was always a battle not to look. Not that he'd been raised to be a gentleman.

She gripped hold of his hand and poured some peroxide from a brown plastic bottle on top. The chemical stung, but he didn't wince. "What's it say?" She nodded toward his tattooed knuckles.

"Angel wings." He didn't elaborate.

Thankfully, she didn't pry further.

Silence stretched between them while she gently stroked his hand with a warm cloth. Tender. Caring.

"You're good at that," he said roughly. "Caring for things, I mean." He glanced away.

She watched him knowingly. He could feel it. From the corner of his eye, he witnessed a small smile curve her lips. She seemed pleased with herself, or maybe with him. He wasn't certain. "The only way I know how to care for someone is serving up a liquor bottle to them and sitting with them in the silence. That's no way to care for a kid." She placed the washcloth in the sink and then returned with the gauze.

He didn't believe what she said for a second, but the fact that she'd cared for him exactly like that for years didn't escape him.

Maybe it was the only way she knew how. Though he'd been telling himself she *didn't* care, that he'd be no more than another notch in her bedpost. He watched as she wrapped the gauze around his hand. Soft. Tentative. She took extra care not to hurt him. Her kind of care wasn't Bo's sweet words or soft affirmations. Trixie would never be good for that. But every month when he'd come into the Coyote, there to pay his homage to the man he'd loved and lost, she delivered the bottle no questions asked and at the end of the night had sat there with him, a quiet presence by his side.

And maybe that'd been exactly what he needed, someone to sit in the silence with him.

Though at the time, he wouldn't have admitted it. Thought it intrusive.

She was no friend of his.

Except maybe now she was. Maybe somehow in that time, he'd allowed his heart to open and let her slip in. Time softened him, made him more pliable.

"There," she said as she finished patching him up with a pleased grin. She returned the supplies to their place in her bathroom cabinet, and then it was back to the plants. Like she hadn't left him sitting on her bed, burning with want. She whispered something soft to a rhododendron. But not him. He'd never been jealous of a fucking plant before.

He frowned. Her passing him the bottle every time he came to the Coyote had gone on for several months—longer even—until he'd been in his grief so long he was certain he would lose himself to it. But *she'd* forcibly pulled him out, practically kicking and screaming. He still remembered the first time she'd taken the bottle away from him, the harsh look in her eyes that said it was time to move on or he never would.

She'd grabbed that damn bottle of bourbon straight out of his fisted hand and said, "That's enough."

He hadn't known two words could be so painful, cut him to the core so quick.

But he hadn't made it easy for her.

She was slipping on a pair of floral purple gardening gloves now. She nodded to the plant before her. "Hemlock," she said in response to his raised brow. Her amber eyes darted to his hand again. "Does it hurt?"

"No," he answered.

She frowned at him, clearly sensing the lie.

He'd told himself her care hadn't hurt then, too. That nothing was as bad as losing Bo.

In a way, that was true, but it wasn't fully honest either.

In the months after she'd started refusing to let him drown himself in a bottle, he'd been a true prick. Snarling, growling, hurling nasty, hurtful words, any insult he could get past his lips with little thought to what it did to anyone, especially the woman who wouldn't serve him. His grief over Bo had been like a living monster that threatened to consume him so completely that he'd never cared, never stopped to consider what that darkness had done to those around him—to *her*.

But Trixie had kept taking the bottle, telling him he couldn't wallow in his pain anymore. He'd tell her it wouldn't work, that there was no saving him, and then one day, like magic, he hadn't fought her because he hadn't needed it anymore. He'd made his way out of his personal hell because she'd made certain he did, ensured Bo's loss didn't kill both of them.

And all that'd been *before* she'd kissed him in that godforsaken alleyway.

Before she'd woken up a part of him he hadn't realized had been dead, a part of him that'd been buried in the caverns right alongside Bo. Something wild, hot, hungry.

He hadn't known he needed it until then.

She removed her gardening gloves, washing her hands in the bathroom sink before digging in a small black makeup bag next to the basin. She pulled out a coppery tube, removed the cap, and freshened her lipstick in the mirror with a ruby-red smack.

He'd had that damn lipstick all over him after that kiss. Hadn't wanted to wash it off.

And what had he done? Only hurt her further, held her at arm's length, blamed her for the mixed feelings she'd stirred in him, which she did… She *did* stir something inside him. No matter how much he didn't want to admit it. All because he was afraid of feeling that same shattering inside his chest whenever she decided that she didn't feel the same. He didn't imagine she was the kind of woman who stuck around for long. Most people he'd been with, men or women, didn't. Save for Bo. Bo had been the exception.

And in the end, even he didn't.

He knew that wasn't fair. Bo hadn't asked to die. But logic didn't govern grief.

"Something on your mind?" Trixie had finished the last of her makeup tending and was zipping up her overnight bag. She asked the question in the way she would to any of her patrons searching for a bartender in whom to confide instead of a priest, but he had more than a passing suspicion that for him, she meant it.

And for once, Malcolm thought about telling her the truth, about what he really wanted and needed from her, what made him so resentful of whatever *this* was between them. But he didn't. What was the point when she'd hurt him eventually anyway?

"You need to tell me what you know about the Grey Wolves," he said.

For a moment, he thought she might have looked disappointed, but he couldn't allow himself to consider it. Not when the lives of his packmates were at stake.

That was why he was really here, wasn't it?

He'd keep telling that lie to himself as long as it worked. As long as it kept whatever this was between them at bay. Maybe then he wouldn't get hurt.

Trixie stiffened. He saw the change in her, the way her glamourous persona slipped back into place, any kindness and caring hidden beneath. He couldn't shake the feeling that subtle sheen in her eyes spelled her own hurt. He supposed both of them were so hung up on protecting themselves from the world around them that there never could have been something between them to begin with.

"I already told you…when we reach somewhere safe, and not a second sooner." She trudged out the door, back toward his bike, hips swaying…

Taking the moment and any chance of honesty between them with her.

Chapter 8

THE RIDE EAST WAS NEITHER QUICK NOR EASY. TRIXIE shivered against the cold night air, drawing close to the radiating warmth of the cowboy in the motorcycle's saddle seat at her front. The mountain air was steeped with the moisture of impending snow. The wind whipped around them as the last of the highway's blacktop changed into a lonely, single-entry road. Despite the leather jacket she'd pulled on at her place, she was chilled to the bone, her legs still baby-bottom bare. Of course tonight had been the night she hadn't opted for pantyhose. Over a decade living in these mountains, but they still proved too damn cold for her southern blood.

She only stopped shivering long enough to recognize the entry road as the west entrance to Yellowstone when they finally slowed for the unmanned gate. The short stop, with signs that warned to drive slowly and watch for wildlife, was their last encounter with any sign of humanity. As they ventured further into the park, the darkness closed in around them, the moonlight and the bike's single headlight serving as the only light on their path.

Against the cold wind, Trixie eased closer to Malcolm's warmth again. Despite the rumble of the bike beneath them and the open road, the bare forest trees and the eerie quiet of the distant mountains gave way to the startling awareness that humanity didn't belong here—that this untouched landscape was as old as it was vast, transcending time and outside influence.

Trixie wrapped her arms tighter around Malcolm's wide frame, another shiver raking through her, this time not from the cold. For once, she felt incredibly small. Like maybe in the scheme of the universe, she and her problems, no matter how big they'd felt when she'd first mounted the back of Malcolm's bike, were nothing more than a speck of dust. The thought stirred a natural awareness inside her, the feeling both terrifying and yet oddly…comforting. There were larger forces at play, things more important than her conflict with Stan. Her problems weren't permanent. Nothing in her life ever was. Though it wasn't every day she had a horde of Triple S assholes who'd gladly have her for dead breathing down her neck.

It wasn't until miles later that they pulled off at the side of the road and Malcolm turned off the bike, the brightness of the headlight instantly giving way to total darkness. She truly felt as if she'd been transported to another world, one unmarred by human hands. The trees and the darkness of the sky whispered subtle sounds around them as the landscape beckoned them back to a simpler time, one wilder and more natural than she'd ever experienced before.

"Where are we?" she breathed into the quiet. The heat of Trixie's breath swirled around her face before quickly dissipating.

Malcolm pushed down the kickstand of the bike as he

allowed her to dismount. Trixie swung her leg over and stood beside where the bike had stopped. The darkness and pale moonlight engulfed them both, making it difficult for her to see. Instinctually, she gripped the arm of Malcolm's leather jacket for reassurance, keeping him close. Though the first bits of winter hadn't made themselves known yet outside the park, nearby a bit of freshly fallen snow sparkled beneath the trees, creating a pale glow. It wasn't enough light for her to see. But it was enough for a wolf. For a creature that belonged to these lands.

"Terra firma, our homeland," Malcolm answered, the deep grumble of his voice thrumming through her. Somehow, he seemed at ease here in a way she couldn't be. In spite of his leather and the harsh lines of his tattooed hands, he belonged here among the forest and the trees. He followed her lead and dismounted, drawing to his full height beside her and the bike. He didn't bother to lock it. There wasn't another soul for miles.

Malcolm nodded toward the forest trees. "Follow me."

Trixie glanced down, but in the darkness she could barely see her own heels. "I would have worn different shoes had I known."

"There's a trail." Malcolm stepped forward, taking her hand as he led her into the darkness. "If it gets too rough, I'll carry you," he whispered.

For a moment, Trixie's breath caught. She tried not to read too much into those words but failed. She quickly swallowed the lump that had formed in her throat, any protest about her footwear forgotten. There wasn't anything more to that sentence, to that graveled whisper that said so little yet made her feel so much. There couldn't be.

She shook her head, pushing away the tumult of feelings Malcolm and this place inspired in her as he led her toward the darkened trail. The sounds of the forest wrapped around them, the rustle of fallen leaves or small animals in the underbrush enclosing them within the forest's bosom. She glanced up at the moon and the starry sky overhead. The inky blackness stretched onward and infinite, and she breathed out a long sigh. She couldn't let herself get caught up like that, convince herself he cared, however briefly. Not after he'd nearly left her to Stan and his goons in the bar. In danger or not, even she wasn't *that* desperate. She wasn't exactly pleased about the way he'd nearly ghosted her, and he damned well knew it.

But he *had* killed for her, saved her and protected her when it counted. Out here in the stillness, that truth seemed all the more important.

Malcolm didn't speak again until a while later, the dark outline of a small log cabin finally came into view, the structure tucked away in the shadows of the trees. Trixie didn't see it until they were nearly on top of it, only steps from climbing its wooden porch.

"Our kind considers this our homeland," he said softly, as if speaking too loudly, too sharply might disturb the natural beauty around them. "Some of the rangers are shifters, friends of the pack. They protect the true wolves, our ancestors, and these lands that were once our home."

Another lump formed in Trixie's throat. There was an

inherent sadness and loss in those words that instantly shook her, but Malcolm didn't elaborate further.

Bending down, he dug a key out from beneath the cabin's old welcome mat. "I called in a favor. The park's entering off-season, so this is safer, more remote than even Wolf Pack Run," he explained. "No one will look for you here." A rustle of key in lock was followed by the sound of Malcolm's boots padding across the wooden floor.

A moment later, a small lamp flickered to life inside the cabin.

Trixie stood in the doorway, taking in the small, enclosed space. The ranger who lived here during the in-season had tastes that were rustic at best, with a single wool-blanketed bed, a rickety wooden table, and an old firewood stove for a kitchen centered around an unlit fireplace. It was far from modern but somehow cozy and charming. A paneled window that looked out over the dark forest covered part of one wall, and a cabin bed that looked nearly as hard and cot-like as the one in her motel room sat adjacent. At least she'd get decent sleep in it. There'd be no way in hell she'd have managed if it'd been anything soft and comfortable, too unfamiliar compared to what she was accustomed to. Rustic and sparse she could work with.

Malcolm threw a few precut logs from near the hearth into the fireplace, kindling a fire with little more than the bare logs and a spare lighter from his back pocket, the way that only a practiced cowboy could. When he was finished, he stood beside the firelight, finally looking back toward her as he leaned against the mantel. The leather of his biker jacket and shitkicker boots looked odd and out of place here.

She cleared her throat. She was grateful to him for all he'd done for her, but savior or not, it was time for him to be on his way. He'd done more than enough for her already. She wasn't used to kindness, from him especially. "Stan and the other bear shifters who were at the Coyote tonight are Triple S," she said, finally disclosing the information she had for him. "South Side Shifter Outfit. You familiar, sugar?"

Malcolm nodded. "I grew up in Chicago."

Where the Triple S reigned supreme. Trixie quirked a brow. A Grey Wolf who hadn't grown up at Wolf Pack Run? She leveled a look at him, showing clear interest. Years slinging drinks at the Coyote meant she was always up for a good story. A girl needed amusement, but when he didn't elaborate, she didn't press. The man had his secrets, but so did she.

Trixie sighed. "Then you know what they're capable of." She tried not to think of exactly how those capabilities would play out if they got their hands on her, considering all the hate focused in her direction thanks to all the money she'd lost them. Boss would be angry with her, but he'd cool off in a few days. He always did.

Stepping farther inside, she pushed the cabin door shut behind her but didn't latch it. A less-than-subtle hint that she expected him to walk out it soon. "Stan and his Triple S goons have been coming to the fights the past several weeks, meeting with Boss. But tonight, I overheard them talking, and from the sound of it, they're partnering with the vamps on something. Your pack was mentioned as their public enemy number one and Stan was not so subtly asking about you and Blaze, so whatever it is, it concerns y'all."

She didn't bother to elaborate that his pack hadn't been mentioned directly. Her magic didn't lie. It may not have served as much protection for her in moments like this, but she had her own talents. They all did.

Malcolm's cold eyes scanned her, considering. "What's their end goal?"

She shrugged. "Hell if I know. You figure it out." She moved closer to the fireside, to the flicker of warmth it was starting to provide. A moment later, she stepped away again, feeling the urge to place some distance between them, but Malcolm blocked her path.

Wrapping one large hand on the mantel's rim, he caged her in place. The large muscles beneath his leather flexed, straining against the material. Inches from her face, the harsh lettering of his knuckle tattoos glared at her. The ink there seemed ever darker in the warm glow of the firelight. "That's it?" he snarled. "I drag you all the way out here on the promise of information, I call in favors to ensure your safety, and that's it?" he growled.

Trixie bristled. Enough was enough. She was over him, this night, and every problem it'd brought with it. "I didn't promise a deluge of details. It's information. That's all I have and now I've delivered it. Do whatever with it you wish, darlin', but it ain't my concern."

She pushed past him again. Thankfully, this time he let her go. If he didn't, she couldn't be held liable for what she and the little bit of magic she had left over after saving Jackie would do. She'd need to rest in order to recharge. She trudged near the cabin's bed before depositing the duffel bag she'd brought with her. Crossing the room to the window, she stared out into the night as she listened for the sound of him closing the door on his way out. She tugged the dusty drapes closed. The door latched with a quick *snick*, but she didn't hear the sounds of his boots descending the few cabin steps as she'd anticipated.

Malcolm's deep, rumbled tenor sounded from the now-closed doorway. "Why are the Triple S partnering with the vamps? What's their purpose?" His voice carried throughout the small cabin space like it could wrap around her, keep her warm and safe, if she'd let it.

Damn him.

"I already told you. I. Don't. Know," she said, exaggerating each word so it'd drill into that thick skull of his. "If I did, I'd tell you. Unlike you, I care about the lives of people I call my friends." She hurled the word *friend* out without thought but then instantly regretted it.

Malcolm fell silent for a long beat, too long, as he watched her. "Is that what I am to you? A friend?" The question seemed to settle into the ether, into the silence of the cabin and the crackle of the fire around them, as much a part of the atmosphere as the quiet promise of soon-to-come snow.

"I meant Wes, Naomi, your other packmates." She waved a dismissive hand.

They both knew she hadn't, but she wasn't about to get into this with him. Not tonight. Not with the sting of the evening's events and all the ire he hurled at her burning like a brand into her heart, and her still like a small babe with sensitive skin. She'd have thought over the years her own hide would've toughened more. But she'd always had too many soft spots for her own good. For snarly, injured creatures like him in particular.

Stepping farther into the cabin again, Malcolm prowled through the tiny space as if it belonged to him. He moved like a stalking predator. Stealthy but also presumptuous. Like he'd catch whatever prey he set those golden wolf eyes to.

She was more than ready for him to leave. She needed time, space, to think and come up with a plan that didn't include him. "What are you doing?"

"Checking the room. Ensuring you're safe. That was part of our deal, wasn't it?"

It was a poor excuse and they both knew it. He didn't want to leave. Hell if she knew why.

She placed a haughty hand on her hip. "You don't trust your ranger friend?"

"I don't trust anyone," Malcolm snarled. His eyes flashed golden. He made his way to the kitchen stove, followed by the closet, checking every space as if he really meant it though they both knew it was a ruse. A moment later, he moved the edge of a mirror that hung on the wall as if he might find something behind it but didn't.

Trixie sighed. What was he playing at? He didn't want this, her. Not really. He'd made that abundantly clear. She crossed her arms over her chest. "I'm fine, Malcolm. There's no boogeyman in the closet that's going to jump out and get me the moment you leave, and even if it did, why the hell would you care?"

His upper lip curled, almost as if he were hurt. "I made a promise to you."

"So that's the extent of it? You made a promise?" She was shaking her head. She didn't know why it mattered. It didn't make two licks of sense. She shouldn't care about his motivation. He'd saved her. As long as it kept her from dead, his reasoning shouldn't matter, but to her, it did. "Caring for me didn't seem all that important when you were about to walk out of the Coyote and leave me to Stan and his goons."

The statement hung in the charged air between them.

There, she'd said it. The accusation had been dancing on her tongue all evening, but she hadn't wanted to do this with him. Not here. Not now. Not when it was certain to end in her heart in pieces on the floor. She knew how this song and dance went.

Last time had left her an indentured servant to a warlock who may have saved her but who'd also damned her to servitude in the process. Boss's deals didn't come with an escape clause. Even when a young girl was trying to save a man she thought she'd loved, even when she'd been too naive, too stupid and blind to see that man she'd been trying to save didn't feel the same. Several embers crackled from the fireplace, settling into bits of ash on the wooden floor.

The sharp, searing gold of Malcolm's wolf eyes turned toward her. "I wouldn't have left you."

"Could have fooled me," she accused. She shook her head in disbelief. "You've made it pretty clear how you feel about me."

"I don't hate you, Trixie," he whispered.

He said the words so softly that for a moment she almost believed them, almost trusted.

"Fine. 'Dislike' then." She waved a hand. "Is that a more palatable word for you?"

He didn't answer.

As silence stretched between them, something inside her toughened, creating an internal distance along with it—to guard and protect herself. She wanted him gone now. Hell, several minutes ago, and if there was one way to piss Malcolm off and get him the hell outta Dodge, she knew it. They'd been playing this same game for several months now. Ever since that damn kiss.

In an instant, Trixie dropped whatever frustration she'd been harboring for him from her face, a soft ease and pliability slipping into her features and loosening limbs. The long lashes lining her eyelids fluttered lower and she placed a little extra sway into her hips. She'd long since mastered her role as the seductress, as the kind of woman that kept men awake at night but who they'd never take home to their parents. She was a looker, a seducer, never the bride or even the bridesmaid. A lady of the night, although she served drinks instead of her body.

That was all there was to her.

Malcolm froze, dark eyes watching her.

She sauntered toward him, steps long and languid. She didn't need to see the fire in his eye to know she looked damned good. Malcolm's heated gaze seared through her—the one that on the surface said he hated the show, but deep down, it burned him sweet. Trixie didn't stop her little strutting display until she stood directly in front of him.

She placed the palm of her hand against the center of his chest. "Is that what you want, sugar? For me to be real thankful and play along like you're the hero?" The teasing whisper in her voice was made of dark secrets, hidden alcoves, and sexy noir heroines who'd been chain-smoking for one too many years. She traced one pink glowing finger over the hardened muscles of his pecs, allowing her magic to caress his skin in a way she knew would both rile and irk him, even as she felt the pleasure of it moving through him.

He tensed beneath the gentle scrape of her manicured nail.

"That's why you followed me in here after all, isn't it? A witch like me knows the truth."

Malcolm inhaled a harsh breath, and she swore she felt the wolf hidden beneath his human form shiver along with it. Coiled, prepared, ready to strike or shift.

She called to both parts of him. Especially here in this abandoned place that was anything they needed it to be.

"I won't pretend like it's some kind of payment for saving me, but if it's sex you want… With you, I'm always up for it." She moved closer, her breasts brushing against him as she drew close. The scent of him was intoxicating, clean and fresh but also earthy, wild like the wolf inside him. "I know you've wanted it since that back-alley kiss."

Malcolm's heated stare fixed on her. "Is that what you think?"

She pressed even closer. "It's the truth. Innit, sugar?"

She moved in to kiss him, crass and dirty. She expected the usual, of course, for him to turn his head, pull away and storm off, or at the very least that her lips would land on his cheek instead of mouth. It was his way of showing her she was a fool, making an ass of herself.

But he didn't.

Instead, her mouth met his, a gentle brush of lips that was so soft and tender it sent a sudden shock through her. Alarmed, she pulled back abruptly, eyes wide. She'd been playing a game of chicken, and this time she'd lost— miserably. She blinked up at him.

There was something sad in his face along with that all-too-familiar heat, not the same as the grief she'd watched him feel for Bo for years, but something new, different. It instantly disarmed her.

"Tell me this is real, Trixie." That gruff command shook her to her core.

He really wanted to know. The truth in his words rang clear.

Trixie struggled to respond, suddenly stricken. "Would it make a difference?"

"Try me," he growled. A shadow from the fire flickered across his face.

She swallowed, hard, so caught off guard that she couldn't bring herself to hide from him. Not at the moment. "I'm real," she said, the words making her feel far more vulnerable than she'd expected. "I may not always show it, act like it, but I am, and I *do* want you," she admitted. Her lips tightened, spread thin with embarrassment. She had no doubt he'd use the words against her, but she couldn't bring herself to care. He'd won. Made her look like a fool, but she was tired. So tired of pretending when everyone else didn't. "All the rest of it is bullshit." She looked away from him.

"I was afraid you'd say that." Without warning, Malcolm grabbed hold of her chin, his callused fingers and rough, cowboy-worn skin contrasting with the gentleness beneath. He forced her to look toward him. "Don't make me regret this."

His mouth was on hers in an instant, seeking, probing, claiming in a way that was so soft she wouldn't have thought the big brute had it in him if she hadn't experienced it herself once before. The warmth of his tongue mingled with hers. He tasted like basil or maybe mint—something fresh, and nice, and green. He used the canines of his teeth to gently nip at the edge of her lips.

At his prompting, she spread open for him, wide and vulnerable. She wasn't thinking or pretending. She simply followed the race of her pulse, the heated beat of her heart, and the growing pressure building between her legs. She pressed closer against him, instinctually wrapping her arms around his neck.

The hardened length of him pushed against her stomach. Unwillingly, she let out a little moan at the thought of him pushing inside her. Not the throaty, sexed-up kind she'd done in bed so many times before, but a soft, honest whimper as one of his large hands darted beneath her skirt and cupped her center. The sound was nothing like her. Or at least the part of her she showed the world. But it was honest, real, some unsung part of herself, and Malcolm must have known it. She felt herself slicken.

Against her lips, she could have sworn she felt something snap inside him. Some feral, wild part of himself she'd always known he'd held back from her unleashed. Malcolm hauled her into his arms, lowering her onto the bed, but instead of falling on top of her, suddenly those large, gentle hands were spreading her legs wide.

Stripping off his leather, he dropped to his knees. Moments later, he was hooking her legs over his shoulders. She sat up, moving to take off her stilettos, but he snarled at her angrily. "Keep the shoes."

And then the next thing she knew, he ducked his head underneath her knees.

Trixie gasped, eyes darting down to where he grinned from between her thighs. The eyes of a wolf stared back.

Chapter 9

Malcolm couldn't explain it, but Trixie's lips tasted of a southern summer—of sweet tea and smoked watermelon and long hours spent in the heat until he was spent for the day. Summer warmth felt like a long-cherished memory in the cold cabin air. And that'd been *before* he'd buried his tongue in the wet, wanting folds of her cunt and felt the heat of her against his chin.

Fuck, she was exquisite. Tangy. Sweet. Smoky. He couldn't get enough.

Even though he knew she'd break him.

Malcolm's hair fell into his face, draping over his forehead as he ate her, the heat of the fire warming them both. He could drown himself in the taste of her pussy, eat her any time she wanted him to—for days and he'd never tire, so long as she allowed it. Oral sex had always been his favorite, pleasurable enough that it made him want to give instead of receive. Hell if he hadn't imagined licking Trixie so many times before, and now that she'd taken their little game of cat and mouse to the next level…

He wanted to fucking play.

To revel in her.

No matter how much it made his fucking heart ache.

His tongue probed and dipped inside her, circling back to the taut bead of her clit, until he found a steady rhythm of giving and then taking away. She bucked her hips forward, whimpering and keening for him to return with each delicious, edging tease. Those sexy-as-hell stiletto boots, covered in dirt from the trail, dug into his shoulder blades. Her hands tangled in his hair. She tugged and fisted at his scalp, his nape, anything she could get her polished, manicured hands on. It gave him a slight tinge of pleasure-pain, enough to take the edge off, let himself enjoy the moment instead of being so swept away he couldn't control his emotions.

How many times had he imagined those same nails scraping his chest, his back? He'd give whatever she was willing to take. Anything to ease the ache.

She'd severely underestimated him the moment she'd leaned in for that kiss, and he was going to make her pay—in pleasure and flushed red flesh. He threw back his head, falling back on his knees again as he licked at the wetness she'd left on his chin.

"Look at you," he purred, only pulling away enough that he could whisper warm, heated breaths against her center. Her folds were blushed with color, a deep, wet pink that made him want to lay her bare, spread her wider. "I want you to see yourself."

Without warning, he stood from where he'd knelt on the marble floor. His knees had started to ache from placing all his muscled weight there. He wasn't built for submission, no matter how much he enjoyed pleasuring her.

He crossed the room to the closet, where a nearby

floor-length mirror hung to decorate the space. Wrenching it from the wall, he accidentally took a nail and a bit of wood with it, but he didn't give a shit. Not when Trixie was still lying on the bed waiting for him, her mini skirt flipped up over her hips giving him perfect, easy access. He'd pay someone to fix it.

It'd taken him all of two seconds to snap the lacy, barely there material of her red G-string. He'd buy her another, if she even cared. She'd dressed as if she'd known the night would lead them there. And maybe she did. He wanted her and she'd known it—wanted her bad enough that it had made him hate her for it, made his chest ache.

Enough that the sight of her open to him was overwhelming. Gorgeous perfection.

More than enough to destroy him, if he let it.

Heading back toward where Trixie lay, Malcolm propped the mirror up against the adjacent wall, her most intimate parts open for him. In the dimmed lights, the mirror framed her in a stunning display. He might have resigned himself to the whims of fate, to letting her cast her spell on him until his need for her felt beyond his control. But it wasn't. He couldn't let it be. He needed to control this. Bend it to his will before he allowed it to break him. He knew it would if he didn't.

As he stepped away from the mirror, she didn't close her knees, didn't flinch at the way he'd put her on a pedestal there. Trixie ate that up, being on a stage, having all eyes on her. He'd watched her do it more times at the bar than he could count.

For *everyone*, but him especially.

"You like that, don't you?" Malcolm stood beside her open legs, admiring. "Being put on display?" It was a crass question, but Trixie reveled in it.

Her tongue darted over her ruby-red lips. That lipstick would look as sexy as it was cheap wrapped in a ring around his cock. She smacked those two red curves together like she knew what he was thinking. "It's novel. I'll give you that, sugar."

Malcolm shook his head. "Don't lie to me." He bent down, getting on his knees again before he sat beside her. He draped one of her legs over his left shoulder, turning so that he could bring his hand up from underneath and touch her while still meeting her eyes in the mirror. "Look at you." He slipped a single finger inside her pussy. She was soaking wet, silky. "You're dripping for me." Malcolm eased in another finger and she pushed down into his hand wantonly. He'd never admit it, but he fucking loved that she wasn't ashamed of her desire, that she was bold, brash, brave. Even if it drove him insane. "Do you like that idea? The thought of other people watching you?"

The mounds of her breasts lifted, still clothed but tantalizing all the same. Her breath visibly quickened from where he played with her. "When it's you, I do."

He growled his approval, the gold of his wolf eyes flashing in the cabin's dim glow. "I'm going to finger-fuck your pussy now, and you're going to watch as I do it."

"You going to ask if I want you to?"

"Do you?"

She nodded as she bit her lower lip. She was a goddamn tease. She'd only meant to stall him. Toy with him again. She knew what it did to him.

He placed his free hand on her hip, anchoring her near the edge of the bed. "Brace yourself, baby." He plunged his fingers into her, rough and unforgiving. In, then out again in a fast, heated rhythm. From where his tongue had warmed her, she was more than ready for him. He slipped inside easily. Trixie threw back her head, blond curls bouncing as she let out a pleasured moan. He loved watching the pressure build inside her, seeing her draw closer to climax in the mirror.

"Tell me what you see, Trixie," he growled.

Still propped on her elbows, her eyes shot open, chest heaving as she breathed in ragged pants. "I see that I want you."

He growled again. "More specific."

"I want you *bad*." She was riding him hard, needy.

He shook his head. In response, she smiled slightly. She wasn't behaving like she was supposed to and she knew it. She was challenging him. He increased pressure, curling his fingers up and in slightly in a way he knew would undo her. She gasped, her cunt clenching around him.

"You're not getting off that easy. You're riding my hand like you haven't been fucked hard in weeks. Tell me what you see," he demanded.

Trixie let out a pleasured little whimper. "I see that she's hungry for you, that she'd let you bury yourself deep if you wanted to." *She* being her pussy.

Malcolm let out a rusty chuckle, shook his head again as he smiled playfully. Who was she kidding? "Who's *she*?" he teased, increasing the pressure again.

He could go on like this for hours.

Until one of them would break.

It wouldn't be him.

If there was one good thing about being a shifter, it was that the strength and stamina for a good, hard fuck came easily. Regardless of whether it was his dick, his hand, his tongue. His muscles were far from weak. Hers, on the other hand, were becoming more pliable by the second. She melted for him, turning molten in his hands.

"Who's *she*?" he growled again when she didn't answer.

"Me," Trixie finally keened as he brushed his thumb over her clit. "Me." She was panting now, skirting the edge of her orgasm and riding him greedily. "*I* want you."

From the fire in her amber eyes, she wasn't pleased to admit it.

"And?" He lifted a brow expectantly. He loved hearing her talk dirty, whisper nasty, naughty things into his ear. His cock twitched eagerly.

Her eyes darted to his in the reflection of the mirror, where he sat underneath one of her legs, fingering her from beneath that too-short flipped-up skirt. His own legs were sprawled out before him, biker boots holding them in place, claiming the space beneath her like he was a fucking king.

"I *like* being put on display," she said brazenly.

She was exquisite. Fierce, wanton, sexy.

A woman who didn't try to hide her desire and who

would tread over any man who said she should. Good girls be damned.

Malcolm's cock gave a heady throb against the fly of his jeans. He'd been hard before but now he was fucking granite. Flesh made steel. His balls tightened with need. "What do you want, Trixie? Tell me now and I'll finish you."

"Everything." She moaned again. "All of you."

He snarled, pleased but still demanding more. He expected perfection. Nothing less. He wouldn't release her until she gave it. "More specific." He increased pressure again. More speed.

She arched against him. "Your cock," she nearly shouted into the quiet of the cabin. He could feel her climax nearing, but it was beyond her reach—until he gave it to her. From the wild look in her eyes, she didn't care if anyone heard them. "Fuck, I want your cock, Malcolm," she snapped. Her eyes narrowed, jaw clenched in sweet, frustrated agony even as her mussed hair fell into her face. She was daring him, daring him to take his hand away from between her legs and see what happened. "Give it to me." Witch or not, she let out a little growl of her own.

Malcolm grinned. He'd known she had it in her. Trixie'd never truly be unsatisfied, because she knew how to take her fill, make demands. Every show was her own. He was simply lucky to be a willing participant.

"Good enough, I suppose." He grinned from between her legs. "I think I'll take pity on you. For today, that is." He angled his hand up and in, driving toward that sensitive spot while his thumb rubbed over the nub of her clit.

His cock twitched, eager to break free. But this was about her.

Trixie shattered against him, coming on a wave of wet heat and pleasure. Her walls clenched around him, leaving his hand soaking in the smooth silk of her desire. She was all feeling. Clawing. Keening. Writhing in the firelight. As raw as he felt each time she teased him. She bucked and moaned, taking her fill of him until with one final, full-body shudder, she collapsed back on the bed, hot and sated. Fuck, she was breathtaking.

Pure sex on display.

Malcolm brought the hand that'd been in her to his mouth, licking her pleasure from his fingers despite the fact that she was no longer looking at him. Unlike her, he didn't *need* the show. He wanted to savor every part of her. Her pleasure could feed him for days. Rising to his feet, he stood over her, still clothed and invulnerable, despite the smell of sex and sweat that hung in the air. He wouldn't be much longer, if that was what she wanted.

Though he thought she might have had enough for today.

He needed to keep his distance, maintain control.

He watched her for a long moment as she lay there, strung out in a postorgasmic glow. She'd ridden high and she wasn't ready to come down yet. Finally, when she opened her eyes, she stared up at him, dark lashes half-lidded and sultry. He had no idea how the fuck a woman who was a natural blond had lashes so dark, even after the mascara she caked on each morning had long since faded away, and to think he'd always thought her hair color came from the inside of a bottle. The joke was on him, he supposed.

He was vaguely aware that where it concerned her, the joke would always be on him. Unless he got in front of this. Like a bronco, he needed to take the reins and control it before it controlled him. She'd top from the bottom if he let her. He couldn't allow that. This wasn't permanent. It never would be.

Even as much as he craved it.

"Are you into kink?" he asked matter-of-factly. He needed to know to make a plan moving forward. He took one of her high-heeled boots in his hand, slowly unzipping it. The arches of her feet had to be aching after bartending all evening, though he supposed by now she was used to it. He'd never seen her wear anything but heels.

"I can be." She shrugged a little. "If you're into it."

"I don't care what you think I want to hear." He moved for the other boot, stripping it off. "Tell me what *you* want."

She stared up at him then, amber eyes assessing. He wanted the truth and she knew it. She laughed. A harsh, callous sound that pierced through him. He didn't know which was worse. That she'd laughed at the question, like a man who truly wanted to know what pleasured her was an oddity, or the knowledge that came with it. The sudden awareness that, based on her reaction, all her previous partners had been selfish idiots. Unwilling to give and only wanting to take.

By his guess, some had probably still been good lays, because she knew what she liked and how to communicate her needs, but they'd never been *considerate*. Not from that amused look she was giving him like he was a novelty, strange. When it came to assholes, the world had plenty and so had she. He'd already known that and yet…

Suddenly, it angered him that she'd let anyone treat her that way.

That *he'd* treated her that way before all this.

"With you, kinky things sound amazing…" she said, though her voice trailed off.

"But?" he prompted. Her eyes were growing heavy, and he understood it. Her life had been threatened, and when someone was hurt that way, the only thing that proved useful was rest.

Or therapy, if he asked Blaze. The other shifter was like an evangelical convert when it came to discussions of feelings these days.

Not that Malcolm was ever going to fucking try it.

Trixie sighed. "But I think I've had enough for one day."

"Then we call it a night." He may have wanted control, to get in front of this situation between them so he could get a hold on it, but he wasn't a monster. Never in that way. "You're in charge of what we do and don't do, Trixie. I don't want to do anything you don't want to. That doesn't appeal to me. If you aren't one hundred percent interested, I don't want to participate. So if the answer is no, don't hesitate. But when we *are* playing, I'm in charge. Understand?"

She nodded. "Understood."

"Consent matters to me. Authenticity too." It was more honest than he'd been with her to date, straightforward and direct. He expected perfection, but that didn't mean he didn't anticipate disappointment. He still remembered every slight against him too clearly. With him, old wounds didn't fade. They simply festered into open, gaping holes inside his chest. But if they were going to do this, they needed to lay down the ground rules, make expectations clear from the start. "Don't ever lie to me." He held her gaze, eyes cold, harsh, cruel. "That's my one rule. You do and we're through. I want honesty or I don't want it."

Trixie sat up, flipping her skirt down to cover herself and attempting to right the mussed look of her hair. She met his gaze. "Got it, sugar. Truth is my middle name." The side of her lips curled as she cast a coy smile at him.

Teasing enough to frustrate, considering she'd taken her pleasure and hadn't wanted to reciprocate. Not that he expected her to, but the oversight wasn't lost on him.

Malcolm grabbed his Stetson from the floor where it'd fallen when she'd thrown herself at him. He shrugged on his leather jacket after that. It'd be a long, cold ride to Wolf Pack Run, especially after *that*. His blood was still boiling in need of her. But they needed some distance for both their sakes. "I'll call and check on you in a few days," he said as he made his way toward the door. No need to linger. "To make sure your safe."

"And if I'm not?" she called after him.

Standing at the door, he glanced over his shoulder at her. The wool blanket on top of the bed where she sat was barely rumpled. Next time, that'd change. "You will be," he promised. He tilted his Stetson as he made his way out the door. "I'll make sure of it."

Chapter 10

It'd taken over twenty-four hours for Boss to come around and answer Trixie's calls. Once he'd finally answered, he agreed to pick her up from Yellowstone, only to bring her straight back to the Coyote. Tables were still overturned, chairs splintered, glass everywhere, and while all the clientele had fled, the coppery scent of their blood hadn't yet escorted itself out when she'd finally waltzed in the creaking back service door.

Boss shook his head at her. His bicolored eyes glared. "You made a real big mess this time, cher."

The routine had been the usual. Her apologizing for interfering, pleading with him not to enact the terms of her contract and destroy her life with the flick of one powerful, magic hand, swearing that she'd never do anything to undermine him again. The song and dance was all familiar. They both knew he wouldn't enact the contract terms. She and her abilities were too valuable to him. They also knew she'd do it again the next time she didn't get her way or he broke a promise to her. It was a mutual understanding. As clear as day but unspoken between them. She'd never been good at obeying without question, even when staring down the terms of her binding spell. Her mother had always said she'd been... What was the fancy word she'd used? That's right...

Recalcitrant.

Nearly a decade together and Boss was used to it by now, but that didn't mean it didn't anger him or that she wasn't skating on thin ice. But she was careful. When it came to the warlock, she picked her battles. It'd be a good long time before she tested him again. She was certain that was why he always let her slide, because her slipups were few and far between and she was more useful than she was trouble. Even on her worst days.

The cleanup had been long and grueling. Full of broken glass and pint shards. She'd seen enough spilled beer and bloodshed for a lifetime. And bodies. At least Boss had taken care of those. She'd gone through ten boxes of lavender-scented garbage bags hauling the debris out to the alley's trash cans. She'd never enjoy the flowery scent again.

But cleanup had always been Boss's punishment.

"You made this mess. You clean it up."

Every time he said it, it reminded her that he really was an old man. Like a father to her—or as close as she'd ever had in their own strange way. He'd even scared off a few of her boyfriends a time or two, ensured they didn't get close enough to hurt her. Sometimes the warlock was old-fashioned, particularly in his punishment, but he was also protective. They both knew full well that magic would have made the business open for operation again a hell of a lot faster. But it was a reminder that money wasn't what was important to Boss. It was power. And he had no intention of helping her when the mess was one of her own making, one that'd taken an opportunity away from him.

He always made that clear.

But at least Jackie had returned home to his family, and a rich man at that. The young coyote shifter may not have won the fight entirely fair and square, but Boss would never acknowledge that. Not publicly. Not without risking the Coyote's reputation and, more importantly, her life. As a result, Jackie hauled in enough cash to care for not only himself but also his four younger siblings for a good long while. The youngest wasn't even ten, and thanks to Trixie, Jackie may never have to step into the ring again. For that, she still wasn't the least bit sorry.

Throughout the long, silent hours of the cleanup, the only thing that ate away at her was the heat that'd passed between her and Malcolm, the change she'd seen in him. When those golden wolf eyes had stared up at her from between her thighs, the wet heat of her center dripping from the stubble of his chin, he'd looked like a savage, wild and feral. More wolf than man. She'd loved that he hadn't cared that she'd been all over him. She bit her lower lip.

Damn if he hadn't even licked his lips.

Trixie let out a long breath, slow and steady as she closed up the bar for the night. Malcolm had been everything she'd wanted him to be and more. Hot. Passionate. Dominating. A true giver like she'd anticipated. And to her surprise, he'd even been oddly…tender beneath all that hardened strength. Like he'd push her but never break her, never do anything she didn't want him to. Hell, he'd even said as much.

Consent matters to me. Authenticity too. His rusty voice thrummed through her, rough and graveled. He'd said it gruffly, like he did everything, but the emotion underneath had been soft, sincere. She'd felt the truth beneath it.

It was like he *cared* about her or something. And wasn't that thought weird? Malcolm, of all wolves, caring about her?

Trixie let out a little harrumph of amusement as she tried to start her car. She kept twisting the key but coming up empty. She hadn't had a man treat her that way in years, like she was worth anything other than a good lay. She'd be lying if she said she wasn't looking forward to a repeat.

Finally, the engine turned over. The old beater sputtered to life.

"Good girl," she whispered, rubbing a hand on the dashboard like the car's engine could hear. It hadn't even taken a bit of magic tonight.

The drive back to her apartment was a long and silent one. Just her, the steering wheel, and the open road. She hadn't driven home since Boss picked her up at Yellowstone, and her car was sputtering something fierce again by the time she reached her apartment, but what else was new? She'd need to let the car cool down before she could take it to a nearby mechanic, and thanks to her little screwup with Jackie, she wasn't about to ask Boss for a cash advance.

Even if he'd likely give it to her. Maybe Dani would give her a ride for her next shift. The poor, sweet thing had been texting her of late. Malcolm may not have liked her since she was a feeder, but Trixie didn't think she was half-bad. Not when you got to know her.

Trixie parked her car at the nearest available spot to her door, sliding out of the driver's seat. Her feet were aching from her decision to wear a pair of even-higher-than-usual heels—clear, platform-like things that occasionally lit up when she walked. They'd clearly been meant for a stripper rather than a bartender, but man, they would pay off in tips once she broke them in.

It wasn't until she went to slide her key into the locked door of her apartment and didn't feel any resistance that her good feeling about the night came to an abrupt end. The door to her room blew open an inch, like it had never been locked to begin with. Trixie froze, hand suspended above the metal handle. Her heart raced. The magnolia scent of her magic came along with it, a subtle means to protect her. Something wasn't right, and years spent dealing with drunks had taught her to trust her instincts.

But there was no one else here. No one else to look inside except her.

She swore quietly under her breath, wishing for once in her life that she wasn't so single and alone, so goddamn self-reliant, before she pushed the door open. The breath rushed from her chest in one fell swoop, like someone had taken a bat to her stomach.

Her apartment was trashed. The shards of her potted plants lay smashed throughout the room. Clothes scattered everywhere. Her signed Dolly poster hadn't only been torn from the wall... It'd been ripped in two. In case there had been any doubt that the destruction was intentional. The mess was nearly as bad as the Coyote had been, except this was worse.

This place meant something to her. It was hers.

Or it had been.

Trixie stepped into the room, wading through the carnage. Tears pooled in the edges of her eyes, but she didn't let them fall. She stared down at her rhododendron, torn from its potted home and displaced. Judging from how dry the roots were, they'd been sitting like this for over forty-eight hours. There'd be no saving all of them. Maybe some, but not others.

Inching farther in, she made her way to the bed. The sheets had been downturned, but it was the only thing left mostly undisturbed. Save for the unfamiliar cell phone that lay atop it. Trixie swallowed down the lump in her throat, hands clenched as she glared at the burner phone. There was already a number keyed in. She knew what would happen the moment she dialed it. But what choice did she have? Boss wasn't going to help her run from this, not when the mess was of her own making, and Malcolm…

She still wasn't certain what she was to him, but it wasn't enough that he'd put his pack at risk, that he'd protect her again.

I didn't do it for you. His words echoed in her memory.

He'd said that after he'd saved her at the bar. Before he'd promised her protection with the subtle tip of his Stetson.

You will be. I'll make sure of it.

Empty words. She'd believed him, but now she wasn't so certain.

Staring down death at the hands of the Triple S changed things.

It'd been a nice thing to say, a pretty lie that she'd wanted so badly to believe that maybe she'd ignored all signs to the contrary. Sure, he might not have hated her, but when it came down to it, could she really trust him?

She was no dummy. She had her and her alone to rely on. No one else. Especially a man. At the end of this little party, there was no way she'd be the one stuck with the check.

Snatching the burner phone from the bed, Trixie hit Call and pressed the thing to her ear. A girl caught more bees with honey than vinegar, and she wasn't above fooling anyone to get her way. The moment the other line connected, she put on her most sugary Georgia drawl. "What do I need to do to get off the hook for this, honey?"

Stan didn't answer at first, just laughed.

She didn't ask how he knew it was her who fixed the fight for certain.

It didn't really matter.

Five minutes later, Trixie hung up the burner, feeling sick to her stomach as she trudged into the bathroom. She threw the phone into the toilet. She watched the water seep into the plastic cracks, beneath the screen. Satisfied, she made her way back through the wreckage of her room, grabbing several outfits and pairs of shoes that'd been scattered in the melee and dumping them into some garbage bags from beneath the sink. When she'd hauled all but the last of her clothes and the plants she could salvage out to her car, she stood for a moment in the doorway. She tried not to let her lip quiver.

"Good riddance," she whispered.

Turning on her heel, she threw the last garbage bag over her shoulder, trekking back out to her car. She tossed it into the back seat, sealing herself in the cab and locking the doors behind her a moment later. Trixie rested her head on the steering wheel.

She needed to get a dog. A huge, monstrous thing that she could take with her everywhere she went. Not a wolf like Malcolm, but a true canine who'd be loyal to her until the end and preferably bite anything but her within a ten-foot radius. And then she needed a plan. To steel herself against the world again. Her lip quivered.

Only after she'd had a good, long cry…

Chapter 11

"THAT FANGER IS A GRADE A PRICK—A FESTERING thorn in all our sides."

The Grey Wolf packmaster grumbled the words from where he'd been poring over his desk once again, his head resting wearily in his hand. Malcolm leaned back in his chair, sinking into the soft leather cushion. Maverick's desk was fashioned out of the trunk of an old oak tree, and it looked the part. But lately it'd been more disarrayed than usual with piles of documents towering at the edges that remained untouched. With the threats they faced, no one gave two shits about the ranch's paperwork.

Slowly, the packmaster's fingers made smooth circles across his own temple as if the movement could ease the tension there. When it didn't appear to help, Maverick tore the gold-rimmed reading glasses from his face with a rough growl, tossing them into the nearby desk drawer before casting a ferocious look at Malcolm.

Malcolm knew without a doubt the ire wasn't aimed at him but their enemies. Cillian, the master vampire of the Billings coven, in particular.

"It's time to end those bloodsuckers once and for all. This has gone on too long now. The time for limited strikes against them ended the moment they chose to help the Volk." Maverick's eyes flashed golden, underscoring the seriousness of his words as he looked at Malcolm. "This is war."

The weight of his alpha's gaze meant Malcolm's own wolf was instantly stirring, eager to break free of his skin. Their kind didn't always need words. A single look could create a silent understanding between them.

Hunt. Maim. Kill. Whatever he had to do.

As long as Malcolm ended this. Struck back. That was his sole task. For all of them.

Malcolm nodded in silent agreement. For once, he couldn't say he disagreed. The bloodsuckers had more than dug their own grave over the last few years, and Cillian, their leader, had been at the helm of all of it. Their assistance had led to the Volk nearly annihilating the Grey Wolves. To the death of Austin and the lost lives of too many.

For the past hour, Malcolm had been sprawled in a chair in the far corner of Maverick's darkened office, having recounted the information Trixie had given him for the umpteenth time as the Grey Wolf packmaster and Blaze, the pack's security specialist, volleyed ideas. All Malcolm needed were his orders, and then he could get to work. He was an executioner, good with his hands. Not an idea man like Blaze.

The Grey Wolves had the best defense any pack of shifters had to offer, along with the protection and alliance of the other shifter clans of the Seven Range Pact, but nevertheless, the events of the past two months had aged all of them, their packmaster most considerably.

The lines near Maverick's eyes had deepened, a result of all the recent death the pack had experienced at the hands of the Volk and the vamps. Mav was still young for a wolf, as vibrant and lethal as ever, but Malcolm could see how the pack's devastation weighed on him. He'd never been envious of the other shifter's position. It was more responsibility than a single wolf should ever bear.

Maverick released a long sigh, shaking his head again, his long hair moving. "First the half turned, the serum, the Volk, and now this. Where does it end?"

"It ends here. Swiftly," Blaze answered, uncharacteristically serious. When it came to the Volk, he always was. He leaned against one of the office's many chairs on the opposite side of the room. "We'll find the right plan."

Maverick was shaking his head again. "What I can't wrap my head around is what a group of supernatural Mafia wannabes from Chicago are doing all the way out here?" Maverick's gold eyes flashed again. "What purpose would partnering with the bloodsuckers and the few remaining Volk serve?"

Their agreement to protect humanity, to keep the bloodsuckers in check in exchange for immunity from the human hunters of the Execution Underground, was always reason enough. The bloodsuckers didn't like being controlled, policed so that they didn't slaughter humans indiscriminately.

Blaze shrugged. "Do they need a reason?" Today he was wearing one of his signature graphic T-shirts, which aptly read *You've Got to Be Kidding Me, Not Again.* "Aside from fucking us over?"

Malcolm smirked in mild amusement.

"Aside from that." Maverick leaned back in his desk chair, considering for a moment while he stared at the dark wood of the bookshelves, as if the large tomes that lined the walls, detailing the Grey Wolves history, would hold an answer for him. The office fell silent, with only the tick of the clock on the wall cutting through the quiet.

After a long beat, the packmaster said, "You don't think it could have anything to do with...?" His voice trailed off, but his gaze fell pointedly on Malcolm.

"No," Malcolm said, shaking his head. "I'm certain of it."

Hell, he hadn't shown his face in Chicago in years. Hadn't made any mistakes or stepped out into human territory, not without being in his assassin blacks or having his face hidden beneath the shadows of his Stetson. He knew the rules. He was a wanted man, and Wolf Pack Run was his prison.

Save for a single outing to the Midnight Coyote a month, a luxury only afforded because there weren't any humans aside from the occasional feeder. He'd been more than careful. Following the exact protocols their front of house, Dean Royal, set out for him.

Not that Malcolm cared to interact with humanity anyway. Not like Dean did. After Bo, as far as he was concerned, there was no redemption for the monsters. At their worst, humans only knew hate, fear, and bloodshed, especially toward anyone or any*thing* different from them.

He'd learned that lesson the hard way, harder than most, in his childhood.

For Bo, that same lesson had ended with him dead and

buried beneath the cavern rock and had left Malcolm alone once again. Nothing but the ghost of the man he'd loved to keep him warm.

"There's no connection," Malcolm said again, reassuring both himself and Maverick. "I'm certain." The Triple S's Chicago home base was pure coincidence. Nothing more.

A moment later, as if his packmate's ears had been burning, the door to the office swung open and Dean stepped in. He smiled at them. The pale tan of the Stetson perched atop his long locs contrasted handsomely with his dark skin.

The Grey Wolf front-of-house director was nearly as quietly charming as he was lethal. That charm played well in his position, since for all intents and purposes, he was the face of Wolf Pack Run, their spokesperson. Only he interacted regularly with humanity, ensuring the ranch's outside business and coordinating their interests beyond the packlands with their ranching contacts as near as Billings and as far as Bozeman, and farther, to the rangers at the ranch's Yellowstone border. He and Malcolm worked closely together, since Dean was in charge of selling and purchasing operations and Malcolm ran the bunkhouse, two jobs that went hand in hand.

Malcolm had always thought Dean was handsome, respected him. He was kind and good-hearted in a way many in the pack weren't, but he was also heterosexual and happily mated. A safe, unexciting attraction when there was no actual risk of his feelings being reciprocated. Not like with Trixie. Nothing about her was safe.

Malcolm cleared his throat, pushing the thought from his

mind and redistributing his weight in the chair where he sat. He wasn't about to examine that thought too closely. Not now.

Not with everything the pack had at risk.

The moment the door closed behind Dean, Maverick's eyes turned to their packmate. "How are things looking from the front? With the humans?"

Internally, Malcolm bristled. At least he'd been wrong about *that*. He supposed a human and a witch weren't the same, but they were still too damn close for comfort. There was something special about shifters, about living more than half a life as beasts that men feared. A man didn't become animal without being humbled, without his voice and all the things that gave him power being stripped away from him. When they were wolf, they were wild, one with the nature around them, powerful in jaws and claws, but also vulnerable. The kind of vulnerability most human males never had to fear.

Not if they were white and heterosexual anyway.

"They're none the wiser. Still ignorant." Dean took a seat not far from Blaze on the opposite side of the room, nowhere near Malcolm. The choice was unconscious, but it didn't escape Malcolm's notice. They all shied away from him.

Even their wolves knew he was a killer.

"The noise didn't carry?" Maverick asked.

Their recent round of battle with the Volk had required the pack to use machine guns instead of their usual handhelds. Volk were more difficult to kill than vampires, but the bloodsuckers had numbers and a hometown advantage on their side. Wolf

Pack Run was relatively isolated, the sheer size of the pack's ranchlands ensuring privacy, but that didn't mean there wasn't still risk living out in plain view, if anyone looked too closely.

That was where Dean came in.

"Nothing to be concerned about. We'll need to be careful, as always. But we're in the clear for now. I've smoothed any questions over."

"Good." Maverick nodded his approval. "That leaves us more room to figure out how to strike against Cillian."

Blaze leaned his shoulder against the adjoining door to the security office. "The MC is on board. They'll be here to fight beside us soon enough. When the bloodsuckers come again, we'll be ready for them."

Maverick shook his head. "We can't wait for them to attack first. Not this time. Not without knowing what the Triple S have planned. We need to understand what they're bringing to the table, and the vamps already dug their own graves by assisting the Volk. This is war now. We strike first."

Dean removed his Stetson from his head. "Still best not to operate without full information."

"Could you press Trixie more?" Maverick asked Malcolm. "See what else she knows?"

Blaze smiled a cheesed-up, teasing grin. "I'm certain he'd love to *press* Trixie."

Without warning, something inside Malcolm snapped, something protective and territorial. He was across the room before he could stop himself.

"Don't talk about her like that." He rounded on Blaze, eyes flashing to his wolf. He snarled, canine teeth bared, drawing up on Blaze inches from the other wolf's face. "Do it again and I fucking end you," he promised.

It surprised even him that he meant it.

Blaze and his other packmates stilled. The threat hung heavy in the charged air.

"Duly noted." Blaze lifted his hands in surrender before he inched a step back. "I'm happily mated, Malcolm. To Dakota. Remember?"

Malcolm wasn't entirely certain why Blaze chose that moment to remind him. But Malcolm backed off, turning his attention toward Maverick again. From the corner of his eye, he saw Blaze mouth a silent *wow* while Dean let out a pretend whistle.

Let them think what they would of him, but he wouldn't let Blaze joke about Trixie. He'd promised her his protection and he meant it fully. The only reason he hadn't dragged her here the moment she'd left Yellowstone was because he was trying to give her space, be respectful of her wishes. She was used to independence. Not him following her every move like a needy bloodhound. What happened between them hadn't changed things.

"She doesn't know anything else. I'm certain," he said to Maverick, refusing to look in his other packmates' direction again.

Maverick was watching him with careful, smiling eyes, like he was seeing Malcolm for the very first time, but the packmaster didn't comment. "Another way then."

Blaze nodded in agreement. "I'll do some reconnaissance. See what I can find, but I don't think it will prove fruitful.

They've gone mostly off-line." He shrugged. "Apparently, they didn't like me using the Volk leader's social media accounts to locate them."

Since Blaze was a former MAC-V-Alpha soldier, they all knew he had done more than simply *locate* them. Apparently, the ordeal had involved several pipe bombs and a planted cyanide pill. Blaze cast the room a charming, wry grin, lightening the mood.

Malcolm rolled his eyes.

Killing wasn't supposed to be showy. It was supposed to be efficient, clean. Not bombastic. Cold and distant was his preference, and in his profession, he *did* have a preference.

"Then we do this the old-fashioned way," Maverick said, ignoring Blaze's joking.

Dean's gaze narrowed on the packmaster, questioning. "What are you suggesting?"

"We find one of those bloodbags and squeeze it until it bursts like a fucking oversize mosquito." Maverick's wolf eyes burned. His heated gaze turned toward Malcolm. "Do you think you can do that?"

Malcolm nodded. "It'd have to be someone lower level. Who they wouldn't notice is missing for a few days." That was one thing he was good at—making people disappear.

"You think someone that far down the ranks would have knowledge of this?" Dean lifted a brow.

"If word's gotten out to Trixie and Boss, then I'd say half the supernaturals this side of Appalachia know. Just not *our* people, and that's deliberate." Maverick stood, pushing back his desk chair.

Blaze opened the joining door to the security office, ducking inside as he called over his shoulder. "So Malcolm targets and shakes down some low-level vamp to see what info he can get out of him. In the meantime, I gather reconnaissance. And then? Once we have the information we need?"

"Not a shakedown. Get the information and then end him if you have to. It'll send a message. A life for a life. For Austin." Maverick placed both his hands on his desk, supporting his weight there. "We do whatever it takes to put an end to this."

A moment later, Blaze ducked back in, a coy grin spread across face. Malcolm lifted a brow because his packmate was directing the full wattage of his smirk at him. "Things just got more interesting," Blaze said, both to Malcolm and the room as a whole.

"What?" Malcolm growled. He'd had enough of Blaze's teasing for one day.

Blaze whipped out his phone and pressed the app that pulled up the pack's security screens, turning it toward Malcolm. "Trixie's here."

Chapter 12

THE NOONDAY SUN HUNG HIGH OVERHEAD, WARMING the cool autumn breeze. The pack truck rattled to a stop, shuddering. Malcolm shifted the clutch to neutral, thankful it didn't stick this time, before he threw the gear into park. He shoved open the driver's side door, and the rusted, old hinges let out a moaning creak. The air smelled of the coming winter, like the dampness of a thawed morning freeze and the dried-out crunch of fall leaves.

Leaning out of the cab, he perched his feet on the edge of the truck's floorboard, balanced between where he rested his elbows on the door and the truck's tin-can roof as he shook his head. He could hardly wrap his mind around the sight of Trixie standing there at Wolf Pack Run's perimeter. Internally, his wolf snarled, fierce and protective.

What the fuck was she doing here? This wasn't any place for her, not with the threat of the vampires and the few remaining Volk drawing near.

It wasn't that he didn't want her here, but he hadn't braced himself for it either, hadn't mentally prepared in any way. He didn't like surprises. Even *he* recognized he was too much of a grump for them. And the sight of her standing there, after he'd buried his face between her legs the last time he'd seen her, hit him harder than he cared to admit. A surprise if there ever was one.

She looked as out of place in the Montana foothills as he did.

At the sight of him, Trixie gave him a sultry little wave, her little four-door junker parked not far from where she stood. She'd clearly made it all of five feet before she'd been surrounded by half a dozen Grey Wolf guards, shifters in human form who were all nearly twice her size and armed to the teeth. Their weapons were poised in her direction, but that didn't seem to faze her. Malcolm nodded to the guards and they lowered their guns.

Trixie's blond hair was done up in her usual curls, not a stray hair out of place. A red handkerchief wrapped around her head reminded him of some rockabilly Rosie the Riveter. A pair of huge Hollywood sunglasses covered her eyes. The jean miniskirt she wore along with her fishnet stockings left little to the imagination and was paired with a strappy little pair of blue heels and a ruby-red blouse that matched her lipstick. The only evidence she had any awareness of the fact that winter was drawing closer by the day lay in the leather jacket with studded shoulders she'd slung across her car's hood. Beside her, a massive male Rottweiler sat on the end of a bedazzled hot-pink leash.

Christ, the woman was as delicious as she was fucking insane.

He'd be lying if he said a small part of him didn't like it.

Even Malcolm had to admit she *was* charming, stand-ing there in her little getup that'd never last a day out in the pastures. Like a fish out of water, except instead of water, the fish belonged in a western bar full of overpriced beer. He made a mental note to get her a different pair of shoes. She'd fall and break her neck in those things.

No way would she get hurt on his watch.

A gust of autumn breeze blew downwind, taking Malcolm's scent with it. The dog sniffed the air and growled, teeth bared. From the gnarled scars on its face, it'd seen one too many dogfights. Trixie smiled at the beast, then at him. All plump red lips and white teeth like a southern, punk Miss America. She patted the dog's head affectionately.

"I thought you said you didn't have a pet," Malcolm growled over the wind.

If anyone could call that mangy, snarling thing a *pet*. It looked more like a dark omen she'd conjured than something cute and cuddly.

"Oh, you mean Dumplin'?" She smiled down at the dog again. "He's new," she called back. "If you're worried, I'm going to put you on a leash, ain't nothing to worry about, darlin.' Don't mean I won't still yank your chain though." She winked.

A few of the guards laughed, instantly charmed.

The chuckle that came from Malcolm's chest caught him off guard. It felt rusty, worn. Fuck if he couldn't remember the last time he'd laughed. He wasn't sure why, but he felt...relieved to see her. Pleased even. He'd checked in on the status of her safety with the wolf rangers at Yellowstone each day she'd stayed there, making certain they checked in on her, remained vigilant, but in the twenty-four hours since she'd left, giving her space had been hard. He hadn't wanted to be impatient—moody and brooding, as she'd no doubt call it.

His laugh didn't go unnoticed.

Trixie beamed. "So you gonna keep starin' or you gonna invite me in, sugar?" she called out to him with a saucy little grin.

He did, in fact, invite her in, and so far, he didn't regret it. Though he *did* regret not checking in on her sooner. The sound of the growl that tore from his throat as she finished describing the state of her apartment was nearly as harsh and feral as that of the mangy mutt now grumbling at him from beside her feet. It'd taken Dakota, the pack's veterinarian, and a whole hell of a lot of coaxing from Trixie and Blaze to get the thing to stop snarling at him.

The fact that it liked Blaze and not him spoke volumes about the canine's intelligence.

Dumplin', his ass. Cujo was more appropriate.

Trixie stirred the cup of hot tea Blaze had made her in a mug Malcolm was fairly certain belonged to Sierra, Maverick's mate and the pack's first female elite warrior. It read, *I make men cry.* Trixie dumped far too much sugar into the steaming liquid, stirring before she took a dainty little sip. Her lips stained the mug rim red. "So I packed my things and I came here," she said, finishing her story as though she'd been sharing her latest vacation plans.

All syrupy smiles like southern sweet tea.

While a Rottweiler slept at her feet.

The woman would be the death of him. The mere thought

of her fear, the state of her apartment, and those damn plants she'd loved smashed to bits made *him* want to smash something. Namely Stan, and also Boss for failing to protect her. Malcolm's wolf stirred inside him uncomfortably. They'd been together exactly once, and already his feelings for her had gone too deep. Enough to give her the power to hurt him.

He'd come to regret that. He was certain of it.

But he couldn't seem to control it.

"And that was it? Your apartment was trashed? No note? No warning? Anything?" Maverick watched Trixie skeptically.

She lifted a sculpted blond brow. "The trashed apartment isn't warning enough?"

She wasn't wrong. It sent a clear message all its own.

Trixie drew another sip of her tea, seemingly unaware of how closely every wolf crammed into Maverick's office watched her. Malcolm, Blaze, Dean, even the Grey Wolf packmaster himself... They were all hanging on her every word. She may not be a shifter, but witch or not, she had her own power all the same.

"Clearly the Triple S is looking for me," Trixie said when she'd finished sipping. "I know you're real important, Maverick Grey, being leader of this pack and all, and a little witch of a bartender like me ain't even a blip on your radar most days, but as far as I'm concerned, you owe me." She held Maverick's gaze from over the top of her tea mug, refusing to look away.

To a wolf, it was a sign of challenge, and considering how many shifters she'd dated and served at the bar, Malcolm was confident Trixie knew that. For a woman whose heels barely made her over five feet tall, she had balls bigger than most for challenging the Grey Wolf packmaster. He'd give her that.

Not to mention a pussy he'd kill a man to taste again.

Malcolm swore under his breath. He was fighting hard to ignore that, but his wolf and his cock weren't having it. She was like a siren to him. The moment she'd climbed into the pack truck's cab and the smell of gardenias and honeysuckle in her hair hit him, he'd been done for.

Maybe he had been from the very start.

Trixie broke Maverick's gaze first, ending their stand-off as she grabbed a carved wooden coaster from the side table next to her. She placed her tea on top of it. "I saved your second-in-command's life and his human mate's. A dead human in the Midnight Coyote in connection with a member of your pack would have caused a real mess for you with the Execution Underground. I didn't have to do what I did, but I saved both of them out of the kindness of my heart." She looked to Maverick again. "Now I'm asking you to kindly save me."

Maverick shook his head. "That was several years ago, and he wasn't my second-in-command then. Nor were they mated yet."

"Only by a handful of days." Trixie waved a dismissive hand. "Let's not split hairs, Packmaster." Not *sugar*. Not *darlin'*. Not when this clever woman was doing business.

Trixie knew how to get her way.

Malcolm might have found it impressive if it wasn't so damn manipulative.

"I'm normally one to offer sanctuary to the pack's—" Maverick's eyes darted toward Malcolm. Blaze had likely filled the packmaster in on the gossip of the tension he'd witnessed between Malcolm and Trixie. The pack was worse at keeping secrets among one another than a knitting circle of old women.

"Friends," Maverick continued, choosing his words carefully. "But the pack is facing extenuating circumstances right now. All our resources are maxed."

"I swear I won't be a bother. I eat like a pigeon and I ain't above crashing on a sofa, and if by circumstances, you mean that the Triple S is partnering with the vamps and the Volk and all three of 'em are gunnin' for you, I can help with that." She folded her hands in her lap prettily. "I already have, as I understand it."

As sweet as sugar but as poisonous as venom.

Malcolm was starting to respect the hustle in that.

Maverick frowned. "Unless you have any further information about the Triple S, we can take it from here." The packmaster was using his I'm-about-to-lose-my-patience voice, which was Blaze's cue to swoop in and lighten the mood.

Blaze thumped Malcolm hard on the back, flinging an arm over his shoulder like they were good pals as he pointed to Malcolm. "Shaking down vamps is Mac's specialty."

Malcolm scowled. "I've told you not to fucking call me that."

Trixie didn't miss a beat. "That's your plan then? To grab one of Cillian's lower-level guys and rough 'em up a bit?" She blinked up at them with those wide amber eyes, thick, dark lashes fluttering.

The room fell silent. Trixie knew far more than any nonpackmember should, simply by the nature of her truth-telling abilities, the manner in which the Midnight Coyote operated, and more than a pinch of quick wits. If Maverick didn't trust her, at least in part, he would have been remiss in even allowing her in the same room as them.

"I can help with that," she said, breaking the tension. The sleeping canine at her feet stirred. She gave it a pat, then took another dainty sip. "I'm willing to earn my keep."

"No." Maverick's word was final. He stood as if he'd heard enough of this.

"It'd be too dangerous. You wouldn't be able to wear a wire," Blaze explained.

"I don't need one. I know how to handle powerful men in a bar, sugar. Whether they're shifters or vamps." She shrugged a saucy little shoulder and dared a glance toward Malcolm. "That's kind of my thing, innit?"

Malcolm refused to meet her gaze. This wasn't his decision to make.

He might have never felt like he was a part of the crowd when it came to the Grey Wolf Pack, but he was more loyal, more indebted to Maverick than most. Outlaw or not, he'd never dare undermine his packmaster.

Maverick glanced toward him, meeting Malcolm's gaze for a moment. For a long beat, the gold of his wolf eyes seared through Malcolm, seeming to ask, *What does this woman mean to you?* Malcolm stared back, letting the answer flow through him.

Nothing. Everything.

He didn't know the answer yet.

Malcolm lowered his gaze in deference. The subtle nod Maverick gave was nearly imperceptible before his gaze turned back toward Trixie. "You're really prepared to go into the Blood Rose unarmed, without a wire, and risk your life, all to be protected by the pack?"

The vampire bar hidden in downtown Billings filled a space that had once been held by the Midnight Coyote. Trixie'd be familiar with its layout, its passageways.

"Yes," she answered readily. "Though one correction, honey." She twirled a glowing pink finger through the air. "I'm never unarmed. Not completely."

"I thought you couldn't see a witch's magic?" Blaze asked. "Isn't it invisible?"

Trixie shrugged again. "The pink is just for show."

Malcolm shook his head. Of course it was.

Maverick frowned. "Either you're more desperate for protection than you're letting on or you're addicted to adrenaline, Trixie. I haven't decided where to place my bet yet." He let out a long sigh. "You can stay, but let that poor thing off its leash." Maverick glanced at Dumplin's collar and scowled.

"That 'poor thing' tried to bite me," Malcolm grumbled.

Maverick lifted a brow in confusion. "So bite him back?"

It was moments like this when Malcolm remembered he was one of the few among them who hadn't grown up surrounded by other shifters at Wolf Pack Run.

Dumplin' let out a loud snore. Finally, relaxed enough to stop growling at him. "Poor baby. He's stressed." Trixie patted the dog's head. "But nobody's bitin' my dog."

"Human canine pets don't work like that, Packmaster," Dean corrected.

"I'm not human," Trixie shot back defensively.

"Close enough," Maverick said, "which is why the only reason I'm allowing you to stay is because half the women in this pack would wring my neck if I didn't."

How Trixie managed to endear herself to all the males of the Grey Wolf Pack *and* their females, Malcolm would never know.

As if she sensed the same question beneath Maverick's comment, Trixie said, "They like to keep me on their good side, since they're all afraid I'll steal their boyfriends."

Blaze let out a harsh bark of a laugh.

Malcolm raked a hand over his face.

"But I have no interest in used goods," Trixie said, as if they were talking tractors instead of many of the Grey Wolves' warriors.

Malcolm didn't want to consider *exactly* how many Grey Wolves, though he wasn't one to judge. He had his own history.

"I'd *never* steal another woman's man. I'm no Jolene."

The venom that dripped from Trixie's words gave Malcolm more than a passing sense that they held a deeper meaning.

"Fine," Maverick answered, stepping away from his desk. This time, the word truly was final. "It's settled then."

Trixie lifted a single finger at him, wagging it as if he were a small child instead of the most powerful wolf shifter in North America. "Hold your horses, cowboy." She smiled sweetly. "I'm not staying unless Malcolm says yes."

For perhaps the first time in his life, all eyes turned

toward Malcolm, and not because they expected he was about to break someone's neck. The idea that his word held more weight than Maverick's wasn't only wrong, it broke all the pack's customs. But Trixie didn't seem to give a rat's ass about that. Dean cleared his throat awkwardly, and even Blaze had the wherewithal to look not only confused but stricken. Only Maverick seemed to take it in stride.

The Grey Wolf packmaster had always seen the value in Malcolm. Even when Malcolm himself didn't.

"Malcolm decides then," Maverick said, ceding the decision to him as if it were nothing.

Malcolm knew without a doubt it wasn't.

The Grey Wolf packmaster moved toward the office door, nodding for Blaze and Dean to follow him. The other two wolves snapped to attention, obedient—at least when they needed to be. The unspoken rule among the elite warriors that Malcolm had never adhered to was simple: Defy the packmaster if needed, but don't get caught.

It spoke to Maverick's sense that no other wolf in the pack was more important to him, no packmember more valued than another. Even him. Being packmaster didn't make him infallible, simply important, and he appointed the elite warriors in his charge accordingly. Malcolm being one of them.

In that moment, he felt the packmaster's trust more than he had in nearly a decade.

"We'll leave you to it then," Maverick said with a hint of a suddenly amused grin, like he knew a secret Malcolm wasn't catching on to. The next look he gave them was calm, serious, as searing in its intensity as the cowboy himself.

Malcolm didn't need Trixie's truth-telling abilities to read the unspoken subtext.

I trust you. Maverick closed the door behind him. *Don't make me regret it.*

There was a lot of that going around of late.

Chapter 13

"I don't know what kind of game you're playing, Trixie, but I'm not certain I want a part in it." Malcolm's dark eyes turned toward her, narrowing in that cold, brooding way of his. If grumpiness were Olympic sport, Malcolm would be a gold medalist. Hands down.

Trixie was certain.

He looked out of place standing there among the dark, coffered wood and full bookshelves of the packmaster's office. Sure, his Stetson fit the bill and he'd traded his shit-kickers for cowboy boots while keeping the leather jacket, but with his chipped black nail polish, tattooed knuckles, and dark eyes that always looked like they were rimmed in guyliner, he still didn't belong here.

Neither did she.

She let out a little sigh, picking up her tea mug again. The rim was stained red where her mouth had touched it. She'd need to freshen up her lipstick after this. But the warm ceramic felt good against the chill of her hands, soothing. The steaming scent of bergamot and orange peel wrapped around her.

With all those other shifters gone, the inside of the office should have felt larger, more spacious than cozy, but it didn't.

Instead, the walls pushed down on her, making her achingly aware that it was only the two of them there, alone together in the silence for the first time since…

She pushed the memory from her mind. She couldn't allow her thoughts to go there, to feel anything for him. Not now that she planned to drop the dime on him and everyone he loved. At first, Stan's demands had felt like simple information. Allocation of resources, striking plans, how the pack had increased and changed their security since their last run-in with the Volk. Simple knowledge to glean for someone whom the pack trusted—for someone like her—but now, sitting here in the packmaster's office, the potential consequences were all too real.

With the Grey Wolves still weakened from the Volk, that kind of information in the hands of the Triple S would no doubt be passed to the pack's other enemies. It was enough to change a battle outcome. Enough for lives to be lost. More of Malcolm's friends for him to grieve.

And Trixie hated herself for it.

"Good to see you, too, sugar." She glanced away to the dog sleeping at her feet before drawing another sip of her almost empty tea. She'd have preferred it mixed with whiskey. A hot toddy would only be the start of what she'd need if she were drinking her troubles away. Anything to stave off her guilt, make her forget her circumstances and Stan.

Bile rose in her throat, the thought of that Triple S bastard sickening her. She'd find a way out of this. She always did. Maybe she'd even be able to keep her pride intact and protect Malcolm and his pack in the process.

She shook her head. Who was she kidding?

She'd only save herself on this one.

What other choice did she have?

She couldn't tell Malcolm the truth. Once she'd agreed to the deal to get the price off her own head, Stan had forced her to meet him at the bar and surprise, surprise used Boss's magic to bind her once again and ensure she couldn't tell the truth. Lord, she'd been foolish to think Stan wouldn't drag Malcolm and his pack into her punishment, make them a part of her penance. She'd thought the hurt would only be her own. But that Triple S-hole must have known Malcolm meant something to her from the moment he first asked about him in the Coyote. Now, whatever he wanted to know about the Grey Wolves, he was going to use her to get it.

Her stomach roiled. It made her sick.

"You should have called me the moment you noticed the door to your apartment was unlocked." Malcolm's words brought her back to herself.

Trixie was already regretting that she didn't.

But lust came easy for her. Trust didn't. That wasn't about to change just because he kissed her like she'd never been kissed before, made her come apart with a single heated glance.

He'd turn out the same as the others. Take what he needed from her and then walk away.

"Why?" she asked, her voice more incredulous than she intended. "So you could save me again?" She said it as much for him as she did for herself. "I don't need anyone but myself to take care of me, darlin'. Besides, you're a difficult man to get ahold of," she said flippantly, changing the subject to distract him. "When I reached the gate, I had no clue who to ask for. For all I knew, there's more than one Malcolm on this ranch."

"There isn't," he grumbled.

She felt him draw nearer then, his presence large and imposing. But she refused to look him in the eye while she lied to him. She owed him that much.

For the flickering ember that'd been the start of their friendship.

Until Stan had come along and forced her to stomp it out, though Malcolm didn't know it yet.

"I wasn't about to ask for 'Malcolm. Just Malcolm,'" she imitated the deep, graveled tone of his voice momentarily. "You'll have to give me a last name. For next time."

He snarled. "There won't be a next time."

The finality in those words captured her, held her hostage in their guttural promise of protection.

She glanced up, taking the full sight of him like a breath she'd been needing for days. Malcolm loomed over her, taking up space in that overtly masculine way men did. She'd thought the other shifters she'd been with had been large, but Malcolm put them to shame, his size instantly dwarfing her. He was a veritable tank in human form. As snarly and mean as she'd let him be.

But sensitive. Always so sensitive. She recognized the pain he wore for what it was now.

Every wound cut him deeply. Each broken promise shattered him. With him, the sting of betrayal never faded, and he used that same pain to keep everyone else at bay. Her included.

Like the dog asleep at her feet, he'd been backed into a corner, caged and made to fight one too many times, and if she betrayed him, he'd never forgive her.

Malcolm held her gaze, gold wolf eyes burning. "I meant it when I said I'd protect you, keep you safe."

Something inside Trixie withered. She tore her eyes from his. She couldn't look at him. Her eyes stung with tears.

Day late, dollar short, sugar.

She pressed her lips into a thin line until her emotions formed a hard lump in her throat. No. No, she couldn't allow herself to believe he cared for her. She'd made the right choice. He'd turn out the same as all the other men who'd only been dark stains on her heart. In the meantime, why not have some fun with him? Where was the harm in it? He'd come to hate her again in the end anyway.

Malcolm must have mistaken the reason for her emotions as a result of his doing, because he said softly then, "Use Grey. The guards will know who you mean."

Trixie sniffled slightly, blinking. "You're related to Maverick then?"

"No."

"Then your last name ain't Grey, sugar," she said knowingly.

"It's the name I use."

"Fair enough." She huffed. She eyed him up and down quickly. "Doesn't suit you though."

"Doesn't have to." He pegged her with a hard stare,

perching on the arm of the chair beside her. Too close, too warm and near. "Why are you here, Trixie?"

She shrugged as if it didn't matter. "Protection. Weren't you listening during that little exchange?" She hated how the lie tasted on her tongue. Acrid and awful. Bitter. "That's what I rescued this fella for." She nodded down to Dumplin'. He opened one scarred eye and looked at her with a grumble that reminded her far too much of the wolf at her side.

"You don't need the Grey Wolves for protection, or a dog. Not when you have Boss," Malcolm said.

The laugh that bubbled up in her chest was genuine, throaty and unguarded. It seemed to catch Malcolm off guard as much as it did her.

"You don't know Boss then. He's the closest thing I've ever had to a father, the closest I've ever come to having someone who cares about me, but he's also an opportunist. He's protected me plenty before, even from my own stupidity, but only when it benefitted him. He makes me clean up my own messes, and *this* mess is definitely my creation, honey."

"For fixing the fight?"

"That seems to be the heart of it." She sighed. "The Triple S don't like losing money, no matter how much of it they have, and a single witch of a bartender makes an easy target."

"And you expect me to believe that's the only reason you're here?" Malcolm lifted a dark brow. She wanted to kiss him there, at his temple, run her fingers through his inky, midnight hair again, taste the sun on his tanned olive skin.

"What else would there be?" she asked.

She was daring him to say it, put a name to whatever this was between them. But he wouldn't. They never did, and in their little game of cat and mouse, he was hardly ever the first one to break. No, he'd be even more stubborn, distant, considering his packmaster had in all but words asked him to keep an eye on her, ensure she wasn't a danger to their pack, and directly in front of her no less. The gall of some men. It wasn't proper.

But hadn't that always been her fatal mistake? Thinking she could protect those she loved?

The last time had landed her in a long-term binding spell with Boss. The terms of which she still had years on, assuming she survived this. This current repeat shouldn't have been a surprise. It was a reminder that she shouldn't allow anyone in her life to become important. She needed to look out for herself first and foremost. Anything less was foolish.

"Do you need me to beg? To plead for a big bad wolf like you to save me? Because if that's what you want, I'll do it, sugar." She met his eyes, willing him to see the truth there. "There ain't a thing I'm above doing. Not if it keeps me breathing. As far as I'm concerned, life is about two things: survival and protecting the things you love, and I love myself enough to survive. I'd think a man of your profession could understand that." She stared up at him.

Please, she pleaded. *Please understand what I'm telling you.*

It was this or die.

This or see Jackie and his siblings tortured.

This or let Malcolm become a target.

Stan was truly a sick, sick fuck.

Malcolm's dark brow lifted uncertainly. "If there was more to the story, would you tell me?"

Trixie felt a burning sting inside her chest, a warning.

"I promised you honesty, didn't I?" In the dark brown pools of his eyes, she could see her amber gaze reflected there. The worry, the pleading, the pain. She was already pushing the limits of Boss's spell. She couldn't push it further. She tore her gaze away, retreated back. There wasn't a way to get through to him. "If being so down on my luck I've hit rock bottom isn't enough to get you to see I'm real, I don't know what is."

It wasn't any kind of answer. But it was enough.

Malcolm stood, crossing the small room.

She'd known the moment Stan had picked up on the other end of the damn burner phone that he was going to make her feel it. She just hadn't expected him to drag all the people she loved into it.

Malcolm headed toward the door of the office, pulling it open. He hesitated, glancing back toward her. "You coming or not?"

He may not have been Prince Charming, but the effect his words had on her was the same. He trusted her enough to let her close. It was a damn shame Stan was going to force her to betray that.

"I know what it's like to hit rock bottom, Trixie," he said. Her magic gave her the sense there was more behind those words than he was letting on. Malcolm's dark stare pierced through her. "It's a long, long way up from here."

Chapter 14

MALCOLM COULD FEEL HIS PACKMATES' EYES ON HIM, the sidelong glances. The uneven ground felt frozen beneath his boots as he led Trixie across the crowded pastures of Wolf Pack Run, her mangy, growling mutt in tow. They breezed out of the main compound, past the mess hall and the training gym, heading out toward the guest cabins. The mountain air was fresh, clear, tinged with the chill of autumn. The temperature would no doubt plummet in the next few days. The fact that they were this far into the season without a true freeze was damn close to a miracle.

The blue snowcapped peaks of the Absarokas loomed in the distance, watching like the eyes he felt tracking their every move. But whether it was Trixie or the dog she was parading around on that hot-pink leash that was earning them so many glances from his packmates, among others, he couldn't be certain. Whatever it was, Malcolm hated it.

Trixie waved at a few passing shifters as they went, keeping an admirable pace beside him despite her wholly inappropriate footwear. A couple Grey Wolves and then a cougar followed by a black bear and at least one of all the seven shifter species currently present on the ranch. Malcolm quickly stopped counting, each tick of the number inside his head fueling his jealousy.

He knew it wasn't warranted, but his wolf couldn't help it. A few of the other shifters had paused at the sight of her, turning to head their way like they would chat and make small talk if given the chance, until they'd caught sight of him by her side, of course.

He tended to have that effect.

With the dual threat of the vampire and Volk that the pack faced, Maverick had called the whole of the Seven Range Pact's warriors here, making the sprawling ranchlands feel more crowded, less private as of late. And all that had been *before* they'd potentially added the threat of the Triple S to the mix. The Grey Wolves had a rough series of battles ahead.

Malcolm veered to the right, apparently too close to Dumplin' for the creature's comfort. The Rottie snarled at him, nearly snapping his drooling jaws at Malcolm's boots. Every time he drew near or even looked at the beast from the corner of his eye, the dog primed itself to attack. Hackles raised. Canines bared. Snarling. Malcolm hadn't had the heart to bare his own lengthened canines and snarl back yet. Maverick's suggestion toyed in the back of his mind.

One look at his wolf eyes and the dog would likely piss itself, but then Trixie'd be pissed with *him*. He sighed, reining his frustration in. At least he and Dumplin' had one thing in common—a drive to protect the saucy little witch.

Even if the dog was confused about how to do the best job of it.

He wasn't a danger to her.

It's everyone else, he wanted to growl at the thing.

"Where are we headed?" Trixie finally asked once they'd been strolling for more than a few minutes without so much as a hint of discussion between them.

"The guest cabins. You'll be lucky if one's available. You might need to double up with some of the other women. Maverick's called the whole of the Seven Range Pact to stay here."

"I figured as much, considering." She gestured at the other shifters passing them. "I guess it goes without saying you're letting me stay then?"

"Looks like it," he grumbled.

"I promise Dumplin' and I won't be much trouble."

"Sure you won't." He glanced down toward the beast. The wide brown-and-black face glared up at him, lip curling. A scar slashed across its muzzle, evidence from one too many fights. His own chest looked the same. He knew the feeling. "Why Dumplin'?" he asked.

No one in their right mind would think the dog was anything close to cute.

Trixie shrugged. "I liked the book by the same title. Lots of my girl, Dolly, in it," Trixie answered.

"You read?" Malcolm didn't intend for the question to sound nearly as surprised as it did. He'd never imagined Trixie curled up on a Friday night with a book instead of behind the bar.

Trixie cut him a side-glance. "I'm going to take that as a statement of fact and not a question. Of course I read. How do you think I learned to take care of all my plants? My mama never taught me any skill worth using."

"Mine neither," he admitted.

Silence fell between them, mutual and comfortable as they walked side by side.

"How do you do it?" Trixie finally asked once they'd ventured a bit farther.

The guest cabins were still but a speck in the distance. But he hadn't been about to suggest she climb on the back of a horse when she was wearing a miniskirt and heels, and to be honest, a part of him had hoped he'd get to talk with her, find a moment like this.

"Do what?" he asked.

"You know what I mean." She gestured to one of his packmates wandering by and let out a low, appreciative whistle. She glanced toward him knowingly. "I can see why you hate it here. So many beautiful men and women in one place. Gettin' any ranchin' work done must be *such* a chore for you," she teased.

Malcolm pawed at the back of his neck. "Who says I hate it here?"

"If you want to lie to me, you're going to have to do a hell of a lot better than that, Malcolm." Malcolm. Not sugar.

He tried not to smile at that but failed. Though if the passing look on one of his packmates' face was indication, it'd appeared more like a grimace. He frowned.

"There's a lot of fine-lookin' men on this ranch. Women too," Trixie continued, "though the women ain't my thing, even though I know you can appreciate them." Trixie cast her eyes toward a particularly handsome male wolf shifter, one of the warriors from the Bozeman subpack. Malcolm couldn't remember his name, but he'd seen him before. Trixie pointed unabashedly as the wolf passed. "I've slept with him. Have you?"

Malcolm growled. He was not doing this. Not here. Not now, but especially not with her.

Trixie ignored his ire. "Don't be jealous. It's just a question."

"I'm not jealous." The words sounded harsh and, well, exactly like what she'd accused him of. *Fuck.*

Trixie laughed. "Sure you're not. Then I guess you don't mind if I tell you I've slept with him, too." She pointed at a passing black bear. "He was real good." She smiled up at Malcolm and winked. "Not as good as you though."

"Trixie," Malcolm growled in warning.

She gently swatted at his arm. "What? Don't be such a spoilsport. That's half the fun of being with someone who's into both men and women, being able to appreciate people together. You're telling me you haven't taken a bite out of some of these fine pieces?"

Malcolm adjusted his Stetson, drawing it lower to block the afternoon sun from his eyes. Sundown came early this time of year. "I think it was you who said you shouldn't shit where you eat."

"But you have before. With Bo, I mean. He was handsome, too." She bumped her hip against his playfully. He tried not to think about how those same hips had felt cupped in his large hands. His tastes had been a bit…singular as of late.

"And how about that cute little Texan?" Trixie rambled on. "What was his name again?"

"Austin, and he and I were only friends." He tipped his Stetson lower. "And he's gone now, too. Like Bo."

That seemed to take the wind out of her sails for a moment. "That's poor luck, darlin'. Truly." They continued on in silence for a moment before she nudged an elbow at him, lifting her brows like she knew a secret he didn't. "But with Blaze, things were different."

Malcolm scowled. "It's not—"

"Don't try to tell me it isn't like that," Trixie said, cutting him off. "Maybe not now, but at least at one point. On rare occasions, I catch you givin' him that same wistful look you give me."

He didn't feel half as attracted to Blaze as he was to Trixie, even though he was an equal opportunist when it came to his taste in women and men, but he wasn't about to confess that fact.

From the way she was staring at him expectantly, Trixie wasn't letting this go.

Malcolm sighed. "Have you seen him?"

Trixie read the true meaning behind those words in an instant.

Can you blame me?

Trixie smiled, wide and pretty. "Oh, I've *seen* and I've appreciated. Only from a distance, mind you."

"It was a brief interest. Before Bo and never since. Since then, there hasn't been anyone except..." Malcolm's voice trailed off. The words he left unspoken hung heavy in the charged air between them.

Except you.

Trixie smiled knowingly.

Malcolm cleared his throat and glanced away. "It was years ago. There's no interest there for me anymore, other than maybe some nostalgia for a simpler time. He's hetero. Let me down easy."

Trixie gave a little shrug again. "His loss then."

"If you want to call it that." He didn't know what possessed him to admit the next phrase that came out of his mouth, but he was saying it before he could stop himself. "Apparently, I have a thing for men and women who like to put on a show."

Trixie stopped in her tracks, looking at him earnestly. Her heels had sunken into the ground a little bit, like tiny drilling spikes. She cocked her head to the side momentarily, examining him. "Because it draws you into the spotlight a little bit," she said knowingly, certain in her assessment. "It feels good to be in the light, the heat of someone else's glow. But it's also easy to hide behind a person who shines brighter than the sun."

Malcolm swallowed hard. This conversation was becoming far more intimate than he'd meant for it to. "Is that how you see yourself? Like a star in the darkness?" He wasn't certain whether the darkness in this analogy was him or the world, but he didn't really care.

As long as she told him the truth.

That was all he'd ever really wanted from her. Honesty. Something real.

"No, darlin'. Not usually." She glanced up at him, her amber eyes still caked with mascara, but he willed himself to see past it. To the real woman beneath. Trixie glanced away then. "But when you give me that heated look, it sure is," she whispered.

To his surprise, she blushed a bit.

Malcolm growled. The warm pink on her cheeks made him think of all the other places he'd made her skin flush with need. He wanted to haul her into his arms, packmates surrounding them be damned. He'd throw her over his shoulder like a caveman if she'd let him, carry her off to one of the pastures, or hell, who cared, and do whatever it took to make her moan again. She was breathtaking when she came, and he wanted to see how many times he could do that for her. He had a feeling she wouldn't say no to that.

"When you look at me like that"—she nodded to where his eyes had turned molten gold—"it makes me feel like maybe I don't need to stand on a stage. Maybe the whole show I put on is only for you. Like you're the only spotlight I need."

His heart gave a hard thump. Like it knew that she held him in the palm of her hand.

How had he let himself get in this deep this fast?

But hadn't that always been what he'd feared? Why he'd pushed her away to begin with?

He'd wanted her too much from the very start.

"Is it?" he asked. "Is it enough for you?"

He wasn't entirely sure what he was asking, but the whole universe seemed to hinge on her answer.

"These days?" She grinned. "Maybe." She glanced down at the ground with a coy little grin before she started walking again. "We gonna talk about the other night or pretend it didn't happen, darlin'? It's up to you."

"I don't want to pretend it didn't happen." The words felt raw in his throat, too honest. Like *he'd* been the one laid bare. "But we don't need to talk about it either. Not yet."

He wasn't a man of many words. She knew that. Talking wasn't his gig. Hell, this was probably the longest conversation he'd had in years. Longer, even.

"Fair enough." She nodded.

She was a few feet ahead of him now, Dumplin' obediently keeping pace beside her as they trekked down a slight incline in the landscape. He watched as her heel drove into the ground again exactly as Dumplin' gave a sudden lurch forward, and then before he could grab her, she slid. Trixie hit the ground hard.

"Shit," he swore, rushing to her side.

She'd dropped Dumplin's leash and the beast had turned around, snarling at his quick approach. His eyes flashed to his wolf and he snarled back. Dumplin' blinked before he growled again. So much for putting the canine in its place.

Ignoring the dog, he turned to Trixie. "Are you okay?"

"I'm fine. I'm fine." She waved him away. "Just made a fool of myself is all." She tried to stand, putting weight on her ankle, and winced.

"And twisted an ankle." Without thinking, Malcolm hooked an arm under her legs and another around her waist before he hauled her into his arms, lifting her with ease. Dumplin' growled again, but a single, sweet hush-now look from Trixie quieted him. He lay down on the ground, placing a paw over his head like he was hiding, and the woman hadn't so much as scolded him. Clearly, she'd already won Dumplin's loyalty, too.

Malcolm turned his attention back toward her. "You never should've worn those damn shoes here," he snarled.

Trixie ignored his protective grumbling. "Look at you. Sweeping me off my feet like Prince Charming." She threw her arms around his neck and snuggled closer, with a minx-like grin.

Her breasts were pushed flush against his chest, and the scent of her hair wrapped around him. His cock stiffened. If she knew all the things he wanted to do with her, she'd never say that. "I'm no Prince Charming, Trixie."

"Of course you're not," she said a little too quickly. She smiled. "I don't want you to be." Her amber eyes seemed to sparkle in the lowering sun. "I thought you told me to keep the shoes," she teased.

The growl that rumbled from his chest this time was pure arousal. "Only when I'm between your legs," he demanded. "The rest of the time, when we're here, you'll wear boots."

Trixie faked a little salute. "Yes, sir."

"If you're trying to put me off with addressing me as a sir, you're failing."

"You like that, huh?" Her arms were back around his neck again. "When I call you 'sir'?"

Malcolm blew out a long breath. He couldn't believe he was doing this, carrying her through the pasture and flirting with her for everyone to see like they were a thing. Like there was obviously something between them. "I like a lot of things."

Things that would make her toes curl, make her let out that adorable *eep* she'd done back at the bar before. For entirely different reasons.

Trixie nodded her approval. "Sure you do. Men. Women. And apparently bossing me around."

Malcolm chuckled, low and dark. "I haven't even begun to get bossy with you."

Trixie beamed. "That sounds like a promise."

"Don't tempt me."

"That's kind of my thing, Malcolm." Malcolm again. Not sugar.

He liked his name on her lips, wanted to hear it again. The next time it'd be on a scream of pleasure.

"I thought we were headed out to the guest cabins," Trixie said, gesturing to the changing scenery around them. They'd headed back in the direction they'd came. Dumplin' trailing along behind them obediently. Maverick had been right. Maybe she did need to lose the leash.

"We were. But with all the extra shifters we have here, the guest cabins are running low on medical supplies, and that ankle needs to be wrapped." He hoisted her higher in his arms. "I'm taking you to the bunkhouse."

"Where you live?" she asked.

He lifted a brow in question.

"Don't look so surprised. You think I don't know you're in charge of the ranch hands? Speaking isn't the only way of communicating."

Malcolm blew out a long breath, struggling to keep his strides steady. This woman. He could think of more than one way he wanted to communicate with her. Namely, burying himself so deep inside her, she wouldn't walk straight for a week—and *not* thanks to that damn ankle. He'd gladly carry her everywhere. Take care of her. Allow her to rest in his bunk. Cook her breakfast and feed it to her in bed.

Fuck, he was in over his head.

They'd nearly reached the bunkhouse, Dumplin' following but stopping to snap at the wind occasionally as if he could bite it. Malcolm's pace was long and quick. Trixie weighed far less in his arms than any of the ranch equipment he was used to lifting, or even his motorcycle. When he'd been younger, his brute strength had made him weird, an oddity in human gym class. But close to human as she may be, Trixie seemed to like it. Hell, even appreciate it from where she was now wrapping her arm around his leather, where his jacket covered his bicep, like she was impressed that she couldn't fit both hands around him. She didn't seem to think he was weird. Too large, too intimidating. A killer or brute.

Just brooding. Maybe a little broken. Those parts were true, at least.

He kicked open the bunkhouse door and carried her in. Dumplin' followed, sniffing the floor like he was part bloodhound, which he wasn't.

Trixie glanced about, arms still wrapped around Malcolm's neck like she belonged there. Dark woods, western decor, like the rest of Wolf Pack Run. A card table sat near a small kitchen and a refrigerator, the open space leading into where several rows of messy bunk beds remained. A couple scattered trunks lined the walls. An ugly carpet with a picture of several horses on it covered the floor between all the beds. It'd seen better days and far too much dirt considering they trampled over it every evening after coming in from the pastures.

Trixie was still in his arms. "It's more communal than I expected."

"I'm not the only one who lives here." He carried her to his bunk and set her down on top of it. "So do the other hands."

"This isn't your home." She said it like it was fact rather than a question.

"How can you be so certain?" Dumplin' had taken up residence right beside Trixie, glaring at Malcolm, but obviously willing to tolerate him now that he'd carried the dog's master all this way. Malcolm headed to the bathroom to the medicine cabinet, more aware of the absence of Trixie's warmth against his chest than he wanted to be. "I sleep here, don't I? Must be home in that case," he called over his shoulder.

He grabbed a rolled-up Ace bandage and returned to where she lay on his bunk. From the looks of it, she hadn't hurt herself too badly—at least this time—but she'd need to stay off it for an evening or risk irritating the muscles worse.

Trixie leaned over the side of his lower bunk, petting Dumplin' affectionately. "A home is more than a place to sleep, and I don't see any of you here." She gestured around them. "It's too western, too country."

"I'm a rancher," he answered.

"Not by choice."

Malcolm stilled, far more exposed than he wanted to be. How could she see straight through him? Like the walls he'd built to protect himself were made of glass and one cut of those amber eyes could make them shatter.

She stared up at him, seeing too much. "Why do you stay here at Wolf Pack Run if you don't want to? You weren't born here, so if you hate it, why stay?"

Because I'm a killer. Because that's all I've ever been good for. Because Chicago wasn't home either. Because I'm not even certain I'd know what a home means.

Malcolm cleared his throat. "It's complicated."

"All good stories are."

Of course she'd think that. What was a bartender but a collector of stories? A priest that delivered absolution in a bottle? "Mine isn't a good one."

"Maybe." Trixie propped herself up on one of her elbows as he sat down beside her. "Or maybe you're simply not done tellin' it yet."

Malcolm took her ankle gently in hand, slowly undoing the strap at her ankle and removing her heel. He unrolled the Ace bandage and began wrapping her foot. "There's a place here on the ranch that means something to me. It's not much, but it became important after Bo died."

It was more than he'd ever thought he'd admit to her, or anyone for that matter.

"Will you take me there?" she whispered.

Malcolm froze. No one had ever asked him something so intimate before. To show them parts of himself he'd never dared bare to the world. Not even Bo.

Malcolm opened his mouth, unsure how he'd answer, but the door to the bunkhouse flew open, and a second later, the cowhands were filing in, all six of them, finished with the day's work. At the sight of Trixie, more than one pair of eyes lit up in familiarity.

"Well, look what the cat dragged in," Miles crooned.

"It was a dog this time, but who's countin'?" Trixie preened, nodding down toward where Dumplin' was now wagging his tail, panting and friendly.

And to think he'd been pleased the Rottie had been warming up to him. If by warming he meant not attempting to maul his leg.

Malcolm's lip curled. *Traitor.*

"Which one?" Miles joked, nodding in Malcolm's direction.

Trixie and the other hands laughed. Malcolm didn't. The joke was on him, he supposed. For ever assuming he'd mean anything—to her or to anyone else.

He finished wrapping her foot, tying the bandage with a secure knot. "Try to stay off it till morning," he grumbled.

"Thanks, sugar."

Sugar again. Not Malcolm.

The Trixie he was accustomed to was back again.

The one he'd always known would break his heart. He shouldn't have been surprised, shouldn't have been hurt by the loss of connection between them, but that didn't mean he didn't feel it. He felt everything far too much. More than he ever wanted to.

Trixie was deep in her flirting with the other hands now, his packmates hanging off her every word and batted eyelash. One of the guys, Chance, whipped out a set of playing cards, suggesting poker, and seconds later, Trixie was up, hobbling on the foot he'd told her to stay off only two seconds earlier. She headed over to the card table, all thought of him forgotten.

"Hey, Malcolm, you want us to deal you in?" Miles asked.

"No. I don't play." The game still reminded him too much of his stepfather. Those drunken nights spent playing always inevitably ended in the human man beating him, taking out his losses on Malcolm's body. Being a shifter meant he'd healed quickly from the blows, but that didn't mean he still didn't remember the pain. He'd told the other ranchers it wasn't his game plenty of times before, not that anyone listened.

Miles didn't even wait for a response before starting to deal seven hands instead of eight. Trixie didn't so much as spare him a glance. His spotlight sure didn't feel like enough at the moment. Dumplin' curled up at Trixie's feet, sleeping.

Placing his Stetson on the hook near his bed, Malcolm slipped out of the bunkhouse without another word, not bothering to look and see if he was alone. He knew he was.

Outside, the sun had started to set, painting the sky a pale purple. Malcolm wandered toward the trees, stripping out of his clothes before he knelt on all fours to shift. Unless his adrenaline was pumping, he still wasn't as fast as the other elite warriors, not when it came to this. They all shifted into their true form as if it were as easy as breathing. It had never been for him. Maverick had always said it was because he'd spent so long living like a human, not knowing what he really was, while most of the pack started shifting voluntarily by the time they were five. It was a matter of practice. But here he was, over fifteen years later and still slower than the rest. To him, it was simply another way he didn't belong.

Beyond explanation, but hurtful all the same.

After a few prolonged moments, he relaxed enough that his shift came. Limbs twisted. Fur sprouted. And he felt the sting of his jaw lengthening, becoming canine-shaped instead of square. He let out a little shivering shake, feeling more himself than he had moments before.

Maybe that was why he never felt at home, because he'd spent so long in skin.

Because his true home was the forest.

Malcolm was running before he'd even decided to, animal instincts taking over. The chill of the autumn night coursed through his fur, ruffling his tail. There was a deer two miles north and he smelled its trail. The musky scent made his mouth water. He followed it by scent, eyes seeing through the darkness in the way only a true predator could. When he was wolf, he didn't know shame, didn't feel guilt for his kills. He was simply one with the trees, a part of a greater ecosystem that not only tolerated him but embraced him, needed him.

More than his pack ever would.

By the time he found the deer, the hunger in his belly was gone, replaced instead by an entirely different kind of need, one it'd take more complex thought to fill. But at least the thrill of the chase had cleared his head. The light of the moon overhead soothed him. He'd let the fawn live for tonight.

Making his way back down the mountainside, he didn't

shift back into human form until he was near the bunkhouse again. He could hear the sounds of his packmates inside, of Trixie's laughter and the roar when she must have bested the men with a particularly good hand.

With her truth abilities, she'd wipe the floor with them.

But Malcolm couldn't bring himself to be pleased about that fact.

Not when he was always on the outside looking in.

Pulling on his jeans, he padded his way across the pasture, barefoot, heading to the one place he knew was his own. When he reached the pack's garage, the doors were already open, allowing the moonlight to spill in. The smell of dirty motor oil and mechanical grease filled his nose. Malcolm ducked inside, careful not to step on any stray tools with his bare feet.

Inside, the cool tones of the moonlight cast a pale shadow over the lifts and toolkits. But it was a glowing pair of wolf eyes that caught his attention. Cheyenne, the pack's mechanic, stared at him through the darkness, silent and knowing. She nodded at him, not feeling the need to greet him. Theirs was a relationship of few words. A mutual understanding between two people who didn't need to interrupt the silence to understand each other.

He nodded to her and she mimicked the gesture, refusing to meet his gaze. With her, it wasn't personal. Eye contact was difficult for her, particularly when she was working and focused, so he knew it wasn't meant to hurt him.

Silently, Malcolm made his way to the back of the garage, the moonlight lighting his path, though his wolf eyes didn't need it. But when he reached the far corner where his paint shelf and supplies were stored, he started to panic. His heart pounded against his chest as his eyes combed the darkness in search. The old sheet wasn't there and neither was…

"Chey, where's—"

"Shhh." She hushed him like he was a small babe. "It's right here." She nodded over to another corner. "I had to move it to get my bench under one of the pack trucks earlier."

"For a moment, I thought you'd…" His voice trailed off.

She stared at him, not able to anticipate where his sentence was leading.

"That you'd gotten rid of it finally," he admitted.

Cheyenne quirked her head to the side like she was studying him. "You know I wouldn't do that to you," she said softly. "She's right there." She pointed toward a sheet in the corner like a ghost. Two wheels stuck out from underneath.

"Thanks." Malcolm nodded.

Cheyenne smiled shyly, though it didn't quite meet her eyes. She didn't bother to ask what he was doing here in the middle of the night, and he didn't ask her the same. That was how it worked between them. Silent understanding while they worked side by side. It was only now that he realized it had been the same with Trixie while he'd been grieving Bo. But something about the silence between him and Cheyenne was different.

Friendship, not attraction.

The presence of another shifter who knew what it was like to be the outsider.

Malcolm wheeled the old Harley back over to the corner

stand where he normally left it, falling into the quiet work of the night as Cheyenne did the same. In the distance, he could hear the sounds of the forest, an owl's hoot, the rustle of leaves, the occasional whistle of the autumn wind. As he took his airbrush and loaded the paints into the canister, the stringent smell of the aerosol singed his nose, contrasting with the sounds of the forest. He had a vague sense that was why he came here each night, for this strange cross-section of worlds that called to both parts of him. Maybe that was why he'd never have a home again. He was too caught between two halves of himself to truly be at peace with either.

Chapter 15

TRIXIE WAS RIGHT BACK WHERE SHE'D STARTED WITH Malcolm, same old song and dance. It was the following evening and Malcolm had barely said two words to her, choosing instead to avoid her throughout the day and well into the start of evening. The moment the sun had crept into the salmon-colored sky that morning, he'd ridden out to the pastures alongside the other hands, leaving Trixie to fend for herself while they gathered the steers for sale.

Whatever the hell that meant.

Trixie settled into the front seat of the truck, the cracked, torn leather of the bench threatening to swallow her whole. A low, crooning country song played on the radio, the raspy tune drowning amid the rumbling of the truck's ancient engine. At least she wasn't the only one with a vehicle on its last leg.

The silence between them seemed to stretch for miles, as long as the open highway ahead. He'd refused to take his bike, grumbling something or other about her being too cold on the ride back and not having the right clothes or shoes. She hadn't been pleased. She'd been looking forward to the closeness of wrapping her arms around him, snuggling close, however fleeting.

The sun had started to set now, the lights of downtown Billings still not seeable in the distance ahead. Trixie cleared her throat.

"So I've been thinking about your last name…"

Malcolm didn't respond. He simply kept his eyes on the road, reached to his left, and switched on the truck's headlights. The two yellow rays beamed through the twilight.

Trixie sighed. "How about White?"

Malcolm ignored the question. Only the slight curl of his upper lip indicated she was getting somewhere, though he was trying hard not to show it. She let out an annoyed huff of her own. *Cat meet mouse.* She shook her head. Except this particular cat was a mean, snarly thing who at the moment was trying to convince her he couldn't be less interested when all she wanted was for him to show a bit of claw. Growl. React. Snarl. Anything.

At least one snarly beast in her life was on her side. Dumplin' had been pleased at the prospect of staying with the pack's cute veterinarian, Dakota, who'd immediately showered him with love and homemade dog treats. Trixie could see why Dakota made Blaze happy, though she still thought Malcolm had the better appeal. Like she'd said, Blaze's loss. Or her gain.

If she ever managed to get him to speak again.

She let another few minutes pass.

"How about Washington?" she said, breaking the silence. "Or Williams? Something with a W. Any of those would pair well with Malcolm."

He growled. "I have a name."

Four words, but it was something. Progress.

She could see the city in the distance now. The dark form of the rimrocks filled the backdrop of Billings, still visible in the early evening light. The upper floors of First Interstate Center and a bank, the tallest buildings in downtown, towered over the others. There weren't any high-rises out here. In that way, it reminded her of back home in the Georgia foothills, before she'd hitchhiked west with nothing but a suitcase and a pretty smile to earn her way.

"I know, I know," she said, checking her makeup in the passenger-side mirror. "Grey, but it's not really yours, is it? Just the name you're using for now. It's kinda like an old library book… You'll have to return it to its rightful owner eventually." She wiggled in the seat, pulling down the hem of her little black dress so it didn't scooch too high on the curve of her thighs—not that it was anything Malcolm hadn't already seen…and tasted. Heat warmed her face. She'd been looking for a repeat, but so far, he hadn't indulged her. "I just think Washington suits you. That's all, sugar."

It must have been the wrong thing to say, because the look he shot her was pure ice. Cold and distant. Eyes so black they looked forged from onyx. "Who says you get a say?"

He said it like she meant nothing to him.

And who was she to say she should?

But that hadn't been the impression he'd given her the night before.

When he'd carried her back to the bunkhouse, he'd been gentle, tender, if a bit overly protective, though she had to admit she sort of liked his grumbly orders about how she should take better care of her feet and watch out for herself more. It meant he cared.

Sure, he probably *would* hate her, given time. But that didn't have to be the case yet, and she was fighting hard not to think about that right now. Not with everything the evening held at stake.

If she played her cards right, maybe she'd help the Grey Wolves more than hurt them while still getting enough dirt to keep Stan and the Triple S appeased. That was the plan anyway.

"Did I do something to offend you?" Trixie asked defensively, her lips pulling into a scowl that matched his own. She'd opted for a darker red than usual tonight—a deep cranberry instead of her usual ruby. Between the black dress and the darker-than-usual lip, the dark colors set off the sun-kissed undertones of her skin and the gold in her hair. She looked downright sultry. Like a ray of sunshine cloaked in night. The kind of woman who belonged on the arm of a vampire instead of a wolf.

That'd been intentional.

There'd be none of her usual boys on hand at the Blood Rose.

"You didn't do anything, Trixie. Anything at all."

She nearly gagged. Malcolm was more honest than most—guarded, sure, but honest—so the falsehood caught her off guard. Lord, lies tasted acrid. Awful. She'd had more than enough of late, of her own doing.

"Don't lie to me. It doesn't suit you." She unclasped the clutch she'd brought with her and took out a breath mint, popping it into her mouth. "Unless you tell me what I did wrong, I can't very well apologize for it."

Malcolm's next words were cold, meant to wound. "Would you? Even if you did know?"

Trixie scowled at him. She was a lot of things, but callous wasn't one of them. She knew how to apologize when she'd done wrong.

"Stop here." She waved toward the side of the road.

They'd reached downtown now. The Blood Rose was only a few more blocks ahead. He pulled over as she'd instructed.

Trixie unlatched her seat belt and slid from the cab, planting her black heels firmly on the sidewalk pavement as if they could anchor her. "If you're going to be an ass, I'll walk from here." She moved to slam the door in his face.

Malcolm's hand shot out, catching it as he frowned. "You shouldn't—"

"No," she said, pointing a finger into his face like she was reprimanding a small child rather than a lethal wolf, a warrior.

Malcolm's eyes flashed gold in his anger. But he didn't dare interrupt her. He had too much respect for her for that.

"You forfeited the right to be worried about my ankle the moment you decided to ice me out, *Malcolm*." She spat his name at him. "I can stand on my own two feet." She slammed the door in his face, then turned on her heel and strutted off toward the bar.

She could have sworn she heard him snarl in frustration and pound his fist against the steering wheel as he cursed at himself, but she didn't dare glance back. She may not have been much, but she was above pleading or begging for the affection of a man who didn't want her.

Grey Wolf reaper or otherwise.

She continued on two more blocks, cutting right and then a sharp left again before she reached the back entrance of the Blood Rose. Malcolm would park the truck on the south side near the mouth of a narrow alley. She didn't need to double-check her plans. She knew these walls from when they'd once belonged to her and the Coyote—before the Execution Underground had shut down their operation, forcing them to move farther west. She had the misadventures of the Grey Wolves' second-in-command to thank for that.

Boss had been salty about that for a time.

Slipping in the back service door, she navigated her way to the front with ease, unnoticed. Even with the redecorating they'd done, she knew this place—the nooks and crannies, its hidden alcoves—almost as well as she knew the back of her manicured hand.

When she reached the front, she eased through the shadows, in favor of blending in over making a grand entrance. She wanted to appear as if she'd been transported there by magic—a diamond suddenly glimmering in the darkness, waiting for someone to reach out and take it, as much a part of the bar's fixtures as the velvet-cushioned furniture.

Quickly, she ducked into the ladies' room, dabbing on a generous amount of perfume to mask the scent of wolf on her skin—no vamp would enjoy the earthy scent—before she slipped back out again. According to Malcolm, she had three possible targets: Andreas, Luther, or Alaric. She spotted the first as she made her way toward the bar, the second as she was slipping into her seat. By the time she was sipping her gin and tonic, the third was making his way to her. She left the bartender a very generous tip.

For her, this would be easy. All she had to do was dangle herself like a juicy morsel in front of them and then let the flies swarm. Or oversize mosquitoes as Malcolm had called them. She'd only made the mistake of having a vamp in her bed once before, and she wasn't looking for a repeat.

Trixie's eyes combed over the bar, taking in the changes to the space. The western decor had been swapped for a more gothic feel, like she was inside a high-end gentleman's club—all dark reds and darker woods, smooth velvet, and hushed whispers. Even the glassware was fancy, top-dollar, cleaned until it was sparkling like the generous array of back-lit liquor bottles behind the bar. There were no taps. No surprise there. Vamps weren't much for beer. It was like the fangers thought it was beneath them.

She didn't feel the warmth of another body slip up beside her as much as she felt a disturbance in the air, like the pressure around her had dropped. A small shiver went down her spine. "I haven't seen you here before, luv. I would have remembered."

She turned toward the vampire beside her, a slow twist of her seat. The bloodsucker leaning on the bar at her side smiled, flashing fang. He was handsome and British, because of course he was, with a sharp blade of a nose and even sharper cheeks and a mouth that looked like it knew how to bite as well as it could kiss. It wasn't the most original of pickup lines. She'd heard better. But for now, it would do.

"First time here," she said honestly. "Haven't been in since it used to be the Coyote."

Better to tell than truth than lies. That had always been her policy. It was easier to stick to a story when that story was real. She still remembered when these walls had crawled with Wild Eight, back when Wes, now the Grey Wolf second-in-command, had been their leader, before the human hunters had followed him there and raided the place.

"Mmm-hmm," the vampire said, nodding with consideration. "And what do you think of the update?" His voice was velvety, cultured.

The kind a woman could listen to for hours and not tire.

But that was how vampires drew their prey in. No one ever said they weren't enchanting.

Trixie glanced around, making a show of taking in the decor. "I think it's too fancy for my tastes. But it suits you." She glanced back toward him, smiling with a coy curve of her lip before offering a gentle hand. "Trixie Beauregard."

No point in giving him a false name; he likely already knew who she was anyway. Working at the Coyote didn't offer much in the way of anonymity. Not in their world.

The vampire reached out, taking her hand. His shake was delicate, smooth, more like a caress than the firm grip of a shifter, but the subtle strength and power that lay beneath was unmistakable. His skin was cold enough to send another chill through her. Though she didn't dare show it.

"Trixie," he said in that thick accent, rolling her name around on his tongue. By her guess, it meant he was old. Damn old. Pre-American Revolution. All the strongest vamps were. Way too powerful to be one of her targets. The older they were, the more dangerous, because it meant they knew how to survive.

Survival was half the battle, even in her world.

"And what exactly about *my bar* is too bourgeois for you?"

He'd meant the indication that he owned the place to throw her off guard, but she already knew. She might have been a bartender, but working for Boss didn't exactly leave her ignorant. Trixie drew a sip of her drink, holding his gaze as she did. "The fact that you use words like 'bourgeois' on a woman sitting at your bar top is a start," she teased.

The joke landed exactly as she intended.

The bloodsucker threw back his head and laughed, a deep chuckle that showed off the pearly white of his straight teeth and, more importantly, the length of his fangs. She supposed she could see the appeal if she were into that sort of thing. Shifters had always been more her weak spot.

"Well, Trixie," he said, "I suppose you have a point." He nodded to her gin and tonic. "The drink's on me."

Trixie smiled, glancing down so she could look back up at him through a thick layer of lashes. "I already paid."

The bloodsucker didn't miss a beat. "The next one then." He pushed off the bar where he leaned beside her and moved to walk away.

"Not a good business model, giving out your product for free," she said, stopping him in his tracks. He wouldn't be good for her target, too old, too powerful, but she wasn't quite ready for him to leave yet. There was something mesmerizing, almost hypnotic about that icy-blue gaze, and she had more than a passing feeling everyone in the room was looking at them. At him and, more specifically, her being the object of his desire.

The power in that was intoxicating.

With a conspiratorial smile, the vampire leaned in close, whispering in her ear as if his words were their little secret alone. "I'm more than happy to pay for a warm-blooded woman to sit at my bar, especially when she's the most beautiful creature in the room. A witch's blood is like milk and honey to a vampire, did you know that?" He pulled back slightly, those cold eyes turning dark with only the slightest hint of danger. Enough to thrill, not scare. "I know what my clients like," he said. "Just do me a favor and get your little feeder friend out of here."

Trixie raised a brow. *Feeder friend?*

Smirking at her confusion, he slipped a business card across the counter. A phone number and email contact, nothing more. As cryptic as the vampire himself.

Trixie raised her glass toward him, uncertain of his meaning. "Thanks for the refill." He nodded, moving to step away again, but she couldn't stop herself from calling after him. "Hey, sugar?"

The vampire paused, glancing over his shoulder toward her.

"I'm sorry, but I didn't catch your name," she crooned.

"Corbin." The bar's proprietor smiled, flashing those handsome fangs again. "But you already knew that."

Trixie's breath caught.

By the time she took another sip of her drink, the owner of the Blood Rose was already gone, blending into the bar's shadows as if he were part of the dark night.

All eyes in the room were on her now. As far as she was concerned, mission accomplished. All she needed to do was make her move. She stepped away from the bar, walking deeper into the establishment. As she approached the booths, she tried to school her features, to stop her eyes from going wide at what she found the farther inside she ventured. There was a concerning number of humans passed out in the alcoves, on the tables. Everywhere. She pretended not to notice, or at least to temper her alarm as she turned in their direction, eager to investigate, but the warm arms flung around her neck a moment later caught her off guard. She nearly spilled her drink, jumping out of her skin as she spun to face...

"Dani?" She stared at the Coyote's other bartender, now bouncing excitedly, clapping her hands with delight.

"Trixie, I can't believe you're here!" Dani squealed. The sound was harsh and piercing compared to the smooth tones of the surrounding vampires and the soft melodies of piano music playing in the background. "You need to meet Cilly," Dani said, grabbing hold of Trixie's hand.

"Cilly?" Trixie lifted a brow.

Cilly like *silly*. What kind of name was that for a vampire?

"My boyfriend, of course." Dani dragged Trixie alongside her.

Dani's pupils were too wide, a sign she'd no doubt been

juiced up with vamp blood. To a human like Dani, it was as addictive as any drug—and she was clearly flying high. Trixie had all of two seconds to keep her cool as Dani yanked her across the bar to a far corner, a nearly hidden alcove, where an ancient vamp, who Trixie had no doubt was *not* named Cilly, waited for them. Trixie swallowed down the curse in her throat.

Not Cilly.

Cillian.

The most ancient bloodsucker on this side of the Atlantic. Trixie schooled her features so she didn't let her jaw drop at the sight of the vamp. He didn't look particularly distinct from any other vampire. Pale complexion. Handsome features. Dark hair. To a human, breathtaking, but in the scheme of supernatural men—a subject in which Trixie had a certain amount of specialization—unremarkable.

But there was an ancient quality about him that seeped into the atmosphere and spoke of power and privilege that could cut deep. It pushed against the warmth of her magic. Trixie could feel it.

And he was dating a little-nobody human like Dani?

Trixie blinked. The thought wasn't meant to disparage her friend, but the difference in power dynamic there was... troubling.

Dani wiggled into the booth beside the ancient vampire, cozying up to him like she was a purring cat and he was her catnip. From how high she was, Trixie held no doubt that was true. What had this vamp done to Dani? She had told Trixie her boyfriend was young, the same age as her, a newbie vamp who couldn't be less important.

Not Cillian, the leader of the Billings coven, who was not only an enemy to the Grey Wolves but a dangerous, sick motherfucker. Either Dani had been pulling the wool over her eyes, a fact Trixie knew wasn't true considering her magic, or the vampire had been glamouring her, using the young human woman against her will.

That didn't sit well in her craw.

"Trixie, this is Cilly." Dani rubbed a hand over the vampire's chest. "My lover."

Lover, her ass. More like serial abuser, but she wasn't about to say that out loud. Trixie plastered the sweetest smile she had to offer on her lips. "I know who he is." Only those who knew her would recognize that greeting as cold, devoid of her usual southern sugar. "Pleasure," she said, careful not to let the venom she felt drip into her voice.

Cillian's eyes raked over her, languid and assessing. Whatever he saw there, he must have approved, because his irises filled with crimson bloodfire. "The pleasure's mine," he purred.

The way he was leering at Trixie spoke volumes about exactly how little Dani actually meant to him.

Trixie had no doubt this bloodsucker was using her friend. It might not have started that way. Maybe it'd even been consensual, but it didn't look that way now. Dani couldn't consent to this fucker biting her or sleeping with her while she was higher than a kite. But from the way Dani had wrapped herself around him, Trixie knew Cillian wouldn't stop her from having her fun once they retired for the evening and he fed her more of his blood. He'd glamour her to forget his true power come morning.

And to think she'd thought this task would be easy.

There was nothing easy about watching anyone use her friend.

She'd been here less than thirty minutes, and already she was in over her head. There was a reason she preferred shifters. In the back of her mind, she was vaguely aware that she too had messed with Dani's head, however briefly, but that'd been to protect her, to save her from dark memories that would be more traumatic than many humans could bear. Not the same.

Cillian gestured to the open side of his booth. "Join us for a drink." From the look in his eye, Trixie had no doubt he really did want a drink—from her.

There was a sprawl of untouched food in front of them. Vampires loved the show of food and drink, but later all that would be regurgitated. The wastefulness brought bile to Trixie's throat.

"I can't actually," she said, faking a little pout of disappointment. "I'm supposed to be meeting someone." Another lie. Bitter. Nasty. But if she knew anything about courting the attentions of powerful men, it was that it was best to give only a little, just enough to leave a lingering taste in their mouth, enough to make them want to come back again.

From the way his crimson eyes were undressing her, Cillian would no doubt want seconds of her, now that he'd gotten a look, the scent of her magic in his flared nostrils.

"Pity," he said. "A shame for all this to go to waste." He cast a hand over the spread before him.

Dani had completely forgotten Trixie was even there in

favor of licking her way across the vampire's neck like she was a panting dog instead of an autonomous human.

Exactly like Cillian thought she was.

"I agree," Trixie said in earnest. She wanted to pry Dani off him and get her friend out of there, but there was no way she could do that without making a scene.

That'd only get them both killed.

"Don't forget to feed her," Trixie nodded at Dani. "Something other than blood."

Cillian lifted his wineglass in acknowledgment.

Without another word, Trixie turned on her heel, heading back toward her seat at the bar. She downed the last of her drink, quickly ordering another. When the bartender delivered it a minute or two later, she drained it. Service was fast due to slow business on a Wednesday night. She slipped the bartender another generous tip, holding onto her glass.

"You see the vampire by the restrooms over there...the one that can't keep his eyes off me?" she asked.

The bartender nodded. She was human, like Dani. But from the look in her eyes far more seasoned and aware of what kind of creatures she worked for. "I see him."

Trixie slipped her an extra bill. "You tell him if he's lookin' for a good time to meet me in the back in five minutes." She nodded toward the bloodsucker. She had no doubt the vampire could see them.

The bartender accepted the bill but shook her head. "I don't think I'll have to tell him. He's going to watch you walk out."

Trixie grinned, chuckling slightly before she patted the

other woman on her warm hand. "That's why we do it, honey." She could feel the vamp's eyes on her as she strutted out, glass in hand.

She only wished the sound of her heels wasn't quieted by that damn bourgeois carpeting.

Chapter 16

THE BACK DOOR TO THE BLOOD ROSE SWUNG OPEN, AND a moment later, Trixie stepped out, the sharp sound of her stilettos clicking against the pavement. Malcolm didn't so much as move in case anyone followed directly behind her. The alley smelled of garbage from the nearby dumpster and like one too many drunks had stumbled out here to take a piss. But for the first time since she'd climbed out of the truck and torn out of there like a bat outta hell, Malcolm felt like he could breathe.

But they weren't fully in the clear yet.

Despite his stillness, Trixie must have sensed him there, hidden among the alley's shadows, because her amber gaze cut straight toward him. At her side, her fingers were glowing pink with a hint of her magic and the look in her eyes was angry. "Alaric's following. Let me work my magic. Give me a crack at him first." She strutted farther down the alley, kicking aside a few crushed cans as she went.

That wasn't his usual style, but he nodded with a single tip of his Stetson. He would follow her lead. He'd known she would make quick work of the bloodsuckers, though he hadn't anticipated it'd be this quick, this easy. A witch's blood was like a rare vintage wine to them, intoxicating in its magic, and having it delivered in a package that looked as good as Trixie didn't hurt either. She'd been dangled in front of them like a gift, wrapped in a pretty, enticing bow of smooth, inky silk that clung to her curves. He wanted to take a bite out of her himself.

If only the bloodsuckers knew that for them, she was poison underneath.

Malcolm smiled, more full of pride than he wanted to be.

"Cillian's a piece of work," Trixie said, leaning against the brick wall behind her and hiking her skirt up a bit higher. She was all about the show. He was vaguely aware that she'd done something similar the first time they'd kissed, but he couldn't think about that now.

Not with the pack's safety on the line.

Her comment caused his twisted pride in her to quickly fade, replaced instead with frustration, concern.

"What?" he snarled, nearly stepping out from the darkness.

"There were a ton of humans in there, passed out all over the place. I can't help but think it has something to do with the Triple S." Trixie was shaking her head now, like she couldn't believe what she'd seen inside the Blood Rose's walls. "And he's dating Dani."

Malcolm swore. "Shit."

"The feeder from the Coyote," Trixie elaborated, as if he didn't already know. "My coworker. The one you treated so nicely."

Malcolm snarled, ignoring the jab. "What the fuck were you doing near Cillian? I told you to stay the hell away from him."

Trixie placed her hands on her hips. "Too late now. Quiet down or Alaric'll hear you," she hissed.

Malcolm gritted his teeth while he resumed his place in the shadows, struggling to control the rage he felt at the thought of Cillian so much as setting his bloodthirsty eyes on Trixie. Thankfully he did, because a moment later, the back door to the Blood Rose swung open again and Alaric stepped out.

The vampire's crimson eyes scanned the darkness, adjusting to the orange glow of the streetlights before that red stare settled on Trixie.

"Hey there, darlin'," Trixie crooned.

Malcolm had heard that fake, sexed-up version of her voice so many times before when she'd been playing their little game that his cock immediately responded. The woman's voice was like a dog whistle, and she'd trained his lower head to be obedient.

Damn, witch. He held down an aroused growl.

If only he'd had the sense to protect his heart as much as he had his cock. At this rate, he'd barely last a few more days before he was so far gone there'd be no saving him. But he didn't have the will to put a stop to it. She was like an addiction—a drug he couldn't get enough of. He craved her. No matter how much she hurt him.

Alaric must have felt the allure of her words, too, because he smiled wide at her, his fangs flashing. He wasn't awful looking for a fanger, but the sickly scent of death on him stung against Malcolm's nose. His wolf stirred, ready to break free.

"I saw you watchin' me, sugar. Could see you wanted to play." Trixie took a lazy sip of the drink still in her hand, watching him with half-lidded eyes.

The bloodsucker was eating out of the palm of her hand, and so was he.

The woman was a siren. Pure sex personified.

His cock gave a heady throb.

Alaric made his way toward her, crimson eyes glowing in the dark. Malcolm's hands clenched into fists, his fingers shifting to claws and digging into the palm of his hand until he felt the warmth of his own blood trickling over them. Alaric approached her. The vampire pressed a hand onto the wall above Trixie, pinning her with his body. Malcolm could barely contain the snarl threatening to escape from his throat.

The vampire reached for her, his grubby palm headed straight for Trixie's breasts, but she playfully swatted his hand away. She knew how to handle handsy men. "Ah, ah, ah." She wagged a single finger at him. "Not so fast, sugar," she teased. "How about we play a little game?"

Alaric's eyes flashed crimson, instantly distracted. "I like games."

"Good." Trixie grinned. "How about this? A truth in exchange for a kiss." She smiled with those dark-red lips.

Alaric laughed. "You'll have to shell out more than a kiss if you expect that to work."

Malcolm had to bite his lip to hold down his jealous growls.

"You'll have to shell out more than some cheap pickup

lines if you expect anything more from me," Trixie said, turning his own words back around on him.

Alaric frowned. "Who says I have to shell out anything?" He leaned in closer to Trixie, close enough Malcolm had no doubt she could smell the coppery scent of blood on his breath. "I find it easier to take." He made a grab for Trixie again, this time trying to put his hand up her skirt. But before Malcolm could tear the bastard to shreds, she shot a brief warning look through the darkness, stepping just out of Alaric's reach as she did.

She could take care of herself, and she didn't need any help from him. Not yet.

"I don't appreciate men who don't ask before they touch." Trixie shook her head in teasing reprimand, but Malcolm heard the change in her voice, knew she wasn't playing any longer. Even if Alaric didn't yet realize.

"Do you know what I like to do with vamps like you, to men who take without asking first?" Trixie whispered, her voice sultry, filled with mock desire.

Malcolm had no doubt she was thinking of him, of his mouth, *his* hands between her legs as she whispered it. That was how she sounded so convincing. His wolf knew it.

"What's that?" Alaric asked, leaning in closer.

Trixie eased forward, wrapping her arms through the air around Alaric's neck, lingering but not touching. Her drink hovered inches above the vampire's left ear. Trixie cast the vampire a seductive smile. "Fuck them, that's what." Without warning, she brought the glass in her hand down on the vampire's head, hard. The old-fashioned glass shattered against the bloodsucker's ear, slicing into the side of his head and Trixie's hand.

She didn't as much as flinch. Just glared with all the rage and hatred of a woman scorned. "That's for pawing me without permission."

Alaric pulled back, shrieking and gripping at his bleeding earlobe. "What the fuck?" he roared.

Trixie's hands pulsed with the flow of her magic, her palms glowing pink. "And this is for sitting by and watching your *master* fuck over my friend, asshole," Trixie growled.

Malcolm would have gladly stood there and watched her own the leech for all he was worth, but Alaric had gathered his wits about him now, flashing fangs. Magic or not, it'd take only a few seconds for him to drain her if he managed to sink his fangs into her neck.

Malcolm didn't think.

He lunged for the bastard, moving so fast his Stetson fell from his head. He pinned the fanger up against the adjacent wall, the blade of his knife shoving against the delicate skin of the vampire's throat. "What do you know about your master's deal with the Triple S?" he snarled.

Alaric may have been a vamp, one of Cillian's lackeys, but he was newly turned, had only been a vamp for the past five years or so. A drop in the bucket for an immortal. He wasn't cut out for this. Malcolm, on the other hand, had been born a shifter, even if he hadn't known it at the time. He'd been born for this, killing much more bloodthirsty men than Alaric since he'd been barely a day older than sixteen.

Alaric might have reeked of death, but it was Malcolm who was hell's angel—the Grey Wolves' reaper.

"I don't know, man. I swear I don't know." Alaric winced as Malcolm pushed the knife harder against his throat.

Malcolm's gaze cut to Trixie.

"He's lying," she said. Not an ounce of reservation or fear in her eyes.

Fear that could have kept her alive, that would protect her from vampires like Cillian if she wasn't so damn brazen, so stubborn and brave.

"You fucking bitch," Alaric hissed. "Satan's whore of a—"

Malcolm shoved harder against the bloodsucker, the tip of his blade drawing blood. The crimson trail slithered like a snake down the pale skin of the vampire's throat.

"Tell me what you know now or I end you. Your choice," he growled. The gold of his wolf eyes flared and he could feel his pupils narrow. "I don't waste time."

His kills were quick, efficient.

"Fuck you!" Alaric spat into his face. "You'll kill me either way."

Malcolm paused only long enough to wipe the spittle away. "Wrong choice," he snarled back. "It's *how* I kill you that matters." He hauled the bloodsucker away from the wall. "I'll be sure to make it painful."

Malcolm sliced across the bloodsucker's neck. Not deep enough to nick his carotid artery, only enough to make him bleed, sputter, and gasp in fear that Malcolm had cut it.

"Malcolm," Trixie warned. "Let me take a shot at him."

The next slice was into its side, straight into the stomach.

For a bloodsucker, it took a severed spine or stake straight through the heart to end them. But for a human, it'd be enough to make them drop. "No." This was for Austin, for every packmember that vamps had helped the Volk kill. The Grey Wolves had never struck first, but there was no such thing as mercy anymore. This was war. This was revenge.

Alaric's features twisted in pain. "You mangy mutt," he hissed.

"Malcolm," Trixie warned. "This is *my* fight, too."

She meant Dani.

"No," he growled again. He wasn't about to risk her that way or, for that matter, hand one of the pack's enemies over to her. That required trust. He wasn't certain they had that yet.

This time, he cut between Alaric's ribs.

"I can make him talk. Use my magic." Malcolm felt Trixie's hand on his arm then, her gentle touch reining him in, making him remember himself. "He can't tell us anything if you kill him."

"We tried your way, and all that happened is this fucker nearly assaulted you." Malcolm bared his teeth. "He's not going to tell us anything anyway."

"You thought it'd be that easy?" Alaric rasped a laugh. "You mutts are so stupid." He turned his gaze toward Malcolm. "I hope Cillian makes you watch. He'll bleed her dry while he f—"

Malcolm didn't allow the leech to finish his sentence. He shifted into his wolf, his adrenaline lending him newfound speed. Fur exploded from beneath his skin. Limbs twisted.

Seconds later, he tore into the vampire's abdomen, his rage lending him strength. He normally went for the throat. The flesh there was softer, easy. But he'd promised the vampire pain. A slow death. For Trixie. For her friend. For Austin. Bo. Hell, so many others.

He wanted the bloodsuckers to bleed.

All of them.

When he'd finished, he shifted back to his human form, standing in the alleyway naked as the day he was born. His clothes were scattered among the trash there, the leftover cans and stubbed-out cigarettes. His front was coated in blood. He swiped a hand over his mouth, wiping the worst of it from his face before he turned toward Trixie.

He expected to find disgust there. At the very least, distaste for the fact that he could kill so indiscriminately. As if a life, even an undead one, meant nothing. Instead, when his wolf eyes settled on her, she was staring at him, her chest lifting and falling in heated starts. Not only was she not disgusted by him, but he didn't see so much as a hint of displeasure on her face.

Instead, he saw desire in the fiery amber of her eyes.

Like he'd protected her. Like he'd been brave—some sort of fucking hero.

Desire mixed with rage for not letting her take a crack at the vamp.

He needed to fix that.

He rounded on her, backing her up against the alley wall in the same way Alaric had, but he wasn't nearly as tentative. Malcolm lifted her into his arms, pinning her between the wall and his body. With a rough yank, he hiked up her skirt, slipping his hand underneath and shoving aside the lace of her thong to find her wet and wanting for him.

He growled his arousal. "I ought to take you up against this fucking wall for disobeying me about Cillian. I told you not to risk yourself."

"I wasn't trying to cause trouble." Trixie's hands explored the bare planes of his chest, undeterred by the vampire blood there. "Sir," she added saucily.

Malcolm's cock throbbed, the hard length of him pushing against her center. "Don't lie to me. It doesn't suit you," he snarled, stealing her words. "This was sloppier than my usual. Him trying to touch you made it personal. Do you know what kind of trouble that will cause for the pack if Cillian notices Alaric missing?" He slid his hand up her arm, settling it on the soft skin of her neck. The thought of that vampire wanting to sink its disgusting fangs into her there tore him to shreds.

"No," she answered, "but I have a feeling you're about to tell me."

He snarled.

"Sir," she whispered, taunting him.

Saucy, sexy little minx.

"No, Trixie. I'm not going to tell you a damn thing." He slid his hand down, over the curve of her breasts. She arched against him, wanting him to palm her there, but she wasn't in charge of this little show. Not this time.

"But I'm going to punish you accordingly."

Abruptly, he released her, spinning her around and

positioning her so that her face pressed against the brick of the wall. "Say the word and I'll stop."

"Don't stop," she whispered.

Spreading her legs wide, he yanked the hem of her dress up and over her behind, pulling her panties down so that her ass and the sweet, wet folds of her pussy were bare. He slipped a finger inside her. "What do you do when you're bad, Trixie?"

"I don't know, sir."

He smacked her on the ass with his other hand, hard enough to leave her pink with pleasure-pain. "I said, what do you when you're bad, Trixie?"

"I don't know," she whimpered, shoving back and onto his hand wantonly.

Another finger. Another smack.

"Don't make me ask again." He started working her, slipping in and out of her center. She was so fucking wet, practically soaking his hand. She rocked back into him, riding his hand like a champ. He wanted to be doing this exact thing with his cock, but fuck if he hadn't brought a condom. He hadn't intended to take her like this, to be so overwhelmed with need.

He took himself in his hand, stroking over his length while he fingered her with his other hand. A bead of moisture pooled at the tip of the head.

"What do you do when you're bad, Trixie?"

"Apologize," she ground out. "I'm sorry, Malcolm," she pleaded. "Please. Just fuck me."

"No," he growled. "Not until you say it like you mean it."

He slipped his fingers out of her, using his hand to gently slap over the sensitive flesh of her pussy. Trixie screamed, coming apart on a wave of pleasure that sent him careening over the edge right along with her. He finished with a guttural groan, spending himself into his own hand. His cum dripped from his palm onto the ground near her stilettos.

Trixie sank back against him. All pleasured sighs and loose limbs.

Momentarily, he propped her up against the wall, quickly pulling on his jeans and shirt before tipping his Stetson back onto his head. Seconds later, he was pulling her into his arms, lifting her up like he was a servant and she was his queen— queen of the sirens, of the wanton women who didn't given a damn what he or anyone else thought of their desire.

She stroked a glowing finger over his chest idly. "I did mean it," she whispered. "My apology. Whatever I did to hurt you yesterday, I'm sorry for it."

Something in Malcolm's chest uncoiled, but he didn't have the strength to probe it, only the strength to carry her home, away from the grime of the city and back to the welcoming mountains near Wolf Pack Run. "Don't worry," he whispered, carrying her. An aroused grin crossed his lips. "You'll be begging for mercy before night's end."

Chapter 17

THE RIVULETS OF WATER THAT POURED DOWN HIS BACK did little to clean him. Malcolm ran his hands through the wet strands of his hair, washing away the shampoo there. The vampire's blood that'd covered his torso mixed with the hot water, pooling in a pink mixture over the cream-colored ceramic before gurgling down the drain. The steady white noise of water against tile soothed him. Malcolm closed his eyes, allowing the water's heat to rush over him, the ache in his muscles, the tightness in his shoulders. Trixie hadn't been afraid of him or disgusted with what he'd done. He wiped a hand over his face, clearing the water there.

He wasn't certain what to do with that.

Once he felt thoroughly clean, he scrubbed some more, isolating himself until the hot water ran cold. Eventually, he turned off the shower. The steam from the water created a fog that remained trapped in the small space, the bathroom mirror cloudy and opaque. Swiping a towel over its surface, he stared at his reflection, trying to assess exactly what it was Trixie saw there, what it was that'd stopped her from turning away.

He couldn't see it.

The coppery taste of blood still lingered in his mouth.

He brushed and flossed his teeth. Bloodsuckers tasted as bad as they smelled, like metallic rust mixed with rotting meat. Disgusting. When he was finished, he wrapped a towel around his waist to cover himself and padded out into the main room.

Trixie was sitting at the card table with a basin of warm water he'd given her and a pair of tweezers in her hand. He'd tried to help her tend to the wound when they'd first arrived, but she'd insisted she wasn't letting him near her again—"not with a ten-foot-pole, darlin'"—until he'd gotten the rest of the vamp blood off him. "Bless your heart, it's unsanitary," she'd hissed with a little wrinkle of her nose. He wasn't exactly well versed in southern euphemisms, but his heart hadn't felt very blessed. He didn't have the patience to point out that everything they'd done in that dingy alley hadn't exactly been the definition of sanitary.

As he approached her spot at the table, she glanced toward him. Her eyes widened at the sight. Him, bare-chested, naked from the waist up. He was vaguely aware this was the first time she'd ever seen him unclothed in full light, having indulged in little more than passing glimpses after he'd shifted. Having been raised among humans, he wasn't as comfortable with nudity as other shifters. He tended to keep his clothes on more than not.

He stood before her, waiting for her response, for her to whistle in appreciation in a way that was brazenly Trixie, ask about the meaning beneath any of the ink that covered his skin, or maybe even wince at the sight of his gnarlier scars— war badges earned over his years spent fighting for the pack.

Instead, her gaze raked over him, slow and assessing. He watched her visibly swallow, a light pink warming her cheeks before she roughly cleared her throat.

A surprise grin pulled at his lips. Who was this woman who could let him take her rough and wild in the middle of an alley but then blush at the first brush of intimacy? She was a seductress, a siren, or so she made everyone think. But the way she glanced away so shyly made him wonder if he'd been wrong to treat her that way. Intimacy and sex weren't always one and the same, though he preferred them to be.

He'd thought that first night he'd pleasured her that maybe he could separate the two. He'd been foolish. For him, that separation wasn't possible. It never had been. He'd given her a part of himself and there was no way he could take it away now, even knowing she'd crush his more fragile innards. If he was going to leave his heart in the palm of her hand, why not make himself truly bleed?

"I need to go get Dumplin'," she said. "He doesn't like being alone."

"Dakota meant it when she said she'd keep him till morning. He'll be fine," Malcolm mumbled.

Refusing to look at him, Trixie turned her back in his direction. She tried to use the tweezers to remove the glass from her hand and winced.

Stubborn witch.

"Let me help you."

Malcolm pulled out the chair beside her, the wooden legs giving a loud scrape against the hardwood flooring, before he did the same with her chair, forcing her to face him. He sat down beside her, taking her palm in his own without giving her a chance to protest. She had washed some of the blood away with the water in the basin he'd given her, but a few shards still remained. She hadn't even touched the gauze, the medical pads, or the warm washcloth. She should have let him take care of her first, *before* his shower, when they'd first returned to the ranch.

He grumbled his discontent. "This'll hurt," he warned. He used the tweezers to remove a larger piece from between her thumb and forefinger.

Trixie hissed.

The sound tore through him. Her pain became his own. He hated that she'd been hurt under his watch again, even if it'd been her own choosing. He should have stopped her, should have protected her from needing to clock that vamp with her glass. He moved on to a piece in the middle of her palm. The shard had pierced her at an awkward angle. The way she winced before he'd even touched the tweezers to the glass surface highlighted how much pain she was in. Stubborn. So damn stubborn.

"You never should have gone anywhere near Cillian," he ground out, trying to distract her as he worked. Blood pooled in her palm, and he dipped her hand into the basin in between each removal to clean it.

"Cillian isn't the reason there's glass in my hand," she snapped defensively.

The subtext seared through him. He didn't need her truth-telling abilities to read it.

You're to blame. For not protecting me.

She didn't say the words, but he felt them, deep in his chest. A sign of his own guilt.

The price of love was always his to pay.

Malcolm tried to steel himself, to ignore it, to push through. "Flaunting yourself in front of him was foolish," he shot back. "Bloodsuckers like him don't know how to take no for an answer. He won't care if you call uncle. If you keep risking yourself like this, you're going to get yourself killed. First, throwing yourself under the bus for that coyote shifter, now this. Volunteering to go into the Blood Rose was dangerous enough, but I wasn't about to pretend I had any right to question your choices. But add Cillian to the mix, and you were in over your head."

"Says you. I know how to handle myself."

Another shard. Another wince. Each sign of her pain shook him.

She *had* handled herself well in the alley, but that wasn't the point.

He growled, low and warning. "You're playing hard and fast with your life. When you bet against fate, no one ever wins. Not in the long run. Death always finds you."

"Or you do." She met his gaze then and held it. "Whichever comes first. Though I've heard it's one and the same." Her eyes flicked to his hands, to the words tattooed across his knuckles, then to the image of a reaper on his upper arm, and back again. "Don't act like you don't do the same to protect those you love."

The fire in her amber eyes flared as he removed the last shard, but this time, she didn't wince. From the hardened look in her eye, she wasn't allowing herself to.

Dropping the piece of glass onto the table, Malcolm slid the nearby gauze across the scratched wooden surface, drawing it toward him to wrap her hand.

He thought about arguing about the difference between wolves and witches, about his kind's increased capacity for healing, a shifter's speed and strength. Those were things a witch could only dream of, but ultimately, that defense would have been a lie.

He'd have done what he did anyway.

"No one would miss me." He dabbed antiseptic over the wound, then wrapped the first layer of gauze over her palm. "For you, that's not the case."

"Like hell it is." The edge in those words caught him off guard. "They'd miss the idea of me, the woman they think they know."

Not the woman they both knew she was. The one who risked her life for those she loved, who tended plants like they were babies because life was important to her, who rescued mean old dogs, and wolves, and made them a less little less mean.

It was the first time either of them had openly acknowledged it—the mutual masks they wore, donned for different reasons but meant to protect all the same.

They were both quiet for a long moment as he finished wrapping her hand.

As soon as he taped the last bit of gauze in place, she tore her hand away from him. "Why were you angry with me? Not in the alley, but before. What did I do to hurt you?"

"It's nothing." He shoved back his chair and stood. "You didn't do anything wrong."

"It's not nothing. Not to you."

He didn't like the way she saw straight through him. He placed his hands on his hips, dipping his head, then blowing out a short breath. "Miles, Chance, the others. The moment any of my packmates step into a room, I disappear," he admitted. "You prefer their company." He placed a hand on the table. "I get it. I don't make it easy, but that doesn't mean I don't feel—"

"Is that what you think?" she said, cutting him off.

His gaze fell toward her, to where she sat, glaring at him. For all the rage in her eyes, he'd have thought she'd be six foot three, not barely five feet with her heels off. "From where I'm standing, that's the only truth I see," he said.

"You've spent so long hiding behind your own pain that you have no idea how others see you, do you?" Trixie was shaking her head. "You try to keep everyone at arm's length, but you don't understand how much you've failed at that." She crossed the room to his bunk, where she reached beneath his pillow. "I did it for you, you big brute." She took the tiny rucksack of bills and coins—her poker winnings— and dropped it onto the game table with a *thunk*. "To start your I'm-getting-the-hell-outta-here fund."

For a moment, all Malcolm could do was stare at the small bag of money.

"It's not like that."

"If you can't buy your freedom, what'll it take?" She placed a hand on the chairback. It was a sexy pose, meant to tease, though right now he knew she wasn't teasing him. "I like to imagine you happy, even long after I'm gone from your life"—she gestured around them—"and happy ain't here for you."

He'd been wrong, so fucking wrong. A lump lodged in his throat.

"There's nothing you can do."

It was the truth, plain and simple. He couldn't live in the human world or show his face anywhere that wasn't frequented solely by shifters. It was the price of being a wanted man. At least at Wolf Pack Run, being a killer didn't mean he was locked away in a human prison.

"You said the same thing when I took that damn bottle from you, and now look at you." She nodded to where he stood in his towel, half-naked before her.

"This is different, Trixie." He shook his head, tried to keep himself from snarling in frustration. It wasn't her he was frustrated with. It was him, for damning himself for the rest of his life this way. It'd been the foolish mistake of the pissed-off young boy he'd once been. "Money, time, none of it matters. I can't escape from here."

Not unless he wanted to spend his life running.

He'd done enough running away in his life. He wanted something he could run toward.

"You said the same then, but you escaped the grief, didn't you?"

"To a point," he admitted.

Trixie drew closer. The scent of her wrapped around him, charging him like a live wire. "You don't have to bear your pain like a badge of honor for all the world to see." Her words were harsh, callous, accusatory. "You don't have to wallow in it. It doesn't protect you, not like you pretend it does."

He snarled, unable to stop himself. His eyes flashed to his wolf. "You're one to talk."

Trixie took a small step back. "Excuse me?"

He stepped closer, closing the gap she'd created between them in two powerful strides. He could practically feel the brush of her breasts against his navel, the warm heat of her body. "You're so disillusioned you can't be real with anyone. I bet you can't remember the last time you dropped the mask for more than a handful of minutes."

She lifted her chin in defiance. Those ruby-red lips puckered with rage, drawing his attention there.

"I may wear my pain like a statement," he hissed, "but you can't stand the way you feel so you bury it, and that's made you so callous you don't even see the point in anything anymore." He thumped a fist against his own chest. "At least I own it."

"Fuck you and the high horse you rode in on." She stabbed a finger at his chest, stomping toward his bunk. Before he could stop her, she was stripping off her shoes, tossing them onto the floor with an audible clack. She pulled her dress down, wiggling the tight fabric over her hips.

Malcolm growled at the sight of her back. Bare golden skin. His cock stiffened. "What are you doing?"

"What does it look like I'm doing?" She turned toward him then, unhooking her bra and tossing it onto the floor beside her so that she stood there in nothing but her panties.

She stared him straight in the eye, gorgeous breasts bared. "It's called hate sex, asshole. It's kind of our thing, innit?"

Malcolm swallowed, the breath tearing from his lungs, all his frustration with her evaporating with it. "I don't want to have *hate* sex with you, Trixie," he whispered.

The words instantly disarmed her.

Trixie's eyes went wide, then watery. "Don't say that," she whispered back. She gave a slight shake of her head like he'd hurt her, lip suddenly quivering. "Not now, damn it."

"Come here," he ordered.

The sight of her standing naked and vulnerable before him destroyed every defense he'd ever built around himself, each brick he'd laid to keep everyone walled away.

She listened, walking toward him but refusing to look him in the face. "Look at me." She did, but not fully. He gripped her chin and forced her head up. "Take it off," he demanded.

"What?" She was already nude and clearly thought he meant...

He nodded to her face. "The makeup, the mask, all of it. Take it off. For one goddamn night. That's all I'm asking."

Trixie shook her head, mouth agape. "I don't know how," she finally whispered.

Malcolm swallowed, the emotion in his throat easing. "Then let me do it for you."

He reached to the table, taking the warm washcloth that still lay there into his hand. Stepping closer to her, he cupped her chin in his palm, gently stroking the terry cloth over her skin. First her forehead, her cheeks. There was a spattering of freckles hidden beneath her foundation and rouge that he'd never seen before. It made her look younger, not that she needed to, and it didn't take much to imagine a gorgeous blond-haired little girl, face covered in those same freckles, mouth dripping with watermelon juice, smiling for a camera.

The southern summer he'd tasted on her skin.

Her eyes fluttered closed as she relaxed into his touch. There were tears pouring down her cheeks, and gently, he swiped them away. When her mascara, eyeliner, and shadow were gone, he laid a tender kiss on each lid. She shuddered.

Finally, when most of her face was clear, he tended to her lips. With her lipstick gone, the pink was still stained slightly, leaving them vibrant, full, like the mouth of a woman who'd been kissed, or who wanted to be. He hadn't yet laid his own mouth there.

"You're beautiful," he whispered.

Another tear ran down her cheek. "I look better with it on," she said softly.

Malcolm shook his head. "Not to me."

He didn't fully understand what her tears were for, but he wanted to chase every one of them away, to make sure no one ever hurt her again. Whether him or anyone else. It didn't matter.

As long as she felt safe. *Was* safe.

He returned the washcloth to the table.

"Do me a favor, will you, sugar?" Trixie placed a tentative hand on his chest as he drew her to him. "Don't be gentle," she rasped. "I'm not certain I can bear it."

"I won't be," he promised.

He pulled her into his arms.

———

Trixie didn't know which was worse: the fact that she was crying like a damn fool, that she'd let him remove her makeup, or that he was looking at her natural face like she was still the most beautiful thing he'd ever seen. She could hardly stand it.

As if he could sense her insecurity, he drew her close. She slipped her underwear off before he lifted her to straddle his waist. She wrapped her legs over the jutted muscles of his hip bones and her arms around his neck. The towel that'd been perched on his hips fell to the floor with a damp little swish.

"You're gorgeous," he whispered, kissing up the side of her neck and reassuring her as he carried her toward his bunk. "The most goddamn beautiful woman I've ever seen."

His words were crass, but the care and complete honesty there stole her breath away. Somehow, that only made her tears come even faster.

She wasn't even certain what she was crying for. For all the times she'd hidden her true face or for all the men who'd made her think she needed to. Or the fact that whatever this was between her and Malcolm, it'd been destined to end before it'd even truly started. She should have told him about Stan, about the threat against her from the beginning.

How had she been so foolish? So selfish?

He laid her out on his bunk, placing a hand on the top

bunk and stepping back to admire her. "I didn't know you had freckles," he said softly.

She smiled through her tears. "I didn't know you had a tattoo there." She nodded to the cross inked above his knee, over the taut muscle of his thigh.

"I got it when I was sixteen." He smiled sheepishly. He pawed at the back of his neck. "Thought it made me a badass."

She chuckled. The thought of Malcolm needing to put any effort toward being seen as anything but one sexy, scary MFer tickled her. Her eyes fell to his hands, the tattooed knuckles there. "Why angel wings?" She'd been burning to ask from the first moment she'd known what the letters read.

Malcolm shrugged, glancing away from her for a moment, eyes distant. "Because I needed an angel's wings to carry me away from there." He looked back toward her. "But I also knew the only way to claw out of that hellhole was with my own two hands."

It was a cowboy's answer. Simple yet moving. She didn't need to ask where *there* was. Chicago. The place that was supposed to be home but hadn't been, the place he never shared, because nothing about it had been worth sharing. At least for him.

"I'm glad you did," she said. She meant every word of it.

His eyes raked over her, sparing no flaw she didn't want him to see. He didn't leave a single curve or blemish untouched. "You're breathtaking."

Another truth. She blushed.

Trixie returned the favor, taking in the wide muscles of his chest, the rippled abs and the thin trail of black hair that led down to the thick, hardened length between his legs. It was only her *second* favorite part of him. Not that she was picking favorites or anything. The first were his eyes, so dramatic and brooding, not the familiar wolf ones currently staring back like all the other times she'd slept with a shifter, but the dark pools of his normal brown, so deep they were nearly black. She'd thought they were cold, uncaring, and they were at times, but when he'd been tending to her hand, she'd seen the depth there, the tender man who hid behind dark fury. A killer with a soft heart.

"You're not half-bad yourself," she teased.

Malcolm threw back his head and laughed, loud and unguarded. The sound broke something inside her chest, like a dam of emotion, every feeling she'd been shoving away, storing under lock and key. It all burst free at the sound of his joy.

For once, she let it wash over her.

When he'd finished, his eyes settled on her again. "Do you want me to—?" He nodded to the bathroom, where his discarded jeans lay within view and maybe his wallet with a condom.

A familiar heat flared inside her.

"I'm clean and on the pill," she whispered, understanding his question.

"I didn't expect anything less." He ducked under the edge of the bunk, positioning himself on his hands so he hovered above her.

"You think better of me than most."

He paused, staring down at her for a moment. He kissed

her then, slowly and deeply. His tongue tangled with hers in a soft, languid caress. He pulled back. "I know you better than most," he whispered against her lips.

This time, the truth there surprised her. He was right.

The prickly scruff on his chin grazed her cheek. He kicked her legs apart, and the head of his cock nudged against the outside of her entrance.

She wiggled her hips lower, his tenderness killing her. "I told you not to be gentle." She was already wet for him, burning with need.

The gold of his wolf eyes flared. "I won't be." Malcolm sheathed himself inside her in a single stroke, filling her so full she gasped for relief.

He didn't give her any time to adjust to the size of him, and she didn't want him to. He drove into her, each thrust of his hips aiming up and inward. Hooking his arm under one of her legs, he hoisted it onto his shoulder, giving him greater access. He drove deeper, harder. There were no words to be had. The splendor of finally joining together left them both speechless, breathless. She was everything.

A few minutes in, the door to the bunkhouse started to creep open, his packmates returning from the evening's fun.

"Shit!" Miles's swear came from the cracked door.

"Get the fuck out," Malcolm snarled.

The door slammed shut immediately. The sounds of his packmates mumbling outside followed. Malcolm didn't miss so much as a stroke. He thrust into her, each continuous blow making her hotter, driving her higher onto the bed. She gripped the tangled sheets beneath them.

"Good to know you can still be mean when you need to be." Trixie chuckled. Reaching around him, she scraped her nails affectionately over the broad muscles of his back. "Who's to say he couldn't join in on the fun?" she teased, searching for a bit of levity now that her tears had dried. But she didn't really mean it.

Malcolm glared at her, eyes filled with open jealousy, exactly what she'd wanted to see there. No pretending she didn't matter to him. Not anymore.

"I'm not sharing you," he ground out, refusing to give her any relief. He saw straight through the bluff. He slammed into her, angling her ass up so he could hit her G-spot. The man already knew exactly how to pleasure her most, and they'd only been together a handful of days.

Trixie moaned, loud and throaty as she always did, exactly as he'd intended.

"You're mine," he growled, wolf eyes flashing. "Now make sure they all know it."

Malcolm didn't make it easy for her to fight it. He pounded into her, working her clit with his hand, the tension building inside her until she was screaming his name. The rickety wooden bunk frame pounded against the wall.

"I guess we're out of a place to sleep tonight, boys," Miles said loudly from outside the door. He sounded as amused as he was annoyed.

Trixie laughed at the devilish grin that crossed Malcolm's lips. The hand he'd been using to support himself dropped to her breast, bringing him flush against her. He palmed her. Even with those massive paws of his, she was more than a handful.

She felt herself clench, the walls of her pussy tightening.

"Come for me," Malcolm ordered. "I want to feel you finish around my cock." He leaned down, tweaking the sensitive flesh of her nipple.

It was enough.

Trixie came apart on a wave of pleasure and sweat and emotion. The shudder that ran through her was unguarded and wild. Malcolm finished shortly after her. She watched his face as he came, drawing in the open ecstasy of it.

When they'd both finished, he collapsed on top of her, rolling and repositioning them a moment later so that she was cradled in his arms against him.

A man who wanted to snuggle her after the fact was novel, new to her, and she felt like a fool again as another fresh round of tears came. One trickled onto his arm before she could stop it.

"Hey," he whispered, his voice rough and raspy. "Hey, what's wrong?" The rough pad of his thumb swiped across her face, catching each tear that fell.

It took Trixie a long time to answer in part because she didn't know what to say. "No one's ever claimed me as theirs before," she said. It was true, she supposed, but she couldn't tell him the true reason for her tears.

Malcolm propped himself on his side, bending down to kiss her. "Their loss is my gain."

Trixie's crying only worsened. The sob that tore from her throat was downright embarrassing because she knew, without a doubt, that he meant it.

Chapter 18

THE EARLY MORNING SUN STREAMED IN THROUGH THE bunkhouse windows. Malcolm lay awake on his bed, Trixie nestled naked and asleep in the crook of his arm, the soft sounds of her breathing lulling him into a relaxed daze. Dust motes floated in the soft, yellow light, the swirls timed with the rumble of the heater that'd kicked in. In a single eve, they'd crossed the line from autumn chill to approaching winter. The temperature had dropped nearly thirty degrees in only a handful of hours.

The Montana cold seeped into his bones, the chill fresh and welcome. Beside him, Trixie stirred, nuzzling closer against his unnatural warmth until her face rested on the thin layer of dark hair on his chest. She felt *good* there, better than good. Like he could lie here like this for days, content to hold her against him, caring for her in whatever way she needed whenever she woke. Comfort, food, sex. Whatever it was, he'd give it to her.

But on the ranch, there was always work to be done, always chores that waited. He brushed a hand over her cheek and allowed his thumb to edge the flutter of her soft blond lashes. Blond, pale, natural. Not the dark obsidian that came from inside a mascara bottle.

Laying a kiss on her forehead, he gently slipped from the bed, borrowing a few blankets from the other bunks and tucking the extra layers around her for warmth. She slept peacefully, hardly stirring, even in his absence. Asleep and with her makeup gone, all the sharp lines of her face softened. He briefly wondered how he'd ever thought her hard or callous. The ruse was so convincing, and yet now that he'd seen behind the veil, it wasn't.

He watched her sleep for a long moment, hands propped on the upper bunk over her head. Rest had never come easy for him. His nights were often fitful, filled with dark dreams of a distant past that still haunted him and softer, warmer memories of Bo that hurt just as bad, even though he cherished them. But last night she'd been his anchor, the feel of her beside him drawing him back to himself each time the gales of his dreams got to be too much. She'd kept him from getting swept away in the emotions, his calm eye in the storm.

He wanted to kiss each and every sun-kissed freckle on her cheeks.

Pulling on his work jeans, Malcolm readied himself for the day, layering up for the cold. His usual routine was a fast one, fitting for the days when they had to rise before dawn. But this morning, he'd cut that time in half. In part because he didn't want to wake her. The other hands would have ridden out hours ago, long before the sun came up, with or without his direction, no matter where they'd chosen to rest their heads the night before. But it hadn't been for the sake of expediency that he'd forgone a shower.

He wasn't ready to wash the scent of her off his skin yet. He wanted to keep her with him a bit longer in whatever way he could manage.

Zipping up his Carhartt, he bent down, reaching for where his wallet lay on the floor. Dean insisted he keep it on him at all times, in case he ever encountered any human law enforcement and needed to have his fake ID on hand. That wasn't often the case out here in the isolation of Wolf Pack Run. Still, he retrieved the wallet out of habit, the old leather billfold floppy and familiar in his hand. As he pocketed his wallet, he caught sight of the little rucksack bag of Trixie's winnings she'd thrown on the card table between them.

The I'm-gettin-the-hell-outta-here fund, she'd called it.

He inhaled a sharp breath, the memory blindsiding him so quickly that he couldn't stop it. Trixie understood him in a way even Bo hadn't. Bo'd been the love of his life, always would be, the first true friend he'd ever made here—or anywhere for that matter. But Bo had been born of these mountains. These hills and Wolf Pack Run had always been home to him, even though for Malcolm, they never would be. Bo had been his home. Not here.

Chicago had been cold, windy, but it'd been nothing compared to the Montana ice that'd crept into his veins. The human hunters hadn't bothered giving him a jacket, like they'd somehow recognized that he didn't need it, now or before. Malcolm clung to the ratty wool blanket wrapped around his shoulders. The only thing that was close to keeping him warm. But it wasn't the weather that froze him.

The snow fell around them in a blur of flurries, obscuring nearly everything in view. All he could see was glaring white for miles, along with the vague outline of an old wooden fence and distant snow-covered trees. The sun's light reflected off the snow-drift, effectively blinding him. He didn't know why, but he felt as if dozens of eyes were watching him, hidden among the trees. The thought was ridiculous, but for once, he couldn't shake the feeling that he wasn't alone.

Not completely.

He stepped forward, nearly tripping thanks to a bank that was deeper than he'd expected. He was naked and shivering, each step causing his bare feet to sink several feet into frozen snow. He'd always been large for his age. A big, wide brute. Muscled yet lean. The hunters had given him clothes when they first found him two days prior, hand-me-down rags that barely fit. They'd clung to him like a second skin, but he ripped through them the moment the hunters tried to stuff him, kicking and snarling, into the back of that old police vehicle. The moment he'd turned into a…whatever he was again.

To his horror, they hadn't been shocked—hell, surprised even—when he'd turned into a creature before them.

Even then, he'd recognized they weren't typical police. Maybe FBI. Ex-military. CIA. Something awful and dangerous. His teenage mind raced, filling in the blanks.

But whoever they were, they were human. Normal. Unlike him.

He was the single, freakish exception in an otherwise homogenous world. Monster and queer, all rolled into one. He wasn't certain which his stepfather had taken more exception to. Not that it mattered now.

The bastard couldn't beat him when he was dead in his grave.

A strange, sick satisfaction filled him at that thought, while at the same time, he was disgusted with it, with his mother, the manipulation, the abandonment, and more importantly, himself. He hadn't been anything more to her than a means to an end, a means to get herself free. From head to toe, he shivered, more from his own fear and rage, confusion and guilt, than from the winter storm raging around them. He hadn't stopped shivering since the blood on his chest and mouth had dried several days prior.

The dried, crusted bits had started to flake away, like little flecks of dried red paint that reminded him of the art pieces from school he'd hidden under his bed to work on at night, horrific but real, yet the dirt lingered, even when his...his... He shuddered again. His fur...had receded.

Fur. Normal people didn't have fucking fur.

Up ahead, in the distant trees, for a moment, he thought he saw a wolf, a large, wild beast, and he was briefly thankful for the gun that was pointed at his back. Then a moment later, a blurred figure emerged. A man, as naked as he was.

Malcolm took one look at the golden eyes that shone through the white desert around him, and in an instant, he knew he wasn't human. Of course, he'd already known, long before now. But the familiar eyes that shone back confirmed it. Yet from the cold look he saw there, devoid of any emotion and feeling, it didn't make a difference. He wasn't any less alone.

The hunter's hand shoved against his shoulder, knocking him down to his knees before the creature. "I think this belongs to you."

A shudder ran through Malcolm, drawing him back from the memory. From the man he'd later come to recognize as Maverick's father, the then Grey Wolf packmaster. They'd never told him he was a shifter, a wolf, but it hadn't taken words to glean that he was like them, one of them, yet not. Some half-breed with a human mother, whose absent father, a drifter likely, didn't know he'd ever existed. Maybe he'd been a rogue wolf shifter, or if he was lucky, a member of one of the subpacks.

No one had any answers. Not that Malcolm had cared to ask.

But he could shift. He was a Grey Wolf. As far as the pack was concerned, that was all that seemed to matter.

Malcolm pocketed his wallet, grabbing his Stetson off the peg near his bunk and heading toward the door. In the days that'd followed his arrival at Wolf Pack Run, he'd also learned the men who had brought him there had been members of a clandestine human organization called the Execution Underground, a group of militia-trained humans whose sworn duty was to protect humanity from the supernatural, from monsters…creatures like him.

They hadn't been kind, or so he'd thought. He'd learned later they could have simply killed him for what he was and, more importantly, what he'd done to an "innocent" human, but he supposed he'd been too young, too bruised and beaten, pathetic and pitiful, for even the worst of hunters to have done that.

So they'd brought him to Wolf Pack Run instead. Dumped him with the Grey Wolves so that he was no longer their problem, then headed back to their Chicago division. Never mind the fact that he'd lived among humans his whole life, that he didn't know anything but humanity. Save for himself. Though humanity had only showed the worst of itself to him.

Malcolm tipped his Stetson onto his head, careful so the sound of his boots didn't wake Trixie as he padded toward the door. He'd slept here that very first night and every night since. He hadn't been able to bring himself to move into the main compound building or even one of the cabins when he'd finally been made an elite warrior, though Maverick had offered. Years later and it still felt too much like charity, so he'd stayed here.

Malcolm paused, glancing around the room. To his bunk, where Trixie still lay sleeping. The Grey Wolves' initiation process had been brutal, unkind, and unforgiving, much like the pack itself. A strange paradox of necessary brutality to any they deemed an outsider and a close, almost stifling love to those who were within its embrace. The pack did nothing in half measure. Theirs was a deep love, as rooted and natural as the mountains and trees that nurtured them and gave them shelter. The three-day test out in the middle of the woods had changed him. He'd been forced to survive in wolf form and to kill small game with claw and teeth, though he'd never held his shift for a handful of minutes before, and definitely never voluntarily.

He'd emerged from the forest wilder than he'd ever been.

And yet somehow better.

Not healed. But different.

"Would you kill for this pack?" Maverick Senior asked him when he'd finally emerged naked and on two feet from the pine trees. The sounds of the pack's howls echoed in the surrounding forest as if in answer. An eerie, haunting chorus. The blood that pooled in Malcolm's hand from the oath felt warm but not foreign. He'd bled for what he was so many times before, at the hands of his stepfather. He simply hadn't known it then.

"I'm fairly certain I already have," he whispered.

His own answer had been honest, foolish, yet also a premonition of the years to come, of the way he'd come to make himself useful, live his life in service to a group of creatures who only claimed him by happenstance, not love. He still wasn't certain whether it'd been a mercy.

And he had defended them for years since. He'd killed for them over and over again, until it stopped being novel, until it stopped hurting each time he did, reminding him of his own mistakes. He'd killed for them until their enemies had become his own and he could no longer count how many bodies he'd lain beneath the ground.

Malcolm slipped out the bunkhouse door, gently closing it behind him and heading out toward the stables.

All in payment of some kind of debt he'd never be able to repay.

Chapter 19

Trixie woke with a start, the quiet of the mountainside unfamiliar and oddly eerie. The sound outside the motel wasn't the same as in a city—not a blustering of constant noise and passersby—but it was a regular symphony compared to this. The relative silence pressed in on her. The bunkhouse heater rattled uncontrollably, fighting to keep the inside of the small space warm despite the cold that nipped at the doors. She was tangled in a mess of blankets, several more than she'd gone to sleep with. No doubt Malcolm's doing.

Lifting up onto her elbows, she glanced around in search of him but came up empty. The blankets fell from her shoulders. Her bare nipples tightened with the onslaught of cold. From the looks of it, he'd ridden out several hours ago. She smiled slightly. Maybe he was more of a cowboy than she'd expected. He might have ridden his bike nearly as much as his horse, but he certainly knew how to hang his hat on a woman's bedpost only to disappear come dawn like in those old western movies.

Wrapping herself in the blankets, Trixie padded from the bed. Malcolm had left out a pile of old clothes for her. A pair of jeans he might have swiped from one of the pack's females and one of his shirts along with his leather coat. She'd no doubt be swimming in them, but they'd keep her warm until she dug for something more weather-appropriate through the garbage bags in the trunk of her car, which was still parked at the ranch's perimeter. She'd normally wear whatever fit her fancy, weather being of little consideration compared to how she looked, but if she did now, Malcolm would never let her hear the end of it.

A grin curved her lips. Bossy and stubborn as he was, there was something strangely endearing about that, about him wanting to protect her and keep her cared for in all ways, even on things she didn't typically deem important.

She pulled on the clothes he'd laid out for her, settling into their comfort in warmth. The pair of female boots he'd scrounged up for her surprisingly fit her petite feet, and it felt odd to be flat-footed. Her arches were used to the curve of her heels, so the boots stretched the calves of her legs in an awkward way, but she'd get used to it.

Thankfully, she'd kept some makeup in the clutch she'd taken with her to the Blood Rose the night before so she wasn't a total hot mess.

Red lipstick painted on, mascara back in place, and curls sufficiently arranged, she headed out of the bunkhouse. It was well into the afternoon. She always slept late. The Coyote's hours meant most days she was lucky to be up before 3:00 p.m. Add in all the times Malcolm had brought her to finish the previous night, and by her guess from where the sun hung in the sky, it was almost four. Malcolm and the other hands would likely return by sundown.

In the meantime, she wandered out to the cabins, where she'd left Dumplin' to stay with Dakota. Surely Malcolm had reported to the pack on their unsuccessful stint at the Blood Rose. She was still feeling salty about the knowledge that Dani was dating Cillian, but she hadn't decided what she was going to do about that yet. She had her own issues to contend with.

One thing at a time.

It didn't take her long to find Dakota and Dumplin'. Though whether she'd ever be able to coax the dog away from the pack's veterinarian remained to be seen.

Dumplin' was asleep on the guest bed in Dakota and Blaze's shared cabin, snoring among a large assortment of pillows that looked more comfortable than anything Trixie regularly laid her head on, the dog bed she'd supplied for him long forgotten. He looked like a canine king.

Beside him, a plate of various kinds of raw game meat had been laid out like some strange, canine charcuterie board, and his collar and leash were nowhere to be found.

When Trixie had asked, Dakota had made such a disgusted face that she had more than a passing feeling the collar and leash had been burned. Or buried by a certain she-wolf's paws.

Trixie tilted her head to the side, watching Dumplin' as he let out a particularly loud snore. She was pleased he'd been treated well, but…

"I think you've gone a bit overboard with the whole dog-sittin' thing, darlin'."

Dakota waved a dismissive hand. "Nonsense. He's one of the pack now."

Trixie didn't have the heart to comment on the fact that the Grey Wolves seemed more concerned with the comfort of a plain ol' dog than the wounded heart of one of the pack's most lethal warriors, but she knew firsthand Malcolm didn't make loving him easy. Though neither did Dumplin', but at least he was more scared than he was mean.

But Malcolm was afraid, too. In his own way. Of being hurt again. So much so he lashed out in order to protect himself. Same as Dumplin' did, though she didn't think he'd appreciate the comparison, even if they were both grumbly, scarred, and a teensy bit snarly.

Her chest ached at the passing thought that when she left here, her parting would do little to help change that fact. Her stomach roiled.

Trixie patted the Rottweiler's head, as much to nudge him awake as to calm herself and ignore her troubles a little longer. "I appreciate you taking care of him. I really do. You didn't need to go through so much trouble."

Dakota smiled. "It wasn't any trouble at all. Poor thing. He's been through a lot." Her brow furrowed with unusual knowing. Like she was looking at a person instead of Trixie's pet.

Trixie quirked a brow. "You…you can't talk with him, can you?"

Dakota shrugged like it was no big thing. "Well, no. Not exactly…but other canine features aren't really that difficult to read when you spend half your life as a wolf."

Trixie glanced toward where Dumplin' was now staring up at her, tongue lolled and panting. She supposed that put her joke about leading Malcolm around on a leash in new perspective. Heat colored her cheeks. If either of them would end up on a leash, it'd be her. In everything they did, he was in charge, dominant. It felt...nice to let someone take care of her in that way. Make decisions so that for a short time, she didn't have to.

Her decision-making didn't have the best track record. Look where it'd gotten her.

Dakota smiled, full of mirth, at Trixie's blushing as if the other woman could read the thoughts in Trixie's head, but she didn't comment.

At least there was one wolf on this ranch rooting for him. Likely more, if only Malcolm would allow himself to see it, if he'd stop wielding coldness like a weapon and allow himself a bit of happiness instead of living in the past. Trixie'd been telling him he needed to move forward for several years, but men never listened. He'd need to come to the conclusion in his own time.

Maybe he would, even without her.

She'd asked Dakota for a tennis ball for Dumplin'. "He wouldn't prefer to chase down some game out in the woods?" the veterinarian had asked curiously before finally ceding to Trixie's request. How the she-wolf had managed to make it through human veterinary school, Trixie would never know. She supposed it involved a lot of awkward questions about wolf vs. canine behavior and confused glances.

Humans tended to sweep stuff like that under the rug, forgetting it easily.

After grabbing some food with Dakota, Trixie spent

the rest of the afternoon wandering around Wolf Pack Run with Dumplin' by her side. Leashless per the pack's request. Occasionally, they stopped and she tossed the tennis ball for him, though more than once, to her shock, it hadn't been Dumplin' that'd brought it back but instead one massive wolf or another.

Vicious warriors, her ass. They were overgrown puppies. All of them.

A part of her had known that from the first time she'd laid eyes on Malcolm. The growling and snarling was only a ruse to protect the soft underbelly underneath the hardened exterior. One that'd be harder to crack in time, considering her situation.

Betrayal cut deep. She knew that from her own past.

The sun hung low in the sky, nothing but a thin sliver behind the snowcapped mountains by the time Malcolm and the other hands rode back in with the last of the steers that'd be put up for sale that season. Trixie watched from a distance as they herded the cattle into the semitruck that'd take them to market. It struck her as kind of sad, which she figured proved that she didn't have the stomach or the desire to get dirt beneath her nails for ranching, but it also wouldn't stop her from tucking into a good burger on occasion. If that made her a hypocrite, so be it.

When the hands had finished their work, they led their horses back to the stables. Trixie stood at the mouth of the stable entrance, Dumplin' by her side as Miles and the other hands filed in. Malcolm brought up the rear.

"You wanna pet him?" Malcolm asked.

"You talkin' about the third arm you keep between your legs or the horse?" Trixie grinned. She said it only to embarrass him, make him laugh. The dark chuckle that tore from his throat was worth it.

"What's his name?" she asked, nodding to the horse.

"Clover."

She crossed her arms over her chest. "Pretty Irish-sounding horse name for a man who looks like he's from the Mediterranean." The olive tone of his skin was still tanned deep even though it'd been months since summer.

"My mother was Italian," he admitted.

"Hmmm, so we're looking for a really romantic-sounding last name then," she teased. "Rossi. Morelli. Tedesco. Resciniti." She ticked each one off on her fingers.

Malcolm scowled, unamused with this game. "You want to pet the horse or not, Trixie?" She knew better than to think he was actually annoyed with her.

He was trying to protect himself, as always.

Tentatively, she stepped closer to him and the animal. She reached out a nervous hand. "Can you believe with all the cowboys I've dated, I've never once ridden a horse?" The heat of her breath swirled around her face in the cold Montana air.

"Never?"

She shook her head. "Never."

"Do you want to?"

Trixie blinked. The idea of her on a horse was novel, new. "I–I don't know."

"Come on. He doesn't bite. Not as much as Dumplin' anyway." Malcolm nodded to the dog at her feet.

Dumplin' let out an annoyed growl. His scarred face twisted until he looked downright nasty. A spittle of drool dripped from his bared teeth. She wasn't exactly certain what the Rottweiler disliked about Malcolm. He'd taken well enough to the other shifters.

"She was mine first," Malcolm said to the dog, holding its gaze in challenge. "Get the fuck over it." His eyes flashed to his wolf.

Trixie let out an amused sigh. Apparently, they were in a metaphorical pissing contest over her, from the looks of it. The truth of which was only highlighted by the fact that Dumplin' circled where he stood before lifting his leg on the side of the stable and peeing.

Malcolm snarled. Wolf eyes flashing and teeth bared.

"Quit it, you two," Trixie said, sounding like she was talking to two tussling children instead of a rescue dog and a Grey Wolf warrior. "I guess I'll give it a try. Why not?" She smiled, maybe a little unconvincingly as she nodded to the horse. "But...it might take me a few minutes to work up to it."

Twenty minutes later, she was out in the paddock with the large beast, Malcolm leaned against the other side of the fence, watching. It'd taken only about two minutes for Malcolm to lead them in there. The rest had been spent waiting for her to build up the courage.

"Still working up to it?" Malcolm made a show of glancing at his wrist, though he wasn't wearing a watch.

"Yes," she snapped, circling the horse like it might rear up at any moment.

It hadn't so much as trotted around the pen, but that didn't mean it wouldn't go wild at any minute. That was how horses worked, right?

Malcolm, more than a bit amused by her reservation, reached over the fence and swatted her on the ass. She let out a startled yelp.

"Get on the horse, Trixie," he said.

"I am. I'm going." She stepped closer. Thank goodness she was wearing these dirty old cowgirl boots instead of heels for this. Though Malcolm likely wouldn't have let her near the beast in anything less than what he deemed appropriate ranch gear. Slowly, she approached. The horse didn't back away, but it was so big. One of those hooves could crush her, or at least do a fair bit of damage, and she didn't heal as easy as Malcolm did. Her wrapped hand was still a reminder of that. Though at the moment, Clover was only standing there, blinking his dark eyes innocently.

"Get on the horse, Trixie," Malcolm said again.

"I am!"

Malcolm cupped his hands around his mouth to make his voice louder. "Get on the damn horse, woman," he called across the paddock with a laugh.

"Quit rushing me," she shot back. She blew out a steadying breath. Better to rip it off like a Band-Aid, she supposed. Slowly, she inched toward the beast, placing a foot up in the stirrup and holding onto the saddle's horn like Malcolm had told her to do.

The horse stirred slightly, causing Trixie to pull back. But from the look of it, the creature was simply letting her know he was aware of her, clued in to her presence. Steeling herself, she tried again. This time, she lifted herself up and over with a small squeak of nerves.

When her bottom settled into the saddle seat, she let out a little whoop of triumph. "I did it," she squealed. She sounded like she was a kid again, first learning to ride a bike, though then it'd been her mother watching from beside the swing on their wraparound porch, a lit Virginia Slims cigarette balanced between her off-white teeth. Not a man who made her burn with need every time he looked at her, who made her feel like she was worth something.

Malcolm was slow-clapping like she'd accomplished something worthwhile rather than an easy feat he did every day. Hell, he could probably do it in his sleep. "You did it," he said, not a hint of patronizing amusement in his voice.

Now that she was settled, the horse started to move, moseying forward to circle the paddock. Trixie plastered herself flat against the beast's neck, wrapping her arms around him so she didn't fall off. "Oh Lord, what's he doing? Sweet Jesus, he's gonna buck me off."

Malcolm laughed. "You aren't going anywhere, Trixie. He knows what to do. Even if you don't."

The horse circled the paddock once, slow and easy, though Trixie didn't dare sit up in the saddle. "I'm riding a horse, Malcolm."

"I see that."

Clover's tail came up from behind and flicked her once or twice. She cringed. "Why's he doing that?"

Malcolm was chuckling again, shaking his head. Okay,

maybe he *was* patronizing her, at least a bit. "You're scared and he knows it. Everything you feel, he feels. Relax a bit and he will, too."

Blowing out a slow breath, Trixie did as she was told, inching upward until finally she was sitting up in the saddle.

"Take his reins. He isn't in charge. You are."

She did. The smooth leather settled into her hands. She could see farther across the landscape from here, the dips and curves. She relaxed a bit, allowing her body to fall in rhythm with the horse's instead of working against it.

"That's it. Better."

Trixie nodded. "Malcolm."

"Yeah, Trixie?"

"I don't know how to get down."

"I got you," he said, chuckling. He hopped over the paddock and came up beside the horse, taking the reins from her. He tugged them gently, bringing the animal to a stop, before he hooked her under her arms and lifted her off.

She wrapped her arms around him, far more comfortable in his arms than she'd been on top of the horse. To her surprise, he kept her there, flush against him.

"That wasn't so hard, was it?"

"Easy for you to say." She glanced down. "Trust doesn't come easy for me."

"Me neither," he admitted. He tilted her chin up toward him. "But you make it easy."

The kiss he laid on her lips was slow and easy. Not the flurry of heat or heady emotion she'd felt from him before. Soft. Slow. Comfortable. The kind of kiss shared with someone who wasn't only comfortable but permanent. Trixie pulled back, emotion caught in her throat. She needed to tell him the truth. Even if it hurt her, she'd bear it, as long as she didn't have to hurt him. He'd already had more than enough pain for a lifetime.

She opened her mouth, trying to find the words, but the buzz of the phone in the pocket of his leather coat that she wore interrupted them.

"Hey, Malcolm," someone shouted in the distance.

Trixie glanced over his shoulder. Blaze.

"Go on," she urged.

Malcolm nodded, heading toward his packmate as Trixie glanced at the number on her phone. She didn't recognize it. Her stomach plummeted. The phone kept ringing, vibrating in her hand, demanding she answer it. She knew better than to think she could ignore the will of a powerful man without him bringing down a world of hurt on her.

Once Malcolm was a safe distance away, joining Blaze, she answered.

"What do you want?"

"*Tsk, tsk, tsk.*" Stan's voice came from the other end of the line. "That's not how this works, Trixie. You don't get to make demands."

She lowered her voice to a hiss, careful so Malcolm or Blaze couldn't hear her. Shifters' hearing abilities were uncanny. "It's not a demand, asshole. It's a question."

"Careful. We've already been through this. I'm giving you this opportunity out of the kindness of my heart."

Sure he was. Trixie's hand clenched into a fist.

"What do you have for me?" Stan asked, not allowing her to even gather her wits.

"Nothing. Not yet. I haven't been here long enough," she said.

"Don't lie to me, you rancid bitch."

The taste in her mouth was vile, but she pushed through it. "I'm not lying," she shot back. "You think the moment I get here they're going to tell me all the pack secrets? I'm still earning their trust, proving myself." And trying her best to help them in the process, though Stan didn't know that.

"You're too busy fucking around with that mutt you call a boyfriend. I always knew you were easy."

Trixie clenched her teeth. As if being easy and enjoying sex was one of the worst things a woman could be. She disagreed. "He's not my boyfriend. He's nothing to me." Another whispered lie. This one even more bitter. She couldn't risk Malcolm hearing her.

"Now I know you're lying," Stan said. The bear shifter had his own talents. No one worked their way that far up in the Triple S without being brutal, ruthless.

Trixie glanced over her shoulder to where Malcolm and Blaze were conversing a safe distance away before she turned back to the mountain landscape before her. Wolf Pack Run was gorgeous, breathtaking. The lands backed up to Yellowstone National Park, and the views were stunning. But at the moment, the open sky felt so large, like it could swallow her whole and no one would miss her. "I'll have something for you. Soon," she reassured Stan. "Just give me a bit more time."

"Remember what's at stake, *darlin'*," Stan said, mocking her accent. "You step one pretty little toe out of line, tell that boyfriend of yours what we're up to, and our little contract transfers to him. I'll own him."

Trixie stiffened. "You're lying. Boss's contracts don't transfer." Not unless someone was stupid enough to accept the debt as their own. The only reason she hadn't told Malcolm already was because Stan had threatened to go after Jackie and his family, and they were innocents in all this. That'd been bad enough.

But the thought of Stan coming for Malcolm…

She'd meant it when she told Stan he wouldn't stand a chance, but would the scales tip if Malcolm didn't even see the attack coming? She couldn't put him in that position.

"You want to risk it?" Stan asked, playing her like the in-love fool she was. That was the problem with caring for someone. It made you weak, easy to manipulate. She'd thought she'd learned that lesson the first time.

"You have less than twenty-four hours. If you don't deliver, your little coyote friend dies first."

Stan hung up, leaving her standing there freezing in the whistling Montana wind.

Malcolm's hand touched her shoulder, making her nearly jump out of her skin. She spun to face him. The fire in his eyes burned through her.

"What's wrong?" she asked, latching onto the first thing she could to distract him, so then he didn't ask her the same.

Malcolm's expression turned grim. "The Execution Underground is here."

Chapter 20

MALCOLM HATED THE HUMAN HUNTERS WITH A PAS-
sion that outpaced his total disgust with humanity. The inside
of Maverick's office felt stifling, crowded with all of them
crammed inside, the scent of shifters and human bodies mud-
dled together in a dangerous mix. The security office or one
of the conference rooms would have been more accommodat-
ing to the sheer breadth of them all, but even with the hunters blindfolded until the moment the office door had shut,
Maverick had insisted he didn't want to risk the human hunters getting the lay of their land. It spoke to how little he trusted
them. In a room this size, with the hunters outnumbered, one
wrong move and any one of the wolf warriors would end them.

Malcolm would be first in line.

Apparently, it wasn't enough that they'd killed Bo—a
misfire during a mutual raid on a particularly nasty cell of
vampires. A supposed accident, according to the paperwork.
A cold-blooded execution fitting of their name, if anyone
asked him. Officially, it wasn't anyone's fault, yet unofficially,
the pack hadn't partnered so closely with the local division
ever since, even with their cease-fire treaty in place. But now
the hunters expected to be welcomed with open arms thanks
to the treaty.

Malcolm nearly growled.

It was the only reason they were all here. The pack might patrol Montana's bloodsuckers to protect humanity in accordance with their treaty with the hunters—a move that offered the shifters of the Seven Range Pact and their associates immunity from the Execution Underground's militant reach—but that didn't mean they trusted the hunters.

Not by a long shot.

"You've got a lot of gall, showing up here unannounced." Maverick stood behind his desk, palms flat against the wooden surface. He addressed the hunter standing before him. His eyes flashed golden. More wolf than any of them. Their fearless leader. "And not alone either."

Quinn Harper, wolf hunter and leader of the Billings division of the Execution Underground, gave a curt nod. He was flanked by another hunter from the clandestine human organization, a wild card the pack had heard of by rumor but never seen before—a fellow wolf hunter named Jace McCannon, with long auburn hair, trench coat, and piercing green eyes. He stank of the city. Whoever he was, he wasn't a cowboy. Not like Quinn.

As if Jace sensed Malcolm's eyes on him, he brushed back his coat, revealing the Mateba tucked into his belt that no doubt held silver bullets. But he didn't place his hand on it. A subtle warning, not a threat. Malcolm swallowed down a growl. Maverick had ordered them not to disarm the hunters in a sign of good faith. But that wouldn't stop Malcolm from tearing out either of these bastard's throats if given the chance. In fact, he was hoping for it.

He sized the other men up. If he hadn't known better, he never would have suspected the two hunters of being human, considering how they rivaled him and his packmates in size. But he supposed their unnatural abilities, a result of rumored government injections, allowed them to rival shifters and vamps alike and keep the supernatural world in check.

"Extenuating circumstances," Quinn said as a means of explanation, tipping his Stetson amiably. He met Maverick's gaze unflinchingly. "We have a mutual problem."

Colt Cavanaugh, the Grey Wolf high commander, scowled. "In other words, there's some mess you want *us* to clean up for you." Colt didn't take kindly to anyone wanting to put the pack's foot soldiers in his charge in harm's way. Not unless it benefitted the pack.

"You never did like to get your hands dirty." That snide comment came from Wes Calhoun. The words to Quinn were personal, meant to provoke, considering Quinn and Wes had a sordid history.

"I seem to remember our dealings differently," Quinn said tersely. Ever the politician.

But Maverick clearly wasn't in the mood to tolerate any pointless posturing. "State why you're here or leave, hunter."

Quinn's gaze cut away from Wes, settling back on the packmaster. "We have reason to believe the Triple S is partnering with the vampires and the remaining Volk."

"Nice try." Blaze rolled his eyes. He was wearing one of his usual graphic T-shirts today that read: *I had my patience tested. It was negative.* "Game over. We already knew that."

"But not the reason *why* or your packmaster wouldn't be asking me what we're doing here," Quinn shot back, undeterred.

He didn't spare Blaze a glance, still focusing on Maverick. So like a human. They thought they knew where the power lay—with Maverick and Maverick alone—but what they failed to understand was that the strength of a wolf was the pack.

They were one. A united front. At least where their enemies were concerned.

Quinn's expression turned dark. "Triple S's goal is for the vamps to help them move a drug into the human market. They call it supe juice. It's a mixture of diluted shifter blood and heroin. It's a way to get humans high like vamp blood, but sellable on the black market. Makes them easier to control."

"Easier targets," Jace chimed in. "Not that the vamps don't already do that fucking well enough with their feeders."

That must have been what Trixie had witnessed at the Blood Rose.

Malcolm growled, but Dean's icy comment took the words right out of his head. "It's always about your precious humans, isn't it? No care or love for any other species."

For anyone who was different from them.

"This product targets us, too," Dean continued. "But you don't care about that, do you?"

"It's not my *job* to care about supernaturals." Quinn spared Dean a harsh but oddly understanding look, his choice of words revealing. There'd been rumors of late about discord within the human organization, a separation between those who wanted to hunt shifters and other supernaturals under the guise of false justice and those who wanted to work amiably *with* other species as true protectors. Apparently, Quinn considered himself the latter. "You all can manage fine without us. It's our job to protect the vulnerable, the underdog, and while you all may consider yourselves hunted in this case, in the scheme of the world, it's the *human civilians* who are truly defenseless."

"We don't hurt humans," Wes muttered defiantly.

"But other supes do." Quinn's nostrils flared, his rage barely contained. "And the fact that you don't is the only reason either of us is standing here." He nodded toward his companion. "We're not enemies."

Malcolm snarled. "Like hell you're not."

Quinn glanced toward him, as if he only now noted Malcolm's presence.

"One of your men killed my mate," Malcolm accused.

Recognition flickered over Quinn's face. But if he felt any remorse over what his associate had done, he didn't show it. "It was a misfire. We've been through this."

Malcolm surged forward. If Dean and Blaze hadn't held him back, he wasn't certain what he would have done. "It didn't seem like an accident considering the bullet landed directly in the back of his fucking skull," he snarled, his voice barely human. "At. Close. Range." He had to struggle to hold in his shift, keep his fur beneath his skin.

"He's not worth it, Malcolm," Blaze hissed into his ear. Malcolm. Not Mac. Blaze knew to cut the jokes when it mattered. "Save it for the battlefield. Bo would want you to."

The look Quinn gave Malcolm then was one of pity.

Fuck him. Malcolm didn't want the hunter's pity. He wanted them to bleed, all of them, the same as he had when he'd cradled Bo's lifeless body in his arms.

"There've been grave losses on both sides." The Adam's apple of Quinn's throat bobbed. The hunter meant his wife, Delilah.

Malcolm bared his teeth. As if a woman who'd deceived her way into a renegade shifter pack that wasn't even theirs and then gotten herself killed for it compared in innocence to Bo. Bo hadn't deceived anyone. He'd always been forthright, honest, a stalwart warrior and friend who had never once hidden his love for Malcolm, even though coming out had put him— hell, both of them—in an unprecedented position within the pack. Bo had been Maverick's former second, and the idea that if something had happened to Maverick, an openly gay Grey Wolf would take his place had been a revolutionary one.

It was the packmaster's unspoken duty to produce an heir for the pack. Bo's coming out had sparked both outrage and support, questions about what it meant to be the pack's leader, about the obligations and duties involved should a gay man become packmaster. The revelation had shaken the pack's politics to the core. Almost as much as Maverick naming his now wife, Sierra, the first female elite warrior. The pack had come a long way in recent years.

But Bo had been loyal, brave in spite of it all. He'd fought for the pack from a place of love, even those who hadn't supported them. He'd been all the things Malcolm had always wished he could be. Kind. Loyal. Compassionate.

The two weren't nearly equivalent.

Malcolm's breath came in quick starts, but slowly he stepped back. Bo would have wanted him to, for the sake of the pack he'd loved, the wolves who'd been his family.

"If it makes any difference to you," Quinn said, his voice uncharacteristically soft, "I personally ensured that hunter was terminated—permanently."

Meaning he'd been put down like the killer he was. Malcolm swallowed. He felt an odd, unexpected sense of... relief at that. But it didn't change the situation, didn't make it right. It didn't bring Bo back, and the look of pure hatred on Malcolm's face must have said as much.

Justice still hadn't been served.

But hatred had never solved anything.

Love did.

Love and enough righteous anger to create change.

Bo had taught him that.

Briefly, his thoughts turned to Trixie. To the look of support she'd given him when she'd gone to join the other females. Maverick wouldn't have wanted her to be a part of this.

But *he* did.

He wanted her to be a part of his life in all ways, with or without the pack. The realization hit him like an oncoming freight train. He'd thought he'd lost everything the day that Bo died. Before he'd lost Bo, he'd counted himself blessed that he'd found one other person who could make him happy for the rest of his days, if he allowed him to get close enough.

Let alone two.

"We're not here to rehash the past," Quinn continued. "We're here to talk about the future."

The clock on the wall ticked steadily, drawing Malcolm back to the importance of the moment. It was a reminder of how little time they had. Days, maybe, before they faced the vampire and the Volk one final time. And it would be the final time. They'd all make certain of it.

Quinn must have sensed the same thing, and he chose that moment to latch onto it. "With the Triple S involved, you'll need allies, and we have as much interest in ensuring their...product doesn't move west as you do."

Blaze scoffed. "We already have allies. We don't need you."

"You're talking about the wolves of the Rock City MC," Quinn said dryly.

Maverick's shoulders visibly tensed. "How do you know about that?"

"We hear things." Quinn shrugged before he nodded at his companion. "And Jace here still has contacts back home in Detroit."

Where the Rock City MC made its home.

Malcolm grumbled. Figured.

"The MC will help, but it's not enough. You need us."

"Our pack has never *needed* you for anything, Quinn. You're simply a means to an end." Maverick crossed his arms and nodded toward the door.

"Then take our deal, our *means*, and end it." Quinn stepped forward, jabbing a single finger onto the edge of Maverick's desk. "Or our treaty with the Grey Wolf Pack is off the table."

The whole of the room went still.

Without another word, Quinn adjusted his Stetson and went to the door. Dean met him there, slipping the hunter's blindfold back into place before leading him out.

His companion stepped forward. "A pleasure to finally meet you..." He extended a hand. "*Packmaster*." The title sounded like a pointed interest in friendship.

Maverick stared at the hunter's hand for a long beat before finally taking it. "I've heard things. None of them good."

Jace released his grip, stepping back. "That's what I'd hoped."

Maverick nodded, some silent understanding seeming to pass between the two men. "You'll have my answer come dawn tomorrow."

Jace nodded once before he made his exit. Dean returned, having passed Quinn off to Sierra and Dakota, and led the blindfolded hunter out.

The lock shut behind them with a metallic *snick*.

"What in the flying fuck was that?" The colorful comment that cut the tension, of course, came from Blaze.

Maverick shook his head. "An ultimatum and a damn good one."

Colt rested his head in his hands. "I've always hated those fuckers, every single one of them."

"You're not seriously considering taking their offer, are you?" Wes asked.

"We don't have much of a choice. This supe juice is a problem for us, too, but even if it wasn't..." Maverick's jaw clenched, like he was struggling not to grind his teeth as he said the words. "It's that or let the treaty collapse. Make the pack vulnerable to their organization, and they're right. The alliance with the MC put us back in the game after the losses we had with the Volk, but with the Execution Underground's help, that would push things over the edge in our favor." He released a long sigh. "I hate to say it, but it's a decent offer."

"Fuck 'decent.'" Malcolm growled. He cut Maverick a look as if to say, *You know how I feel about this.*

Maverick looked sympathetic but undeterred. "I can't allow personal feelings to get in the way of protecting the pack. Partnering with them is for the greater good."

Blaze opened the adjoining security office door, glancing inside toward where the wall of monitors lay. He was likely watching to see the exact moment when Quinn and his associate, Jace, left the ranch. "But what did he mean by end it?" the security specialist asked. "If they're partnering with us against the vamps, when the final battle comes, they'll be standing beside us."

"He's referring to what comes before," Maverick answered. "He wants us to take out Cillian. Cut off the head of the vampire's leadership, and with all our allies in place, the following battle will be easy, even with the Triple S and the Volk involved."

The room fell silent for a moment.

"I don't think there's a single one of us who *wouldn't* want to take out Cillian," Blaze said finally.

"He doubled-crossed the Wild Eight, created the half-turned vamps." Wes placed a hand on his brother's shoulder.

Colt nodded in agreement. "He ordered Lucas to torture me, tried to use my blood to make that fucking serum."

Maverick glanced toward a picture frame on the mantel that held a picture of him and his younger sister. "Mae's too. Then the conflict over the serum itself put the pack in a"—he chanced a look toward his office door where Quinn had exited—"tenuous position."

Blaze turned away from the security cams. "Then the Volk. Austin."

"Even Bo," Malcolm added. If they hadn't been trying to keep Cillian and his vampires in line, Bo might still have been alive. "Everything links back to him."

"It seems there's a score we *all* need to settle." The voice seemed to come from the room's shadows, and a moment later, Rogue stepped forth.

Maverick snarled. "What the fuck are you doing here?" Maverick shot a questioning look toward Blaze.

Blaze shrugged. "He's always been good at getting around the pack's security. It's kind of his thing, being a criminal and all, remember?"

Rogue glanced between the two shifters as if he were bored. "If you think I don't keep tabs on what you're up to, *brother*, think again."

Maverick frowned at the noun choice. The fact that Maeve, his sister, had run off with a man who'd once been his enemy was still a sore point. But being brother-in-law to the unofficial leader of North America's packless rogue shifters had its advantages.

"What interest do you have in Cillian?" Maverick asked.

Rogue glanced down at his nails coolly. "You forget. He tried to kill my wife."

Maverick growled again. "You mean my *sister*."

"Yes, I suppose she was *your* sister, but now, she's *my wife*. She made her choice." Rogue smirked, driving the point home. "But Mae's her own woman, of course."

"It's a risk," Colt said, as if he'd already assessed the strategic possibility and what it would mean for the pack's warrior ranks.

Wes shook his head. "The Seven Range Pact won't be on board."

"They don't need to be." Rogue's face darkened. He had never been fond of the Seven Range Pact and their politics. "My men are willing to lend support. We do this alone."

"Before the Rock City MC arrives," Blaze agreed.

Maverick held up a hand, silencing them all for a moment like he needed the space to think. A few beats passed, every warrior in the room seeming to hold their breath, before finally he turned his attention toward Malcolm. "Do you think you can do it?"

"Not alone." Malcolm shook his head. If he could've, he would have done it years ago. Cillian was too well guarded. "But if you tee it up, I can take him out without question."

Rogue grinned. "From the sound of it, it won't be a chore for you." The packless wolf shifter knew a thing or two about revenge.

Malcolm cut Rogue a passing look. "It won't be."

He'd do it for Bo. For Austin. Exactly as he'd sworn to.

"One last raid?" Colt asked Maverick. "For old time's sake?" The two had been best friends since they were children, always looking out for each other. Their partnership leading the pack's elite ranks had been inevitable.

Blaze lifted a finger before Maverick could voice any dissent or issue any caveats. "This time without pipe bombs." He grinned, anticipating exactly what Maverick had been likely to say.

"The rogue wolves are willing to stand beside you. On this and against the Volk. They pose a threat to us as well," Rogue said.

Maverick nodded in approval. "Then for once, I agree with…" He nearly choked out the other wolf's true name. "Jared," he grumbled begrudgingly.

Blaze let out a little whoop of triumph. "Yes, I love a good raid!"

"Shut up," Malcolm grumbled.

"Killing Cillian will be easy. It's the retaliating battle to follow that will be the hard part. But we're ready for them this time, more than we've ever been. It's time to end this."

The elite warriors nodded.

"I think you forgot something, Packmaster." Dakota stepped in through the open security office door, wrapping her arms around Blaze's neck and laying a quick kiss on his cheek.

The other females followed in behind her.

Naomi strode in toward Wes. "You need a way in."

"A decoy." That addition had come from Mae, who, like her new husband, seemed to have developed an uncanny ability to emerge from the shadows like she was a part of the office's woodwork. Apparently, she'd been standing there, not far from Jared's side, all along.

Belle was next, still in her physician's coat, having come

from the clinic. She cradled one of her and Colt's children on her hip. "We need to make sure no one gets hurt."

"And for that, you'll need more than just a bunch of alpha males." Sierra made her way in, her hands placed on Trixie's shoulders as she steered the other woman forward.

To Trixie's credit, she didn't look like a deer caught in the headlights but a veritable seductress of a witch, a magical demoness in her own right, a woman who knew her own power and didn't hesitate to use it. Dumplin' trailed at her heel like a hellhound ready to attack at her beck and call.

She smiled at Maverick and then gave Malcolm a knowing look as if the plan they were about to disclose had been her doing. "The Grey Wolf Pack is nothing without its females."

Chapter 21

"ARE YOU CERTAIN YOU WANT TO DO THIS?"

The alley behind the Blood Rose felt different this time. Cleaner and less empty. Like the moon overhead was watching over them, casting her pale glow onto the darkened streets of downtown Billings and making a cityscape with her beautiful gaze. The sounds of a nearby western bar, a tourist trap that sat along the main drag and always thumped with the latest western music, played in the distance. Billings wasn't Nashville, but sometimes it tried to be if travelers threw enough money at it. Trixie lifted her head a little, basking in the moonlight's glow like *she* was the shifter instead of the massive alpha male beside her.

But witches had their own relationship with the full moon and her magic. She let herself enjoy it for a minute, let it charge her up for the night's events to come.

"Like I said before, it's my fight, too," she answered Malcolm finally. Lowering her head, she reached out and gripped his hand with a reassuring squeeze. "I was a part of this the moment he drew Dani into it."

Malcolm nodded like he understood. He knew her secret now. Not *all* her secrets—there were too many for that—but one of them, the most important. Callous and uncaring as she might seem, she'd do anything—even risk her own life—to protect those she loved.

Including him.

He simply didn't know that detail yet.

She'd thought she could sell him out to Stan no problem, to protect Jackie and his family—and, more importantly, herself—but she couldn't do it. Not after all the intimate moments they'd shared, after she'd let him see her without her makeup. That'd changed things.

As soon as he'd ducked into that private meeting with the pack's elite warriors and the Execution Underground, she'd picked up her phone, called Jackie, and warned him to get the hell out of Dodge. Boss's binding spell hadn't extended to him technically, so warning him hadn't been an issue. That little clause had only applied to the Grey Wolves and their pack. She hadn't done that sooner because she hadn't wanted to upend her friend's life that way and also because of the risk it posed for her. But she'd bear any risk if it kept Malcolm out of harm's way.

Surprisingly, Jackie hadn't simply understood... Hell, he'd been grateful.

She supposed after all was said and done, she *had* secured his family's future by fixing the fight in his favor, and it wasn't the first time Jackie'd had something to run from. At least this time, she'd given him the monetary means to do it, and comfortably. Apparently, it played into his plans to return back home to South Korea, the country of his birth. The next step for her would be telling Stan. When her time was up, she'd deliver the news. It would be satisfying to tell him to go fuck himself, even if it'd get her killed in the end. Hell, maybe she'd manage to escape and stay on the run at least for a while.

She was good at being slippery.

Not that it'd change things with Malcolm.

If he ever found out what she'd intended, even if she hadn't gone through with it, he'd never forgive her. No lying: that'd been his one rule, and she'd broken it from the get-go. With a wolf like him, there was no coming back from that.

It made her heart ache.

And wasn't that a new feeling? She hadn't felt that way about anyone in a long time, too long. Seven years, thirteen hours, and twenty-eight minutes to be exact. She knew the exact time and day she'd locked up her heart, because she'd been counting the minutes until she was free again ever since. Until her binding agreement with Boss became a part of her past instead of her present. It was a shame she likely wouldn't get to experience true freedom again.

Trixie cleared her throat. "The pack will offer Dani protection? Help her get away from here?" She'd had terms of her own in order to help them. She would have done it either way, but that didn't stop a girl from negotiating. She knew a thing or two about verbal contracts.

Magical or otherwise.

"Maverick gave you his word." There was an unusual hint of admiration in Malcolm's tone. "The Grey Wolf packmaster is a lot of things, but he'll keep his word."

Unlike her.

Trixie tried not to let that thought show on her face.

She schooled her features, adjusting the sticky silicon pads that held the girls in place—her dress required she go braless—before nodding her approval. "And this time you won't ice me out?" she asked.

"I didn't trust you before." The truth in that hurt, cutting through her. "Not fully," Malcolm admitted. "But I should have." He looked regretful, apologetic even. It was a new look for him. One that spoke of how their dynamic had changed, deepened. They'd shown each other parts of themselves no one else had seen, both physical and emotional. That meant something.

"I trust you now, Trixie," he whispered.

She felt the honesty in that, the sweet tang of truth on his lips as she leaned in and kissed him, but with the knowledge of what lay ahead of her, it felt bittersweet, not triumphant as it should be. Lord, she didn't want to break his heart, but there was no way around it now.

"Good," she said quickly, pulling back from their kiss. She was ready to move forward. No sense in crying over spilled milk tonight. She'd never been one to wallow. "On my cue then."

The Blood Rose was empty when she stepped inside. The business card Corbin had slipped her had proved more than useful, and when she stepped in, the smooth-talking vampire anticipated her. He waited in the bar's back wings. Over the phone, he hadn't given the reason he was willing to clear his club for her and Cillian's meeting, nor why he'd volunteered his personal security detail to Cillian and had been willing to send them away at her and the Grey Wolves' request, selling out the vampire master to the first and highest bidder.

He'd simply said he'd had "enough of the old bastard" ruling Billings and that he was "fond" of Dani. Whatever the hell that meant. It was a dangerous power play.

But she and the Grey Wolves had seized upon it.

The owner of the Blood Rose was a shark, circling for the earliest sniff of blood in the water. His bar was aptly named. Corbin might have looked pretty, but he'd sink his fangs into any enemy as soon as look at them, fellow bloodsucker or otherwise. But thankfully, he had no problem sitting back and allowing Malcolm to make the kill.

As long as it ended with Cillian dead.

"He's waiting for you," Corbin said smoothly. His crimson eyes flashed through the dark, a stark contrast to his handsome features. "Make him bleed, little witch," he whispered affectionately, a little too gleeful at the idea of someone being murdered in his bar for Trixie's taste, before he disappeared into the club's kitchens.

Once again, she was left alone. Trixie cursed the damned bourgeois carpeting, all plush and red as she made her debut. Her heels on the Coyote's hardwood always made for a far more dramatic entrance. Not that her role was all that important. She was simply a decoy. A seductive distraction while the Grey Wolves circled and closed in for the kill like the wolves they were.

She only had to keep Cillian talking.

He was in the same booth where she'd left him and Dani last time. Only this time around, there was no food and Dani was already passed out on the carpeted floor beside him. She looked thinner, gaunter than she'd been even days before, and the usual blushing of pink had drained from her hollowed cheeks, making her look almost as beautifully corpse-like as Cillian.

There was blood on her lips from where he'd fed her, whether his own blood or some supe juice, Trixie couldn't be certain. A familiar bite mark marred the tender flesh of Dani's neck. Fresh and swollen. The red looked angry against the pale tones of her skin. A trickle of Dani's blood had seeped from it, running down her chest like a solitary tear drop.

Normally, the healed-over scabs she sported on her neck at the bar didn't bother Trixie. In her mind, Dani was a big girl who knew how to make her own choices. It was Dani's decision on whether she wanted to date a vamp, a risk for any human, but Trixie knew Dani was in over her head with Cillian, stuck in a power dynamic no human could fairly navigate. That power gap was only widened by the way Cillian was glamouring her, and he'd clearly fed Dani enough of whatever he'd been using to get her high so that she was likely addicted to it now. She couldn't stop even if she wanted to.

She needed someone to save her. A friend who cared enough to pull her out, since she was past the point of being able to help herself.

Cillian glanced at his watch. For him, the hands probably seemed to move at a nonstop pace, ticking by as fast as a vampire could blink. Not that they often did. Time was a frail concept to an immortal as old as Cillian. The passage of years made little difference.

"Fashionably late," he said with a small grin of approval. His wasn't a British accent but something far older. Trixie had never been much when it came to school and history. But she knew the ways of men, vampire or otherwise.

"I like to keep an element of mystery." She smiled coyly.

She didn't slide into the booth across from him right away, instead letting him take in the full sight of her and admire her curves. The dress she wore was a barely there contraption. Little more than two thin pieces of fabric stitched together. The silk left her skin open to the cold winter air. Difficult to move in or feel comfortable, but it showed every part of her. The curve of her back above the Georgia peach of her ass, a plunging neckline that drove down almost to her navel, and the open swatch of her breasts that highlighted her long, elegant neck. The naked, virgin skin there was the only part Cillian really cared about.

Malcolm had taken one look at her and nearly come out of his skin, dragging her back into the bunkhouse until she had to put the thing back on again.

She smiled to herself, thinking of him and their old game. She'd used her femininity, her sexuality as a weapon to conquer more than one powerful man. If that made her a whore or easy, so be it. She didn't need society's approval to own her own power. If you asked her, it was men's fault for being so easily led about by their dicks.

They made it too damn easy.

All of them but Malcolm. Nothing had been easy about him.

Cillian's gaze raked over her as he took in his fill. To his credit, he didn't hide that he was objectifying her. He was open about it. She appreciated honesty in all its forms, even when the truth made her skin crawl. But she'd been admired by villains before.

Their tips were never great.

"Please, sit," Cillian said, gesturing to the seat across him, clearly having gotten his fill.

For now.

Trixie slipped into the booth across from him, fighting hard not to let her eyes fall toward Dani again, to give herself away or, worse, lunge toward her friend and check to see that she was still breathing. Overdosing on vamp blood caused a person to become a vampire only if they died and then were buried for several days, a slow and arduous process, but when heroin killed a person, they didn't come back. Ever.

Even if it was mixed into supe juice.

She was still cursing herself for not noticing Stan's mention of it the night of the bar brawl at the Coyote. It would have saved them all a lot of trouble and prevented her from having to slice open her hand. Belle, the pack's physician, had ensured she was healing properly. Malcolm had taken good care of her.

Trixie settled into the booth like she had all the time in the world. "I'm sure you're wondering why I asked you to meet me alone here."

Cillian tilted his head a little, but his face remained expressionless. A wall of beautiful ice or marble. Stunning to look at, but devoid of feeling. Frozen. "On the contrary, I'm not surprised. Your Boss is rather fond of having you do his dirty work for him, so I hear."

Boss as in the proper noun with a capital B. Trixie fought not to look as surprised as she felt. Not that Cillian knew she worked for the warlock, but from the way Cillian spoke of him, the two men were acquainted, on a first-name basis. She'd never known Boss to meddle in the affairs of vampires. He'd said the undead made him uneasy. Ask anyone down in the swamps of New Orleans. Warlocks and vamps didn't mix. Even if the French Quarter was full of them.

"You seem surprised by my mention of him."

"Not at all," Trixie lied. A waiter appeared with a glass of merlot for her and she latched onto it immediately, drawing a small, tentative sip. "Everyone knows I work at the Coyote."

"Not everyone knows you're bound there against your will." Cillian said it as if it were an offhand comment, not her darkest kept secret. "Another two years by my estimate, or so I hear." Down to the exact time.

Now he definitely had her attention.

No one knew about her and Boss's binding contract. Not even Malcolm. She didn't make a habit of telling people. She wasn't an open book about her past or the inevitable details of exactly *how* she'd ended up both in Boss's servitude and on his payroll. That was between her, the warlock, and the devil who'd sanctioned the deal as far as she was concerned.

The man upstairs was nowhere to be found for a witch who made dirty deals at the crossroads like she had. Powerful women, witches, were always within the purview of the guy belowstairs, or so the tales went. No one really knew their origin story. Not even the Grey Wolves.

Those of their kind were all so old they could only speculate.

All she knew was she'd been born with her abilities, hadn't asked for them.

"That's some dirt you've dug up on me there. I'm going to guess Boss himself told you."

The part she couldn't wrap her head around was why. Boss used her abilities to his advantage. Most knew she was a witch, but not a veritas witch. Boss kept that part of her to himself typically. For his own benefit.

So why had he spilled her backstory to Cillian? It didn't make sense.

She took another sip of her drink.

What have you gotten yourself into, old man?

Boss might be ancient, but in the supernatural world, she knew better than to equate age with devaluation. For a vamp, warlock, or witch, age was a sign of power. A life spent surviving. Like shifters, their bodies didn't age as fast as their minds did. She was a babe compared to Boss and Cillian, only as old as she looked, which wasn't much.

Cillian didn't affirm or deny her assumption. Instead he said, "You're here because you're hoping for a way out of it."

That wasn't at all why she was here, but she'd let him keep talking. Both out of curiosity for how deep Boss's involvement in this went and also to play her role with the Grey Wolves. She knew better than to think Cillian's offer, whatever it was, would be in any way appealing to her. She wasn't about to trade her remaining time from one powerful man to another. Even on his worst days, Boss was still good to her, looking out for her in his own way. He'd saved her after all from her own foolish mistakes.

Hadn't he?

Not this time, something inside her whispered.

But definitely before.

Naturally, she'd known since he was dealing with Stan, he'd planned to be involved with Triple S and the vamps in some way, but she'd figured he was only a third party—meant to broker the deal and leave like usual. But something about the way Cillian referred to Boss made her think that she'd been wrong.

It made her question exactly how deep Boss's involvement went.

"I won't say the warlock's magic will be easy to get around, but there are ways. If you know the right people, have enough money to pay."

She'd known that, of course. But she paid her debts honestly. "I don't have any money."

"Of course." Cillian smiled, flashing fang.

Which meant he expected to pay and then she'd pay him with…other means. Favors. Sexual in nature, and in her own blood from the way he was looking at her. Fucking and feeding: vampires often paired the two activities. A witch's blood was intoxicating to vamps, lending them the temporarily thrill of magic coursing through their undead bodies. Her one-time vamp boy toy had once told her that it made him feel alive again.

It hadn't made her eager for a repeat.

That was a kind of flirting with danger even *she* wasn't into. She prided herself on being up for almost anything once, but she didn't have a death wish. All it would take was one vamp who was a little too hungry, who lost control, got a bit too thirsty for her, and she'd be a goner. No way in hell.

She'd broken it off with him shortly after that. Boss had ordered Frank, the Coyote's bouncer, to throw him out on his undead ass when he'd shown up at the bar a time or two after, trying to win her back. It'd spooked her for a time, but Boss was good about keeping her old boyfriends at bay, even if that didn't always stop the patrons from getting too handsy on Friday and Saturday nights. She'd add another five years or more to her contract with the old warlock before she took her chances with Cillian or any bloodsucker like him.

Shifters were more her thing. A certain growly Grey Wolf executioner in particular.

Cillian was still talking, yammering away without even realizing she wasn't listening. Undead or not, men like him loved to hear themselves talk. Finally, he ended with, "But I think something can be arranged between you and me."

He reached across the table, extending a beckoning hand toward her. Not a handshake, but the kind of open-palmed gesture extended to a lover who was about to swept onto the dance floor. She was one hell of a dancer, but not with him.

It took everything in her to reach out and place her cold hand in his, but as his grip tightened around her, the hairs on the back of her neck prickled and she knew without a doubt nothing in her life ever went this easily.

Cillian's fingers tightened around her, hard enough she had to grit her teeth not to cry out. That'd only make Malcolm go wild, get sloppy, and she was no damsel in distress.

"Silly little witch," he said. When Corbin said it, it was

affectionate, but how it slipped from Cillian's lips was demeaning, meant to make her feel small, insignificant. "I knew from the moment you waltzed in here you were working with those mutts. You reek of them."

His grip on her hand tightened. Any more, and the bones there would crush.

Trixie reached down inside herself, summoning her magic forth until she was practically humming with it. Even the strands of her hair stood on end. "Corbin sent your security detail away. It's all you now. Alone. None of your coven to back you up. Those *mutts* will end you. Easily."

Cillian laughed with genuine amusement. "You think I didn't count on that glorified bartender stabbing me in the back the first chance he got? Corbin may be a vampire but he's no better than the beasts you bring into your bed."

Which meant the pack was in for more of a fight tonight than they'd bargained for. She'd need to conserve herself to lend an extra hand. But she had more than enough magic to fuck over Cillian.

"You can tell a lot about a man by how he treats the waitstaff." She gripped Cillian's palm back, cupping her free hand over it. Her glass of merlot spilled across the white tablecloth. "And about how *little* he considers the threat of an angry witch."

Cillian glanced down at their locked hands, at the flesh-filled fingers that'd transformed into rotted bone. He wrenched back in alarm, staring down at the rapidly disintegrating flesh there.

"I'm the veritas witch," she hissed. "And the truth of it,

Cillian, is that you're *already* dead." She smiled, all ruby-red lips. "Bless your heart, my only job is to show you what's behind the curtain."

Trixie opened both her palms, allowing the thrum of her magic to course through her and into Cillian. He stumbled back out of the booth, trying to place distance between him and her, but it was no use. As he did, he caught sight of himself in the mirror, at the decrepit, ghostly face that stared back, all the illusion that he was still living stripped away. Vampires were nothing more than glamour and rotted bone, held together by the force of human lifeblood.

She couldn't kill Cillian with the truth, but she could scare him. Give him pause.

And it was enough.

The doors to the main room finally flew open, Malcolm and the others obviously having been delayed by Cillian's anticipation of their arrival. Several of them were naked from having shifted, their clothes lost in the melee, Malcolm included, and they were all already covered in blood, snarling like the wild beasts Cillian had accused them of being.

Trixie loved it.

It all happened so fast. The room exploded in a burst of movement. The Grey Wolf elite warriors singled out Cillian in a matter of seconds. The pack worked as a unit, moving as one so thoroughly that teamwork didn't seem to be an accurate description.

They *were* one. All of them, and for a moment, Trixie's magic slipped due to her awe of it. A second round of Cillian's men stormed in behind them, prepared to tear into her wolves. She couldn't allow it. She dug down deep inside herself, all the way from her head to her toes. Trixie released her focus on Cillian, sending out a single pulse of magic, every bit she possessed. It emanated from her like an air wave reverberating through the room, stunning every vamp in her immediate radius. Not that the pack needed it.

Wes and Colt held Cillian down.

Rogue headed them off, throwing a stake into another outstretched hand.

Maverick and Blaze crouched in wait, prepared to fight off the other shifters with fang and claw, while Sierra and Dakota rushed to Trixie's side, protecting her with bared teeth.

But it was Malcolm, blood-soaked and snarling like a feral beast, who ruthlessly drove the stake Rogue threw him into Cillian's heart, claiming his revenge.

The ancient vampire exploded in a disgusting spray of blood and guts that caused bile to burn at the back of Trixie's throat.

Oversize mosquito indeed.

The moments that followed were...strange. A chorus of all of them panting, most of the room's habitants soaked and bloody, and her in the soiled dress Mae had loaned her that she thought might have been Gucci. Trixie stumbled out of the booth.

Malcolm's wolf eyes turned toward her, assessing her for any wounds.

She cackled, far more stereotypically Halloween witch than she'd usually allowed herself to be, but the last of her magic was still seeping from her pores, and she was drunk with it. She gestured to the room around them, chuckling like a madwoman. The club was littered with stunned vampire bodies.

A satisfied smile curled her lips, even as she felt her legs wobble beneath her. "Who were you calling a human again?" she snarked, and then she was falling.

As Trixie mentally braced for the impact, she was only vaguely aware that Malcolm had already caught her.

Chapter 22

THE EARLY MORNING SUN SPILLED OVER THE BLUE-ridged mountaintops, streaming through the pines until their shadows grew tall. Trixie closed the bunkhouse door behind her and trekked out into the cold, alone. It was well past dawn now, the ranch starting to come awake in small bustles of sound and movement. The whinnies of the horses in the nearby stable carried on the light wind. The sharp crow of a rooster. The occasional rev of one of the pack's truck engines.

The echoing howls in the forest had long since quieted.

She walked out toward the trees, where the source of her ire had originated. All night, those howls had kept her awake in the moonlight, pacing. She hadn't slept a wink. Not that wakeful nights weren't her usual. With her bar schedule, she was a night owl, both by nature and necessity. Nearly as nocturnal as a wolf. But she'd been too wired, too nervous to sleep, even if she'd tried. She'd worried about everything—about Malcolm and how she'd break his heart, about whether Jackie and his family made it out okay, about Dani recovering in the pack's medical center, and of course, about her own long list of troubles. Even though her momentary blackout had left her exhausted from draining her magic dry, those damn howls had haunted her.

They were a reminder.

That there was too much at stake. Of all her shortcomings. Most her own doing.

Trixie huddled inside the oversized Carhartt coat Malcolm had loaned her, blowing a heated breath out into the chilled air. The vapor swirled about her face, then dissipated. She pulled her hands up into the too-long coat sleeves, wrapping her arms around herself to keep warm. Her mascara was a black, smeared mess. Her hair mussed. She'd told Malcolm she'd needed a minute to clear her head. But in truth...

Her twenty-four hours were up.

Trixie watched in the distance as one of the packmembers opened the stable doors, an audible creak of old wood and hinge. Spotting her, he gave her a curt nod. She lifted a half-hearted hand in greeting, though she wasn't certain who it was, before she ducked her head in the opposite direction and quickly turned away. She both wanted to be alone and didn't.

She nudged a rock with the toe of her boot across the frozen short grass. For the first time in a long time, she wished her mother were here to stand beside her, her bad hip jutted out as she leaned against some surface or another. She'd offer her one of those damn Virginia Slims like it would solve all her troubles, even though Trixie didn't smoke and never had. Her ma would rasp at her that she'd gotten herself into this mess, and she could damn well get herself out without the help of any man.

Trixie wasn't so certain that was true this time.

She shook her head. She supposed it was fitting that a witch only had her ghosts to help keep her warm.

The phone in the pocket of her jeans buzzed from an incoming call, but she ignored it. She needed to tell Malcolm what Cillian had said about Boss, about…everything, but she didn't know where to start.

How could she tell the man she now loved that she'd been lying to him?

And she did—love him, that is.

Trixie let out another exhausted sigh. She hadn't counted on that, on feeling so deeply for Malcolm, among other things. She'd compromised her plans and hadn't realized the price was too much to pay. Her thoughts turned to her conversation with Cillian, to his taunting. From the beginning, she'd suspected Boss might have been more involved than he'd let on. She'd almost known it when he agreed to forge the binding spell between her and Stan on the Triple S leader's behalf.

She'd headed west at seventeen after one of her mother's boyfriends had gotten a bit too handsy. Though the first time she'd set foot in the Coyote, she hadn't been a day over twenty; nowadays, if anyone asked, she was forever twenty-nine. The first time she'd walked into the Midnight Coyote's smoke-filled dark, the bar had been dead.

Boss sat at the bar top, a lit cigarette hanging from his lips as he counted the cash drawer. It'd been well past close, but the old warlock had made the mistake of leaving the door unlocked and it'd been easy for her to slip in. She'd stood there for several long minutes in the bar's entryway, watching him tally the drawer and the credit receipts.

It reminded her of nights spent as a child, her mother at the kitchen table, barely visible through the crack in Trixie's bedroom door, counting her tips from the diner. Dawn would come soon after and when Trixie would rise, she'd tuck her mother in, wrap a blanket over her on their sofa, and tiptoe out to the bus stop or to the car of whatever boy she was flirting with those days.

After several minutes, when he still hadn't looked toward her, she cleared her throat.

"I know you're there, cher." Boss lifted his cigarette from his lips, flicking the ashes into the mountain-shaped ashtray beside him, some novelty gift from a nearby Billings tourist shop. "We're closed."

"Those things are gonna kill you, you know. Always told my mama the same thing."

With a resigned sigh, Boss reached for a Guinness pint glass full of pens near the register and plucked one out. He scribbled down a figure on a scrap of receipt paper and turned his attention toward her. His smoky exhale wrapped around him, and then he butted his cigarette out. He didn't scan her up and down, just took in the whole of her in one glance.

She'd liked that.

"And what's a pretty young one like you doing standing here in my bar, giving me advice, girl?"

She hadn't been world-wise enough to place his Cajun accent then.

She stepped forward and placed the cashier's receipt on the bar top beside him, then stepped back again. "I'm here to pay a debt."

Boss picked up the cashier's receipt, glanced at the number written upon it, and didn't so much as blink. It was the whole of her life savings, not that she'd lived very long, but she'd stored away some money from cleaning dishes at the diner for her mother over the years. Occasionally, she'd taken over her shifts when her mother had been too worn out and the arthritis in her knees got too bad.

"This debt isn't yours, cher," Boss said. "I've never seen you in here before. Who roped you into paying for him?"

Trixie bristled. "Tony Degaetano. He's my boyfriend," she said defensively. "And he didn't rope me into anything."

Tony'd sworn he'd pay her back, make it right. She believed him. He was still working on the smaller amounts from before, but debt collectors had put him in a bad way and she had a steady paycheck coming in. She knew how it was to always be short on cash. Her whole life, it'd always seemed to be gone only moments after it came into her hand.

There was always someone looking to make a poor girl pay.

Boss shook his head. The look he'd given her then had been one of pity. "Tell me you weren't so stupid as to use your magic to take on that fool's debt."

Trixie stiffened. "I ain't much, but I ain't stupid."

She'd managed to make it through high school, get decent grades. A lot of her friends hadn't. She hadn't wanted to take on Tony's debt as her own, use her magic to transfer the remaining balance to her, but what choice did she have? If Tony didn't pay, this asshole warlock's debt collector would tear Tony to pieces, and she'd already known he was in a bad place, trying to get back on his feet.

She loved him. That was what you did to help the ones you loved. Made sacrifices, even when it wasn't convenient. He treated her real good when he wasn't too deep in the tables to pay attention. Took her out on real dates, to the movies and dinner and everything when he had some winnings. He told her she was beautiful. Not sexy, but beautiful. She liked that.

So he was a gambler?

Nobody was perfect.

Lord knew she wasn't worth much herself.

Nothing more than a pair of good legs and tits, *her ma's old boyfriend had said. Will had been his name. A truck driver from San Antonio who'd shacked up with them for a few days before hitting the road again. He'd been one of many.*

She'd been fifteen. Ma hadn't bothered to correct him.

But at least he hadn't touched her.

Boss let out a long-winded sigh, collecting the stacked bills on the bar top and placing them back into the drawer. He picked up the cashier's check again, looked at it, and set it back down. "This isn't enough."

Trixie blinked. "What do you mean, it isn't enough? There's a full five thousand there. Every bit of my savings and then some." She'd had to take out a small personal loan and a cash advance on her next paycheck from her job as the night attendant at the Exxon gas station out on I-90 and empty out her checking account. She'd be behind on this month's rent, but Merle would front her, and if he didn't, she'd figured she could stay with Tony.

He'd never taken her back to his place, but he would if she asked him.

"Did you use your magic for him, cher?" Boss asked again.

Trixie opened her mouth but didn't answer.

The warlock sighed. "Yes or no?"

"Yes," she finally breathed. She still wasn't used to openly discussing her magic. Her mother had never had a coven, and most of the men she'd brought home from the diner had been human. When she'd asked why, her mother had said it kept them safe, kept the power dynamic even. Human men were easy to handle for a witch, but that'd never stopped Ma from letting any of them hurt her.

"Let me give you some advice, cher." Boss was still shaking his head. "Men like Tony will take you for all you're worth."

Trixie's stomach dropped, but she wasn't certain why. She didn't question if what he said was true because something inside her knew already. "What do you mean?" she whispered.

Boss laid the last stack of bills back inside the register and looked at her. That prolonged stare, one eye green and one blue, was unsettling. "He made a deal with me at the crossroads, cher. Five grand was just the start." Boss's nose flared as he released another long sigh. "He bet on his soul, his life, and you were stupid enough to take on his debt as your own."

Trixie felt as if she'd been gutted. Her pulse raced. She felt her chest constrict as she struggled to breathe.

"You have fifteen years left."

Fifteen years. Fifteen years was over half her life. She'd barely gotten started living.

Fifteen years…

"Before?" Adrenaline caused her to be reckless, ask a question she didn't want answered. She regretted it the moment it'd left her lips.

Boss didn't answer her. He didn't have to. He just gave her that sad, pitying look.

Fifteen years before the hellhounds came for her. Until her soul belonged to the devil. Boss's mismatched eyes suddenly made sense now, along with his rumored penchant for binding spells. He wasn't simply a necromancer, a warlock. He was a crossroads demon.

Fifteen years. Bile rose in her throat.

"And he's married."

Three words. That'd been the final nail in the coffin. The realization Tony hadn't loved her. She'd been the other woman, and he'd played her for a fool.

The pitying look in Boss's eyes suddenly felt like too much. She hated him, hated herself. Tears poured down her face, but she couldn't bring herself to say anything.

What else was there to say?

"What kind of witch are you, cher?" Boss asked, the question catching her off guard. He stood from the barstool he'd been perched on and made his way toward her then, assessing her like she was an object to be possessed, like a car he needed to repo.

Though she supposed in fifteen years, she would be.

Trixie gaped at him, struggling to answer, torn between running for the door, though she wasn't certain her feet would carry her there, and dropping to her knees and pleading that he spare her. "I—I'm a veritas witch."

Boss had laughed, full and throaty. Deep belly laughs. He'd looked like a villain then. Like the man who'd been sent to damn her. Not save her.

The irony of her situation wasn't lost on her either.

She was supposed to be able to tell truth from lies, but she'd been played as a fool. Magic worked like gut instinct. It only worked if you trusted it. She hadn't wanted to believe.

So she hadn't.

Boss clapped her on the shoulder, gripping her frail, shaking body in his large hand and leading her over to the bar top. He didn't need to tell her to sit. She lifted herself up onto the stool, flats sliding over the metal ribbing of the bottom frame. That'd been the last time she ever wore anything but heels. Boss rounded the bar top, grabbing a tumbler and pouring her a finger of whiskey. She'd taken it in her hand but hadn't known what to do with it.

She wasn't even old enough to drink.

In the background, Dolly Parton's "Jolene" played quietly on the jukebox.

Boss eyed her wearily as she took a sip of the whiskey and coughed, hands still shaking.

"I think we can come to some sort of arrangement, cher." He nodded. "But this'll be the last time I clean up your mess."

The second sip had gone down smoother.

Trixie shivered—whether at the cold or the memory, she didn't know.

Having her clean up her own messes was one thing. Handing her over to the supernatural Mafia was another. Why would he do that to her, if not for his own benefit? How else had Stan found her apartment? She paid her rent in cash tips the landlord pocketed directly in order to keep her name off the motel's books. Shifters weren't the only ones who needed to keep themselves scarce and hidden from humanity.

Still, Cillian's confirmation of Boss's involvement had felt like a betrayal. A betrayal of... Well, she didn't know what. Trust wasn't what had held her and the old warlock together all these years—magic was, their mutual agreement, and some weird sense of obligation that she somehow owed him for saving her from herself. Even if it'd been *him* she'd needed saving from. Even if he'd used her.

He meant something to her all the same.

After all they'd been through, could she really drop the dime on him to Malcolm?

She and Boss were family after all.

Family was always fucked up.

The phone in her pocket continued to buzz incessantly, not taking no for an answer. She reached for it, picking up the call only to immediately hang up again. The move would infuriate Stan. But she had nothing to say. She glanced back toward the bunkhouse.

Not to him anyway.

———

Malcolm had ordered the other hands to clear out of the bunkhouse again, and at this rate, he was going to have to take Maverick up on his offer of claiming his own cabin. He sat on his bunk's thin mattress, elbows resting on his knees and eyes locked with Trixie's damn dog. The early morning light streamed in through the thin slider windows near the bunkhouse ceiling, illuminating the space in a pale, white glow.

Malcolm adjusted his weight uncomfortably, only causing Dumplin' to growl louder. He shot the dog an annoyed look. His bunk was more like a cot than a true bed, and his folded-over position was less than comfortable, but that hadn't stopped him and Trixie from making good use of the mattress last night. The bed frame had been groaning and creaking well into the early morn. At one point, it'd banged against the wall so hard he'd been certain they'd break it.

The thought had been a strange point of pride for him.

Malcolm shook his head, resting his face in his hands. He'd intended to let Trixie rest after that brief blackout at the Blood Rose, but she'd insisted it'd been a result of her magic draining, nothing more, and though they'd tried to rest, sleep wouldn't claim either of them. He'd still been high on the adrenaline of taking out Cillian, the result of which would cause the bloodsuckers to retaliate, maybe even scare the Triple S enough to cause them to back out, and he was eager to make use of what little time he had left with Trixie before their next battle. She had said she was alright, feeling good even, despite her brief blackout, so he'd trusted her judgment. In part because he realized he trusted *her*.

From across the room, Dumplin' stared at him, lip curled and grumbling. The Rottie had been oddly quiet throughout the nighttime hours, only opening his droopy lids and giving Malcolm the occasional angry side-eye whenever Trixie had let out a particularly loud moan, but as soon as Malcolm had risen for the day and pulled on his clothes, work gear, and weapons, Dumplin' had resumed his position as guard dog. Not that he was very good at it.

"You let us spend all night fucking and then growl when she's not even here?" he asked the beast. Unlike when he was in wolf form, Malcolm knew the canine could only understand a handful of the words he was saying, instead reading the feeling, his tone of voice, and his body language more than anything, but that didn't stop him from addressing the thing like they were...well, one and the same.

They'd both gladly let Trixie lead them around on a leash. *Fuck.*

Malcolm let out a long sigh, running his fingers through his hair before he raked both hands across the scruff on his chin. Blaze had been right. He'd been a goner from the start. "Look, we need to make peace, okay? For her sake," he said to Dumplin'. Goddamnit, he couldn't believe he was doing this. He was sitting here *talking* with her dog.

But he'd do anything for Trixie.

Be anything. Say anything. More importantly, *do* anything. Actions spoke louder than words. Whatever she wanted, he'd give it to her. It'd been the same way with Bo.

Because that was what he did for someone he loved.

Malcolm cleared his throat with a rough, raspy cough. He wasn't certain when he'd realized it. The thought had settled into him like it was as much a part of him as his fur or his leather or his tattoos. Maybe it'd been sometime last night, between her riding his face like *she* was the cowhand instead of him and he was nothing but a hungry animal for her use, or maybe when she'd grabbed one of his and Bo's old toys from the trunk at the foot of his bed like the true siren she was and then bent *him* over the game table like *she* was in charge.

Shit, maybe she was. He shook his head. Top from the bottom, exactly like he'd predicted. He blew out a brief sigh. He couldn't bring himself to feel sorry about that.

He raked a hand over his face again. Maybe the change had been the moment he'd taken off her makeup and seen her freckles, those little kisses of color spattered across her cheeks that made her look like she belonged in the warm sun instead of a bar's darkness. She kept the best parts of herself hidden from the world. But not from him.

For him, she'd been open and honest, willing to show herself. She'd put her trust in him. He wanted to do the same. Anything to make her happy.

There'd been a fear in her eyes last night that he hadn't understood. Not when they'd been making love, but in the moments in between their shared pleasure. Last night, he'd been her distraction from whatever it was that had plagued her. In those quiet spaces, she'd stared up at the ceiling, naked and relaxed in his arms, listening to the familiar howls that filled the nights at Wolf Pack Run, and more than once, he'd seen tears in her eyes.

He hadn't asked her what was wrong. She'd tell him whenever she was ready. He'd simply done what she had for him so many times before and sat there in the silence with her, held her against him so that if she'd needed to break, he'd catch the pieces of her in his hands and put them back together.

Pushing up from his seat, he stood, only causing Dumplin's growls to increase.

He sighed. "Look. I mean it," he said to the dog. "I'm willing to make nice if you do." He lifted both hands in a sign of surrender and stepped closer to where Dumplin' lay at the foot of the opposite bunk.

The Rottweiler's growls grew louder still.

Immediately, Malcolm eased back, willing to go at the animal's pace. He watched the dog carefully, his eyes following the canine's to where Bo's blade was nestled in its sheath at his hip. The other Grey Wolf warriors hadn't been fully armed when they'd approached the rescued animal, not with their knives anyway, but *he* had been.

For a long moment, he simply stared at Dumplin'. He watched the dog's lip sputter and curl, mouth dripping with slobber. The dog's bad eye was cloudy, white with a cataract and recessed with a jagged scar that cut through it. Both the good eye and the scarred, misshapen one from where he'd been wounded tracked Malcolm's every move. At quick glance, Dumplin's raised hackles looked like rage, aggression, but the longer he stared, the more the dog's growls looked like fear. Fear that he was going to be hurt, should anyone come any closer.

Malcolm swallowed. He knew the feeling.

"Is that what's bothering you? Did someone hurt you with something like this?" he asked, nodding toward Bo's sheathed blade at his hip. He didn't expect the dog to answer, but something inside him felt compelled to ask the question anyway. He'd assumed the scars the other beast bore had been from his fighting days, from another dog's claws or teeth while whatever human had abused him forced him into the ring, but now...

Now he wasn't so certain.

A scar like that could have easily been made by human hands. By a blade meant to injure.

"I'm gonna take it and put it on the table, okay?" he said to Dumplin'. "It'll stay there. You can trust me. I promise." Slowly, he reached for the blade.

The moment his hand connected with it, Dumplin' was on his feet, shoulders hunched and snarling like he was about to charge Malcolm and tear a chunk from his leg to protect himself, but the darkness before dawn was always the most terrifying. Malcolm knew that firsthand. He quickly tossed the weapon on the table, abandoning it with a clatter, before he lifted both his hands again to show Dumplin' there wasn't anything in them.

"See. Kept my promise."

Dumplin's eyes darted between where Bo's blade lay on the table and where Malcolm stood, unarmed. Immediately, the dog stopped growling. His mouth opened and he panted several fast breaths. His hackles lowered and he relaxed slightly. Still fearful, but more tentative than aggressive. The stance the Rottweiler held was one that said he could run, if needed, but he trusted Malcolm enough that for now, his feet remained firmly planted in place.

"I'm gonna come closer now, okay? Try to pet you, if you'll let me?"

The Rottie blinked at him.

When Malcolm took a step forward, the dog jumped back, startled. But another step and this time the canine stayed in place. Malcolm inched toward him, and before they both knew it, he was crouched beside Dumplin', near eye level with him. He reached out and brushed a hand over the smooth sheen of the dog's fur. Dumplin' relaxed into his touch, slowly trusting him.

A moment later, Malcolm was wincing at the wet nose that was suddenly shoved into his face as Dumplin' sniffed him from head to toe in a hurried frenzy. He had to nudge the beast back when shortly after, a wide, wet tongue connected with the side of his face.

"Ugh," he groaned. "No kisses. I draw the line at kisses." He wiped the slobber from his face. But Dumplin' was in his lap a second later, staring up at him with suddenly affectionate eyes as he panted. Malcolm chuckled. "You really are a softie, aren't you?"

He wasn't certain whether he was speaking to the dog or himself.

A moment later, the bunkhouse door opened and Trixie blew in along with a gust of winter wind. She'd returned from her walk and was now flitting about the bunkhouse kitchen like a hummingbird. Finally, when she glanced in their direction, her eyes grew wide.

She blinked. Then blinked again. "Am I...seeing what I think I'm seeing?" she asked.

Malcolm shrugged, turning his head away slightly with another grumble as Dumplin' pressed his wet nose against Malcolm's cheek again. "We made our peace, I guess. For you."

Trixie stared at him for a long moment, silent, before she smiled. If Malcolm hadn't been paying attention, he wouldn't have noticed her chin quivering.

His heart plummeted into his feet.

"What's wrong?" He hadn't wanted to ask her the night before, to pry, but now he couldn't stop himself.

To Trixie's credit, she didn't hesitate and draw the pain out. She flayed him open with little more than a sentence. "I–I can't stay here, Malcolm."

This was it then.

Malcolm blew out a long breath, his hand resting on Dumplin's head like it belonged there. He had known this moment was coming from the first minute she'd set foot on the ranch. He hadn't known exactly what she'd been running from then, because she hadn't told him, but he'd known it was something more than she was saying. He'd recognized the desperate look in her eyes. The one that Dumplin' had had only moments ago. Fear fueled by a drive to survive.

He'd seen it reflected in his own eyes once, too, reflected back in the windows of that repurposed police car. Rock bottom had a look, a smell, and a taste that only those who'd been there could recognize, because they'd lived there, experienced it. Grief changed a person.

He'd known there was more to her situation with the Triple S than she'd let on. So had Maverick. How could there not be? Still, the Grey Wolf packmaster had trusted that whatever it was, Malcolm would handle it. He'd make it right with the pack's blessing. Whatever it might be.

He'd known from the moment he'd first slept with her

that she was going to break his heart. He was too sensitive for her not to. He'd simply decided the pain would be worth it for the memories he'd have long after she was gone from his life. Memories seemed to be all he was destined to have these days. The details of Bo's face were already fading from memory along with the few photographs he had. Why not Trixie's, too?

"I would if I could, but I can't... I–I made a mistake, a big one, that I can't take back," she said. "It was before I knew where...where this was going, and I..." She struggled to hold in her tears, keep her mascara from pouring farther down her face. "I'm sorry, Malcolm. I never counted on this."

This being loving him. She didn't have to say it for him to know.

He'd known the moment she'd let him see her true face beneath the makeup. Not saying the words out loud didn't make it any less real.

He couldn't blame her. He hadn't said it either, hadn't counted on it. But he'd forgiven her from the very start. "Let go of your tears, Trixie." He met her gaze. He didn't enjoy her crying, but he needed to see the real emotion there, see what he meant to her.

Trixie's chin wobbled, tears streaking down her face with it. A moment later, he was on his feet, moving toward her, pulling her in to his chest at the exact moment those tears turned into racking sobs. "Don't you want to know what I did?" She sniffled, for once seeming to take little notice or consideration of how her makeup had smeared. "How I hurt you?" She hiccupped.

Malcolm shook his head. "It doesn't matter."

"It does. It *does* matter."

You matter. He heard the truth there, as if her magic had become his own, though he knew that was impossible. He simply knew her, better than most, like he'd told her before.

"Not to me," he said gruffly. He held her tighter for a moment before pulling back. A knife wound was a knife wound no matter the kind of blade. He gripped both her shoulders, staring down at her. "Whatever it is, will telling me make you feel better? Will it make you stay?"

It was both a question and a subtle plea.

Don't leave me.

I promise I'm worth the risk.

Trixie shook her head. "I can't stay, Malcolm. Even if I wanted to."

The grief that cut through him stopped his breath short, but he resigned himself to it. "Then I don't want to hear it." He stepped away from her, putting a bit of distance between them, even as he held onto her hand. His thumb traced slow circles over her palm, the smooth lacquer on her manicured nails. Her hands were so soft, unworked. Not worn and ragged like his.

Trixie sniffled again. She swiped at her tears with the sleeve of the Carhartt he'd loaned her. It was so big on her that she was nearly drowning in it. "You're not going to try and s-stop me?" she sputtered. "Try to convince me not to walk away?"

"No," he grumbled. "I won't treat you like that." He didn't beg. He didn't plead. Even when he'd held Bo's body in his arms, he hadn't prayed to a god he wasn't certain existed. That wasn't his way. Fate dealt him his hand and he accepted it. "You're a grown woman, Trixie. I won't try to make those kinds of choices for you." He gave a rough clear of his throat. "If you say you need to go, that it's your only option, I believe you." He met her gaze. "I trust you."

Trixie was trembling from head to toe. "I think that trust's misplaced."

Malcolm shook his head. "I don't."

Trixie inhaled a shuddering breath through her mouth. "You will," she breathed.

It was a warning, but he didn't need it.

Malcolm nodded. He'd accept whatever she gave him. No matter how much it hurt. "Well until then, there's nothing else left to say." His thumb stopped tracing circles on her hand, and before he could stop himself, he was gently leading her along behind him, out of the bunkhouse and into the freezing Montana cold. "There's something I want to show you."

Chapter 23

Trixie didn't know where Malcolm was leading her, but she sensed its importance. She inhaled a ragged breath. The chill in the air made the damp tearstains on her face feel like ice against the winter cold, but with Malcolm's hand in hers, the heat from his body kept her warm. She'd lied to him and he knew now—at least in part, though he hadn't yet faced the worst of it—and still he was trusting her with whatever meaningful part of himself he was about to show her. The gesture humbled her.

Even if it was only temporary.

Running would keep her safe, would keep both of them safe.

Though he'd resent her in the end.

Malcolm didn't stop until they came to a large, red wooden building with a frozen metal garage door. Another entrance sat off to the left for standard entry. He made his way toward it, picking out the correct key from the ring on his belt. He pushed the key into the lock, lifting the door up by the handle and pushing it inward with his shoulder as though he was used to it sticking. When it came loose, he stepped inside with a nod for her to follow.

The inside of the garage was unlit. The floors and rafters

of the open space smelled of motor oil, wiper fluid, and rubber tires like so many others she'd been in anytime her car needed to be fixed. But this one was cleaner, well maintained and meticulously organized. She wasn't sure why, but something about the clean floors and the gleaming red polish of the tool chests gave her magic the sense of a woman's touch. But she pushed the thought aside.

Malcolm flicked on the lights. The fluorescent panels blazed to life overhead. The garage was large, intended to accommodate the breadth and width of the pack's trucks and ranch equipment. A large tractor was parked in the first available space, followed by a tiller and a forklift. But Malcolm didn't pay any mind to them. He was headed to the far corner, a tucked-away space, and she followed him, careful of her step.

When he finally stopped, they stood in front of a motorcycle covered in an old paint-stained sheet. From the length and spread of the body between the front and back wheels, Trixie recognized it as a chopper. A shelf lined with half-used acrylic paint bottles, an airbrush machine, a few spare rags, and a siphon waited beside it. Malcolm laid a hand on the handlebars beneath the sheet.

"It was Bo's," he said into the quiet. "A restoration project. But I've…finished it for him."

Trixie's breath caught.

"Do you want to see it?" he asked. He glanced toward her, dark eyes vulnerable and hopeful. As if he feared she might not be interested.

"Of course," she breathed. She knew without asking that

he hadn't shown it to anyone else, and she wanted to see every part of him, know him like no one else did. No one still living anyway. But she'd have been blind not to realize this was hard for him. "Take your time." She placed a soft hand on his arm. Her fingers brushed against the flexible, grainy material before she dropped it again. Leather had a distinct oaky smell and it lingered on him.

Malcolm nodded, staring down at the sheet momentarily like he wasn't certain he could do it. She wouldn't have blamed him. Unlike her own secrets, this wasn't only his to share. The man he'd loved was still a part of him. She knew he'd loved Bo deeply. He always would.

Malcolm pressed his lips together, nodding to himself in reassurance as if he knew it was time, before finally pulling the sheet off. Trixie covered her mouth.

The chopper was a testament to the beauty and artistry one devoted person could create with patience, paint, and chrome. The careful detail work on the gas tank and fender stole her breath away.

Unthinking, she reached out, almost touching it before she stopped herself. She glanced toward Malcolm hesitantly. "May I?"

He nodded, features heavy as he watched her.

Trixie inched closer. She ran her hands over the polished gas tank, crouching a little to see the full detail there. It was a dark nightscape. A side view of the open road. Billings's rimrocks hovered in the background. The Montana sky in the picture stretched before the rider depicted there, its depth seeming to go on for miles. In the image, a man who she recognized immediately as Malcolm rode on a dark chopper while beside him, the ghostly image of Bo, sheer and haunting, galloped alongside on a horse, smiling at the rider like a reminder he'd never be truly alone. Trixie's fingers traced over the uncanny depiction.

She'd considered Bo a friend.

To think, she'd always thought the dark stains on Malcolm's nails had been chipped black nail polish, but she recognized it now as paint—paint he'd used to craft his grief and love onto the backdrop of a wide night sky.

Trixie's eyes watered, but she blinked back the tears. "He would have loved this, Malcolm."

Malcolm dropped his head slightly, looking at his feet as he scrubbed at the back of his neck. "I put the finish on a few nights ago. When you and the hands were playing poker."

She nodded, suddenly understanding. No wonder he'd been hurt.

He'd meant to bring her here.

Open himself to her.

She was thankful he still had, that she hadn't scared him away. She realized now that he took to heart every word she said. With him, she needed to be careful, sensitive, offer solace.

Straightening, she stepped toward the back of the bike, running her hand over the smooth leather seat and watching her distorted reflection in the custom chrome tailpipe. The continued starscape on the fender was as stunning as the gas tank. Who knew Malcolm was an artist?

She shook her head. He was so talented and no one but

her seemed to know it, seemed to see him for anything more than what others told them to believe.

A killer. An outlaw. A cowboy.

He was all those things and yet none of them. Not at his core.

"Do you want to sit on it?" Malcolm asked sheepishly. He nodded toward the empty seat.

Trixie's gaze snapped toward him. He was being serious, genuine.

"I'd offer you a ride, take you out, but"—he gestured to the garage door and the whistling winter winds outside—"it's not exactly the right weather."

She didn't know how to tell him that offering for her to sit in the seat was more than enough, more than she'd ever ask of him.

"Are you certain?"

Malcolm nodded. "Yeah, I'm certain."

Slowly, she made her way back to the chopper's side, placing her hands on the high-seated gorilla bars and carefully swinging her leg over. The motorcycle was enormous. She'd never be able to balance it by herself, especially not in her usual heels, but thankfully its wheels were locked onto a solid red dolly rather than balanced on the motorcycle's narrow kickstand.

She chanced a glance toward Malcolm, smiling.

He nodded in quiet appreciation. "You look good on it. It suits you."

Trixie struggled to know what to say.

"Malcolm, I—"

"Trixie—"

They spoke at the same time.

"Oh shit, sorry." He let out a raspy cough, like he was embarrassed to have interrupted her.

"No, please." She placed her hands on the gas tank, his artwork. "You go first."

Malcolm nodded slowly but didn't look at her. "There's... some things I need to tell you, and I need you to hear them, so...listen close because I'm only going to say them once, okay?"

Trixie's breath fled from her lungs. "Okay."

Malcolm stared down at the bike's gas tank, the image of him and Bo. "My last name's Marchetti," he said, refusing to look at her. "That's the name I was born with anyway. All my fake IDs say Grey now." He let out a long exhale through his nose, as if that single sentence had taken everything out of him, but he didn't stop there. "The Execution Underground dropped me off here when I was eighteen. It was a grace, a mercy. I'd been raised by my human mother my whole life and didn't know who or what I was."

Trixie's throat felt like it'd close around her own emotion. Being a teenager in the supernatural world was hard enough, but being one among humans, when he hadn't known what he was felt...unfathomable. She couldn't imagine that kind of loneliness.

"The reason I can't leave Wolf Pack Run," Malcolm continued, "is because there's a warrant out for my arrest, though I figure you'd already gathered that much."

Trixie nodded. "I had." She'd met enough ex-cons and

men running from the law at the Coyote to know the signs. Reserved. Secretive. Guarded. Unhinged when threatened.

Malcolm ticked all those boxes and then some.

"But...I–I need you to know why, need you to hear it from my mouth to your ears." He lifted his head and looked straight toward her. His eyes were the burning gold ember of his wolf. "When I was eighteen, I killed my stepfather," he said without hesitation. "I shifted for the very first time, though I didn't know that's what I was doing then, and I mauled him. He deserved it. He was an abusive fuck who'd hurt me for over half my life. My mom, too, when she wasn't so strung out she didn't give a shit about anything or anyone, but that's not why I killed him."

Trixie knew how to school her features, to keep the shock from her face like she did whenever anyone was confiding in her at the bar. She was part bartender and part wayward preacher. There to take drunken confessionals. "Why'd you do it then?"

Malcolm didn't seem surprised by her question. "Because my mother told me she was pregnant with that bastard's baby and I–I stupidly believed her. I couldn't let him hurt another helpless kid like he'd hurt me." A growl started to rumble in his chest, but he sealed his lips shut, jamming it back down inside him with his wolf, where it belonged. "The next time he lifted a hand to her, I saw the look of fear in her eyes. Her hand fluttered to her belly and I–I lost it."

His eyes burned with hatred. "I wish I could say I don't remember doing it. That I blacked out, but I *do* remember. I remember every second of it." He gritted his teeth. "And I remember the way my mother laughed afterward. Like I'd done her a favor." The deadpan expression he gave her sent a chill down her spine. "She lied to me. She wasn't pregnant. She knew what I was even before I did and she used that to her advantage, exploited it."

Trixie struggled to wrap her head around that. Her mother had failed her in many ways, but never like that. Only two people had ever betrayed her, and the first wasn't family.

Maybe Boss wasn't either.

"Why are you telling me this? Why now?" she whispered.

She needed to know. She couldn't walk away without knowing, no matter that doing so would protect him and his pack. All of them.

"Because I wanted you to hear it from me. Because when you leave here, I don't want you to take me for granted, believe any of the things other people say about who I am or what I've done." He swallowed, smacking his lips before they settled into a grim line. "I want you to see *me*, Trixie."

She reached for him. "I do see you. I see all of you." He stepped toward her and she grabbed his hand, drawing him close. "You're not a monster, Malcolm."

"How can you be so sure? My own mother thought that of me." The laugh he gave her was bitter, cold. "It's only a matter of time before you think it, too. Everyone does."

"No," she said harshly, swinging her leg over the bike to sit astride. "No. Not everyone. Not Bo. Not me. Not Austin or anyone who dared to draw close enough to try to coax you into letting them in." She reached up and cupped his cheek. He leaned into her touch. "I see you, Malcolm. Killer or not, you don't look like a monster to me. Bo never thought so either."

It must've been the right thing to say because suddenly she was his arms, and he was kissing her for all she was worth. His tongue parted the seam of her mouth, greedily seeking entry, and she opened for him readily. He kissed her until they were both out of breath, until her lungs were screaming, but she didn't need air. Not as much as she needed him.

She knew he felt the same.

As he kissed her, he cradled her back, leaning over where she sat in the motorcycle's saddle seat. One large hand snaked to her front, palming her breasts. He paid equal attention to both of them, kneading and tweaking the hardened peaks of her nipples through the thin fabric of the long-sleeved T-shirt she wore, an old Social Distortion shirt he'd loaned her. Malcolm kicked her knees apart and she knew exactly where this was headed. A fire lit inside her.

She pulled back, gasping for breath and placing a hand on his chest to stop him momentarily before she lost herself to her own need. "There's some things I should tell you, too," she panted. So many things that she didn't know where to start, so she went back to the beginning. "Boss owns me." She felt Malcolm's muscles stiffen with protective anger beneath her hands. "I work at the bar because it's part of a binding contract. I took on an old boyfriend's debt. I was stupid and young enough to believe he loved me, but turns out, I was the other woman."

Beneath his Stetson, she could see the gears turning behind the golden irises of his wolf eyes, the way he was putting pieces of her together, reconstructing like he had the bike beneath them. She knew the confession explained a lot and also not enough.

"Foolish, huh?" She shrugged like it was nothing. It'd been over a decade and still she felt every bit the fool she'd been taken for—naive, forever placing someone else before herself.

"Not foolish." Malcolm placed a hand on her face, brushing the rough pad of his thumb over the edge of her lips like he wanted to smear the red makeup there. "Love makes us do reckless things."

She stared up at him. "Like trusting a witch who doesn't deserve it?"

"Exactly like that." His hands were at the button of her pants now. She nodded her approval. He yanked her zipper open and lowered her jeans down around her ankles while she worked his belt buckle to do the same to him. Moments later, the hardened length of his cock pressed against her entrance, where she was seated and spread wide on the chopper.

He rocked his hips forward slightly, eager to claim her. The erect head nudged apart her wet folds. "I love you, Trixie," Malcolm whispered into her ear.

She shivered. "I love you, too, sugar," she admitted. "I've loved you since the moment you first let me sit with you at the bar, since you first kissed me," she whispered back. "I haven't been able to get the taste of whiskey from my lips since."

Malcolm growled his approval. "I'm not certain either of us deserve it." He sheathed himself inside her, rough and claiming.

Trixie cried out, though she was more than ready for him. She angled her hips forward, leaning back against the bike seat where he cradled her as he drove deeper, took her harder. Malcolm fucked her in long, hard strokes until her nails were scraping across the leather bike seat beneath her as she struggled to hold on. He'd made love to her before, but this felt different, like a collision between their pasts, present, and future. A future she wanted to be a part of, even though she knew she couldn't. A pang of sorrow clutched inside her chest. A familiar pressure built inside her, but Malcolm was already nearly over the edge.

"Don't wait for me," she whispered in his ear, encouraging him.

Malcolm came on a rough guttural moan, emptying himself inside her until she was full to the brim with him. The smell of lemon soap and leather on his skin. The earthy undertones of the forest, and the hot warmth of his seed inside her. She shuddered, near her own release, but not quite there. The coiled tension in her muscles was tantalizing. Oh, so sweet.

But she needed more.

Malcolm pulled out of her, grabbing an unsoiled paint rag from the shelf behind them and cleaning himself off. He didn't wipe away the remnants of himself on her pussy.

"I want to taste myself on you," he growled, starting to drop to his knees, but she grabbed the sleeve of his leather jacket to stop him.

"Not this time," she said, shaking her head.

Immediately, he froze. He lifted a brow in confusion but

didn't move an inch further. Trixie fought back a chuckle. "Remember that night at Yellowstone?" she asked.

Terra firma.

Malcolm nodded, though the furrow in his brow highlighted that he wasn't certain where she was going with this, but he was indulging her. That was his way after all.

"You pleasured me that night, but I didn't return the favor." Trixie smiled, licking her lips suggestively. "Now, it's your turn." She gripped the front of his shirt, lifting him to his feet before they switched places.

"Trixie," Malcolm breathed.

"Don't try to tell me you prefer my pleasure, because I won't listen to a word of it. No matter how true." She pushed him down into the motorcycle's seat. "This is about you. Me giving you everything you deserve. I want *this*." The moment she dropped to her knees before him, he was ready and hard again. Trixie grinned to herself, glancing up at him from where she was on her knees. That was another thing she loved about shifters.

They could go on for hours. Long past what her vibrator's batteries would have endured.

But there was only one who she ever wanted to share her bed with again.

Trixie knelt on the garage floor before him, spreading Malcolm's knees. The look of his eyes was one of wild, feral anticipation mixed with tender gratitude—appreciation for the fact that she hadn't forgotten him. She'd remembered him. She always would.

She cupped his balls in her hand, rolling around the soft

weight of them. She felt them tighten. She gripped the base of his length with her other hand. She could barely circle him. He was thick and ridged and beautiful. She laid a kiss on him there, leaving a little lip-shaped imprint, where she planned to give him a good long lick.

"There's a reason I wear red lipstick," she whispered against his skin. "And I'm about to show you."

She drew him into her mouth, wrapping her lips around the head of his cock and working him until he threw back his head and howled. The sound of his finished pleasure echoed across the mountainside.

Chapter 24

TRIXIE'S LIPSTICK WAS SMEARED ALL OVER HER MOUTH, but to her surprise, she didn't care. It felt like a public sign of how she'd submitted herself to him, a declaration of her devotion, and from the fiery appreciative look in his eyes, Malcolm fucking loved it.

When they'd finished in the garage, they'd both righted themselves and their clothes. Malcolm had hesitated only for a moment before covering Bo's refurbished chopper with the sheet again. It hadn't taken much to close up shop after that. As they'd made their exit, before they'd locked the door, Trixie had taken his face in both her hands and made him promise he'd take the bike out for its virgin ride come spring, though she wished she could be there to enjoy it with him.

The truth—that she wouldn't be—filled her with regret. But he'd sworn he would and she knew he'd never lie to her.

She watched Malcolm's wolf eyes dart over the planes of her face, grumbling in heated approval as he took in the mess of red lipstick around her mouth. With a small smile, she gripped hold of his hand and squeezed. The winter winds whipped around them as they walked back toward the bunkhouse, though she was far from cold. He kept her warm.

I love you, his eyes seemed to say through the silence, heating her. Over and over again.

They didn't need to share words to understand each other. She'd always known that. When they were alone like this, she didn't need to put on a show for him or anyone else, didn't need to guard herself or her heart, and in return, he didn't need to try to be anything he wasn't—didn't need to hide his grief or his pain or every soft, tender part of himself he kept hidden behind a hardened exterior, all for fear of being hurt.

She'd already done him worse than he'd likely ever imagined, yet he still loved her.

For now. In this moment.

Trixie watched a rustle of movement somewhere in the forest trees, certain it was from another wolf, one of his packmates. If she was honest with herself, she'd known where she and Malcolm were headed from that night he'd kissed her outside the Coyote, the night she'd first started to fall in love with him, slowly, painfully, yet the years since had gone by in the blink of an eye.

Love couldn't stop time, but it sure could make it pass quickly.

Even though she'd tried to resist it.

They walked near the tree line, sheltered from the wind in part by the trees' branches. Their steps left imprints in the snow. The pines shivered. But she felt the reassuring heat of Malcolm's presence beside her, keeping her warm. She glanced in his direction and caught him looking at her mouth again. She'd made certain he'd see the red streaks of her lipstick on him long after she left. Those would be for his eyes only.

She bit her lip. Her heart dropped at the thought. Despite the sated afterglow in her muscles, she was trying not to think of her impending departure, trying to enjoy the last minutes she had with him. If she focused on him hard enough, she could ignore what she'd said—or hadn't—to Stan and what the consequences of her actions would prove to be. For both of them. The future held little hope, but right now, the present was all that mattered.

"What do you want from life, Trixie?" Malcolm asked, surprising her with the sudden question. "What's your I'm-gettin-the-hell-outta-here fund for?" he asked.

Trixie wasn't certain any man she'd been with had ever asked her what she wanted before, had ever cared to know her hopes and dreams. "I want to be free," she answered. "From here, from Boss. And I want to own my own bar, like the Coyote but all mine, and none of the gambling, none of the secrets. Drinks and food only."

She'd never told anyone that before.

Malcolm smiled, squeezing her hand. "Then I hope that happens for you."

Something in how he said it sounded far too much like goodbye.

Up ahead, the bunkhouse sat not far in the distance. As they approached, a few wolves darted from the trees, circling, but it wasn't the sight of them shifted into their true form that concerned her. It was the sight of their packmaster standing outside the bunkhouse in human form with several of the pack's elite warriors beside him. Maverick reached down and brushed his hands through each of the circling wolves' fur. The beasts nuzzled against his palm, eager to be marked with their alpha's scent and touch. But his eyes never left Trixie's as she and Malcolm approached. The unmitigated fury there sent a chill down her spine.

She didn't need to ask what was wrong to know.

Their time was up.

As they drew closer, Malcolm swept her behind him, placing himself between her and his packmaster like a shield. He sensed the pack's tension, too—by her guess, more keenly than she ever could. He was one with them in a way that couldn't be replicated, even during the moments he was inside her. She'd never know him like that, on the base predatory level his packmates did, and for a brief moment, she understood why he'd once said she might as well be human. No matter what she was to him, she wasn't a shifter, wasn't pack.

She never would be.

For the first time ever, she resented her magic, how it kept her separate from him, put them at arm's distance from each other.

Malcolm didn't say anything, simply watched Maverick and waited. Wes and Blaze flanked the packmaster along with the other circling wolves. The look on Blaze's face was so unlike him, so serious and distant that it unsettled Trixie, and from how Wes stared at her, wolf eyes unblinking, the former Wild Eight who'd once been her friend would tear into her the moment his packmaster gave the word. She knew that look.

Maverick nodded toward Blaze. He was holding his phone, which she wasn't surprised to see had access to the pack's security systems and, more importantly, what she presumed was a satellite they used to monitor all private telecommunications on the ranch. She should have known the pack would use technology like that, particularly now that the ranch was full of all the other warriors of the Seven Range Pact. The Grey Wolves trusted their allies, but they also weren't foolish enough to think that allies couldn't become enemies with the right incentive.

Like she had.

Of course they'd monitored her calls, though Blaze's monitoring had likely been delayed by a few days thanks to her assistance at the Blood Rose. They'd used her for what they needed from her and let the pieces fall where they may. She shouldn't be surprised. Pack shifters held privacy in little importance. They shared everything. They were one after all. They would have been remiss, blindly trusting, not to have that option available to them, should they need it.

And she wasn't one of the pack. They'd never trusted her to begin with. That pack mentality was what had helped the Grey Wolves and so many other species like them survive for so long, proliferate like so many other supernatural species hadn't.

Blaze pressed a button, and a moment later, her voice—or a garbled, recorded rendition of it, from the first conversation she'd had with Stan—cut through the silence and the wind. When the recording finished, Blaze cleared his throat. "Our enemies are on their way."

From where Trixie stood behind him, she saw Malcolm's shoulders tense beneath his leather. His hand fell from where it'd been on her arm moments ago and she flinched. But he didn't turn toward her, didn't move from where he stood between her and his packmaster.

She couldn't bear to see the look of betrayal in his eyes.

Maverick's gaze fell on her. She felt the wave of power behind the packmaster's words as if he himself had magic, though she knew he didn't. His power lay in the wolves now circling her, in Malcolm, the loyalty of his people, his friends and family. That was something she'd never have.

"A life for a life," Maverick growled. He gave a brief nod toward Wes to indicate exactly which life she'd once saved. "That's the only reason you're still standing."

Trixie swallowed. She wanted to reach out and take Malcolm's hand for reassurance, but she feared he'd only pull away from her again. She couldn't face his rejection. Not without falling apart when she desperately needed to stay together, to survive this. She was back where she'd started, cold and alone. She had no one but herself to rely on, and this time, it'd been her own doing. She should have trusted Malcolm from the start.

Trixie opened her mouth, struggling to know what to say, but Blaze's next words stopped her short.

"An alliance gift for the updated agreement," he said before pressing the next recording again. "From the Execution Underground."

Again, the voice was familiar, but not hers. On the recording, Boss rattled off her address to Stan, outing her before launching into renegotiating terms. He didn't even sound like he regretted it.

The pain in Trixie's chest intensified, making it hard for her to breathe. Boss had sold her out. Like she suspected, but worse, he'd not only brokered the deal between the vampires and the Triple S but also orchestrated it. He'd been the catalyst for its creation, pushing the groups together, though she still didn't understand to what end, which meant the pack had killed Cillian for nothing. Sure, they'd wanted him dead, but doing so wouldn't stop the vampire's alliance with the Triple S or spook the South Side Shifter Outfit into pulling out of their end of the deal. It'd only set them up for hasty retaliation—by all involved parties.

She hadn't needed to betray the Grey Wolves, to give any information to Stan.

Boss had already done it for her.

This'll be the last time I clean up your mess, cher.

She'd known what that meant, and yet she hadn't expected him to sell her out like that. But that was what she'd always been to him, wasn't it? The spoils of a debt he needed paid. A pawn for his use. Exactly what she'd been to Tony.

Slowly, Malcolm turned toward her. The hurt in his eyes tore her in two.

"Is it true?"

Trixie drew in a shuddered breath, then nodded.

His next question hurt even worse. "Were you coerced?"

Deep down, some part of him still trusted her, still wanted to believe in her.

She didn't deserve it.

"Y-yes," she managed to sputter out. Tears coated her cheeks. "I didn't tell them anything, I swear it. Boss and Stan made me enter into another binding spell. They said—"

"Binding spells don't work at Wolf Pack Run," Maverick snarled. His wolf eyes blazed. "It's one of the pack's many secrets. Secrets you deemed yourself privileged to. You think I'd be foolish enough to allow any of our pack to enter into that bastard's agreements if they held true?"

Trixie gaped at the packmaster. Her eyes darted to Malcolm's right hand, the one he'd used to make a deal with Boss the night of the brawl at the Coyote. For the first time, she noticed the binding magic there had faded. The inky black tendrils had vanished from the olive tone of his skin, the time-faded tattoos still there, though she knew the pack's deal with the Rock City MC Wolves was far from over. She and Malcolm had heard the roar of a dozen of their motorcycles arriving at the ranch late last night. Her eyes turned to her own palms. The deals written there were also decidedly absent, but she always used a small portion of her magic to keep them hidden.

She willed the magic away, trying to see the onyx mark-ings, but they refused to appear. Trixie loosed a startled breath. She'd been free this whole time, able to make her own choices as soon as she'd set foot into the sanctuary the pack had created here. But she'd been too terrified of trusting anyone but herself to tell Malcolm the truth.

Somehow, that only made what she'd done worse.

She reached for Malcolm. "I—I didn't know. S-Stan said he'd kill me, kill Jackie and his siblings and you, too, if I didn't. Malcolm, I'm so sorry. I—"

Malcolm lifted a single hand to silence her.

Trixie trembled beneath the weight of his gaze. He'd made his decision. Whatever it was, he didn't need to hear anything further from her. He knew what it was like to be manipulated, used for a dark deed he'd never have done without provocation. But she'd lied to him. Just like his manipulative mother. She'd broken the one rule he'd given her.

"Don't ever lie to me." His eyes had been cold, harsh, cruel. *"That's my one rule. You do and we're through. I want honesty or I don't want it."*

He was through with her. *They* were through. She saw it in the tightness of his shoulders, the flex of his hand she'd held only moments earlier. He didn't need to say it for her to know.

Malcolm looked over his shoulder toward Maverick, his face calm, resigned. He was silent fury. "I'll make it right, Packmaster," he reassured Maverick.

Without warning, he drew Bo's blade from his hip.

Trixie shook from head to toe, but she didn't shy away from him. He wouldn't hurt her. Not if he'd still had a choice. Better this than a life spent running, constantly looking over her shoulder, better death at the hands of a man who'd once loved her enough to fight his way through the darkness of his grief in order to claim her. Anything was better than what Stan held in store for her. Malcolm would show her mercy, make her death swift and painless.

He clutched Bo's dagger in his hand. His eyes held hers. "Did you mean what you said? That'd you'd stay if you could?" he asked. The unmitigated hope seeded there ripped her to shreds.

"In a heartbeat," she breathed.

Malcolm nodded, solemn yet pained. "I trusted you."

"I know you did." Trixie pressed her lips into a thin line as she closed her eyes. Tears streaked her face. "I'm sorry."

"Me too." Malcolm drew her hand into his. His palm was warm, comforting against hers. "I'm sorry I can't give you a choice in this."

Trixie braced herself. For death. For the end of it all.

Pain sliced through her palm instead, her blood pooling hot. In her hand. Only her hand.

Trixie's eyes shot open. She was still standing, still breathing though she trembled from head to toe. She watched as Malcolm lifted his own palm and repeated the same action. Blood dripped from his hand. It speckled the gleaming white snow beneath their feet with a shocking crimson.

He gripped his hand in hers, their blood mixing together. Turning to face his packmates, he leveled a harsh, challenging gaze at Maverick. "I claim her as my mate," he said, eyes unfaltering. "Her punishment is my own." His eyes turned back toward her, but instead of anger, all she saw was his forgiveness, forgiveness she hadn't earned.

Trixie struggled to speak. "I–I don't understand."

"Don't you?" Malcolm shook his head. *I love you*, his dark eyes seemed to whisper.

"*You're* my pack, Trixie," he said. "One mistake won't change that."

Chapter 25

TRIXIE WAS PLEADING, HER HAND STILL GRIPPED IN HIS, and Malcolm couldn't stand the sound of her pain. "I can't let you do this. Malcolm, I can't let you—"

Malcolm shook his head, growling a subtle warning at her. "You don't have a choice, Trixie." Didn't she understand? *She* was his pack, his everything. Exactly as Bo had been. Not the Grey Wolves, despite the debt he owed them, despite the years of loyalty he'd given, his years of service. They'd never once been a part of him, not like he felt when he was with her. She was all the happiness he needed. He had no other choice.

It was either this or let her die. This or throw her to the wolves he called his packmates. He'd accept any punishment they could give him as long as it kept her safe, happy.

Her debt was his own, and he knew the action wasn't without meaning or consequence to her. She'd done the same for someone once before, only to find out she hadn't meant anything to that monster. But to him, she meant something. She meant the world. He only wished he could have done the same for her, shown her that and protected her from Boss all those years ago. Maverick could choose to end Malcolm's life or cast him out, exactly as Boss could have done with her, but it didn't matter. This ranch had never been his home. His home had been with Bo, and now it was with her. A single lie, no matter how hurtful, wouldn't change that.

His only regrets were that he'd ever made her think that it would and that he'd taken her choice to be his mate away in order to protect her life. But he'd had no other options. It made him feel like he was no better than Boss, claiming her as property. He only hoped she could forgive him, if she chose to stay. If she wanted to leave, he'd let her.

As his and Trixie's blood mingled, Malcolm felt whatever it was inside them that made them other, different—not human—shudder and connect like the union had been there all along. The pack considered it a rare blessing to find a true fated mate. Two in a single lifetime was unheard of. But he had never fit in among their crowd.

Malcolm watched the muscles of Maverick's throat contract as he swallowed, such a subtle sign of emotion, but present all the same. It wasn't like the Grey Wolf packmaster to show it. His role didn't allow him to, but for now, Malcolm was still connected to the Grey Wolves, and he knew Maverick could sense the link between him and Trixie, knew that insofar as Maverick was his friend, he'd be happy for him. He only hoped the packmaster would show him enough mercy not to break that same bond, and if he did so choose, to take his life instead of hers.

Malcolm held Maverick's gaze. "Spare her life in place of mine. You owe me that much."

For all the times I've killed for you. For all the times you made me your villain.

Maverick gave a silent, solemn nod.

Malcolm turned toward Trixie, pulling her into his arms momentarily. She rested her head against his chest. They didn't have much time. Not before the pack's enemies arrived.

It took everything in him to pull away from her, pluck her from the security of his arms. "Take this. For protection." He placed Bo's blade in her hand, still dirty with the blood that'd bonded him and Trixie instead of his vengeance against their enemies. Bo would have wanted it that way. For him to find someone who made him happy, made him feel whole again. "Go get Dumplin'," he directed. "Run to the pack's perimeter. Don't stop to talk or converse with anyone on your way. Just get in your car and drive, Trixie. Go to the cabin."

Their secret place. Their safe space. Terra firma.

She'd be safe there.

"I can't. Not the last part anyway." Trixie shook her head. "There's…something I need to take care of first."

She loved him, but whatever it was, she didn't trust him enough to tell her.

For fear he might try to stop her.

He wished he had time to tell her he wouldn't. She was her own woman, her own person. He wanted her to feel and know that from now on through the rest of her days. No one controlled her. Not him. Not Boss. No one. Whatever she wanted, even if it was to run from him because she didn't want forever, he'd let her go.

"Do whatever you need to do then." He knew she could feel the true meaning in his words as he spoke them.

And whenever you're through, I hope you come back to me.

"I will," she said. "I promise."

Malcolm released her from where his hands gripped her shoulders. Dumplin', who'd been growling at the circling wolves from the open bunkhouse doorway, came to her side. Malcolm couldn't bring himself to turn and watch her go. He faced his packmaster, though Maverick wouldn't be his packmaster much longer.

Maverick released a weary sigh. "I knew it would come to this from the moment you threatened Blaze for her."

Blaze cleared his throat. "Which…by the way, you still haven't apologized for." His packmate cast him a sheepish look. Underneath his open Carhartt, he was wearing a shirt that read *Bye! You were pretty bad at your job anyway*, which he'd no doubt chosen for this exact occasion.

Malcolm shook his head, fighting not to chuckle despite the iron grip of fear in his chest. Fear Trixie wouldn't return to him. But surprisingly, for the first time, he appreciated the levity his packmate's joking could bring, and he knew that even if he lost her as he had Bo, somehow he'd be okay.

"Don't for a second think this means you won't pay for my meals again," Blaze said.

Both Malcolm and the packmaster ignored him.

Wes shot Blaze a silencing look. "The Peer Council and the Seven Range Pact will have very real concerns about your…new mate and the way she planned to betray us," he ground out, reminding them of the harsh, cruel reality. "Someone will have to take the fall for it."

Maverick nodded in agreement. His wolf eyes flashed,

bright and glaring against the backdrop of white Montana snow. "You'll be cast from the pack."

Malcolm nodded. "I know, *Packmaster*." He said it as a quiet means to show his respect, no matter what Maverick chose. These lands may not be his home, but the Grey Wolves would always have his respect and his gratitude.

"I think it can wait until after our next battle," Maverick said, placing a hand on one of the circling wolves beside him. Malcolm recognized the she-wolf's markings—Sierra—alongside the other wolves who made up the Grey Wolves elite warrior team. There'd be a vacant seat to fill upon his departure. He hoped it would go to a female or maybe another queer packmember.

"The intel from the human hunters says the vampires plan to close in before the day's end," Blaze warned. His eyes darted to where the sun was starting to set in the western sky.

"Stand with us one last time?" Maverick asked. To Malcolm's surprise, the packmaster reached out and placed a hand on his shoulder. Malcolm didn't flinch away from the other man's touch.

His gratitude could have filled the whole of the foothills.

He tipped his Stetson. "One last time."

At Maverick's signal, his soon-to-be-former packmates dispersed, heading toward the main compound in preparation for the impending battle. If the pack faced death one last time, they'd face it with honor and bravery, exactly like they'd taught him, because death wasn't truly the end. Malcolm felt Bo's presence, as sure and real as if his mate had been standing beside him. He wished Trixie could have been there to experience it with him.

Maverick stood across from him, the two of them now left alone near the start of the forest and the mountainside. Malcolm turned toward the west, to where Trixie had disappeared in the distance.

"Do you think she'll come back to you?" Maverick asked softly.

"I don't know," Malcolm answered.

All he could do was hope.

Chapter 26

TRIXIE FOUND BOSS SITTING ON THE SAME BARSTOOL he'd been on nearly fifteen years earlier, fourth one down from the right side of the bar, near the register. The layout of the bar and the location might have changed since then, but the old rickety stool the warlock favored was the same. He was stooped over the cash drawer and the bar's open financial books. Whatever servers he'd hired in her and Dani's places hadn't managed to keep the place up to snuff when it came to cleaning, and the air reeked of stale beer like it was a busy Friday instead of a dead Wednesday weeknight. The purple and orange on the new jukebox screen flashed, glaring and bright among the bar's shadows.

Trixie had entered through the front entrance, not the service door, using her key with Dumplin' at her side. The choice had been intentional. It was well past nightfall, and she was thankful her car had managed to make it from Wolf Pack Run over Idaho state lines in record time with little more than a hope, a prayer, and a bit of magic. The bar closed early on Wednesdays, and she'd hoped to find Boss here counting the drawer, exactly as he was.

The old warlock raised his head at the sound of her approaching heels clicking against the hardwood floor. He took one look at her and raised the brow above his eye. The green one, not the blue. "Didn't know you had a thing for animals, cher." He nodded toward Dumplin' beside her.

Trixie placed her hands on her hips momentarily before giving Dumplin' the signal to stay. The dog sat obediently. "Apparently, there's a lot you don't know about me." She made her way around the bar top, slipping her hands into the pockets of her short cutoff jeans. Her ass cheeks were nearly hanging out, and they'd been freezing since she'd stopped for gas at the Marathon station and changed on her way in, but the distraction the look created was intentional.

It always was.

She rounded the bar top as Dumplin' waited obediently by the door. "Like the fact that I don't take kindly to being sold out to the supernatural Mafia," she continued. She grabbed one of the clean mixers and scooped some cubes from the ice bucket into it. "I'd thought Stan saw me cast the spell. But he didn't. *You* told him it was me. You knew he'd kill me and still you told him, sold me for dead like I'm nothing to you."

"It was me or you." Boss watched her, yellowed eyes weary. "It was business, cher. Nothing personal."

Of course. Boss was always the opportunist. She'd never really meant anything to him, not truly. She'd tried to convince herself she had, only because it'd made things easier, made the way she was stuck with him easier to bear, made her feel a little less alone. But she'd been lying to herself. Now she knew what it was like for someone to really care for her, and it wasn't someone who cut shady deals with her only so he could use her for her magic.

Trixie stood on the tiptoes of her heels, grabbing down the white rum from the shelf. She poured it into the mixer. A generous enough share to cover up other tastes. "Of course, it's always been business with you, Boss. That shouldn't be news to me." She shook her head and sighed. "The problem is that I was ever foolish enough to hope it was anything different." She added the simple syrup. She pegged him with a hardened stare. She'd cleaned up her makeup for this specifically and she knew she looked good. Better than usual even.

Self-worth could do that for a woman.

"Kindness, compassion: you don't have it in you, do you?" she asked. She'd hoped once he had, convinced herself for her own comfort.

Boss's brow drew low before he flashed her a white-toothed grin and laughed. "'Course I do." He chuckled and picked up his ledger pen. "For the right price."

From beside the door, Dumplin' let out a growl, sensing the tension between her and the warlock, but Trixie shook her head at the sweet Rottweiler. Dumplin' was eager to protect her, but this fight was hers. It always had been. She just hadn't realized it.

Boss looked back down at the books again, as if she and her troubles were of no concern, and Trixie poured the final ingredient into the shaker. Twisting the top closed, she made a show of rattling it around for a few moments before grabbing a highball glass to pour it into. "Is that why you did it?" she asked Boss. "Power? Money?"

She shouldn't be surprised. That was his usual way, of course.

The necromancer turned his attention back toward her. "If I've told you once, I've told you a thousand times, girl. Money talks." Boss wrote down a figure in the books, then looked back toward her again. "But you forget… That pack is responsible for moving the Coyote out here to this hellhole." His mismatched eyes flashed with dark rage that been suppressed for too long, and Trixie could see his magic emerge like dark tendrils, born out of the bar's shadows. But he wouldn't hurt her.

Not any more than he already had anyway.

"I liked Billings better," Boss said in explanation.

So this had been years in the making. Figured. Trixie shook her head, trying to hide her disappointment.

Dumplin' let out a whimper followed by a growl. The scent of Boss's magic snaked throughout the bar. There'd been a time when she found the familiar scent soothing. Coconut and mango mixed with anise, like licorice. But now the sick sweetness of it made her stomach turn.

"If you ever cared for me, then let me out of my contract," she said. "Please. If you do, I'll turn around and walk out of here. You won't hear from me again. We can let bygones be bygones."

Boss lifted a dark brow toward her. "We both know I won't do that, cher. You've asked plenty of times before. You're too valuable."

"You mean my *magic* is too valuable to you." Anger built inside her then, quick and unexpected. Not the devastating resignation she'd felt so many times before. "Then call off the Triple S. Tell them the deal's over with." She'd give him this last chance to save himself, a tribute to whatever familial love she'd once felt for him. When she spoke, her voice sounded dark, the voice of a witch, not a sweet, southern seductress. "I've never tried to get out of our contract because a deal is a deal and you did help me, even if it was to serve your own means. But it's one thing to hurt me. That I can take. I've stomached it for this long. But if you hurt the man I love or his pack, I'll end you." She leveled Boss with a hard stare. "Call them off."

Boss laughed. "Where do you think you're gonna get that kind of power, girl?" He chuckled.

Trixie smiled at him, soft and sweet. Pliable, like she'd once been. She'd been so used to bending to the will of powerful men so she didn't break that she'd never dared to consider her own power. "I call it the Dolly." She pushed the new drink she'd mixed across the bar toward him. "Try it."

Boss eyed the chilled highball glass before he drew it into in his hand and took a hearty sip. How many times had she done the same for him before? She couldn't count.

He nodded in approval. "It's a good one," he said, like she was still working for him, still his to control. She'd known he'd like it. She'd made it with all his favorite ingredients.

Custom to taste.

Blowing out a long breath of tension, Trixie strutted out from behind the bar, heading toward the jukebox. The credits from the previous machine had been transferred over, so thankfully she didn't need the handful of coins she'd stored in her pocket for this exact moment. She pressed a few buttons, and a moment later, Dolly Parton's "9 to 5" started belting through the bar's speakers. Dolly's high-pitched soprano rang out for a moment, quickly leading into the chorus.

Trixie had played the song for Boss plenty of times before, but this time felt different.

Last calls always did.

She turned to face the old warlock. Boss had already consumed about half of the drink she'd given him, and he let out a rough, choked cough.

"You shouldn't have come for the man I love," she said.

Boss shook his head, coughing again. Smoking would do that to a person. Make their lungs weak. "Didn't I"—another cough—"teach you better than to be so naive, cher?"

"You did," she answered. She smacked her lips together, giving him an innocent look. "But apparently I never taught *you* that you should be careful who you let serve your drinks."

Boss's eyes went wide, darting to the drink in his hand and then back to her at the exact moment he started to rasp and cough again. Suffocation was an awful sound. Boss's eyes bulged and he pawed at his throat, but the look of anger in his irises said he'd kill her if he had the chance. Too bad she hadn't given him one.

"Hemlock," she said, explaining. "You never took much interest in my love of poisonous plants."

Boss fell from the barstool, clawing at his throat and twitching in a struggle for air. His hands pulsed black as he struggled to use his magic to get out of it. But it was no use.

Magic didn't outpace nature.

It was why shifters rather than witches reigned supreme.

"You should have let me out of my contract," Trixie said again. A stray tear rolled down her cheek, and she swiped at it with the back of her hand. "Here, you can have these to remember me by." Bending down, she slipped off the first pair of heels she'd ever owned, walking over and thrusting them into Boss's curled arms as he fought for his last breath. "I'm never wearing those fucking death traps again." Trixie turned on her bare heel, arches flat and ground against the floor, and walked out of the bar. She took her pride and dignity with her.

A moment after she left, with Dumplin' at her side, she placed a hand on the dog's head. She knew the moment Boss was gone, because a weight she'd felt for too long lifted and she smiled to herself. Finally, she breathed a sigh of relief.

She was her own woman.

———————

The moon hung high in the night sky, casting her cool, pale glow down on the snowcapped mountaintops. A prickle of energy ruffled through Malcolm's fur, down to his skin. He lay in wait for the pack's enemies, the bustle of the other warriors cloaked in the forest around him nearly imperceptible. But he could feel them there, sense them like a part of himself.

Most of the pack had already shifted into their true form, their weapons hidden among the hollows of the trees and the surrounding brush. Tonight, they fought together as one, and for this, only fang and claw would do. They were as prepared for battle as they'd ever be.

Without warning, a rustle of leaves sounded to his right.

Malcolm snarled, harsh and fierce in warning, but a moment later, Blaze emerged from the brush on all fours. His packmate sniffed Malcolm, drawing up with him muzzle to muzzle in friendly acknowledgment before he shifted into human form. The air bent and folded around him as his fur gave way to human limbs and feet, his ability to use verbal language restored.

"Maverick thought you would want to know..." Blaze stared down at him, naked despite the surrounding snow. "Apparently the Triple S chickened out. The scouts out past the ranch perimeters said only the vampires and the remaining Volk are on their way." The wry smile Blaze gave Malcolm was filled with more than a hint of twisted glee, like he couldn't wait for what he had to say next. "And you can thank your mate."

Malcolm didn't need words to answer. He nudged his nose against Blaze's hand in approval, snapping his jaws when Blaze laughed and tried to ruffle his fur. Malcolm jumped over some brush, spry and enthused, before he threw back his head and howled. The whole of the pack answered. Wes. Colt. Blaze. Maverick. Hell, even Rogue and so many others.

And for once, Malcolm didn't feel so alone.

Blaze nodded in the direction of the pasture, shifting back into wolf form to signal it was time for them to take their places. Malcolm followed his packmate into the dark, running with a wild abandon he hadn't felt in far too many years.

When they reached the pasture, the packmaster and the

other elite warriors were already waiting for them in wolf form, Maverick leading the small group at the helm. As they waited for the vampires to make their appearance, the packmaster took care to mark each one of them, sealing their kinship with his scent. When he reached him, Malcolm half expected the packmaster to turn away. He wouldn't be one of the pack much longer after all, but instead, Maverick didn't hesitate.

The packmaster drew up on him, marking Malcolm with his scent before exposing the vulnerable fur of his neck. The hair on Malcolm's back prickled in awareness. For them, the gesture wasn't without meaning.

We are one, and we always will be.

A sound from the darkness drew the wolves' attention as their enemies swiftly approached. At the signal, they shifted into human form, Maverick and Colt standing naked at the front of the pack of elite warriors as they all faced their enemies one final time.

A large band of bloodsuckers stood across the pasture, looking toward them. Every leech and fanger in the state of Montana who counted the Grey Wolves as their enemies stood before them. By appearance alone, they outnumbered the Grey Wolves three to one. A handful of the older vamps, those close in age and power to Cillian, stood at the front of the crowd. One of them stepped forward, some nameless face Malcolm didn't care to remember.

"This is what's left of the Grey Wolf Pack?" he sneered. "A mangy ragtag group of mutts you call warriors and two of their bitches."

Sierra and Dakota both snarled.

But Maverick raised a hand, causing them to fall silent.

Wes chuckled his amusement.

Colt glanced toward Maverick from where he stood at the packmaster's side. A sparkle of chaos flamed in his eyes. "Should you tell them or should I, Packmaster?"

At least the vamp who now fancied himself their leader had the heart to look confused.

Maverick held the bloodsucker's gaze, stepping forward as he flashed the gold of his wolf eyes. As if by magic, the deep thrum of his voice seemed to carry across the mountainside. "You forget, leech, that wolves circle before they go for the kill."

At that moment, the darkness of forest and hills, the whole of Wolf Pack Run, seemed to come alive with movement as the rest of the pack and their allies closed in on the coming battle like the rush of an incoming wave. Chaos broke loose as the two groups charged each other.

The sounds of shouts, howls, and bloodshed rent the night. Malcolm charged forward along with his packmates, shifting into his wolf as he met the first bloodsucker in his path with teeth and claw. He showed not an ounce of mercy, ripping into the vampire with all his strength.

The bloodsucker took a cheap shot, going for the soft skin of Malcolm's underbelly with his blade. But the leech didn't stand a chance. Abruptly, Malcolm shifted back into human form, faster than he ever had before, gripping the leech by the throat and crushing his windpipe. The leech crumpled onto the pasture in front of him. He wouldn't be the pack's reaper for much longer, but watching his enemies fall would always be fucking satisfying.

Beside him, Malcolm caught a glimpse of Sierra as she tore apart a bloodsucker with her teeth.

Her *human* teeth.

She turned to him from where she crouched over the vamp and smirked before shifting back into her wolf. As he watched the fray, the triumphs of his other packmates quickly followed. Malcolm laughed. *Maybe they don't need an executioner after all.*

A moment later, he was drawn back into the melee, only staying in skin once someone finally tossed him a blade. He dropped another bloodsucker with ease. Followed by the next. Another. Then another.

It was dawn by the time it was finally over, by the time they'd searched out every leech that hadn't fled and finished them. For once, little of the blood shed had been their own. The vampires had fought as fiercely as they ever had before. Tactics that had worked in the past, but this time, they didn't, because the pack knew a secret their enemies didn't. Change was inevitable, and history was only kind to those brave enough to change with it.

Malcolm certainly had.

Now that his duties to the pack were fulfilled, he raced on all fours out the perimeter gate, the cold mountain air like a stark relief against the warmth of his fur. He shifted into human form, eager to leave the ranch and find Trixie, but he wasn't at all surprised to see her there instead, sitting on the hood of her car, Dumplin' at her feet beside her.

He padded naked through the snow toward her.

"You look surprised to see me here, sugar." She smiled.

She'd changed her lipstick from red to a subtle pretty pink. More natural.

It suited her. Though he thought she'd looked great in anything.

"Don't worry," she said, noticing the way he looked at her lips. "I'll keep the red for certain occasions." She gave him a sultry wink.

Malcolm growled his approval. Fuck, he loved her.

Trixie pushed off the car's hood as he came to stand before her. She wrapped her arms around him, pulling him against her in that less-than-subtle manner of hers. "You think I would miss all these naked men prowling about post-battle?" She nodded toward the mountainside and gave him a coy grin. "Not my style, sweetheart."

Sweetheart, not sugar. Long ago, he'd noticed she reserved that one only for him, on the rare occasions he'd pleased her or showed her a glimpse of himself. He hoped there would be more time for that in the years to come.

"I'm not surprised," he grumbled. "Just grateful."

"Mmm-hmm," she purred against his lips, pulling him down over her on the car's hood. He was already naked and ready for her. "Why don't you show exactly how grateful?"

Epilogue

"You're certain you want to do this?" The hesitant question came from the Grey Wolf packmaster himself. Maverick and the other elite warriors stood beside Malcolm, prepared for his final send-off. The sun shone high over the mountaintops, and a golden glow had taken over the Montana foothills. The last of the winter's snow had melted only a few days prior, and the air felt damp with morning dew. Malcolm and Trixie had rolled Bo's chopper out of the garage for its virgin voyage early this morning, and now his art on the full gas tank and the chrome gleamed in the sunlight, ready to go and on display.

"I'm certain," Malcolm answered, passing the packmaster his Stetson. He wouldn't need it where he was headed. Not anymore.

"I understand." Maverick's lips pulled tight with disappointment. Not his but the pack's.

Malcolm knew his now-former packmaster was happy for him. The other wolf drew Malcolm into a brotherly thump of a hug, and Malcolm returned the gesture in kind.

Once the heat of their final battle with the vampires had calmed, the pack had waded through the bloodsuckers' records regarding their brief interlude with the Triple S.

Time and some coaxed (i.e., bribed) file digging by Blaze had eventually shown Trixie had been telling the truth all along. She hadn't crossed them, even if she'd intended to out of fear for her life and his, though Malcolm had never doubted her. As a result, Maverick had decided that Malcolm would be allowed to stay, if he wanted, even with Trixie, though the pack would never fully trust her.

But home wasn't here. Home was where he planned to rest his head with Trixie. The pack would never welcome her with open arms, though they tolerated her now that they knew she wasn't a threat, but he was eager for the two of them to create a home of their own—in the apartment above the side-by-side speakeasy and custom bike shop they planned to open not far southwest of Detroit.

He wasn't joining the Rock City MC wolf shifters, despite their invitation, though Dom, Rigs, and the other nomads did intend to ride out east beside him and Trixie, having stayed at Wolf Pack Run for a handful of months. Trixie had insisted it was good for bar business to have a pack nearby, even if that pack wasn't his.

He'd given her the money from his savings to start her dream of operating her own place, of course, mixed with a bit of the tips she'd stored away from both Boss and the IRS. All the years spent working Wolf Pack Run and spending so little had paid off in the end, in getting to see Trixie happy and filled with a sense of newfound purpose. Him too. He'd been eager to put his executioner days behind. It'd been the right decision for them both.

Trixie kept insisting she was going to pay him back, that

she never wanted to be in another man's debt, but he'd told her he wouldn't hear of it. It was a gift, not a loan. She didn't owe him anything. Besides, he was more wolf than man, not like a human. He'd finally accepted that, embraced it. He'd keep his word, keep her safe.

Trixie leaned against the side of the chopper where she and the other riders were waiting for him. She'd damned near begged him to get a sidecar for Dumplin' to ride in, but finally, they'd both agreed that Dumplin' would ride in the front seat of Trixie's car, which Dani had volunteered to drive behind them. She'd managed to make it through detoxing from the vamp blood okay and was working hard to recover, to heal. She'd said the open road might do her some good. She needed to get away from the West, and Malcolm had known Trixie didn't have it in her to refuse a friend. She'd do anything for the people she loved, the ones she let in and trusted, the small circle of people she cared for.

The trunk and back seat of the old beater were stuffed full with their shared handful of belongings. Dumplin' let out a bark from the front seat, where the window was rolled down. Dani sat in the driver's seat beside him, smiling at them.

It wasn't much, but it was theirs.

Trixie lowered her Hollywood sunglasses and peered at him. "You gonna draw this out or you ready to hit the road, sweetheart?"

He loved it when she called him that. Malcolm drew her into his arms, claiming her mouth with his. He kissed her with his whole soul, every broken and scarred part of him she'd help make whole again. Trixie sighed against his lips, going soft in his arms. When they pulled back and her amber eyes met his, there wasn't anything cold and callous about them. Instead, they were full of hope, joy, and sunshine.

Sunshine that only made the visible freckles on her cheeks more apparent.

Trixie pulled back a little, giving him room to swing a long leg over the seat of Bo's bike. Malcolm settled into the motorcycle saddle before Trixie hoisted herself up and over onto the back seat with ease thanks to the flat-heeled biker boots she wore. She wrapped her arms around him as he tested the throttle, revving the engine.

An echo of farewell howls sounded from the depths of the forest.

Trixie squeezed Malcolm's shoulder as he nudged up the kickstand with his boot, drawing his attention.

"Before we go, I have something I want to give you," she whispered against his ear. She wiggled behind him a bit, retrieving something from the pocket of her jeans, but the feel of her breasts pressed against his back made him growl with arousal.

A moment later, she passed two small cards over his shoulder to him. One plastic and one paper. A Michigan state driver's license with his picture on it and a social security card. New fake IDs.

"You said I was your pack," she whispered against his ear over the rumble of the motorcycle's engine. "I figured that meant your name needed to be Beauregard. I had to use some of Boss's old contacts, but they assured me your case had long since gone cold so they didn't think you needed to be worried about running from the human law."

Malcolm ran the gloved leather of his thumb over the name on the ID. Her name that she'd given him.

"It suits you better than Grey ever did anyway."

The gratitude, joy, and love he felt for her was unlike any he'd ever known. She'd made him whole, complete, given him a place in her world, stood alongside him, and that was more than he ever could have asked for.

"I love you," he growled to her over the sound of his bike and the wind. His eyes flashed to his wolf from the wild strength of his emotion.

Malcolm felt her smile where she rested her head on his shoulder, arms wrapped around him. "I love you, too," she whispered. "Now let's ride, cowboy."

Acknowledgments

The problem with waiting until the final book in a series to do an acknowledgment is that there's so many people to thank and I'm terrified I'll leave someone out, so if I do, please forgive me. It may only take one person to write a book (or six books in the case of this series), but it takes a whole team of people to publish it, and for that, I'm so incredibly grateful to each and every person who's been a part of my team or, dare I say, my pack.

To my editor, Deb Werksman, who believed in my idea for the Seven Range Shifters from the start, and during the later books in the series, editors Jocelyn Travis and Christa Désir. I'm so thankful for your insights, good humor, and the love and care all of you have given both to me and to this series. I'm so grateful to have been able to work with you.

To my copy editors, Heather Hall and Diane Dannenfeldt, among others, thank you for never complaining about my overuse of commas and for tolerating my occasional misplaced modifiers and other grammatical errors, and to the whole Sourcebooks team, Susie Benton (who helped manage my sometimes off-schedule deadlines and helped coordinate all the amazing maps inside the front covers), Stefani Sloma and Katie Stutz (marketing extraordinaires), Dawn Adams and team (for the amazing covers), Dominique Raccah (for founding an innovative, independent publishing house that's been such a pleasure to work with), and everyone involved in the production of the series, I'm so incredibly thankful.

As always, one of my biggest and deepest thanks also has to go to my literary agent, Nicole Resciniti, for reading and editing all the early drafts, letting me make her laugh by turning her husband into a secondary character, always going to bat for me (even when I made her participate in editorial discussions about humorous humping horses, which unfortunately didn't make the cut in book four), and for not missing a beat on our phone call back in 2016 when I scoffed and said "Cowboy wolves? Really?" To which she responded that I should give it a try because I could be great at it and "It makes sense if you really think about it. Wolves live out in Montana near Yellowstone, so why can't they be cowboys?" Nic, I never would have thought we'd end up here six books later with me feeling sad and a bit heartbroken to let this ragtag pack of cowboy wolves go. You've believed in me since I was basically still a baby—What kind of amazing, crazy-woman superagent signs and believes in a writer who's only nineteen? Who *does* that?—but I adore you, and it may have been over a decade since we first started working together, but I'm still as eternally grateful for you now as I was then. Thank you for all the amazing opportunities you've created for me.

To my mom, for paying to send me to my first writer's conference years ago and always believing I could do anything I set my mind to, and to my aunt Jackie, who alongside my mom, encouraged my love of reading when I was younger—particularly for all things fantasy and paranormal. Mom, you may have let me read Aunt Jackie's Laurel K. Hamilton books when I was a bit too young, and the scorching heat level in this series is probably the result, but I'm glad you did, and better yet, that you've never been the least bit embarrassed by my writing, only proud. That's how we create intergenerational romance readers and writers, folks. No shame!

To my author friends Mara Wells, Jax Cassidy, Tracy Goodwin, Marisa Cleveland, and so many others along the way, thank you for always being there to lend an ear or cheer in support when I needed it. Mara, throughout this series, you've become one of my most important creative advocates and, more importantly, one of my closest friends. I'm so grateful for all the brainstorming sessions and the seed of an idea that grew into the cave scene in Maverick's book in particular. That's still one of my favorite moments in the series, and it wouldn't have come to me without you. I'm so thankful for all the support you've given to help get me to this moment.

And last but certainly not least, to my family. To my two beautiful sons, Jackson and Jamie, thank you for understanding that Mama not only needs to work but that often I want to since doing this whole author thing is my dream. You're both still so little as I'm writing this, but both of you are wise beyond your years. Thank you for saying you're proud of me each and every time I finish a book or even come in from my office to report that I've gotten words on the page. "Eighty gazillion thousand!" as Jackson loves to exclaim.

I love you both, and watching you grow while writing

these books has been one of the hardest parts of saying goodbye to this series.

Jackson, you were only a toddler when I wrote the first proposal for this, and yet you jumped up and down and celebrated with me when the first three books sold and did it again for the later leg of the series. I love you "more than anything," as we love to say.

Jamie, you weren't born yet for the first bit of this, but I still remember doing copy edits on *Cowboy in Wolf's Clothing* while I was in early labor with you and then holding you in my arms (you were only a handful of days old) when *Cowboy Wolf Trouble* made its debut. You and the book release shared an arrival date, but you were far more important and made your debut a couple days early. I wrote most of *Wicked Cowboy Wolf* with you snuggled against my chest in the Tula while you were still nursing, and I have to tell you, your sweet little snuggles were the perfect complement to balance writing that devilish, dark cowboy wolf. I love you.

And to Jon, my love and, as the Grey Wolves would say, my mate, so much of you is in the heroes of these books— Blaze, in particular, as you know. But I couldn't have written about these amazing, handsome, wholehearted, funny, brave, tragic, fierce, and loyal heroes if I hadn't had a partner who was all those things and more himself. I love you, always.

And to my readers—don't think for a second that I forgot you!—thank you for taking a chance on me and my work. This wouldn't have been possible without you. I hope you've enjoyed reading this series as much as I've enjoyed writing it, and I hope you'll join me again on whatever adventure comes next.

About the Author

Kait Ballenger hated reading when she was a child because she was horrible at it. Then by chance she picked up the Harry Potter series, magically fell in love with reading, and never looked back. When she realized shortly after that she could tell her own stories, and they could be about falling in love, her fate was sealed.

She earned her BA in English from Stetson University—like the Stetson cowboy hat—followed by an MFA in writing from Spalding University. After stints working as a real vampire a.k.a. a phlebotomist, a bingo caller, a professional belly dancer, and an adjunct English professor, Kait finally decided that her eight-year-old self knew best: she's meant to be a romance writer.

When Kait's not preoccupied with writing captivating paranormal romance, page-turning suspense plots, or love scenes that make even seasoned romance readers blush, she can usually be found spending time with her family or with her nose buried in a good book. She loves to travel, especially abroad, and experience new places. She lives in Florida with her librarian husband, two adorable sons, a lovable mangy mutt of a dog, and four conniving felines.

Readers can find more information about Kait or sign up for her newsletter at kaitballenger.com.

WHILE THE WOLF'S AWAY

Dive into *USA Today* bestselling author Terry Spear's ever-fascinating world of sexy shapeshifters with heart in this thrilling Arctic wolf romance.

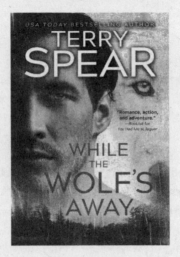

David Davis and his fellow Arctic wolves are seeking a new life in the wilds of Minnesota, away from the controlling pack leader who exploited them. Elizabeth Simpson helped David escape, but the pack leader won't let her go. It'll take everything David and Elizabeth have to get out and make a new home...together.

"Spear takes readers on a pulse-pounding ride."
—*Publishers Weekly* for *SEAL Wolf Christmas*

TRUE WOLF

New York Times and *USA Today* bestselling author
Paige Tyler's STAT: Special Threat Assessment Team
fight paranormal enemies and fall in love once again.

As STAT agent and wolf shifter Caleb Lynch investigates a case of
stolen nuclear weapons, Brielle Fontaine is his hottest lead. Brielle's
supernatural abilities are a force to be reckoned with, making her
one of STAT's biggest threats and a most useful ally. He'll have to get
close to her, but when the team comes under fire from supernatural
terrorists, the growing attraction between them could lead to something much more explosive…

**"Unputdownable… Whiplash pacing, breathless
action, and scintillating romance."**
—K.J. Howe, international bestselling author, for *Wolf Under Fire*

For more info about Sourcebooks's books and authors, visit:
sourcebooks.com

THE LEGEND OF ALL WOLVES

For three days out of thirty, when the moon is full and her law is iron, the Great North Pack must be wild... Don't miss this extraordinary series from Maria Vale

The Last Wolf

Silver Nilsdottir is at the bottom of her Pack's social order, with little chance for a decent mate and a better life. Until the day a stranger stumbles into their territory and Silver decides to risk everything on Tiberius Leveraux...

A Wolf Apart

Thea Villalobos has long since given up trying to be what others expect of her. So she can see that Elijah Sorensson is Alpha of his generation of the Great North Pack, and the wolf inside him will no longer be restrained...

Forever Wolf

With old and new enemies threatening the Great North, Varya knows that she must keep Eyulf hidden away from the superstitious wolves who would doom them both. Until the day they must fight to the death for the Pack's survival, side by side and heart to heart...

Season of the Wolf

Evie Kitwanasdottir leads the Great North Pack into new challenges, like taming the four hazardous Shifters they've taken into custody. Constantine, the most dangerous, is assigned to Evie's own 7th echelon, but if anyone can show what true love, leadership, and sacrifice looks like, it's Evie—the Alpha.

Wolf in the Shadows

Once a spoiled young Shifter surrounded by powerful males who shielded her from reality, Julia Martel is now a prisoner of the Great North Pack, trusted by no one and relegated to the care of the pack's Omega, Arthur Graysson. But being the least wolf has its advantages...

"Wonderfully unique and imaginative. I was enthralled!"
—Jeaniene Frost, *New York Times* bestselling author

For more info about Sourcebooks's books and authors, visit:
sourcebooks.com

MAD FOR A MATE

Beloved and bestselling author MaryJanice Davidson
is back with a hilarious and heartfelt shifter romance.

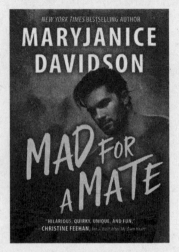

Verity Lane might be a Shifter who can't shift (known as a "squib")—
but woe betide anyone who tries to tell her who she is or what she's
capable of. She's a proud member of a club for squibs out to prove
themselves by participating in dangerous stunts. Which is probably
how she ended up on this strange island…

Magnus Berne is determined to sniff out who's been targeting
squibs on his island. He won't let any more get hurt, especially Verity,
who has charmed him with her wild spirit.

"Hilarious, quirky, unique, and fun."
—Christine Feehan, #1 *New York Times* bestselling author,
for *A Wolf After My Own Heart*

PRETTY LITTLE LION

Sexy, action-packed paranormal romantic suspense—the
Third Shift series from award-winning author Suleikha Snyder

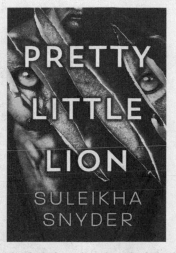

Lion shifter and Third Shift co-founder Elijah Richter is on a mission: seduce arms dealer Mirko Aston's gorgeous girlfriend, use her as an entry point to the organization, and discover what the global terrorist is planning. It should be simple. Then he meets Meghna Saxena-Saunders—influencer, celebutante, ex-wife to a handsome Hollywood hotshot, and a highly trained assassin—and all his plans are blown out of the water.

"Clever, romantic, heroic, and filled with hope for a better future. Suleikha Snyder has crafted an amazing world."
—Alisha Rai, award-winning author, for *Big Bad Wolf*

For more info about Sourcebooks's books and authors, visit:
sourcebooks.com

A WOLF IN DUKE'S CLOTHING

A delicious mix of Regency romance and shapeshifting adventure in an exciting new series from author Susanna Allen

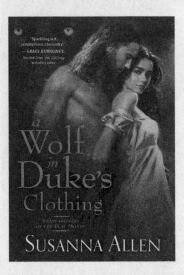

Alfred Blakesley, Duke of Lowell, has long been an enigma. No one dares to give a man of his status the cut direct, but there's simply something not quite right about him. What would the society ladies say if they learned the truth—that the Duke of Lowell is a wolf shifter and the leader of a pack facing extinction if he doesn't find his true love? So now he's on the hunt...for a wife.

"Sparkling wit, scrumptious chemistry, and characters who will go straight to your heart!"
—Grace Burrowes, *New York Times* and *USA Today* bestselling author